Thurber's Light

Diana Lee Whatley

PublishAmerica
Baltimore

© 2003 by Diana Lee Whatley.
All rights reserved. No part of this book may be reproduced, stored in a retrieval system, or transmitted in any form or by any means without the prior written permission of the publishers, except by a reviewer who may quote brief passages in a review to be printed in a newspaper, magazine, or journal.

First printing

ISBN: 1-59286-351-5
PUBLISHED BY PUBLISHAMERICA, LLLP
www.publishamerica.com
Baltimore

Printed in the United States of America

For the lightkeepers who served their lives often in isolation and earning meager wages, for those who now race to preserve our precious lighthouse history, and for all who keep hope alive.

Acknowledgments:

Claire Webb, without whose advice this book would not have been possible, John Lee, Jim Dunlap, Lens Preservationist, Scott T. Price, Historian, U.S. Coast Guard, and Donald L. Nelson for sharing their invaluable knowledge concerning lighthouses and lighthouse history, and the Lee County Library Interlibrary Loan team for finding the near-impossible.

Chapter One

"We'll be doing the locals a favor. This land is useless in its current state!" Brett Jarrett laughed with a slick smile, his arms open wide in an overly dramatic gesture as the two other people present watched.

It was true that the place was in rough shape. The landscape seemed almost alien. Once home to an impressive stand of sprawling, southern oaks, it was now overgrown by a layer of vines. A thick, matted tangle of kudzu spread solidly over much of the terrain. The imported weed grew rampantly, with its thick foliage coating most of the other plants and smothering all that it covered. Its tough appendages reached for the very top of even the oldest trees, bending some limbs with its spiraling cling and breaking others with its weight. The last of the oaks were in danger of being completely covered by a blanket of green.

"We'll just scrape it clean and build our estates." Then he added with a laugh, "and who could possibly object?" The fit, middle-aged Brett looked at his two companions and expected complete agreement. His suntanned frame holding the pose of sensational exhibition, he waited for a response from his new partner, Troy McGovern, and McGovern's friend and assistant, Darcy Vornack.

Roughly the same age as Brett and also athletic, Troy was slightly taller than his fellow business investor and stood a few inches over six feet in height. Though his expression was at first pensive, he folded his arms and nodded in agreement. A soft smile slowly broadened on his handsome face. His stance was both casual and confident. If the man had any reservations about the proposal, they did not show.

Brett's brow furrowed in mild frustration as he watched Troy's assistant. Darcy stood next to her comely host, trying to avoid Brett's direct gaze. She pursed her lips and examined the dirt below her. She moved the sandy soil around with little kicking motions of her leather work shoes and sent the loose, granular material in between the vine stems.

"Do I sense some disapproval? Don't think two actors know a sound investment?" Brett's eyes sparkled as he spoke. Though he continued to smile, there was something slightly sharp in his tone. His theatrical pose gave way to a milder posture.

Darcy hesitated for a moment, feeling a bit out of place. Her jeans and t-shirt were conspicuously less expensive than the casual, but costly, attire of the two men. Her facial features revealed that she was slightly younger as well.

"Well," she started slowly, "I'm sure you have done plenty of research on this project…and have given it much thought." She raised her eyes and looked around the area. Glimpsing only the very top of a deteriorating, rusty, round roof rising above the vine-cloaked trees, she asked, "What about the old lighthouse?"

Brett showed no affection in his quick reply, "That creepy thing? It's a goner…outta here. It's a possible safety hazard. That ugly, old thing should have been demolished years ago. It would be just a matter of time before it came down on its own, in some storm or something. Besides, we can put up an eight million dollar estate on that beach."

With deliberate words and some caution, Darcy countered, "I'll agree that the tower is in bad shape, but it could be recoverable…with some work." Again she averted her eyes away from Brett's confident gaze. She gently moved her foot to untangle it from a green jumble created by the numerous shoots of a voracious kudzu vine. Looking around her at the lump-laden landscape, the sturdy young woman had a growing curiosity. The vine had covered some areas so thickly that what laid underneath was a complete mystery. She speculated aloud, "This might make a nice spot for a park. Some of the trees might even be savable."

Jarrett half snorted, "Aw, get real, girl! The way this land is, no one would be willing to do that kind of work! Let alone, stay out here."

"I would." There was a firmness in Darcy's voice and she now sharply met Brett's eyes. The actor had stepped on a nerve and in doing so, increased the resolve in her. Though younger than Brett, Darcy was in her late thirties and far from being a pliant little girl. He wasn't accustomed to this kind of woman.

"You expect me to believe that you would stay out here by yourself? This place is eerie as heck." Brett forced a laugh and half joked, "Those vines might grow over you in your sleep. And it's like…I mean…the nearest clothing store is over forty miles away." He shook his head, causing a blonde lock to fall casually toward his eyes. "Just because you could survive being a production assistant on one of our movies doesn't mean you can survive with complete social deprivation. It isn't quite the same thing," he paused to snicker to himself and then added, "though maybe some people might think it's close." He reestablished his line of thought and continued, "What have you got out here...a tiny general store, a few old houses, a couple of sweaty fishermen...and even all that's a handful of miles away, across the bridge." He swept the stray lock of hair upward from his grey eyes, with a pass of his hand, and asked, "You would really stay out here?"

"Yes." Again there was a defiant firmness in Darcy's tone. Her sight strayed back to the forlorn tower.

Brett retorted, "I don't believe you!" His eyes narrowed, as he looked at her.

Troy smiled lightly and looked from his assistant to his fellow actor, "That sounds like a challenge to me."

Bypassing his partner's comment, Brett propped his hands firmly on his hips and smirked at the obstinate assistant, "It's that nasty, old lighthouse, isn't it? It's going to come down, whether we knock it down or not."

"It isn't nasty," Darcy contended, "it just needs help."

Troy interjected, "How about a friendly wager? Say, if Darcy stays on the land for a period of time, maybe a week or two, without spending the night elsewhere...she gets the lighthouse and the lot." Troy had always been one to take calculated risks and he figured the odds were good on this bet. If he lost the damage would be minimal...but if he won it would be payback for the trouncing Brett had given him at the Pro-Am golf tournament.

Brett scoffed and gave his partner a disbelieving look.

"The State has already agreed to sell to us and we're getting the land for next to nothing as it is. The project area is large enough, it won't hurt us if she wins. And anyway, you don't think Darcy will be able to make it, do you?" Troy's words were spoken calmly, but with a carefully trained, provocative inflection. The very tone of the actor's voice dared his partner.

The prodding hit home and Brett spat out, "Heck no!" He had total faith in women being the frailer, lesser sex. No woman would ever be able to face the rigors that only an outdoorsman could. Darcy would not be capable of staying in such an uncomfortable and eerie location without the assistance of a man, let alone without her modern amenities. He mused that it would be pure pleasure to hear her admit it after she gave up the challenge. Just for insurance, he added, "But it's three months...three whole, uninterrupted months. If she makes that then she can have the lighthouse, the lot it sits on and the connecting land, from here to the tower…with my blessings!" After a beat, he flatly added, "And no RVs and no trailers, either."

Speculating, Darcy mildly asked, "What about a tent?"

Brett drew a sharp breath and was about to respond in a negative blast, but stopped short as he caught the look on Troy's face. Exhaling with a bit of a snort, he begrudgingly said, "Okay, fine, a tent."

Darcy did not hesitate, "You're on!"

~~~

On a crisp, spring morning in 1937, when Martin Thurber arrived to assume his duties as the new principle keeper of the Saint Rosabelle Lighthouse, his green eyes gleamed as he viewed his new home and the tower which would be the center of his responsibilities.

The lighthouse sat at a distance down the wide expanse of sandy beach on the shore's point and could be seen across the inlet from the village. The tower was not an exceptionally tall lighthouse, standing only 70 feet high, but had served its purpose well for a number of years. Its nighttime light and prominent profile by day guided the numerous local fishing vessels, small cargo ships and ferries safely into the active, little port. The cylindrical building's appearance was one of sturdy dependability and precision with its masonry of white-washed bricks. Ebony paint protected the metal railings of the high balconies, the slender window frames of the lantern room and the tapered roof, topped by its spherical heat vent. Even the neighboring brick structure of the keeper's house and the wood frame assistant keeper's house were an impressive display of regular maintenance and care. He reached into his pocket to tip the old boatman Dinkle who had shuttled him across the inlet in a dinghy, but the crusty seaman declined the offer. Having removed his shiny black shoes, Martin collected the entirety of his gear, a single duffle bag, from the little boat. He stepped barefooted from the vessel into the edge of the water. Two strides had him on the moist sand of the beach and he began walking the distance to the facility. The tiny outboard motor sputtered behind him and the boat pulled away, leaving the U. S. Lighthouse Service employee on his own. He carried his canvas bag in one hand and his polished leather shoes in the other. As his feet nestled into the soft sand with each step, he felt lucky to get this assignment.

This station was in a far more temperate climate than his last post and the light was within a reasonable distance to a community. The beach was unspoiled and imbued with natural beauty. Small, salt-and-pepper colored plovers ran ahead of Martin's steps only to eventually take wing. They circled wide across the water and then back, to land behind the lighthouse keeper. A great blue heron and a snowy egret avoided Martin, stepping aside as he passed by. Thick stands of graceful sea oats gently rustled in the breeze, their golden tassels swaying freely. In spots shells were piled in drifts as high as Martin's calves, marking the tide lines.

He saw the wooden dock from a distance. It would have easily accommodated the dinghy, but Martin was happy with the walk. Slightly inland, the white tower stood firmly, over two hundred yards from the water. Nearby, the American flag hung still, but proudly, from the top of its pole. As the tall lightkeeper neared the buildings, he paused long enough to slip on his shoes and watch for any signs of activity. A young chap, perhaps not even twenty, hollered and waved to him. Martin's arrival at the lighthouse was far from unexpected. He was here in response to an urgent request issued by the local authorities for a new keeper.

The youthful man strode forward and extended his hand, asking, "Mister Thurber?"

Martin straightened himself up and firmly accepted the handshake as he replied, "Yes."

The lad introduced himself as Robert Carlo Bowsen and with some pride explained that he had been operating the light on his own for nearly all of the last two weeks. Prior to that, he had only served as an assistant keeper for less than a month. The change had come when his superior failed to return from an excursion across the inlet for supplies. The body of the head lighthouse keeper was found a day later, drowned.

After a contemplative moment, Martin asked what had become of the keeper's family. Bowsen explained that the widow and son had moved to Charleston where they were staying with relatives. The youthful attendant then inquired, "When can we expect your family's arrival, sir?"

The new principle keeper simply stated, "I don't have a family."

Martin was efficient and insisted on performing an immediate examination of the facility in order to make an assessment of its operation. First inspected was the tower itself. Martin followed the energetic lad as he climbed the structure's nearly one hundred stairs. As they mounted the spiral flight the assistant keeper was eager to show his knowledge and explained, "The lens is rotational. It has the characteristic of a continuous light, with a flash twice every minute."

"I see," Martin replied and inquired, "and how many other lights on this coast have that same pattern?" His ascending pace was steady, but not as accelerated as that of his youthful guide.

Bowsen slowed, having noticed his rate exceeded that of his new superior. "Um," the lad answered with a slight tinge of embarrassment, "I don't know."

Martin calmly answered his own question, "None. That allows mariners to not only use the light as a warning of danger, but as a position marker for navigation."

They reached the top of the stairs and then climbed the few rungs of a metal ladder to the lantern room. The very heart of the lantern room was the kerosene lamp and the third-order Fresnel lens that surrounded the lamp. Just over five feet tall, the beehive-shaped, leaded crystal Fresnel served to funnel the light into a beam and send it outward, often reaching eighteen miles out to sea during good weather. Martin nodded to the assistant, who responded by pulling open one portion of the beige curtains that completely lined the lantern room windows. As the sunlight streamed in, the keeper gave the massive, crystal prisms of the Fresnel a studious eyeing for damage, dirt or any other obstruction that would limit its functionality. He removed a linen hanky from his trouser pocket and with a painful gentleness removed a small smudge from one of the curved components. Without looking at the young man, who was standing stiffly with a nervous, military stance, Martin stated, "The lives of people depend on this light."

"Yes, sir." Bowsen's reply was somewhat cracked and Martin paused to glance over his shoulder at the fellow who was barely beyond boyhood. The principle keeper became aware of the age difference between himself and the lad. Martin was in his late thirties and his face showed signs of a life in both the hot, bright sunlight and the cold, cutting wind. Creases had begun to show at the corners of his eyes. His dark hair was no longer as thick as it once had been. The keeper again stood straight and moved to examine the windows, which were actually the glass walls of the lantern room, held in place by strong ironwork. Satisfied at the cleanliness, Martin lead the way back down the ladder, leaving Bowsen to pull the curtains closed in order to protect the lens. Having completed the task, the assistant keeper caught up to his superior on the stairs.

Martin allowed Bowsen to lead the tour around the rest of the grounds and out-buildings. The lean young man showed the principle keeper to the oil house where the fuel supply for the lamp was stored, the boathouse and short wharf, the foghorn building, work shed, a small barn and the two water cisterns. Martin gleaned as many details about the buildings and their history as he could from his assistant. At the end of the rather staunch inspection, the light's new keeper paused and nodded. He smiled at Bowsen and stated, "You have done a good job, Robert."

The youthful assistant's face filled with an eager pride. As Martin turned to enter the keeper's residence, he was stopped by Bowsen's questioning voice, "Sir?"

"Yes?" Martin turned to again face his new co-worker.

"Most people just call me Robby." Bowsen shuffled a little, his face adorned with a wide smile.

"Well, okay…Robby. Why don't you call me Martin…all right?" Martin watched as the assistant keeper nodded enthusiastically and then, as he again turned to enter the residence, he punctuated with, "All right."

~~~~

Riding in the comfort of Troy's suburban utility vehicle, Darcy sat next to the driver. They followed Brett's Hummer down the dirt road which led to the paved, county road that was the main passage through the rural area. Sitting on the plush, front seat of the new, metallic silver SUV, the twosome kept glancing at each other. Despite the repeated, clumsy looks, it took a few minutes before either of them spoke. Eventually Troy broke the silence and asked, "So you're really going through with this?"

"Yeah." Darcy spoke softly as she began to think about what she had just committed herself to. She wore a lopsided smile and apologized, "I'm sorry if I'm causing trouble."

Troy's face brightened with a toothy grin. "You're not. I'm the one who started the bet…remember? But three months? That seems like a long time to spend out there. I've been on extended camping excursions before, but it was always somewhere scenic. I can't think of one redeeming thing about that land back there. Those vines have killed all the natural beauty and, to be honest, I've got to admit that it gave me a weird feeling. Is it just the challenge?" His prods were well placed, as usual.

"Not exactly." Darcy spoke hesitantly, her voice filled with deep contemplation as she thought of the desolate lighthouse, "There's more than that. There's just something about the place…I got this really strange kind of…well, yeah…feeling, like it needs to be healed or something." She shook her head, trying to rid herself of the peculiar sensation, and then decided on a more logical explanation. Perking up a degree, she said, "But really, I've never owned property before. Never even really had a place of my own. I've always moved from apartment to apartment…sometimes bunked in with friends…sometimes with relatives." She looked at him with an awkward expression, her light brown eyes filled with an intensiveness. She asked, "Is that too hard to imagine?"

"I figured that it was something like that." McGovern smiled while still watching the rough path of the road. With an unmistakable honesty, he added, "I haven't always had money, you know."

"Yeah, I know." She viewed him with a certain admiration, but still with an amount of puzzlement. She asked, "Why did you agree to this? You know…I can't possibly pay you back, as it is. Once your development is underway, the price of that property will skyrocket."

"Because I like you, that's why." The actor gently pressed the brakes of the luxurious transport and brought the SUV to a near-stop at the intersection of the dirt road and the county throughway. Having checked for the remote possibility of any traffic, he resumed driving and pulled the vehicle onto the pavement. Troy continued his explanation as he applied pressure to the gas peddle, "You're a hard worker. We've worked together on three productions, right?"

Darcy nodded and responded in a quiet voice, "Yes."

"And you've been one of my personal assistants on two of the three." McGovern gave a subtle glance to his helper and added, "You've helped me through some tough things and…I appreciate having people around me I can trust."

Darcy was a little overwhelmed by this and not sure how to respond. She spoke with a measured reply, "Well…thank you."

"Hold on, lady!" Troy's eyebrows arched and he laughed, "You haven't won the bet yet."

"No…I mean, thank you for the trust." After a moment of silence she asked, "Troy, what happens if I lose?"

"Well, Brett will brag a lot. I will probably have to buy him dinner and maybe a round of golf. That tract of land will be cleared for construction along with the rest of the project area and the lighthouse will be demolished, maybe a year or two before it would collapse naturally." He paused, having noticed his companion's discomfort. He breathed deeply and then continued, "I don't think Brett would do anything to hurt your career. He isn't that mean."

"If you say so." There was a skeptical edge to Darcy's voice, but she smiled just the same.

Thanks to Troy's intervention, Darcy was given a three-day reprieve in the city to prepare before beginning occupation of the coastal land. She had reasonable accommodations in the metropolitan area which suited her modest needs. The entertainment production worker had recently had a good run of employment and was able to rent a second story efficiency from her older sister, Gwen. The arrangement had thus far worked out smoothly despite, or perhaps because of, the sibling relationship between the landlord and tenant.

Taking the first day to relax and think, she tried to imagine every possible situation that might occur while she would be staying on the oceanside plot. Darcy created lists as she thought of things and wrote down the items in a notebook. By that evening, she was running out of ideas and hoped that she had thought of all the contingencies. She had contemplated heat, rain, food supplies, wildlife and the task of improving the usability of the land...the land which would possibly become her own. Darcy smiled to herself and thought, *This might be worth documenting*. Win or lose, she would record the effort in all of its various stages. She scrawled at the bottom of one of the lists, "Bring camera."

With her thoughts clear on what had to be done, Darcy began shopping the following morning. She went first to a sporting goods store.

She already owned a tent which she had used for temporary lodging during her work on low-budget films. It was small and not of the best quality, but she had used it on a number of occasions and it was serviceable. She also owned a couple of tarpaulins, but given the age and limited size of her tent she decided to get a few more of the durable, weatherproof covers. She added extra tent spikes to her inventory to go with the tarps.

Darcy added a new portable shower to her purchase. The simple contraption was specially designed to hold enough water in its storage bag for a quick shower and the showerhead had a mechanism to stop or release the water flow. A cord and support bar at the top would allow the bag to be hung just about anywhere. To go along with the shower she bought environmentally-safe soap and shampoo.

She picked up a healthy supply of "sure start" fire sticks to use with her camp stove and foldable wire-frame grill. She had learned in past misadventures just how valuable the "sure start" sticks could be. Darcy remembered one particular foggy night in a remote campsite on the northern California coast. All the firewood in the area was saturated with moisture from an earlier rain and refused to catch flame. Even the paper scraps she tried to use to start a fire had been dampened by the fog's heavy mist. However, her tiny supply of the specially treated, reconstituted, wood products allowed dinner to be cooked after all.

She ventured into an area of the store that she was not at all comfortable in, but on this rare occasion she had need of. Finding a clerk standing at a counter that displayed hunting knives, she asked about "snake leggings." The man gave her an odd look of disbelief, then took her to the appropriate rack. The store had a few selections, but the leggings were mostly meant for use by men. They were designed to cover the lower portion of the legs, strapping on like the canvas-covered pieces of armor that they were. Darcy tried them on and found that even when strapped as tightly as possible the standard sizes were too large. Patiently smiling at the amused clerk, she asked that he go to the storeroom and get the smallest size they had. After a number of minutes he returned with a size that at least would be serviceable to his smaller-than-usual customer. They weren't pretty, all drab green, but they worked. Pleased, Darcy thanked the clerk for his time and happily purchased the protective attire.

Next she visited a warehouse store…wholesale supplier. Checking her list, she collected a variety of dried, easy to prepare foods that would be easily kept without refrigeration. She then stopped at a hardware store and gathered an array of items there. Among her purchases was an inventory of weapons to use against the kudzu: a handsaw, an axe, a machete and shovel.

Her final shopping excursion, late in the afternoon, was to a discount store. Having shopped for supplies most of the day, Darcy found herself becoming weary of the city traffic and crowded stores. As she assembled the final items, her thoughts began to wander. An image of the solitary lighthouse, its red-brown, exposed brickwork entered her mind. The metal railings and floors of the balconies were thinning and brittle, eaten away by ravaging rust. A few of the jagged shards of glass, all that remained of the lantern room's great windows, clung precariously to their deteriorating frames. Weathered plywood and boards covered the few small lower windows. Even these barricades were worn to the point of decay, scoured by years of sand and wind and rain. The tower seemed dark and lonely. Though she had only seen the tower briefly, this vision was as vivid as if she stood on the beach at that very moment.

She stopped and picked up a number of emergency candles, plus a few larger, pillar candles that would burn for a long time. A couple of disposable lighters joined the wax burnables. Darcy looked at a kerosene camp lantern and her daydreams continued. Who had kept the lamps lit in the tower so long ago? What kind of person would stay there and serve that kind of duty? Why was no one there now? Images of the rushing waves encroaching on the abandoned silhouette flooded her thoughts. She placed the lantern into her shopping cart.

By the end of the three days Darcy felt prepared for anything. She had collected everything from rope to a complete first-aid kit, from bleach to pasta, from plastic bags to insect spray. She had tied up as many personal loose ends as possible and during her preparations had talked with her sister about the pending three-month venture. The night before leaving town she wrote out information, including emergency contact phone numbers and approximately where she would be during her absence, and gave it to her sister. Darcy did not own that much to begin with, so it took her little time to pack and store those things she would be leaving in town, just in case Gwen rented the efficiency while she was away. The car was packed and loaded with the equipment Darcy intended to take with her. There was nothing more she could think of that needed to be done. She was ready to go.

The next morning, the two actors and the production assistant again journeyed from the city and returned to the edge of the overgrown lot. They had driven the distance during the early morning hours and had arrived on the coast about mid-morning. This time the two thespians had traveled together in the Hummer, leaving Darcy to follow in her old Chevy. Her aged car, filled with her supplies, moved at a slower pace than the unburdened all-terrain vehicle.

The Chevrolet Impala had been given to her when she had graduated from college. Her parents had thought that it would last for maybe a couple of years before completely falling apart. Darcy nursed the car through a number of minor breakdowns and grew accustomed to its lack of modern devices. The large trunk was perfect for hauling all the stuff that went along with working on films and commercial productions. When she began to earn a fair income, her family assumed that she would be getting a new car. Perhaps partially in defiance of their insistence she instead began to refurbish the Impala. Now the automobile was in fine operating condition and even sported a new paint job.

She found that the two men had slowed drastically as they neared the destination and had allowed her to catch up to them. Leaving the paved road and making the final turn of the trip, Darcy noted that somehow the dirt road that lead out to the property had seemed a lot smoother in Troy McGovern's SUV than it did now in her automobile. As the vehicles reached the end of the unpaved road, the dirt trail disappeared into the tangled cover of foliage. The Hummer crushed through the vegetation and turned about, leaving room for the car to pull forward. The travelers disembarked and stretched their legs, stiff from sitting.

Brett Jarrett announced in a bright and overly cheerful tone, "Well...here we are!" He smiled broadly and taunted Darcy, "You can back out now...just say it."

"No...I think this will be fine." The feminine adventurer reflected the oversized smile back at Brett, denying him the satisfaction of a quick victory. She glanced over at Troy who was silently doing calisthenics.

Brett deliberately surveyed the surroundings. "I've been told there are snakes out here...spiders too, big ones."

"So I imagine." Darcy seemed undaunted by all of the man's efforts of dissuasion.

Shaking his head, Brett gave a slight laugh and shrugged his shoulders. He looked into Darcy's determined brown eyes and jeered, "Darn, girl. Just you wait...."

"You know," she pondered aloud, "if you both are going back to California, how are you going to know if I hold up my end of this?" Though she had addressed both men, Darcy deliberately aimed the question in Brett's direction.

"Oh, don't you worry about that. We'll know." There was an assured edge in Brett's voice that told Darcy he had cooked up something.

She simply replied, "Okay, then."

The actor's sharpness was becoming more and more obvious. He pulled in a deep breath and made one last attempt, "Okay, well...no last minute reconsideration?"

"I'll see you in three months." Darcy's words held a finality in them as she leaned against her parked car.

Accepting that she would not be talked into allowing him a win by default, Brett grunted and headed for the driver's door of the large, off-road vehicle. Troy removed an opaque plastic shopping bag from the floor of the passenger side of the Hummer and stepped up to his occasional attendant. Placing his hand on Darcy's rounded shoulder, he eased her defensiveness. Her sharpened expression melted as she relaxed. He smiled and looked warmly into her eyes. Drawing close, he quietly asked, "Are you all right with this?" Troy watched as Darcy returned his smile and simply nodded. He gave her shoulder a gentle massage and then handed the grey plastic bag to the new rural resident. He requested, "Call if you get into trouble." She accepted the bag and glanced inside, finding a new cell phone and car adaptor. Looking back at the movie actor, she again nodded without speaking words. Giving her a final pat on the arm, Troy turned and walked to the waiting Hummer. He boarded the already idling vehicle and it pulled back onto the dirt passage.

Darcy watched as the all-terrain vehicle left and headed back toward the main road, nearly a mile away. As the dust settled and the last sight of the actors was lost, she looked around and surveyed her surroundings. The vines were so thick that there was not even a place to set up her tent. There were no open paths to the beach or lighthouse. There were no obvious signs of recent human occupation of the land. There were just the vague shapes of objects that lay underneath the thick coating of kudzu, the top of a couple of trees yet to be totally smothered by the vine and the barely perceptible, old roof of the lighthouse, which stood at some distance beyond all the vegetation. An odd silence overtook the area, broken only by the distant soft lap of waves and a sweet breeze that rustled the leaves of the great, green expanse. Alone, Darcy quietly spoke to herself. "Oh boy, you've done it this time."

Chapter Two

When she got up that morning she had dressed in a well-worn pair of jeans, an old t-shirt and sturdy, leather shoes. But now Darcy Vornack strapped on the snake leggings and donned the leather gloves that she had owned for years. She had work to do. There wasn't even room on the kudzu-covered ground for her to set up her small, domed tent. She opened the automobile trunk and unloaded her arsenal of tools dedicated to vegetation combat. As she prepared to begin her work, she remembered her vow to document her efforts. Accordingly, she fetched the camera and snapped two "before" photographs that captured the smothered landscape on film. Stashing the 35-mm safely away, there was no reason for her to delay the effort further. Darcy began the task of clearing the space needed to set up a base camp. That seemingly simple chore was harder than she had expected. It took over three hours to make a viewable hole in the vines. She merely managed to remove some of the surface growth, chopping off the thinner strands and runners without dislodging the strangling weed's main trunks or roots.

Gathering the cut segments and piling them next to the car, she took a break and consumed a short lunch of dried fruit and a bottle of water. The sun had removed all hint of the morning's coolish conditions and only a slight breeze stirred the warm air. Darcy already felt gritty from the weeding effort. Her clothing had begun to cling to areas of perspiration. Swallowing the water, she found it tasted better than it had earlier. It soothed a thirst that had arrived without notice.

After resting for about a half an hour she renewed her efforts. She was determined that this time she would remove entire plants. She waded through the tangle while tracing a large, woody stem. Tracking the runner led her into vegetation that was often over her knees and she lumbered forward until she found what she believed was the vine's origin. It lay in the shadows cast by the overhanging branches of a nearly-choked oak tree. To her astonishment she discovered not one, but four large vines growing from the very same spot in the ground. Even more to her amazement all four of the green beasts were no less than four inches thick at the base. Darcy refused to be dismayed. Attacking with the hand saw, she began working on the kudzu trunks. Her arms were unaccustomed to this form of labor and soon started aching. Severing one plant she pulled at the vine, hoping to reel it in like an untied rope. However, there was no give from the stout, woody tendril—absolutely none. She leaned over to see what the problem was and discovered that the vine was attached to the ground by runners at nearly every foot of length! At these joints more new runners reached from the ground and headed in all directions.

Bending the cut trunks to the side as best she could, Darcy decided that she would go after the root system in order to prevent the vine's regrowth and ultimately to smooth the surface of the ground. She fetched the shovel from her car, waded back through the tangle to the one severed trunk and set about attacking the weed's stump. Digging down one side, she found a solid mass of root. With the results of that tactic less than desirable, she began removing dirt from all sides of the tuber. As Darcy cleared away the first foot of earth she discovered that her foe was not one, but close to ten tubers, and the main anchor was wider than her fist. She wiped the sweat from her brow with her dirty fingers and sighed.

Kneeling and looking at the roots she thought she noticed something unusual about the earth. She spotted some odd items among the expected soil components of sand, a trace of clay, and an amount of detritus. There were small white flecks in the dirt. A closer examination revealed these fragments to be brittle and often having distinctive shapes. It took a moment of thought for Darcy to recognize these particles as fish bones. The dirt was rich with the tiny bone remnants, bleached and broken through time. She returned her attention to the tubers and momentarily dismissed the discovery as nothing more than a curiosity.

Standing up, she resumed digging, heaving hard on the shovel. Cutting through the sandy soil she again worked all sides of the monstrous root system until the hole was another foot deep. Darcy laid the shovel aside and grabbed the roots with her gloved hands. She braced her feet and pulled hard on the tuberous mass. She strained for several seconds while applying her entire strength, becoming red, then white in the face. The roots held against her best efforts. Letting go an explosive breath, she released her hold on the stubborn plants.

Again Darcy straightened and then flexed her back. Soaked with perspiration, she rested her hands on her hips and drew a few deep breaths. Then she picked up the shovel and once more went to work. Her hands were becoming quite sore, but Darcy would not admit defeat. She shoveled away yet one more foot of earth which was now harder, more compact than before and lacking the fish-bone content. With this done, she dropped the digging tool and again took hold of the root. She strained with a mighty tug and groaned in her effort to budge the insidious tuber. Not one millimeter did the root yield.

Darcy strode back to the car while cursing the plant's roots all along the way. She found the machete and took a vise-like hold on the hilt. Half an hour later, the crown of tubers lay loose on the soil surface after having been chopped crudely below ground level. Despite all her efforts, the very base of the tap roots remained secure in their earthen home. Darcy sat on the ground next to her adversary. Sweat ran down the sides of her face and she guzzled more water from the plastic bottle. Examining the source of the dislodged vine while she rested, she decided that she would not try any more root removal soon. She looked up into the ailing tree and the cords of runners that hung from the branches. There would be no roots up there!

After having relaxed for a spell, Darcy slowly got up and singled out a length of dangling vines. She cut the growth off at the bottom and then used both hands to hold the entwined runners. As she began slowly pulling downward on the mass, it yielded slightly with smaller connections breaking free from twigs and bark. The progress was momentarily halted as her pull met the strength of thicker segments which wrapped over themselves along the limbs of the old tree. Optimistically Darcy pulled harder and when the vine did not surrender she applied her own body weight to the effort. She heard a slight snapping sound from above and looked up in time to see a substantial limb beginning to fall. Releasing the vine, she scrambled to avoid the impact. Her legs worked furiously, but were slowed by the snags and snares of the kudzu. She found herself on all fours and did not bother to try to stand again. Reaching forward she pulled herself out of the way, hand over hand. The limb crashed into the bed of vines some three feet behind her. As her adrenalin slowed and she realized that she was mostly unharmed, she managed to regain her footing. Looking at the downed and decaying tree limb, she realized her mistake in not perceiving the true extent of the vine's toll on the trees.

Darcy retrieved her tools and made her way to safe ground to regroup.

This time she armed herself solely with the saw. She realized that she had been diverted from her original task of clearing an area for the tent. She had lost a good portion of the day by tracing the one runner and only then finding out the depth of the task of root removal. Refocusing her efforts, she contented herself with an attempt to simply clear a section of the property near the dirt road. Now, if a vine was within Darcy's immediate reach it got sawed off, whether it connected to anything or not. For all of her efforts, a space of approximately four feet by six feet was cleared of the kudzu runners by the end of the day.

When dusk came, Darcy was beyond tired. As she removed the protective gloves she discovered her hands were red—in some places they were raw. She also had nasty blisters. Too exhausted to do anything else, Darcy decided not to bother cooking that night and instead ate a bit more of the dried fruit and a few pretzels. She piled all the contents that were held in the back seat of her car into the front seat and opened the car window just a crack to let in fresh air. Backing out of the car, she closed the door behind her and then glanced at her attire. After attempting to brush off some of the layer of dirt that now coated her clothing, she crawled into the rear of the vehicle. Darcy closed the car door behind her and stretched out on the back seat as much as she could. Her legs were still bent and rather folded, but it did not matter. The seat was comfortable enough…and she was exhausted. She fell asleep listening to the distant sounds of the ocean surf.

~~~~

An eerie humming sound saturated the air as Martin sat down at the simple wooden, roll-top desk in the keeper's residence. Withdrawing the log book from the side drawer and opening the official journal, he found the page of his last entry. He picked up his fountain pen and began his daily entry:

"Weather calm. Cleaned tower windows and lens. Area plagued with heavy numbers of biting insects during twilight and dark hours, limiting outside efforts. Myself and assistant keeper forced to seal ourselves into the tower during the night."

Somberly Martin looked to the window. At first glance, the glass pane appeared to be painted grey, but on closer inspection he could see the outside surface moving with a coating of live mosquitoes.

~~~~

Darcy stirred abruptly and slapped at the side of her face. The night was still dark, but its peacefulness had been shattered. Sitting up in the car she was surrounded by the buzz of small insects. The vehicle had filled with hungry mosquitoes. Wearily looking beyond the side window, Darcy saw that it was even worse outside of the automobile. Reluctantly she opened the door and went outside to the rear of the car. She unlocked the trunk and raised the lid, digging into the well-planned layout of contents. Finding the repellent, Darcy doused herself in the stinky spray. She closed the rear compartment and then turned the pungent mist toward the interior of her car. She gave the sheltered area a heavy dose and waited a moment for the insects to leave. With mild satisfaction she took the repellent with her and climbed back into the rear seat of the car, shutting the door behind her and rolling the windows closed. Once more at peace, she did not wake until dawn.

Opening her eyes to the pale grey of early morning, Darcy looked out of the car window to see the tops of the strange kudzu forms and the clear sky. The world seemed to have an unnatural stillness. The air was so placid that not one leaf moved. She sat up and rubbed her arms, removing the chill that had settled in during the night. A realization came to her and she smiled with private delight. She had made it through her first complete day and night on the property.

As Darcy stiffly climbed out of the car, she stretched heartily and glanced over at yesterday's work area. She could not believe her eyes and walked over to the cleared patch of ground where the remaining vine bases were still rooted. From a number of the chopped remains grew brand new, thin sprouts, bright green and filled with life. Overnight new tendrils had begun to spring from the kudzu and some were already inches long. Grumpily she remarked, "No wonder they call this 'the vine that ate the South!' "

Throughout the second day Darcy worked at a slower pace. She excavated the ground around the thick, kudzu stems, this time only digging to a depth ranging from five to eight inches. With the bases exposed, she then cut off the wood below the ground level. She had been engrossed in her labors for a few hours and was in the midst of sawing away at a chunk of kudzu root when a very peculiar feeling came over her. Darcy halted her motions with the saw still resting in its cutting groove, halfway through a vine tuber. Her senses became absolutely alert, peaked beyond normal. It was as if she could feel the stare of a stranger gazing upon her. She released her grip on the tool and gradually straightened, looking over the flat, open space that was covered by kudzu. Her ears suddenly filled with the sound of whispering, unintelligible urgings from an unknown male voice. Darcy spun about while surveying the scenery for the unannounced visitor. She looked down the dirt road, then to her car, then to the line of trees bordering the expanse of vine, then to the foliage-draped shapes within the growth. She searched everywhere that she thought the voice might be coming from. There was no one in sight. To her confoundment, she could not even detect the actual, single direction from which the muddled whispers might be emanating. The words were indistinct and somehow muted beyond recognition. Even straining to listen, Darcy was only able to discern the slightest amount of what was being said: the words "light" and "three boats." She continued to search for the source as the whispering continued for a full minute, gaining exigence and volume, but no more clarity. Just when it seemed that the whispers might reach the level of shouts, they swiftly faded away to nothing. The sounds left as quickly as they had come, leaving the lone occupant of the plant-snarled clearing both alarmed and baffled. She continued to look around her in every possible direction. After several minutes of failing to see anything out of the ordinary, Darcy attempted to dismiss the event and knelt again to resume her work. She assured herself that the event was just a fluke. Perhaps a boat had passed offshore with its radio turned too loud. Maybe a vehicle equipped with speakers was blaring an announcement along the highway. While continuing to work through the day, however, Darcy was unable to rid herself of the uncomfortable feeling of being watched.

By the end of the day, she had managed to clear an area just large enough to allow her to set up her tiny tent. The tent was designed to sleep one to two people, but only one person could use it comfortably. Darcy spread a tarp on the ground where she planned to place the tent, so as to provide some protection to the floor of the domed, nylon structure. Having securely planted the metal stakes and inserted the fiberglass support rods, she forced the rod tips into their nylon sockets and raised the structure. Though small, the little nylon shelter and the sleeping bag would be more comfortable than the cramped back seat of her car. The faded, blue tent was not much, but for now it was home.

Although she was tired Darcy thought it wise to use the camp stove and fix a simple evening meal. Fueling the burner compartment of the stove with dry leaves and twigs, she boiled water and cooked a handful of pasta. The dish was adequate—enough to fill Darcy's stomach, if not satisfy her pallet.

After cleaning the dishes, Darcy took a few minutes to organize the cut lengths of kudzu. She quickly developed a system of sorting the cuttings by approximate diameter and length, establishing separate piles for the different sizes. She was unsure of how she might use the detached vines, but she knew that she would eventually think of something.

On the morning of the third day, Darcy's body was one massive ache. Her hands were swollen and raw from the abuse. They had continued to blister, despite the leather work gloves and assorted small bandages that she had used the previous day. Her back, shoulders and arms were twinging with sensitive muscles that were unused to doing the labor that they had been engaged in. Even her legs were stiff. Darcy acknowledged the need to recuperate. She decided to take a leisurely drive to the village and stop at the general store, all of some five miles away. She would check to see what they had in stock and maybe learn something about the local area.

Darcy was in no rush this morning. Before leaving the camp she made use of the portable shower, refreshing herself and washing off the gritty combination of dirt, bug repellent and sweat that she had accumulated during the last two days of work. Darcy selected clean clothes to put on, the nicest of the work clothes she had brought with her. As she pulled on the shirt she suddenly felt observed, just as she had the day before. She was unsettled and glanced around the area. Despite her thorough scrutiny, she could find nothing amiss in the scenery. There was no one there but herself. Finishing getting dressed and giving the camp site a careful examination, she determined that it was secure enough to leave without great risk of disturbance. Darcy made sure she had her camera with her when she left, as it was probably the most valuable thing she owned beyond the car. Besides, she might have fun taking a few tourist shots.

As she reached the junction of the dirt road and the paved county highway, she was somewhat surprised to find what had happened there since her arrival at the property three days earlier. The lot on the right-hand corner of the junction had been cleared of most vegetation. The stripped bit of land was now occupied by an old trailer. Dented and tarnished, the once-chrome mobile home was parked a few yards from the roadway and faced the dirt road. The crumpled remains of three or four beer cans littered the ground not far from the door. Darcy stopped her Chevy so that she could examine the trailer more carefully. As she sat in her car surveying the area, the ragged drapes of one of the trailer windows parted just long enough for an unshaven, disheveled man to peer out. He spotted Darcy watching him and quickly let the faded fabric fall back to its hanging position.

Darcy laughed and lightly jeered, "So that's how Brett will know. Well, that's fine with me." She pulled the car onto the main road and proceeded down the narrow thoroughfare. Driving across the long stretch of the baffle bridge, she looked out across the coastal scene. Great golden-green reaches of sawgrass lined the shores of the inlet, hiding an uncountable number of tiny lagoons and creeks. Looking beyond the partially sheltered, rippling waters, Darcy could see the open blue of the ocean. Leaving the rhythmic hum of the causeway behind, the roadside was lined with southern Live Oaks often adorned with strands of Spanish moss and aerial bromeliads. Moving further along the route she passed a two-story building that looked to be nothing more than someone's home, but a sign in the yard claimed the shingled building was actually "The Mockingbird Inn." If the structure with only a dirt driveway and in need of maintenance was indeed a guesthouse, there was no indication of its active use. She passed half a dozen back roads that were marked only by their own short line of mail boxes and then at the side of the road she saw a plywood sign which read, "Antiques."

On an impulse Darcy steered off the road at the marked driveway. The approach to the small business was dirt and grass, just like the entrance to the Mockingbird Inn had been. She parked her car and disembarked to look around. There was no sign of life other than a truck that was parked to the side of the antiques store. Curious, she walked over to the front door. Finding it locked Darcy looked through the dirty windows and strained to see inside. Though her view was obscured she could see a plethora of dusty bottles, rusty objects of iron, green and corroded items that might have been brass or copper and crab trap buoys. She decided that she would have to return at another time to explore the shop when it was open, even if it seemed that there was more junk than possible items of value.

Approaching the village nestled next to the inlet she reduced her driving speed and matched the marked speed limit of twenty-five miles an hour. When she came to the only other paved road she knew of in the area, she slowed the car further. Looking down the secondary road, aged and declining warehouses were matched by docks with sagged, worn boards. Some of the metal buildings were marked on the side by barely discernible, faded letters, painted there many years ago. Moored to the dubious docks were a handful of steel-hulled fishing vessels, most of which desperately needed fresh paint. Piles of crab traps were erratically placed and stacked in varying degrees of neatness. Tall, steel frames supported fishing nets, untangled and drying in the morning sun. On one corner of the intersection, across from what seemed to be a restaurant or an ale house, was the Campbell & Hoffer General Store.

The store was housed in a tin-roofed building with a broad front porch that was supported by wooden beams. The exterior of the building was armored in corrugated metal siding that was not particularly new. A weathered dullness covered the outside of the store matching the metal that the local warehouses wore. Everything here was touched by corrosion born from the saltwater spray carried on the wind. A large, drab metal chest marked with the word "ice" sat on the right side of the building entrance. In front of the building was a simple, two-post sign. Its tacked-on letters, hanging askew, read, "GENE AL STORE." Hung over the porch was a carved wooden sign with flaking and faded paint announcing the store's name and the phrase, "Since 1923."

~~~~

"Since 1923." Having read the cleanly painted sign, Martin climbed the stairs to the store. The street in back of him was lively as people went about their daily business. Some ladies walked by engaged in whispered conversation and with sly glances studied Martin in his Lighthouse Service uniform. A boy peddled on a bicycle and was followed closely by another lad on a home-made kick scooter. A fisherman pushing a cart filled with nets greeted the busybody women and then laughed to himself as they recoiled from the odorous gill mesh.

Martin entered the store and closed the door behind him, causing the dangling, small brass bells attached to the doorknob to chime. Looking across the store the keeper's eyes fixed first on a gathering of young women. The eldest of the trio was probably in her early twenties and was quite possibly one of the most beautiful lasses Martin had ever seen. The young woman's radiance caught his total attention. Her laugh completely captivated him—a delightful tone, more melodic than the tinkle of the door bells. Though she was standing and talking with two other pretty young women, for the keeper neither of the others were as lovely as she. Her skin was beautifully fair and her hair sparkled with a sheen of silky gold.

Martin was surprised by the older woman's voice beside him, "Good morning, sir. Is there something I may help you with?"

Momentarily disoriented, Martin glanced about, then turned awkwardly to face her. For a horrible moment he found that he had forgotten why he had come. She watched him with a prudish, knowing expression. The grey-haired woman was plainly dressed in a crisp maroon frock. The keeper stammered and then forced himself to say something, anything. "Uh, yes ma'am. Yes...I need chicken feed."

"I see. And you must be the new lighthouse keeper."

"Yes. Yes, I am." He smiled, remembering he was in uniform.

"Well, welcome to our store, Mister...?" The woman deliberately allowed the greeting to trail off and gave the customer an expectant look.

The light keeper played to the social cue and responded, "Thurber…Martin Thurber."

"Welcome, Mr. Thurber. I am Mrs. Caroline Campbell…and that is my daughter, Iris…her friends Becky and Doris." Caroline directed herself to the threesome of gossiping, giggling young women, "Ladies! Iris has work to do!"

~~~~

An old man sat straddling a stool on the left side of the porch. His attention was directed toward a game board and he did not bother to look at the newly arrived vehicle. Darcy got out of the car and walked up the three stairs to the front porch. The door to the business was closed and she could not see inside. She addressed the elder, "Hello. Is the store open?"

He slowly looked up from the game of checkers which was balanced on a small, unfinished, wooden table. Inspecting the woman in her jeans and t-shirt, he made no attempt to rise. "No," was all he said before looking back at his game in which he had no visible opponent.

"Oh," Darcy hesitated before inquiring, "What time does it open?"

The man took his time in reacting to the question, choosing first to move one of the black checkers forward before waving a weathered finger toward the door. He made the pointing motion without looking up from his continued contemplation.

Glancing back at the portal Darcy spotted the small piece of paper taped on the inside of the door's window pane. It was yellowed from age and faded from years of sunlight, so it required some effort on her part in order to be read. "10 AM - 6 PM Monday thru Friday, Noon - 5 PM Saturday, Closed Sundays."

She found herself having to count the days back in order to figure out what day of the week it was. After a moment, she decided that it had to be Tuesday. She looked at her watch and it read 9:30 AM. Resigned to the delay she stated, "Looks like I'm early. Guess I'll have to wait."

"Yep." The man looked up from his game and again pondered the newcomer standing by the door. After a moment he asked, "Play?" He motioned to the game board and then to a nearby stool.

Darcy raised an eyebrow, smiled and replied, "Sure, why not." She took hold of the stool and drew it close to the rustic table as the man cleared the board. Once seated across from the man she got her first good view of him. He was old, but not frail. His face was creased, but not at all pale; rather, he was tanned and leathery from years of too much sun exposure.

He displayed two checkers in one open, callused hand, one red and the other black. Darcy caught the implied question and responded, "Black, please."

With the board reset the pair started the game. It had been quite a while since Darcy had played checkers and she attempted to give her advances proper deliberation. Her opponent had no hesitation in his moves and placed his checkers with an unnerving confidence. As the game progressed Darcy found herself repeatedly losing game pieces to her cunning adversary's strategies. A second and third game showed the same results. Finally in the fourth game she spotted her chance. She proudly moved her black checker, jumping a vulnerable, red game piece and exclaimed, "Got ya!" The old man just shook his head and grinned, his pale eyes twinkling. He reached forward and taking hold on one of his red checkers, proceeded to jump one black checker, a second and then a third. Darcy pursed her lips and stared at the game board in disbelief. His move was perfectly legal and well-planned. She folded her left hand over her mouth and cheek, propping her elbow on the table. Looking up at the fellow who was smiling broadly, she began to quietly laugh and shake her head in near awe.

The elder was about to set up for a fifth game when much to Darcy's relief a station wagon pulled up to the front of the building. When the door to the tan vehicle opened, a lady got out. Her hair was an assembly of long, milky white strands that she had pulled back and braided. Darcy guessed that the trim and firmly-built woman was maybe in her early sixties. Dressed in shorts, a matching top and deck shoes, the new arrival almost sprinted up the stairs and began to unlock the wood frame door to the general store.

The older woman looked over in Darcy's direction and in a sing-song voice announced, "Good morning!"

Darcy stood and smiled, replying in a softer tone, "Good morning."

Freeing the keys from the door and opening the entrance, the woman nodded at the potential customer and said, "Go on in." As Darcy strolled toward the door the shopkeeper passed her along the porch and embraced the shoulders of the seated elder.

The interior of the store was unlike anything Darcy had ever seen before. The floor was crowded with racks and shelves, squeezing every possible inch of space into use. In the midst of all the goods were maritime relics. High on one wall a magnificent bow maiden dating most likely from the turn of the nineteenth century was securely mounted. The carefully carved lady's brown eyes gazed over an assortment of spooled ropes that were displayed on a tall rack. There were bins containing a variety of nails and screws, numerous tubes of glue, caulk and other sealants, plus pulleys and cleats. Further down the wall were strung the remains of an expansive fishing net that was used as decoration. Hung within the mass of heavy mesh was a selection of trap floats showing wear by wind and sea. Below the net was a line of coolers and freezers containing perishable foods including, not surprisingly, a notable amount of seafood. Fishing lures, bobbers, hooks and monofilament line were next to the various packaged food supplies with their tins and plastic bags arrayed on shelves.

A number of signal flags hung from the wooden rafter beams, most faded with age. Darcy did not know how to read them, but she knew that each represented a different letter in the alphabet. On the center beam was mounted a massive ship's wheel. The steering mechanism showed wear, but was kept clean and was lovingly polished. A metal shelf which held used paperback books and a few old video tapes for rent was adjacent to the dog food, cat food, and bags of chicken and rabbit feed. Near the center of the store was an aisle with liquid detergents, laundry soap, bath soap and batteries, plus paper towels, trash bags, toilet paper and baby diapers. A spattering of tourist trinkets and a wire frame stand displaying outdated, sometimes tacky postcards were near the front of the store. Darcy stopped and picked up a snow globe, shook the plastic toy and watched as the white flakes swirled around the captive, black and white, generic lighthouse. She placed the object back among the other snow globes and moved on. On one side of the register was a ship's bell that shined from being keenly polished and was as tall as Darcy's forearm was long. It was set in a dark, lustrous, wooden framework. On the other side of the register was a glass counter which displayed all the available candies. The selection ranged from Snickers bars to canisters of individually wrapped, hard, sugar candies, such as peppermints and root beer drums.

~~~~

As he was presented with a bag of chicken feed, Martin's attention was momentarily distracted by the actions of a boy who was just entering his adolescence. The lad was standing at the front counter in which a variety of candies were displayed, all carefully sorted in glass canisters. It seemed that the child was in negotiation with the beautiful lass with the golden hair. Iris stood behind the counter and adamantly whispered, "No, Ben. I can't...."

The child pleadingly whined, "Just one...."

"Benjamin Louis Campbell! What did I tell you!" Mrs. Campbell's voice was stern and the boy's posture became stiff as he turned around and saw the irritation on his mother's face. The child's expression was half-beseeching and half-fearful at having been caught in the act. Mrs. Campbell sighed and then waved the boy toward the door, "Leave your sister alone…go on. Go sweep the porch!" Lethargically the lad turned and went out the door. "Sometimes I don't know what to do with the child, Mister Thurber. He is too young for his father to take out on the boats, but he is old enough to find trouble."

As Martin and Caroline walked toward the front of the store, the lighthouse keeper inquired, "Your husband owns boats?"

Iris preempted her mother, "Father owns five of the finest fishing boats in the port. All of the fish and crab we carry are from his fleet!" The young woman stood proudly behind the counter and began to ring up the merchandise which Martin had laid on the wooden surface.

Caroline was incensed by her daughter's airs and scolded her, "Iris!"

"Well, it's true, Mother." The lass smiled, more for the pleasure of her customer than that of her parent. There was a twinkle in her blue eyes.

"And what of those boats owned by Mister Hoffer and his son? They bring in their catch, too." The elder woman gave the lass a scornful look, then directed all of her attention to the register as Iris punched in the prices.

"They hardly bring in anything these days." The young woman spoke with a lightness in her voice that Martin thought seemed to grace the air with its sound.

Mrs. Campbell was not amused, "Hush yourself. Mister Hoffer is part owner of this store and I will abide no disrespect toward him."

Iris gently shook her head and replied, "Of course not. I didn't mean any. Fishing is a hard business and catches invariably fluctuate." Turning to Martin, she looked directly into the moss-green eyes of the tall light keeper and asked, "Anything else, today?"

Martin felt his breath catch in his throat and for a moment he could not look away. Swallowing, he forced his eyes away from hers and glanced down at the contents in the candy display case. "Yes," doing a quick search of the canisters, he spotted the glass container with the lemon drops. Pointing to it, he requested, "Please, five of those."

Martin could not help but smile as the lovely lass knelt to fetch the desired sweets. He sensed the older woman moving away and busying herself with tidying the merchandise on the tables and wooden shelves. He glanced briefly toward the back shelves where a variety of used paddles, oars, rope and other various riggings were neatly stocked. In an attempt to continue conversing with Iris, Martin quickly surveyed the store, then commented, "I notice that you have a number of used items in the rear of the store."

Carefully placing the lid back on the clear cylinder, Iris rose from her stooped position and handed Martin a crisp, waxed, little bag containing the yellow candy. "Yes. Father does some salvaging and we do some used-items exchanges. He cleans the items up and then we sell them here."

"I'll have to remember that," he smilingly lingered on the thought and then continued, "in case I ever need to replace an oar." Again her eyes met his and he became very self-conscious. Suddenly embarrassed, he looked down while digging for his wallet. After he handed Iris the money for the purchase, he glanced over his shoulder and noted that Mrs. Campbell was now heading for the back of the store. He quietly said to Iris, "Your father is very fortunate."

As Iris hit the sale button on the register and the machine sounded its tiny chime, she responded, "The Depression taught us to be very frugal, sir."

"I mean," Martin paused and then boldly followed through, "your father is fortunate to have such a beautiful daughter." As the words came from his mouth, he could not believe that he had actually just said that! His head momentarily seemed to spin and his stomach clutched in sudden anxiety. He felt like an awkward schoolboy. When he looked back at the young beauty she had a curious smile on her face and her eyes showed a surprised appreciation. Though still disbelieving his own actions, Iris's pleasure made Martin glad that he had spoken his thoughts.

With a hint of blush gracing her cheeks, Iris graciously replied, "Well...thank you." She handed Martin his change. He tucked it into his trouser pocket. But before picking up the sack of chicken feed, Martin opened the little bag of candy and handed one of the lemon drops to Iris. She quickly glanced to where her mother had gone. Mrs. Campbell was concentrating on straightening the stock. Iris responded softly, "Thank you, again." Martin just gave an ample, toothy smile.

Leaving the store, he found Ben sweeping the front porch of the building. Martin stopped and once again opened the bag of lemon drops. He called to the lad and then offered him one of the sweet, yellow treats. The child eagerly accepted and popped the candy into his mouth, without pause. Ben beamed with delight and exclaimed, "Thanks, mister!"

"You're welcome, Ben." Martin smiled and wandered down the stairs to the roadway.

~~~~

Finally, after having explored the entire stock of the store, Darcy ran out of excuses to prolong the shopping trip. She had taken so long in her exploration of the wonders in the store that the older lady had turned her attention to other activities. Having gathered a tube of Ben Gay, a pint of one percent milk and one of the outdated postcards, Darcy wandered to the front of the store. Her eye was caught by the antique candy counter and she paused, contemplating the bags of Creme Drops, small boxes of candied peanuts, caramel Cow Tails and other treats.

The shopkeeper was restocking the cigarette shelves on a cabinet behind the register when she noticed that Darcy was standing in front of the counter. Setting aside the carton of tobacco products she smiled and asked, "May I get you something?"

Pursing her lips, Darcy delayed for a second before responding, "Some of those Boston Baked peanuts, please." After a moment of thinking she added, "I need to fill a couple of jugs with drinking water. Is there some place local I could do that?"

The white-haired lady reached into the case and removed one of the small, dark red boxes. Placing the candy on the counter, she replied, "There's a spigot around on the side of the store…a gas pump too…if you need a fill-up."

"Thank you, but I'm fine on gas for the moment." Darcy commented, "I would like to take some photos of the boats, so I can share your area with my sister. She doesn't come out to the coast much. Would there be any problem with that?"

Totaling the purchase on the electric register and using multiple function keys, the shopkeeper explained, "Most of our boats are out today, but I don't see why anyone would object." She took a breath then added, "You be careful though, if you go back to the docks. Some of the guys like to party pretty hard when they get in, you know, after being offshore for a while. I'm not sure, but I think some of the things they like aren't always legal." She smiled softly, "Just watch yourself, that's all." Hitting a final key, she announced the sum to her customer.

Darcy gingerly removed her wallet from the rear pocket of her jeans, being careful not to further injure any of the blisters on her hand. As she opened the wallet she noticed the shopkeeper intently watching her cautious movements. Handing over the money, Darcy displayed her palm and explained in a reticent fashion, "I use my hands a lot."

"Ah." The lady nodded with perhaps a hint of uncertainty showing in her expression. She entered the transaction in the register and handed the change to her customer. Pulling a small plastic bag from below the counter, the shopkeeper put the purchased goods neatly inside, taking care with the postcard. As she finished the bagging she said, "Well, I hope you have a good trip."

"Oh, I'll be staying in the area for a while." Darcy carefully slid the change into her front pocket, again being careful to avoid the injuries on her hand. She continued, "I'm helping a couple of gentlemen who are buying some land nearby."

"Really?" There was a tone of intrigue in the older woman's voice and a look of curiosity in her eyes.

"Yeah." There came a sudden comprehension to Darcy that the locals might not approve of her friends' doings and that it might not be in the actors' best interests for too much information to get out too soon. Seeking a way out of her self-made situation she gathered the bag from the counter and began to back toward the door. She attempted to punctuate the exchange and said, "Well, I'm sure I'll be back in again."

"Okay, then. Bring the bag back and we'll reuse it." The sound in the lady's tone was now one of puzzlement. She added, "Have a good day!"

As Darcy trod down the stairs of the store, she nodded to the aged gentleman who was intently studying an arrangement of red checkers. Depositing her purchases in the front seat of her car, she picked up her camera and began walking down the side road. Though the area remained seemingly peaceful, there were now indications of daily activities taking place in the warehouses and on a few of the docked boats. She walked the entire length of the pavement and passed a total of eight warehouses before even opening the cover on her camera. At this point she noticed a truck being loaded from one of the old warehouses. The composition of the truck, the wooden crates, the loading bay as well as the late morning light enticed Darcy. She snapped a few frames of the scene, before moving on. Finding an access to the docks, she ventured onto the planks and discovered a pair of trawlers moored behind the metal building. To her quiet pleasure she saw that there were some crew members on one of the boats. They were a scruffy lot with unkempt beards and wearing faded jeans or overalls that were sometimes covered by work slickers. The fishermen were unloading wooden crates from the boat onto the dock. Men from the warehouse lifted the cargo from the old planks and carried it into the building. She knelt and focused the lens of her camera. Pressing the shutter release, she caught the local industry in action with all of its crusty flare.

With a third snapping shutter release she caught more than an image. One of the dock hands noticed her presence and pointed her out to another of the warehousemen. As he began to move in her direction, Darcy capped the lens and loosely covered the camera. The seasoned worker hailed the female intruder, "May I help you?"

"Oh, no thank you." Feigning a naive smile Darcy warmly replied, "I just wanted a couple of photos to take back to the city with me…to show my family."

The rough-looking man gave the photographer a stern glare and responded, "Well, it can be a bit dangerous back here and I think it would be better if you didn't stay."

"Oh, okay. Sorry." She turned and moved down the boardwalk away from the stone-faced dockhand.

As she progressed along the planks, she could overhear the man behind her comment, "Just a stupid tourist." There were a couple of other boats moored back toward the intersection and she found more congenial circumstances with them. Darcy was glad to find the first boat was unattended which allowed her more time to capture the weathered grace of the vessel. The second trawler had a lone individual onboard who was dressed in a classic, yellow slicker and rubber work boots. When asked if it would be okay to take a photo of the boat, the aging fisherman said, "Yep." He even posed for a picture of himself on deck. She grinned at her good luck, snapping a couple more pictures.

Still smiling to herself about the playful seaman, Darcy returned to her trusty car. As she was climbing in she saw the old man on the porch look up from his checkers board. She waved a farewell to him and he happily returned the wave. She smiled broadly.

Slowly rounding the corner onto the dirt road Darcy spotted the resident of the bleak trailer seated in a lounge chair in front of the mobile housing. Given his unkempt condition, it was hard for Darcy to accurately gauge the man's age, but she finally decided that he was probably in his late forties. She deliberately gave an exaggerated smile and waved to the fellow who was dressed in faded shorts and a stained undershirt. Without a change in his unshaven, blasé expression, he simply watched her drive by.

It would take Darcy another day and a half to cut a simple, narrow foot path through the thick expanse of the kudzu to where she could enter onto the edge of the beach. On the evening of that day, her fifth day on the property, she forged through the growth and broke free from the tangled foliage. She laughed with delight as she stumbled onto the beach and into the open expanse of pale, loose sand. She pulled off her leather shoes and thick socks, letting her feet feel the soft give of the beach floor. Again she laughed and was filled with the triumphant joy of the moment. She strode barefoot toward the water's edge. The vapor of salt water made the air seem sweeter in some way and the full sound of the gentle waves now seemed delightfully playful. She spun around with dancing steps, stretching her arms wildly wide.

Something drew her attention. Still laughing, she glanced at the base of the lighthouse tower which stood some thirty yards away. A man was standing there just to the side of the aged building, watching Darcy's antics. His expression was not one of happiness, but one of puzzlement and possible concern. He stood approximately six feet tall and his attire was dark, dark blue, perhaps some odd kind of uniform. His eyes were shaded by an unusual, billed hat.

Startled, Darcy stopped where she stood. She stammered aloud, "What…? I didn't think that…." She quickly glanced from side to side and down the length of the beach in each direction in an attempt to spot a boat, a vehicle, any means by which the man might have come here. Seeing nothing obvious, she looked back at the base of the lighthouse. The man was gone.

"Huh? Wait…hello?" She felt an urgency growing inside her and she was drawn toward the building. Scanning around for signs of the stranger Darcy's mind raced for an explanation. She called out while she strode toward the structure, "Hey…excuse me…sir!?" As she approached the base of the conical tower, she noticed for the first time the awful graffiti that was emblazoned in multicolored spray paint across the aged bricks and the exposed pilings where erosion was removing the very ground the building rested on. Though offended at the defacing and stunned at the disrepair she was more concerned by the peculiar man's vanishing. Darcy began circling around the lighthouse, heading first in the inland direction…the side closest to the dense plant growth. She examined the border of the sand beach where it met the plants. Certainly she would have heard it if the man had ventured into the foliage. She saw no trace of his forging through the vines.

A step further and she found the one ground-level entrance into the tower. The deteriorating, wooden door was closed and padlocked. The planks of the barrier were crumbling around the edges and misshapen from the extremes of oceanic weather. The wood revealed sizable cracks that were filled with sand. The lock was severely corroded. Surely the door had not been opened in years. She pushed at the door and, though it was rotted and worn, it remained firmly in place. No one had passed through that opening in a long time.

Darcy continued to move around the building and looked down the length of the beach to the channel. There was no sign of anyone. She was very befuddled and just stood there while trying to figure out what had just happened. She had no doubt that she had seen the man in the uniform. He had been right next to the tower. An idea came to her…she was on a beach so all she needed to do was trace his footsteps in the loose sand! Again she turned and now examining the ground proceeded to retrace her own steps next to the tower. She made the complete circle around the building and then stopped, having located her own origin. Impossibly, the man had left not a single footprint.

"Who are you?" He did not know this person, this interloping woman, and he watched her from above. "Why have you come here?"

Chapter Three

For a number of days the mysterious forms underneath the growth of foliage, like ancient tombs shrouded by emerald jungles, had fascinated Darcy. Some of these lumps were quite large indeed. A couple of the plant-smothered objects appeared to be much taller than she was. One was nearly twenty yards across. Resolving to find out what their secrets might be, she decided to carve a path that would lead in between the two largest bulges of the greenery. That would afford her the option of choosing which one of the masses she would investigate first.

She began early in the day and whacked her way forward, detaching segments of vine as she went. With practice Darcy had begun to develop a method for creating open spaces in the plant coverage. First she cut the stalks off a few inches above the ground, then if the stems were anchored elsewhere, she severed the loose sections close to the next set of roots. It was still hard work, but she wasted less effort.

She was nearly halfway to the hidden objects when there came a noise from some distance in front of her, off in the foliage. She paused and watched intently in the direction of the rustling. There was definitely something there. As Darcy held her gaze and maintained a rigid, tense pose, the mat of kudzu shook once, then twice. She yelled firmly, "Who are you? What are you doing in there?"

There was no immediate response to the questions. The trailblazer stood her ground. Again she spoke, "Come on out of there!" Nothing happened. She demanded, "What do you want?" All that could be heard was the distant surf and the wind gently moving the leaves. A minute passed and there was no further activity. Darcy relaxed somewhat, but remained perplexed. With added caution she resumed her activity and slowly progressed toward her goal.

Not attempting to expand the width of the path at all, simply moving forward through the tangle, by late morning Darcy found herself nearing her goal. She worked her way between the two lumps which were some fifteen yards apart. Finally she began to remove the cut stems from the path in order to create some work space.

Darcy had an idea as she hauled the severed vegetation down the path to place it on the ever-expanding piles. Maybe she could string her tarps between the two landscape features and use some of the more stout, cut stems to support the covers in both front and back. That might give her a bit more living space. In its current location the tent, while small, barely fit the ground that had been cleared for it. There was hardly any space available for stepping from the tiny, nylon shelter before encountering kudzu. It would be good for her morale to have a bit more room to move about in and live in.

When the foliage was cleared from the immediate work area Darcy concentrated on widening the open ground between the green lumps. As she pulled on one massive strand of vine she noticed something whitish grey underneath the foliage. It was to the rear of the largest obscured form, possibly two feet tall, near the beach side of the property. If it were not for the difficulty in stepping through the kudzu, the pale mass would be only about five paces away from her. Again she tugged at the vine, managing to dislodge it to a minor degree. The covered object was some kind of smooth, stone surface that seemed heavy enough not to be moved by the bulk of the greenery. She stepped into the jumble of vines and made her way to the hidden item. Pulling the smaller stems of the rampant weed upward she used the machete to sever them. She pulled the loosened strands as wide as she could and looked at what was revealed. The stone face was low to the ground and she knelt on the vegetation to get a better view. She gently brushed away an accumulation of dirt and detritus from the surface. Her gloved fingers found what she first thought was a texture, but then realized it was a carved groove. Now with some apprehension she further completed the cleaning. With a gasp Darcy realized that she had discovered a grave marker. The stone was large enough for an adult, but was more briefly inscribed more like a child's—simply, "M. L. T. 1939."

A deepening tide of sadness overcame Darcy as her fingers moved over the initials. The feeling was inexplicable. She did not know who this person was, but she felt a deep emotional pain for whomever it may have been. She tugged at the voracious flora to reveal the whole of the stone lest it be lost overnight again to the vines. Something pulled at her attention and she glanced over her shoulder at the lighthouse.

She was being watched! The mysterious man wearing the dark uniform was back and was standing at the top of the tower, behind the rusty railing outside of the lantern room. Darcy quickly stood and as she caught her balance she again looked at the tower. The man was gone.

Cursing in frustration Darcy ran down the path. Somehow her feet missed the remaining, treacherous kudzu trunks. Breaking through the vines, she was soon on the beach and proceeded directly to the lighthouse. Reaching the door of the tower, she breathed heavily from exertion mixed with excitement. The door remained as it had been, locked and unmoving. Again she examined the beach for any signs of unusual activity. There were no footprints to be found except her own.

Darcy was thoroughly flustered. How could someone just disappear like that? No one could just come and go like that without leaving some kind of evidence. People have to leave footprints. It is physically impossible not to leave them…unless the person isn't really there…not physically there. The thought came to her like the prickling of a mild electrical shock and Darcy sucked in a deep breath. She murmured aloud, "He's a ghost. Oh my gosh, he's a ghost. This place is haunted." Darcy had believed in angels and ghosts all of her life, though she had never actually seen a spirit before.

Troubled by her discoveries Darcy no longer felt inclined to remove more of the vine that day. She slowly retraced her steps down the narrow trail and returned to her base camp. She was so agitated by the morning's events and her latest discoveries that she unzipped the tent door flap and crawled inside to flop down on the sleeping bag. She didn't know what to do. If she left now, she would forfeit everything. Though the ghost's presence made her uneasy, for some reason she was not actually afraid of him. Darcy reasoned that at least he had not tried to harm her, so far. She decided to stay and maybe the specter would leave her be.

After she had a chance to relax Darcy began thinking about the tombstone and then remembered her camera. Gathering her strength, she forced herself to rise and fetch the Minolta from under the car seat. She returned to the grave and took a photo of the forlorn, solitary headstone. While Darcy had the camera in hand she went back to the beach and photographed the graffiti on the lighthouse base. She took four or five snapshots of the structure while attempting to capture all of the sprayed writings.

Returning to the campsite Darcy stowed the camera away having decided on yet another chore. Examining the piles of kudzu cuttings, she pulled out stems that were approximately seven feet in length and at least somewhat straight and rather thick. While seated on the hood of her car Darcy began removing the leaves and smaller side growths from the selected stalks. After the lengths were stripped of appendages she stood them vertically and studied each piece for strength and overall straightness. Then if the limb met her approval she sharpened one end of the makeshift pole and prodded it into the sandy soil.

~~~~

The wooden stake was driven into the loose dirt by Martin's repeated pounding with the flat of a shovel. On the side of the stake near the very top he thumbtacked the empty seed packet marked, "Sweet Carrots." He viewed the newly-seeded row in the garden patch while wiping away an accumulation of moisture from his brow. His blue work shirt showed his sweat.

Robby approached the garden as he carried two large watering cans that were filled and heavy. He watched his footing to avoid spilling the limited resource. As he neared his destination he glanced up to Martin and commented, "You know, my father is a farmer."

"Really?" Martin took a step toward the assistant keeper, relieved him of one of the weighty cans and replied, "No, I didn't." Moving to the freshly sewn row, he carefully began moistening the soil.

"Absolutely! I grew up milking cows and feeding chickens." There was a tone of pride in Robby's voice as he continued, "My father…he grows some of the best tomatoes in the area." The bright-eyed, young man gently tilted his watering can and sprinkled a row of tender, green sprouts. He asked cheerfully, "How about you, Martin? Where did you grow up?"

Martin continued with his watering and responded, "In a lighthouse…up north. We did a bit of gardening, but nothing like the farm your father must have." He moved down the seeded row one step at a time while keeping a close eye on the shower of water. When the can was empty he looked at Robby and asked, "Do you think that you would make a good farmer?"

"As good as my father? Maybe. I don't know." Emptying his own can Robby looked back at his superior and inquired, "Why?"

"Because these plants will be the bulk of our winter food supply."

~~~~

In the cool of the morning Darcy renewed her efforts aimed at clearing away the vines between the two large forms. Though still sore in some places, her hands were becoming callused and accustomed to the rough usage. She noted happily that this was her seventh day on the property. She had been in residence a full week!

She first began cutting the vines covering the object nearest the beach, which also happened to be the larger of the two covered forms. Feeling like a bit of an explorer Darcy pulled away some of the jumble and was not entirely surprised to find a brick wall. The size and shape of the hidden structure could easily be that of an extremely modest, small house. With some humor Darcy thought to herself that she had seen larger garages.

Rather than proceed to defoliate the newly uncovered discovery she turned instead to the other mysterious form. It was as tall as the first, but vaguely cylindrical in shape and about half as wide. The shape of the vine-choked feature had Darcy completely puzzled. Sawing her way across the expanse, she cleared a footway to the sizable object. As she separated the stalks she again found a brick surface. She still had no idea what this structure had been used for, what purpose it may have served. It would have to remain a mystery for a while longer.

With her curiosity at least partially satisfied Darcy set about dislodging the kudzu at an energetic pace. Removing the chopped weed from the expanding open area, she lugged the cuttings back to the organized piles of severed flora. Each time she returned to the area designated as her future refuge she carried something with her, be it a jug of water, a rope, a tarp or some other useful item.

Darcy was stacking a handful of cut runners on one of the piles when she heard a ringing sound. It took her a moment to realize what the tone was, then she sprinted to the car and opened the passenger door. The ringing noise continued as she tried to trace its source. She dug her hand under the driver's seat and emerged with the cell phone that Troy had given her. Pressing the activation button, she answered, "Hello?"

The voice on the other end was familiar despite a bit of static. "Hey, Darcy, ready to go home yet?"

"Hi, Brett," Darcy smiled to herself while backing out of the car and answered, "No, not yet...sorry." Holding the phone in one hand she picked up four of the pointy, kudzu poles in the other.

The actor taunted her over the long distance connection, "I hear the mosquitoes are horrible in the evening...."

Darcy began to walk while talking into the device, "Nothing that a little repellent can't take care of." She took her time and followed the trail through the vegetation. From the other end of the connection the sounds of a dining area were faintly audible in the background. Assuming that Brett was calling from California she knew the meal must be breakfast.

"Seen any snakes yet?" Brett sounded chipper as ever as he continued his playful harassment.

Deliberately sounding unconcerned she responded, "One or two…but I leave them alone, so they leave me alone." Somewhere in the midst of the restaurant noise Darcy thought she heard another familiar voice.

Trying a new direction in which to antagonize the homesteader Brett prodded, "I bet it's really humid…."

"Mmm. A little bit, but the sea breezes have been really nice." She strolled while still holding the kudzu poles. Casually looking at the cut areas of vine along the narrow path, she checked for any new growth that needed to be clipped off. Darcy laughingly commented, "They seem to have helped clear up some of my sinus allergies."

"But I bet there's been a lot to do there," the satirical twist in Brett's voice was meant as provocation, "like watching the vines grow. That kind of stuff…."

Resisting the temptation to play into the man's game Darcy lightly began, "Really, it's been quite…."

She stopped where she was. Suddenly aware of a rustling coming from beneath the covering of kudzu she lost the thought behind her sentence. There was something large moving under the vine strands attached to the remains of one large tree. In an instant a grey, grunting animal burst through the vines and charged forward, aiming directly at Darcy. She shouted, "A boar!"

The cell phone fell to the ground.

Troy McGovern set his coffee cup on the table and reached for the cell phone in his friend's hand. Growing impatient he complained, "Come on, let me talk to her."

Brett huffed and switched the phone off. Setting the device on the restaurant table he met Troy's condemning stare. Shrugging his shoulders the actor said, "We were disconnected…but she said the place was a real bore!" He laughed out loud.

Chapter Four

Darcy saw the red and blue lights flashing in her side mirror and muttered, "Ah, crud!" She pulled the aged automobile off to the side of the road and slowed to a stop. Shaking her head she resigned herself to the inevitable and cast her eyes downward. Only then did she truly realize the condition of her t-shirt and jeans. She was covered with the blood of the wild boar.

The officer approached from the driver's side of the car while carefully watching the occupant. He was African American with strong, pleasant, facial features. Judging by his athletic build he was accustomed to regular fitness workouts.

Darcy rolled down her car window and sheepishly started to ask, "May I help...." The officer's eyes grew wide as he saw her condition. When he realized the blood was not Darcy's own he made an instant decision and jumped back from the driver's door. In a flash he had his pistol in hand, aiming it in the blood-marked woman's direction. Dumbfounded and aghast Darcy sputtered, "Uhhhh...."

In a deep, booming voice the officer commanded, "Get out of the car and keep your hands in the air!" Nearly swallowing her tongue in fear Darcy opened the vehicle door and eased her way from the interior of the car. Unable to look away from the barrel of the gun she tried not to panic though everything in her certainly wanted to. She was barely on her feet when she heard the man demand that she face the car. As soon as she had turned she was shoved hard against the metal surface. The officer's voice seemed to ring within her ear as she heard him shout, "Hands on the roof! Legs apart!" Darcy immediately responded by raising her arms fully and placing her hands on the top of the car, then shuffled as the inner side of her feet were kicked to insure their wide separation. She stood stiffly as she felt the frisking begin to take place. After a number of seconds of being roughly patted down there was a pause. Then the lawman demanded, "I'll need to see your driver's license."

Not knowing whether to remove it herself or if she should just stay still Darcy meekly offered, "Um…it's in my rear pocket." After another moment she felt her wallet being removed from her jeans as she remained rigid.

After a seemingly extended period of time Darcy heard, "All right, Ms. Vornack, you can turn around." Very slowly Darcy turned to face the officer. She was scared, and it showed. She found the man standing only a few feet from her and much to her relief she saw that his gun had been placed back in its holster.

"Ma'am, what's all this blood on you? It doesn't seem to be your blood. And where were you going in such a hurry? Do realize at what speed you were driving?" He stood with a stiff posture while copying the information from her driver's license onto a hand-held pad. His face was the picture of sternness. Watching the violator swallow hard, minutely shake her head and glance toward the truck of her car, he continued, "You were doing nearly seventy in a fifty-mile-an-hour zone." He paused and waited for her reaction. When he failed to get an intelligible response from Darcy, he shook his head and handed back the wallet with the driver's license. The officer asked, "What's that in your trunk?" Moving toward the rear compartment of the passenger vehicle, the uniformed man glanced at the makeshift closure that was tied with nylon cord. Wooden rods protruded through the slight opening of the trunk.

Regaining a little of her voice, Darcy responded, "A boar."

"Excuse me?" Even his questions sounded like commands.

"A wild pig." Darcy was still apprehensive and moved with a painful slowness in the direction of the trunk.

With his eyebrows arched the lawman asked, "Do you have a hunting license?"

"No," her voice was a near squeak and she felt herself on the verge of tears. She attempted to explain, "It…. It attacked me! I didn't know what…I mean…it…just…and…I…."

Trying to loosen the knot the officer looked over at Darcy while struggling with the cord. Watching her, he saw that her face was now moist and he spoke in less harsh tones, "Just calm down, ma'am."

The knot gave way and the hood of the trunk drifted open. The officer glanced at the interior of the compartment and then did a double-take. He stared for a brief moment into the holding area. With an astounded look he asked, "You speared it to death?"

Darcy's stomach churned and she was almost ill as she responded, "Yes…it was the only way…that was the only thing I had to defend myself with."

"What's the boar doing in your trunk?"

"I didn't want him to go to waste, I mean, now that he's dead and all. I don't have any refrigeration where I'm staying. I didn't want him to spoil." She pulled in a great breath and continued, "So…I was taking him down to the store…to see if they could do something with him."

"Like what?" The officer now stood with one elbow propped on his other arm, his hand nearly covering his mouth. His amusement was plain.

"Oh, I don't know." Still upset and flustered Darcy inquired, "Can people eat wild boar? Officer…?"

"Deputy Lester McKay." He propped himself on the edge of the open trunk and answered, "Yes ma'am, people eat boar all the time…and you would be willing to share this?"

Darcy responded emphatically, "Of course! Absolutely! I just don't want it to spoil!"

McKay laughed, "Well, I guess this is a bit of an emergency." He loosely tied the trunk closed and asked, "Where are you staying…that doesn't have a refrigerator?"

"I'm camping out." Seeing the lawman give her an inquisitive look she added, "At the old lighthouse."

"That's State property. Do you have permission to stay out there?"

"Well," she hesitated, but answered, "that land is about to be sold…if it hasn't been already."

"Really?" With his dark eyes watching Darcy, McKay asked, "And who would the buyer be? You?"

"No." Not seeing any way out of the question Darcy told the unembellished truth, "Troy McGovern and Brett Jarrett."

Recognizing the names, the officer was suddenly more serious and countered, "Don't get smart with me!"

"No…no, I'm not joking…honest!" Darcy swallowed and tried to explain, "I've worked with them in Hollywood," then trying to be earnest she amended her statement, "well, more with Troy than with Brett."

No longer amused by this strange female traveler, McKay responded in a sour tone, "Sure, lady." He started to move on her again and aimed to once more push her to the side of the car.

Darcy automatically raised her hands in submission and blurted out, "I have Troy's phone number!" The uniformed man paused at hearing the rebuttal and allowed her to continue. Not wasting the given opportunity she proceeded,

"You can call him and confirm it! His number is in my wallet...on a scrap of paper...with his initials." She handed the wallet back to the officer and pleaded, "Please, call him."

McKay gave Darcy a deeply skeptical stare, but then searched the folded, vinyl wallet and found the shred of notebook paper. Taking the note he handed the wallet to the uncomfortable civilian. He cautioned her, "You had better not be telling me stories!"

Relaxing slightly once more Darcy responded, "It is the truth, I assure you."

Giving her a prolonged look the deputy finally said, "Well then, come on...let's get your pig gutted and on ice." He turned and headed for the patrol car.

Darcy followed Deputy Lester McKay's car across the lengthy bridge that spanned the inlet and banks of lush sawgrass, then down the road to the Campbell & Hoffer General Store. As before, the old man sat on the porch studying the checkered game board. The tan station wagon was again parked in front of the building.

Getting out of the patrol car Lester called to the porch sitter, "Ben, give us a hand here!"

The white-haired man stood up and studied the situation, then proceeded down the wooden stairs at a hearty pace. He looked hard at the blood stains coating Darcy and expressed a true concern. He asked, "Hurt?"

The officer laughed and replied, "Don't worry, Ben. Ms. Vornack just killed herself a boar." He untied the knot that held the Chevy's trunk closed.

"Darcy, please. I'm not that formal." The smudged and soiled camper looked momentarily at her filthy clothing then at the aged gentleman. "I'm fine, I think...just a bit dirty." She added with a smile, "Thank you, though."

The trunk hood sprang up and the two men looked inside. Ben stood at one side of the open trunk and studied the animal's carcass on top of a spread tarp. With a slightly wrinkled brow he said, "Small."

"Small?" Darcy was astonished. "You mean, they get larger than this?"

Lester responded in place of the elder who simply nodded, "Oh yes, quite a bit larger. This fellow is only about a hundred and a quarter...maybe one fifty. They can get up to three hundred pounds." He worked to remove the kudzu poles from the body of the boar. As he pulled hard on one of the pieces of wood he commented, "It's a good thing you thought to put the plastic under him. You would never get your trunk clean if you hadn't." Having freed the last of the makeshift spears he pulled the sides of the tarp up and attempted to roll them together so they would not fall open. He mused, "Maybe we can get through the store without making too much of a mess." Motioning the old man to one end of the pig the officer took hold of his side of the hefty bundle and said, "Any time you're ready, Ben."

Together the men lifted the pig out of the truck and carried it up the stairs of the building. Darcy preceded the pair as they worked to keep any dripping blood from escaping the tarp. She opened the door of the business and held it as the fellows entered carrying the carcass.

"Good gracious alive! What on Earth?" The shopkeeper stood behind the counter with her mouth gaping as she watched the awkward entry of the two men with the large, cloaked bundle between them.

The officer grunted, "We're going to need to use your cooler, Abigail." Not stopping to talk the two men moved on toward the entrance of the walk-in cooler. Lester led the way while walking backward and firmly holding the front end of the animal while Ben supported the rear. Darcy kept pace with the men and opened the metal door to the cooler.

As the men disappeared into the walk-in, refrigerated compartment carrying their load, Ben finally answered Abigail's question by simply calling out, "Pig!"

"Pig? Of all the…and in my cooler?" The aging lady came from around the checkout counter and walked down the store's aisle.

"Boar, actually," Darcy answered. She noticed the safety latch on the cooler and released her hold on the thick, insulated door. With a cockeyed smile she explained, "It charged me."

"Good heavens! Are you all right?" The shopkeeper looked at Darcy from head to toe…examining the blood-spattered shirt and pants.

"Some scratches…I guess. A few bruises…nothing that won't heal." Glancing down at her shirt, she said, "It's more the boar's blood than my own."

Stepping from the refrigerated closure Lester asked the shopkeeper, "Do you think David would be willing to fire up the smoker? Ms. Vornack…."

Darcy cut off the lawman's sentence and, extending her hand to the store operator, interjected, "Darcy…please." She gave the officer an apologetic smile.

"Abigail Hoffer-Brown," the local store operator responded and clasped the newcomer's hand.

Continuing from where he had been interrupted Lester explained, "Ms…Darcy…indicated to me that she would be willing to share the pork, hoping it won't go to waste."

"Yes, please...I have no way to keep it." Darcy watched as Ben quietly slipped from the cooler and went to fetch a large knife and plastic bag. She continued, "And even if I did, I could never eat all that by myself."

"Why, I'll certainly call and find out!" Abigail paused and then asked, "Are you sure? That's mighty generous of you."

A smile brightened Darcy's smudged and dirty face, "Yes...I'm sure."

"I have some work to do, ladies." Looking to the storekeeper the officer said, "I'll join you this evening, if I may."

"Of course, Lester." The older woman spoke in warm tones, "You know you are always welcome at my home."

"Thank you, Abigail." Turning to the pig-fighter the officer added, "Darcy, I would ask that you not leave the area for a while...at least until I confirm your...contacts. You don't really need a hunting license for killing boar. However until I find out whose boar it was I would suggest not killing any more. In case you get the urge to try your hand at other game...well, you would need a license for killing deer."

"I don't plan to kill anything else...and I'll be around for awhile."

Once the lawman had taken his leave Abigail wasted no time in getting on the phone. The word was quickly spread that there would be a smoked pork supper that night. She gave the newcomer a simple map of how to find the evening rendezvous place...the shopkeeper's own home. When Darcy asked if there was some place she might do a load of laundry she was told that there was a washer and dryer in a shed behind the store. She was more than welcome to use them.

~~~~

"Yes!" Robby hollered exuberantly, "We have company!"

Martin straightened from his position where he had been wiping the Fresnel lens. Looking at the young assistant who was standing at the great windows of the lantern room with a rag in his hand, he asked, "Well...who is it?"

"Becky Darwell! ...And Iris Campbell...and her little brother...Ben, I think his name is...." His words trailed off as he descended the ladder and headed down the stairs, "...and some other kid."

With a growing smile Martin folded his linen cleaning cloth and glanced out of the tower windows. The launch was being tied to the wharf and the young ladies were disembarking. He watched as his junior partner crossed the beach with springing strides in order to greet the guests. Martin took a moment to remove the white, full-length cleaning apron and pull closed the lantern room drapes. He combed his fingers through his hair and then pulled the uniform hat on to his head, attempting to make sure that it was straight. Feeling presentable, Martin went down the stairs.

~~~~

Having freshly bathed with her shower bag and in a clean set of clothing Darcy followed Abigail's hand-drawn map. The lines were clear enough, but Darcy noticed that none of the roads on the map had names. In truth none of the roads did have names or at least there were no signs to indicate any names that they might have had. Darcy followed Abigail's written directions with little problem despite the map's vagueness. She was adept at finding her way and was observant of landmarks that included an old boathouse and a cattail marsh. The sprawling home was off a dirt road which was off a larger dirt road off the main throughway.

The residence of Abigail Hoffer-Brown was a sizable southern-style structure built of red brick. Both the house and its land offered a feeling of timelessness. The building had the stature of long-term, rural well-being. A long drive to the front of the house was lined with sprawling, old live oak trees. Their gnarled limbs were draped with misty grey Spanish moss that swayed gently in the late-day breeze. As the new guest parked and opened her car door the scent of hickory smoke filled the air.

Azaleas lined the walkway to the front door, adding a leafy lushness to the entrance. Reaching the front stoop Darcy found herself momentarily studying the beveled, leaded glass inlay in the front door before she rang the doorbell. She was greeted promptly by her hostess who eagerly invited her in.

Entering the expansive home Darcy was introduced to Abigail's son, David, who was on his way out to the backyard armed with a basting brush and an unmarked Ball jar of sauce. David's wife, Linda, shook Darcy's hand, noticeably realizing the rough condition of the visitor's palm. Her expression revealed her surprise though she said nothing. Linda was not extraordinarily beautiful, but was stately and gracious. She introduced their two children, Eric and Kim. A lean youth just in his mid-teen years, Eric had almost escaped the formalities by heading out of the room. As he heard his name being called, he knew that his mother had spotted him. He paused long enough to look back and acknowledge the new arrival before continuing on his way. The younger of the two children, Kim, was attentive just long enough to be introduced before also disappearing into the depths of the house. Linda explained apologetically that the children were ages fourteen and nine…and quite independent.

If the general store with its collection of nautical items had impressed Darcy, then the house was beyond compare. Accented with a large dose of seasoned and polished wood the living room alone offered antiques worthy of any museum. A large, mounted globe that was more than likely from the turn of the century sat next to an overstuffed, leather couch. A heavy harpoon nearly the height of a man rested in one corner of the room next to inlaid shelving that was also of lustrous wood. Old texts filled the shelves save for the center piece…a telescoping, brass spy glass. Darcy could only guess how old that item was. An ornate sextant and a large piece of scrimshaw were placed on a luxurious, wide mantle. Above the mantle was an original coastal map from the 1890s that had been mounted, framed, and sealed behind plexiglass. Darcy's jaw dropped and she commented to the hostess, "I'm impressed. This is beautiful."

Abigail accepted the compliment. "Most of this has been in the family for some time. Both of my parents and their parents before them were seafaring folk."

For lack of something better to say the guest responded simply, "Wow."

Darcy smiled as she saw Ben setting up his checkers board on the expansive back deck where the gathering was to be conducted. The deck lay just beyond French doors that lined the far side of the living room. The elevated wooden surface of the porch had a beauty all its own and was edged with ceramic pots filled with blooming plants. Yellow pine tables had been pushed together, creating an eating area spacious enough for over a dozen people. Citronella was burned in decorative holders to ward off the evening insects. Beyond the impromptu dining area was a cozy garden which was planted in part for beauty and in part for food and herbs. On one section of the small lawn surrounding the garden were two hefty, steel-barrel smokers that released the wonderful, hickory scent which blended with the smell of the meat. The scent set mouths watering and taste buds tingling in anticipation of the pork dinner.

The gathering continued to grow in number as two women arrived. One carried a glazed orange cake and the other a large bowl of homemade potato salad. As the apparent guest of honor, Darcy was introduced to the women, and they in turn were introduced as May Baker and Gretta Behr. A tall woman of supple build, May was fighting middle age. Her hair color was quite vividly blonde and Darcy could not help but to think that it came right out of a dye bottle. Gretta was short and her figure was rather stout. Also middle age, she made no attempt to disguise the fact. From the rapport between them, Darcy gathered that they had been neighbors of Abigail's for years.

With David tending the smokers, Ben and Eric engaged in a round of checkers. Linda and her daughter set the dinner table. Darcy offered to help, but was told rather to make herself at home. Reluctantly agreeing she returned to the deck. Unlike many of her fellow film workers Darcy was not completely comfortable with social gatherings. She lacked a performing artist's smoothness at light conversation and tended to feel awkward at times when left alone with strangers.

With the ladies tending the side dishes and the others intent on their respective activities, Darcy found herself momentarily unoccupied. Wandering off the porch, she began examining the garden. She had not been long from the deck when Linda headed her way seeking flowers for the table. As she joined Darcy in the garden, she pointed out different varieties of blossoms. This in turn attracted the attention of the two neighbor ladies who also entered into the examination. Spotting a beautiful crimson geranium Darcy commented on the flower. Linda chimed in that her mother-in-law truly had a way with plants. May offered, "My mother used to grow those too and they would get over six feet tall." In near unison the collection of women turned and looked at May in disbelief. Straightening in posture May defended, "Well...it's true."

Just then Abigail's voice rang out, "Dinner is served!" The platters of smoked and seasoned meat were presented as all present sounded their approval. The meat was accompanied by the homemade potato salad, cole slaw, baked beans, apple sauce and slices of white bread. There were enough pitchers of iced tea and cold drinking water to satisfy any thirst.

The chatting heated up as people dug into the platters and bowls of food, helping themselves. Abigail's son, David, was the first to take charge of the conversation. He was most likely in his late thirties and was not particularly tall. What he lacked in stature he made up for with upper body muscle. His suntanned face was comfortably appealing in a rugged way. Addressing the regional newcomer he inquired why a lone woman was staying in the area.

Darcy had anticipated that there would be unavoidable questions and she was right. "I..." Suddenly feeling the spotlight of the people's attention she chose to swallow her bite of slaw before proceeding, "am cleaning up some land...removing kudzu."

"Kudzu?" Abigail seemed shocked by the response and exclaimed, "Why, now, we hardly ever have that on the coast."

David stuffed a chunk of bread in his mouth and commented, "Lots of it inland."

Eric scoffed, "Kudzu doesn't grow near saltwater!"

"Well..." Darcy hesitated before replying, "I wish you would tell that to the vines I've been cutting on...because that's what I've been working—no, struggling— to remove." She separated a piece of tender pork with her fork and added, "This sure is good!"

Gretta called from the far end of the table, "Have you tried herbicides?"

Eric quipped, "That'll just make them grow faster." Darcy had earlier noticed that the youth had wavy hair that hung just below his shoulders. She figured that the hair length was no doubt a response to his father's own short cropped hair style. Now she saw that he had pulled his hair back for dinner.

Gretta scolded the young teen, "That's ridiculous!"

"No. For real!" The lad objected, "I read it on a government web site. Some herbicides make kudzu grow better."

Darcy noticed the portly woman's consternation and injected, "I really didn't want to work with poisons...."

"You shouldn't use poisons where they can run off and pollute the water." The matter-of-fact statement came from the previously silent Kim who was by far the youngest member of the gathering.

"Well, that's right." Darcy smiled and added, "But also...I was kind of hoping to plant some nice things when the vines are gone."

In between shoveled bites David asked, "What kind of saw have you been using?"

This question threw the guest as she had no idea what manufacturer had made her saw. Dumbfounded, Darcy replied, "I'm not sure." She spread her hands approximately three feet apart in display and said, "It's about this long."

An audible laugh came from Eric who was attempting not to choke on his mouthful of pork. He blurted, "You've been doing all that by handsaw?!"

Darcy slowly nodded and answered, "Yeah...." Rather than being offended by the boy's snipe she too found the amusement. It had never even occurred to her to use power tools as she did not own any kind except a drill. She consumed a forkload of beans, relishing their sweet taste.

Linda was not at all amused by her son's behavior and redirected the conversation, "Where on earth is kudzu growing around here?"

Darcy swallowed and answered, "I'm across the water...near the old lighthouse." She chased the beans with a gulp of iced tea.

Before anyone had a chance to respond there came a man's voice shouting greetings and all at the table turned to see a fellow approaching from around the side of the house. He was a comely chap, dressed in casual yachting attire. He was in his early thirties and would have been quite attractive had it not been for his wildly uncombed hair and stubbled appearance. He carried a bottle of white wine in one hand.

David wiped his mouth and scolded, "Late as usual, little brother." His tone could have been mistaken for playful, but there was a sharp, cutting look in his eyes that showed his disapproval.

Abigail stood and put her arms around the late arrival. She gave him a warm hug and said, "I'm glad you could come, Peter." Releasing him from the embrace she remembered introductions, "Peter, this is Darcy...."

The guest caught the hostess's hesitation and so filled in the gap, "Vornack." She wiped her fingers on a paper napkin and extended her hand to the man. She received a healthy handshake.

Continuing with the formalities Abigail stated, "This is my other son, Peter." Unlike his brother David, Peter was fair complected. They both had dark, brown hair, but where the younger brother's skin was light David's skin seemed dark and tanned by comparison.

"We were just talking about the old lighthouse property." David cut short the interruption caused by his sibling.

The matriarch encouraged her youngest, "Sit, sit." There had been two spaces saved at the table and Peter's arrival reduced the empty chairs to one.

David continued the review, "Darcy is removing kudzu that has grown up there."

Peter asked while filling his plate, "That belongs to the state, doesn't it?"

"Are you a state employee then?" Gretta studied Darcy with the sense of having found some novelty in the visitor from elsewhere.

Darcy reluctantly conceded, "Well, no...."

Eric was blunt as ever and flatly asked, "Then why are you out there?"

The lad's mother began in warning tones, "Eric...."

May seemed oblivious both to the boy's question and that he was being scolded for it. She brightly inquired, "Volunteer, then...?"

Despite her best efforts Darcy started to laugh with her mouth full. She raised her hand while managing to swallow. Her gesture silenced the inquisitive group and she choked out, "Okay...okay." She paused, not knowing how these people would respond to what she had to relay about the tract of land and development plans. Darcy felt trepidation, but knew that they would not be satisfied until she offered information. She asked, "Would you like to hear my story?"

A chorus of half-full mouths pronounced in disorderly agreement, "Sure," "Yeah," "Okay," "Of course!"

She nodded. Being aware that she had the complete attention of the table made her slightly nervous, but she drew a deep breath and began, "Okay. The land is being bought from the state by a couple of fellows that I have worked with on occasion." Darcy allowed that concept to take hold and then continued, "I got into a bet with one of them and we made a deal…that if I managed to stay on the land for a period of three months then I could have a small piece of the property…and the lighthouse. I knew that the land was covered in this kudzu before I agreed to this. I just didn't know how mean this vine really was."

Gretta voiced her disgust for the weed, "You said that, all right." Her portly face screwed up into a grimace before she took in another large bite of meat and wiped her mouth with an already stained napkin.

David was blunt, asking, "So…who are these new owners?"

There was no way around it and even if she did try and hide the truth it would be found out soon enough. Darcy responded plainly, "Brett Jarrett and Troy McGovern."

Voices collided in a jumble of astonished gasps and exclamations with a sprinkling of utter disbelief. Eric's voice rose most discernible from the group, "You mean…like, the movie stars?"

Darcy had anticipated the overwhelming response and donned a slight smile. She nodded and answered the question, "Yep, the same."

Abigail was still doubtful, but watched her guest's expression and inquired, "You're not joking…?"

Slowly shaking her head Darcy replied, "No…."

Peter smiled wildly and exclaimed, "Oh, man!"

May seemed overwhelmed by the concept as she asked, "You know Troy McGovern?"

A familiar, booming voice came from the side of the building, "She sure does!" Now dressed in civilian clothes Lester McKay strode across the distance. "I verified it myself. Troy also confirmed that Carl has permission to stay on the corner lot. When Carl told me that Brett Jarrett had hired him I had no reason to believe him and so I gave him a deadline to move the trailer. Looks like I'm going to have to offer him an apology."

"Good evening, Lester." Abigail pointed to the empty chair, "We have been saving a seat…just for you. Please, help yourself! There's plenty of food left."

Rather than direct his question to the off-duty officer David continued his inquiries to the guest from out-of-town who seemed to be the harbinger of change, "What do two movie stars want with a piece of rural property covered in kudzu?"

Darcy took her time in answering and everyone at the table became relatively quiet. After a moment she drew in a long breath and responded, "They're going to build a beautiful, exclusive housing development."

Peter's response seemed to be an expression of the universal thought at the table, "No way! Out here?" All of the diners looked at one another. They seemed to be questioning what they had just heard.

"Well...." Again she paused and thought her words through before continuing, "The coast is prime property. Housing is going up in a number of locations. People like living near the water. Look at the North Carolina Outer Banks and around Wilmington. People flock there and build very nice vacation homes."

"This is great!" Eric began to figure the possible outcome of the future population influx, "All these new people will need to buy things…and to eat somewhere!" The lad turned to his grandmother and commented, "Your store is going to have a lot of new customers."

David toyed with his fork and rather somberly said, "Yeah, a lot of things will change in a hurry if this happens." He jabbed at a shred of tender meat.

May noted, "You don't seem terribly happy about that."

David shook his head and said, "Change is only good some of the time...." He consumed the fork's load and chewed the soft pork before swallowing it down.

Peter took the bait without hesitation and asked, "Meaning?"

"This is just one more reason we should incorporate now. Once these new people move in, our community will never be the same. They won't have the same ideas we do…or the same kind of values. And we will need the extra money. The county doesn't give us that much right now and the state barely helped last time we were hit by a hurricane. With more people there will most likely be more congested roads. Extra traffic will mean that the roads will have to be widened and repaired more often. And you're right, Eric, these people will want to shop some place. Chances are good that other businesses will probably spring up all around the place, chains like McDonald's and Wal-Mart. That can make it harder on the locally-owned businesses. As more and more buildings are built we may lose local landmarks. It could become nothing but hotels and condos. Unless a local government takes an active stand a lot of the natural areas probably will be built over and the wildlife will go too, as they lose their habitat. Do you want to trust the county officials with that? You know all they want is more money filling their own pockets."

Kim looked up from her piece of white bread, "Suddenly this doesn't sound so good."

"But think of the profit," Peter offered, "if we just ride the tide of growth!"

Eric asked, "What about the fishing boats?"

"Oh come on, David." May was completely flabbergasted with disbelief and exclaimed, "Now, how can all of that happen...out here? No one has ever had any interest in this land other than for farming and fishing."

Abigail was perplexed by her son's fatalism, "How can you be so sure about all of this?"

"I watched the same thing happen in south Florida." David spoke in flat strains and his disillusionment was plain. "I remember going down there with Dad when I was still a kid. Remember? He would move part of the fleet for the winter and he would take me along?" He watched as Abigail nodded. Darcy noticed that Peter deliberately paid more attention to his food at this point than to his older brother. David continued, "It was beautiful there. There were wading birds everywhere. There were a few towns and a number of fishing camps sort of like ours now. The older I got, the more people were there. Those areas that were already official cities were at least able to control some of the growth that happened, but those areas that weren't incorporated were just consumed. Big ol' condominiums went up right where the best shell collecting had been. Colonies of sea shells where the mollusks lived and bred were covered over with fill dirt. I hear that estuaries are now being destroyed because of saltwater intrusion. That never would have happened if not for the construction going on. Last time I went down there it had gotten to where you could drive along the coast and never see the water because of all the high-rise buildings. It seems like all the fishing camps have disappeared now, too. I hear that some of the shrimp boat operators have survived, but they're surrounded by marinas that cater to the wealthy yacht owners. In some ways it's still a neat place, but it isn't like it used to be." With a tinge of bittersweetness, he added with a muffled laugh, "And you know...no one ever thought that people would want to live where there were so many mosquitoes...or want to buy swamp land...but they did!"

Eric spoke up, "Why didn't somebody stop the building?"

David answered, "Well, they couldn't. Because the land was not in a city it was up to the county officials...and all they saw was the money to be made. They never considered the long-term effects...like running short on drinking water or endangering wildlife or completely altering the way of life of the longtime residents of the area."

Gretta inquired, "And you're saying this is going to happen to us?"

Trying not to sound overly judgmental, David replied, "I'm only saying it's possible...."

The table fell quiet, as all in attendance gave thought to what had been said. Darcy swallowed hard. She had been unprepared for David's perspective, but felt that she needed to say something. Attempting to not sound defensive she slowly said, "Well...I'm certain that Troy and Brett have taken into account environmental conservation as much as possible...and I believe that the development will be in excellent taste."

"Of course, I'm sure it will be," Abigail responded, trying to reassure her guest of her welcome. "We...that is, the community...have been discussing incorporating for some time. It seems that we just don't get the funds that the towns and cities get."

Gretta added, "But we also don't have the taxes either."

"Saint Rosabelle was once an official town...back during World War II," Eric eagerly shared his knowledge, "but the town was later legally dissolved because there was not enough money to pay for the services."

After a moment David looked to the guest of honor and asked, "What happens if you lose the bet?"

"Well, I won't get the land." Darcy thought that was obvious enough, but then expanded on the scenario by adding, "The bulldozers will remove all the kudzu...and everything else there...including the lighthouse. It will all become part of the housing development."

"No!" The abrupt reaction came from Ben who up to that moment had been quietly consuming his fair portion of the feast. This was his first word of the whole evening.

Noticing the hurt look in the man's eyes Darcy attempted to soften her unfortunate response, "Afraid so, friend...."

Abigail was also not happy with the possible outcome. "Why would they want to tear down the lighthouse?"

"Brett thinks it's unsafe...and it probably is." Darcy shifted her eyes downward and admitted, "The pilings are very exposed."

David tried to sound optimistic, "It's made it through a lot of storms."

His son added, "Yeah...and each time we have one of those storms more of the beach washes away from it."

May sighed with resignation before lamenting, "It will be a shame if it's destroyed."

Again there was a lull at the table as no one felt the urge to say anything further. On a sudden impulse Darcy spoke with her customary spunk, "Well…who says it has to be destroyed?"

Peter smiled with slight bemusement and countered, "You yourself said the pilings were exposed. The weather will take it." Reaching for a platter he added, "And I'll take a bit more of that pork."

With her usual sense of determination Darcy responded, "People are always restoring historical places."

Eric quipped, "Yeah, well…this is one historical place that is about to have no land under it."

Abigail began to think on the matter and commented, "Beaches can be restored."

"Not at Cape Hatteras. They had to move that lighthouse inland." The teen became sour, "Anyway, why should we care about some ol' stupid tower…if it falls apart?"

The lad's comment drew irritated expressions from both his parents, but before they had a chance to chastise the young fellow Darcy shot back, "Excuse me?"

"Well, what does it have to do with me?" He questioned, "Who cares?"

"I care!" Darcy wasted no time in answering the youth, then remembered that she was a guest in this home and moderated her voice as she continued, "And maybe you should, too."

Eric shifted in his seat and laughed, "Get real!"

His father was growing angry and slammed his napkin on the table. In a heated voice he proclaimed loudly, "All right…that about does it, Eric!"

"Wait, please." Darcy smiled at the agitated man and gently raised her hand in a request for patience. Again she addressed the teenager, "Fine. I'll tell you what's real." She waited until she was sure that she had the lad's complete attention, "I get the feeling that seamanship runs in your family."

The boy was reluctant to give the visitor any positive response, but begrudgingly agreed, "Yeah, I guess…."

Darcy deducted, "So maybe your grandfather went to sea as a fisherman or merchant sailor or a member of the Navy? Yes?"

Abigail answered, "His grandfather, my husband, managed a good fleet of fishing boats." Then she explained with a bit of pride, "Both of my grandfathers were also fishermen."

David picked up where his mother had left off, "Dad managed the combined fleets and I manage the boats we have today. Eric may someday have them."

Darcy nodded in understanding and then continued her dissertation, "They took their boats out to sea sometimes at night, I bet. That lighthouse gave them a point of reference. It let them know where home was. Without that light they could have lost their way…might not have been able to find the inlet. They could easily have run aground on sandbars and been stranded…or lost during storms. And perhaps they might not have lived to have families…to have children."

Eric's father brought the point home, "And that means you wouldn't exist."

"Yeah…but," the boy was not inclined to give up easily, "it's been out of operation for years…all my life anyway. I mean…there are automated beacons now…and satellite systems."

"Enough!" The table resonated from the impact of a fist and all present were speechless as the old man rose from his chair. With a remarkable firmness and his jaw set tight Ben placed tremendous effort and emphasis in his words, "We…must…keep…the light!" Having completed his struggle he shoved away from the table and strode away from the group. He went directly into the house, leaving the whole gathering stunned. It seemed clear to Darcy that the fellow did not have any form of classic speech defect. His words had been perfectly spoken and not stuttered or slurred, but it was certain that the act of speaking was an extraordinary effort for Ben. Any doubts she might have had about it were dispelled by the number of dropped jaws and gaping mouths found among the dinner guests.

Peter was the first to recover with an ever-growing smile and glibly announced, "I guess that settles that!"

~ ~ ~ ~

By the time Martin reached the dock Robby had already helped the ladies from the boat and the quintet was proceeding along the timber boards of the wharf. Led by the young women the assistant keeper carried a sizable picnic basket that was heavy with content. He was flanked by the two young boys.

Martin cheerfully greeted the visitors as he met them along the boardwalk, "Welcome to our lighthouse." He relieved Iris of the blanket she had been carrying and commented, "It's nice to see you again, Miss Campbell. We met one day at the store."

"I remember…and from now on, please call me Iris." She smiled warmly,

"This is my friend, Becky Darwell. Becky, Mister Thurber is our new principle lighthouse keeper."

"My pleasure." The lightkeeper gently took the lass' hand for a friendly shake, but in the corner of his eye caught a look of apprehension from Robby. Martin kept the contact between him and the young woman short, but his smile never diminished. He announced brightly, "If we're to be on a first-name basis, then you both should call me Martin."

Giggles came from behind the ladies and Iris turned to see the grinning faces of the lads. Pulling forward the elder of the two boys she asked the keeper, "You remember my brother Ben?"

"Yes, I certainly do! How are you, Ben?" Martin extended his hand to the youngster. The lad was all of twelve years old, with freckles and unruly blonde hair. Ben gave a good, strong handshake. Looking back over his shoulder the adolescent motioned for the other boy to come forward. The younger child, who looked to be about ten, approached shyly and then peered up at the tall man in the uniform hat. The boy had dark, mocha-colored skin. His brown eyes showed true trepidation as he looked at the government employee. Oblivious to the possible concerns of his companion Ben proudly stated, "Mister Thurber, this is my friend, Vern."

Iris spoke up and quickly explained, "Vern's mother does all of our cooking."

Surprised momentarily by the child's ethnic background Martin paused, simply because the racial groups in Saint Rosabelle rarely mingled, but then once again smiled and offered his hand to the dark-hued youngster. The child was at first timid and slowly extended his own hand to meet that of the lightkeeper. As he took hold Martin said, "I'm glad to meet you, Vern."

As his confidence increased the lad sprouted a beautiful smile and pumped the keeper's hand firmly. Vern's eyes shone with happiness as he replied, "I'm glad to meet ya', too, sah!"

The contents of the picnic basket had been emptied and mostly consumed. Ben and Vern now fed the remaining pieces of bread to a gathering of seagulls. The birds called out their shrill, staccato cries between each toss of the morsels. As a shred of bread would leave the boys' hands a chaos of flapping grey wings and snapping beaks descended on the treat.

Nearby the adults lounged comfortably on an oversized blanket spread wide on the soft sand of the beach. Becky was full of gleeful enthusiasm as she asked, "Could we go up and see the lens?" Her auburn hair and girlish smile captivated Robby's attention.

Hearing the question Ben excitedly chorused after the young woman, "Could we? Could we, please?" He emptied his hands of the last of the bread, leaving the birds to squabble over the crumbs as he returned to the blanket. His eyes were shining with a playful joy as he looked to the men for an affirmative agreement.

"I don't think there's any regulation against it." Robby looked to his superior for some leeway in his usual, strict observation and enforcement of the rules.

"I don't know." Martin was dubious, "We have to be very careful of the mechanisms and the lens. They're extremely sensitive and can be easily damaged."

Vern had finished feeding the birds and joined in the pleading, "Please, sah, we won't hurt nothin'." He was just as eager as his partner.

Iris looked at the skeptical keeper and impulsively placed her hand on his arm, "It would be nice...."

He glanced at the alluring young woman and his glance turned into a gaze, his eyes meeting hers. The feel of her touch on his arm was a kind of sensation almost alien to him, but one he liked.

Pulling his eyes away from Iris, Martin looked directly at the boys and gave a begrudging smile. He sighed and relinquished, "Absolutely no touching the lens!"

With a jubilant cheer the lads stood immediately and took off running for the tower. Iris yelled after them, "Wait a minute!" The boys came to a quick halt and waited anxiously for the grown-ups to follow.

"Wait for us at the bottom of the ladder," Martin commanded of the boys. Agreeing heartily the children scampered off and were trailed by the strolling adults.

The adult foursome entered the tower and began to climb up the stairs. As they continued to spiral upward the steps narrowed in width while conforming to the tapered shape of the building. Robby explained to the guests that there were nearly one hundred stairs. Becky breathed heavily from the effort of the climb and in a gasping voice exclaimed, "And you climb these every night?!"

The youthful man answered, "Several times a night." He beamed as Becky looked at him in amazement. "You get used to it after a while. Martin should know...he grew up in a lighthouse."

Iris inquired of the lightkeeper, "Really?"

"Yes," Martin replied. He methodically took the stairs and brought up the rear of the group while explaining, "I'm a third-generation lightkeeper."

"Was it wonderful?" Becky called from beyond the keeper's sight somewhere up the stairs, "Growing up in a lighthouse?"

He answered, "It was good in some ways...bad in others."

Iris looked back at Martin who was following her closely. She asked with a genuine interest, "How do you mean?"

"It was beautiful...with the ocean constantly there. There was room to play and being isolated made the family very close. We never had to worry about crime...or door-to-door salesmen." Martin grinned as he heard Iris chuckle and he continued his march up the stairs, following the others. He carried through with his explanation, "But on the other hand, it didn't offer much variety in a choice of friends...and some of those you might only see a couple of times a year...if that often. Life wasn't always easy and there was a lot of work to be done. The winters could be especially brutal," as he reached the top of the stairs he added, "which is why I got myself transferred here where it's a bit warmer."

Finding the boys exactly where Martin had asked them to wait the gentlemen assisted the ladies up the ladder first with a warning for them to watch their step. The children followed the women and climbed the iron bars of the ladder quickly. The keepers mounted the last ascension and joined the others in the lantern room.

Robby pulled open a section of the beige drapes and allowed the sunlight to stream in. Another tug on the expansive drapes and the panoramic, coastal vista was revealed. As their eyes adjusted to the light both ladies sighed in awe, seeing the view from the tower. It seemed that they could nearly see forever into the distance. The view reached far out to the ocean horizon.

The room was an extremely tight fit for the group as it was designed for the sole purpose of housing the lens and lamp. The mighty Fresnel was central in the area and there was just enough space for one person to shuffle carefully past another without bumping into the glass windows. Outside of the light room was an extremely narrow, iron balcony that wrapped full circle around the uppermost section of the building.

Both of the young lads examined the crystal lens with their eyes wide with wonderment. Ben edged close to the large, glistening structure and peered at the prisms. Martin watched as the boy came near to being in contact with the lens elements. The keeper sharply yelled, "Ben!" The boy jumped and turned in fear toward the man. Martin diminished his vocal tone somewhat but remained firm as he said, "That's close enough."

Robby gave his superior a sour look and commented, "Martin...he didn't touch it."

THURBER'S LIGHT

Sensing the assistant keeper's dissension Martin's response was stern, "I know!" Looking back at the paralyzed boy the principle keeper repeated in a softer tone, "I know…and there's no harm done, but we must be careful." Allowing himself to relax a bit he began to show a slight smile and asked both of the boys, "Would you like to know why it is so important?"

The children looked at each other and then nodded. The possibility of learning attracted Iris' attention as well and she joined in the audience. Not at all interested in listening to his superior's dissertation Robby motioned to Becky and the pair descended the ladder to exit onto the lower balcony. Ignoring the couple's departure Martin picked up the white apron from where he had left it. He showed it to the boys and said, "Anytime either Robby or I work on the lens we wear one of these." He put the apron on and tied it around him. "It covers our belt buckles, the clasps on our suspenders, the buttons on our shirts, because even the slightest brush against the crystal could scar it and the lens would be permanently damaged."

Vern felt unconvinced and asked, "Jus' by a button?"

"Just by a button." Martin looked at him earnestly and told him, "As a matter of fact the aprons…and all the cloths we use to clean the lens…are made of linen because we can't take the chance of using cotton cloth. Cotton cloth might still have some plant parts in it that could scratch the crystal."

"Well," Ben looked puzzled and inquired, "what happens if the lens does get damaged?"

"It doesn't work as well." Martin thought for a moment and tried to figure out the best way to explain. "Say you have a candle and you light it in a dark place. The light from the candle goes everywhere…out in all directions and all angles, right?" The boy contemplated the image and agreed. Martin continued, "Okay…that is what it would be like if we didn't have the lens. Our light would go out in all directions. When you walk away from the candle it gets harder to see the light coming from it…and eventually you can't see the candle at all. That is because some of the light isn't coming toward you…it's going up or down or in some other direction. All that light is wasted. But we want the light to be seen way out there on the horizon. That's where it is needed." Martin lifted his hand and motioned to the oceanic panorama. His eyes momentarily strayed to the distant blue horizon. As he returned his sight in the direction of the boys he noticed that Iris was watching him intently. There was a warmth in her gaze and an earnest enjoyment in hearing the explanation, or at least the politeness and kindness to make it seem so to him. He found himself having to make a deliberate effort to shift his view from

Iris and back to the boys. Refocusing on the topic, he continued, "In order to send the light out to sea we have to make the most light possible go in the direction we want it to. The lens captures all the light that would be wasted if it escaped up or down…and forces it to go out all in one direction…in one bright band of light." Martin's eyes became deeply intense as he spoke, "If the lens is damaged then that scratch sends some of the light somewhere else outside of that single beam…and it doesn't reach out to sea…to those people who need it. People count on this light. Sometimes their very life depends on seeing it." He paused and placed his hand on Ben's small shoulder. "We have to help them find their way home, Ben."

As Iris watched Martin she could see that he had more than just an employee's interest in his duties. It was more than just a job to him. There was a personal aspect, an emotional conviction. He truly believed in the importance of what he was doing and Iris found a curious sense of pleasure in this. She stood and watched the play of light on the delicate, crystal form as it refracted and blazed into rainbow colored bands that were trapped within the curved prisms. In a wispy, quiet voice Iris commented, "I think it's the most beautiful thing I've ever seen." In order to get an overall view she backed away a step or two from the beehive-shaped structure that was as tall as she was. Her eyes shifted and she saw the principle keeper smiling at her.

"If part of it gets broke," Vern asked, "can't you jus' replace it?"

Before Martin could answer Robby interjected as he returned from the lower balcony, "No, sir!" He assisted Becky up the ladder and proclaimed, "That lens and all of its parts were 'specially made for this lighthouse and came all the way from France."

"All the way from France?!" The young man's companion was captivated by the concept, "Where the war took place?"

"That's right…and each piece is crafted special…optically perfect and set for a unique light formation." Bowsen looked at the young woman's face as if he had been speaking of her rather than the lens.

Ben looked at Martin with innocent curiosity, "Sir, why do some of the men on the docks call you and Robby 'wickies'?"

Her eyes suddenly wide, Iris attempted to silence her younger brother, "Ben!!"

"No, it's all right." Martin reassured his guests, despite his momentarily hurt expression. "The term 'wickie' was given to lighthouse keepers long ago, because every day we need to trim the wicks of the big lamps inside the lens. If the wicks aren't trimmed, then the lamps create a lot of greasy smoke that coats the lens and blocks the light. Once, it was an honor to be called a wickie." He sighed and shook his head, "Now...well, it's used more as an insult."

"Gosh, lamps, lenses...I don't know how you ever take care of such things." Becky sounded overwhelmed as she twirled her auburn hair, "I know I never could."

Martin was taken aback by the lass's statement and pondered aloud, "Why on Earth not?"

Iris came to her friend's defense, "This is a man's work, Martin."

"Nonsense." The keeper ignored the skeptical gaze of his coworker and said decisively, "You're both intelligent, healthy, young women. There is nothing here you couldn't learn...given a little time." The three listening adults looked at Martin as if he had gone mad or had suddenly contracted a bad case of the mumps. "Honestly...Iris, you run the register at the store. This is no harder. There is a bit of carrying that has to be done, but I think you could handle it."

Becky remained skeptical and questioningly said, "I don't know...."

Martin sighed and tried once more, "You've never heard of the Lady of Lyme Rock? Ida Lewis? Or how about Abbi Burgess?"

"No...." Iris gave the lightkeeper a curious look and her friend shook her head seconding the response.

"Ida Lewis was just one of the most famous lighthouse keepers, ever." Not seeing any signs of recognition from either of the two attractive women he continued, "She tended the light at Lyme Rock...in Newport, Rhode Island. She started helping take care of the light when she was not much older than Ben is now. During her years she not only kept the light burning, but she saved over two dozen lives...all on her own. Abbi Burgess also tended a light...on an island in Maine. There have been a number of women who tended lights." He looked at Iris and gently added, "You can do anything...if you really want to."

The sun had fallen low in the sky. The two keepers waved as the motor of the launch shifted gears and their company pulled away from the dock. The boat increased speed as it headed out from shore to deeper water and then paralleled the length of the beach heading down toward the inlet. The men watched as the watercraft rounded the corner and disappeared from view.

Reluctantly the keepers turned and began walking the length of the wharf to return to the duties that awaited them. Martin broke the silence and commented, "You seem to have quite an eye for Becky."

"Yeah," Robby grinned, "I do."

They continued to walk and another silence set in which allowed the sounds of the surf slapping the shore to penetrate the air. After a prolonged moment Robby said, "Martin…I think I should tell you something."

"What's that?"

Robby hesitated and his fellow keeper looked over at him. Swallowing he haltingly replied, "I've heard that Iris is betrothed."

~~~~

The ladies helped Abigail clear the table of emptied plates, used silverware, serving platters and bowls. In the midst of the busy women Eric made an effort to be of assistance and rinsed the eating utensils as they were deposited in the sink. He still seemed troubled by the evening's events and mused, "Man…I have never seen Grampa Ben like that. He never says more than two words glued together about anything."

Abigail explained to her grandson, "Ben is old enough that I think the lighthouse was still functional when he was a child. It was like Darcy said earlier, people relied on the lighthouse for their safety and for the safety of the people they loved." She added, "It probably means a lot to him."

Lester ventured into the kitchen carrying his own plate. He teased Darcy with a delightful smile, "Now see there…boar's quite good eating, don't you think?"

Darcy returned the man's smile and answered, "No argument here."

"Where's your aluminum foil?" May fumbled through a kitchen drawer until guided by the hostess.

"Might it be possible," the dark-eyed gentleman asked, "for me to take a plate of these vittles to my grandparents. You know my granddad…he just loves that pork."

"Why, we've plenty left…." Abigail looked to Darcy questioningly for a confirmation.

It took Darcy a moment to realize that the choice was being left for her approval. Catching on, she exclaimed, "Oh…of course! Please! You know that I can't keep it and we can't let it go to waste." After a moment of thought she asked, "What did you say his name was? The guy in the trailer…Carl?"

Lester nodded a positive response as he set his silverware in the sink.

"Maybe I should take him some…."

The reaction of groans and scoffs was notable and Gretta was not bashful in saying what she felt, "Why him!?"

"Well...." Darcy hesitated and looked around the gathering of displeased people before slowly replying, "It seems that he's going to be my neighbor for the next three months or so. I just thought it might be nice to be on good terms with him."

"You're probably right," Gretta gruffly rebutted while wrapping foil over one of the plates heaped with food for Lester to take, "but understand that the guy is nothing but a bum. It will do you no good to try and be friends with him."

"Ah." Not knowing how to respond Darcy simply said, "Okay...well...now I know." She attempted to redirect the conversation and asked, "Does anyone know who M. L. T. was? I found a grave on the property with that carved on the headstone."

Eric perked up and responded, "That must be 'Crazy Thurber.' He's a bit of a local legend." Having run out of silverware the lad began to rinse plates and set them on the counter to be loaded into the dishwasher.

With her curiosity growing Darcy could not help but ask, "Crazy Thurber?"

"Martin Thurber," the hostess answered, "the last lighthouse keeper."

Linda commented with a touch of dramatic flare, "They say his ghost still haunts the grounds." She had bent over to search for more space in the refrigerator in which to store some of the containers of leftovers.

Seconds passed. Then Darcy replied, "I've seen him." Her statement was matter of fact and she was aware that it drew a number of probing gazes. She asked, "Why 'crazy?'"

Gretta wrapped the second plate in foil and replied, "He went nuts...destroyed the light."

"What?!" It was Darcy's turn to be stunned with disbelief.

"Yeah...they say he lost it." Lester recalled the story, "The woman he loved jilted him. He went insane...freaked out and busted the lamp. He really wrecked the place...then took his own life." Lester arched his eyebrows and darkly embellished the tale, "He jumped from the tower and fell to his death."

Chapter Five

On the way home Darcy saw that a light was still on in the old trailer. She pulled her car onto the dirt road and then slowly brought it to a stop off to one side. As she had predicted, Carl, the disheveled and stubble-faced man who had been hired to keep tabs on her, abruptly parted the faded curtains in the tiny window. He watched Darcy as she exited the car and approached carrying a package covered by aluminum foil. Before she had a chance to knock on the door it opened and Carl stood there in his dirty undershirt and plaid boxers with a cell phone propped to his ear. Not looking at the visitor he said, "She's back." Switching the phone off and setting it on a counter he turned to look at Darcy but said nothing.

Feeling slightly daunted she held forth the foil-wrapped bundle. Giving the offering a skeptically careful examination and then looking back at his visitor, Carl slowly reached to take what she was holding. Darcy said, "It's...smoked pork. I thought you might like some." She smiled faintly as the man took hold of the shiny package and nodded to her. With the delivery made, the visitor backed off a step and Carl closed the door.

As she stood there in the dark Darcy mused to herself that it could have been worse. She remembered Gretta's warning that the man was not known for his friendly behavior. At least he had not rejected the gift nor thrown the pork back at her. Heaving a sigh she turned and headed back to the car. What had begun as a normal day of vine removal had become a social event thanks to the charge of a wayward boar. She truly hoped never to have to skewer another creature the same way even if it did provide a great meal.

The following morning was Sunday and it arrived with a light mist in the air. Darcy had not been able to transfer her tent location the day before and truth be known there was still an awful amount of work that needed to be done before she could make the move. Enough of the kudzu had been cut between the two brick structures to give room for her tent, but there were still stubs sticking up from the ground that could puncture the vinyl floor and would undoubtably quickly regrow into vines. *This should be a day of rest,* Darcy thought, but she could hardly afford to allow the vines to begin reclaiming territory.

    Slowly she wandered down the path she had cut through the greenery and trimmed off the new shoots growing from the kudzu trunks. Following the path she turned the corner and progressed toward the brick buildings while working at stooped angles all the way. Though she was thorough in her trimming and gave thought to her pruning, she could not help but cautiously glance around for any signs of movement and remained ever wary of another unannounced animal attack. Discovering the dropped cell phone with the power now drained from the device's battery only served to remind her of details from the prior day's events. She was more on edge than ever. Every noise caught her attention. A crow sounded with a jarring "caw!" from one of the vine-covered trees and startled the camper. She jolted upright with her heart pounding. Darcy saw the black bird as it spread its large wings and took flight. She stood filled with anger not only directed at the bully of a bird, but more at herself for allowing her nerves to be so tight. She knew that she had to find a way to relax.

    After completing her trimming chore she decided to take time off and ease her mind by relaxing on the beach. Strolling along the shore for a while, she glanced at the small piles of shells and found herself occasionally picking up a tiny treasure. As she returned to the area of the lighthouse, Darcy decided that she would make a habit of walking the beach at least once a day. Settling on the dry, soft sand Darcy watched the moving water for a few minutes and then slowly closed her eyes. She began a meditation using the sounds of the seashore as a calming sedative. The waves methodically lapped on the beach and gulls called their laughing song lulling her into comfort.

    Her meditation was broken as Darcy realized that a vehicle horn was being blown. She had no idea how long she had been sitting there undisturbed on the shoreline. Getting up she brushed off the sand from the rear of her pants and walked back toward her camp. As Darcy walked down the narrow path she recognized Deputy Lester McKay in his street clothes. His off-duty transportation, a Ram truck, sat where the Hummer had previously crushed down foliage when Darcy had first begun her occupation of the property. The muscular man was surveying the surroundings and looking at the kudzu-covered forms. She hailed Lester and went to greet him. With a light laugh she joked, "It's a pretty good growth, you think?"

    "It sure is." He continued to scan the smothered trees and added, "It's the darndest thing, though. I've never seen kudzu this close to the shore."

"I've noticed that it doesn't grow beyond a certain point. It stops right at the tree line. I guess there is too much salt in the soil closer to the shore. I'm beginning to have a theory," she said, "as to how it got established so well."

"What's that?"

She bent down and scooped up a handful of the soil. Holding it up to show Lester she poked through it with her fingers and separated out some of the little white objects.

With a befuddled look in his dark eyes the lawman questioned, "Fish bones?"

"A lot of them." Darcy dumped the dirt back onto the narrow pathway and wiped the palm of her hand. She continued, "It's like someone used this place as a dumping ground for organic material. You couldn't get a better fertilizer than fish emulsion."

A curious smile graced Lester's strong features as he asked, "You think someone was deliberately trying to get this stuff to grow?"

"I don't know." Darcy laughed, "Whether it was deliberate soil enrichment or whether they were just doing some dumping…the kudzu sure liked it!" Shaking her head she added, "None of the bones are new. They've all been here a while."

Lester said, "It might be near impossible now to find out why they're here." He altered his stance and disclosed, "I actually came by to relay a message."

"Oh?" Darcy smiled inquisitively at the lawman.

"I told my grandparents about your battle with the kudzu," he explained, "along with the rest of the story and Granddad decided that we should offer to lend you a goat."

Puzzled Darcy replied, "A goat…?"

"To help eat the foliage," he added, "that is…as long as you haven't used any chemicals."

The light of understanding brightened the camper's face and she responded with exuberance, "I would love to have a goat!" She added quickly, "And no chemicals, none. I don't like using that kind of thing."

Lester displayed a warm mien and remarked, "They loved the pork, by the way."

"I'm glad." She paused for a contemplative moment and then ventured, "Would you be willing to do me a favor?"

Attempting to be noncommittal Lester responded honestly, "Well…ask and we'll see."

Darcy inquired, "Have you got a pair of lock busters in your truck?"

"Sure...of course." Looking around at the lush leafage of the vines he attempted to think of how metal cutters would be used in this setting. He questioned, "What lock do you want broken?"

Darcy's answer was blunt, "The one on the lighthouse door."

Losing part of his smile Lester replied, "Oh." He chewed the inside of his cheek while thinking about this proposal. "The sheriff locked that tower up a number of years back to keep vandals out...and to keep people from getting themselves hurt."

"It may have kept the vandals out, but it didn't stop them completely." Darcy's voice matched her tart expression as she added, "The outside of the place is awful."

"Seeing as how you're connected with the new owners I reckon we can remove the lock...but I think I should first inform the office that we're going to open the place." Lester looked earnestly at Darcy and said, "If I were you, though, I'd buy a new lock to replace the one that's there."

"All right." She nodded, "I can agree to that."

Monday dawned with a beautiful blue sky. There had been some sea mist in the air when Darcy had first gotten up, but by the time she had dressed and eaten her morning serving of dried fruit any sign of sea fog had gone. Having spent a fair amount of the prior evening removing the stumps between the two brick constructs Darcy resolved that she would take the day and do something other than removing kudzu. Her heart told her there were other important tasks that needed to be done that morning. The old lighthouse tower was a sad sight with all that spray paint on it. She had to work on that.

She would need a few supplies in order to make any real impact on the vulgar spray paint. Turpentine or mineral spirits would be needed and rags for wiping. Taking her time she drove across the inlet bridge toward the one local store. From the concrete expanse Darcy was delighted to watch one of the fishing boats with its net outriggers towering vertically from the ship's deck heading for open water.

Again she found that she was early for the opening of the Campbell & Hoffer General Store. This time she anticipated the pleasure of being resoundingly beaten at a few games of checkers. Waiting in his usual place Ben was more than happy to oblige the visitor. He welcomed her with "Morning!" He had managed to earn a few victories without one more word spoken by the time Abigail Hoffer-Brown came to unlock the door to the business.

Greetings were exchanged as Darcy entered the old building to begin her survey for things that she would need. On her way down an aisle she spotted a boxed set of checkers. Pricing the game she decided to buy it. She would set it up later and practice playing against herself.

The turpentine was near the caulk, but Darcy had to ask about the rags. Abigail confirmed that the store did not have any for sale, but seeing her customer's disappointment she offered some that she had in the back of the store for cleaning purposes. When Darcy offered to pay for them the storekeeper just smiled and said, "They're just old t-shirts. Don't worry about it."

Lastly Darcy asked about padlocks. Abigail checked the shelf and found that the last one had been sold. Apologizing she explained, "We'll have to order some in."

"That's okay…it can wait a while." Darcy paused and glanced out the window. She softly inquired, "Has Ben always been so quiet?"

Abigail nodded and answered, "As far back as I can remember…yes."

"Any idea why?" Darcy continued to keep her voice down and added, "I mean…there's nothing wrong with it, but it is a little unusual."

"He was involved in some kind of boating accident when he was young. I remember being told that he nearly drowned." Abigail shrugged and commented, "We've never talked about it to be honest."

"Hmm." Darcy gave a thoughtful smile and then after delaying a moment said, "I guess I'm being too nosy…."

The store operator patiently watched her customer and replied, "Not at all. It's nice to know you care."

"The other night I got a bit confused," Darcy proceeded, "Eric called Ben 'Grampa Ben,' but David talked about his father as if he were not there."

"I'm divorced." Abigail watched as Darcy looked a little sheepish, then continued her simple explanation, "My husband remarried and now lives down in Miami. We don't see him much these days." A bittersweet look shown in the older woman's eyes.

Almost regretful that she had asked Darcy said quietly, "I'm sorry."

Abigail said flatly, "Don't be." Looking out the window she remarked, "Ben is my uncle. He has been more of a grandparent to the kids than my ex ever could be."

The answer caught Darcy by surprise and she mused aloud, "Your…uncle?"

Seeing Darcy's amazed expression Abigail offered a clarification, "Yes. He's fifteen years older than I am."

THURBER'S LIGHT

"Ah. Okay." Backing toward the door Darcy said, "Well, thank you."

Near the base of the lighthouse Darcy partially unfolded the green tarp and spread it on the sand. She looked up in time to see a flight of three Brown Pelicans with their wings spread wide, their large, avian bodies gliding at treetop altitude with little apparent effort. Smiling, she knelt and set the portable radio on the tarp, then turned on the power switch. It took a few seconds of turning the tuner dial to find a suitable station, but she finally located a setting that offered current pop music. It was the first time during her stay that she had turned the radio on. Pleased with her find she adjusted the volume upward and then straightened to examine the work ahead of her.

Darcy set about removing the awful graffiti that marred the lighthouse's structure. Armed with one of the t-shirt rags and turpentine she began the cleaning effort. "Wreckers 1980." "T.D. + S.H." "Kilroy 92." "Fish Lords." There were layers upon layers of spray paint with one message covering another in jarring shades of black, red, blue and green. It was obvious that the graffiti had taken place over a number of years. Darcy could not fathom how anyone could want to deface such a noble building. "Fck U."

As she worked she got into the musical groove offered by the radio and began to hum along while moving the rag in time with the beat. Abruptly the music vanished only to be replaced by static. Darcy stopped her actions and cocked her head to listen. The static altered and a blur of radio voices came and went, soon to be replaced by opera. She was baffled by the sounds and muttered aloud, "What the...." Leaving her work Darcy wandered over to the radio and examined the tuner dial. Somehow the radio had been reset to a new frequency. She turned the nob and again tuned the chrome trimmed, little grey box to the pop music station. Satisfied that she had gotten the strongest signal possible she set the radio back on the tarp and returned to her cleaning.

An ugly patch of red and black paint smeared into a fading area of pinkish grey with the wiping of Darcy's turpentine-soaked cloth. Her nose filled with the fumes of the solvent. As she continued to gently rub the blemished spot again Darcy worked to the bouncing melody coming from the radio. She picked up on the rhythm and began to rub in time. Bluntly the melody was cut off by a rapid succession of static and voices that peaked then were squelched. The opera resumed.

Now truly vexed Darcy tossed her rag down on the turpentine can and marched over to the radio. She snatched the appliance from the tarp and examined the tuner dial. Sure enough...the station had been changed again. With clenched teeth Darcy rotated the nob and once more reset the device to receive the pop music station. With purpose she firmly and deliberately set the radio back on the tarp and stared at it for a moment. Taking a deep breath she turned around and began trudging back toward her work location.

Darcy had not even made it as far as the tower when the music evaporated entirely and was followed by a solid, clinking thud. She turned around and looked at the tarp. The radio was lying face down on the plastic ground cover. Darcy felt a wave of anger come over her, but she worked to calm herself. Taking a few deep, slow breaths she regained her composure. Speaking to no one but herself, she muttered, "It's a beautiful day. I am not going to let...some ghost...spoil it." Walking back over to the tarp she asked into the air, "What do you have against rock, anyway?"

He said flatly, "I don't like it." His words were for his own benefit, not hers. The woman seemed completely oblivious to his nearby presence.

"So okay...my ghost doesn't like pop music." Almost laughing Darcy added, "He likes opera." She sat down on the green surface and picked up the radio. Examining the receiver she found that it had definitely been turned off, but otherwise the case seemed undamaged. Darcy shrugged and clicked the power on. Her beat-laden pop music came forth. She steadily turned the tuner dial until she had located the classical strains of a tenor voice. Sighing and placing the radio back on the tarp she looked toward the tower and said, "Okay...well, I hope this is better."

Smirking, he replied, "Thank you." Then he looked away and shaking his head spoke bitterly, "Why do I bother? She can't hear me. They never hear me."

"Can't spend all day arguing over the radio. There's work to be done." Standing up from her tarp seat she walked back over to the tower and picked up the rag. Refreshing the turpentine on the cloth she began rubbing the stone surface with the force of the operatic music filling the air.

~~~~

He wiped the rag in circular motions on the lantern room's sparkling window. In the grip of Martin's strong hand the cloth moved with all the strength of the musical strain. Filling his lungs to capacity the lighthouse keeper did his utmost to equal the opera singer's performance and blasted forth the lyrical strains in adequate, but sometimes imperfect, tones. He was at ease in the mid-day sun with his regulation pants held up by blue suspenders and his hat pushed back on his head. For the cleaning duties there was no need for the wool uniform jacket. The breeze softly eased the warm temperature of the day and the elevation of the lantern room lessened the heat reflected by the sand below. Martin industriously, but thoughtlessly, went about his cleaning chore. His mind was filled with the drama of the music.

In mid-note he suddenly realized that he had an audience. His breath caught short as he suddenly swallowed his robust vocalization. In his surprise he froze his position of balance with his shoed feet on the railing bar of the lantern room balcony while one hand gripped the metal handhold of the window frame. With wide eyes he gawked in a momentary loss of comprehension.

"Martin, that was wonderful!" Iris was attired in a light blue patterned frock and smiled at the keeper from the other side of the window. Sensing that she had caught him off-guard and in a possibly precarious situation she spoke loudly over the radio's continued song, "I'm sorry. I didn't mean to startle you."

"No...please," Martin's face erupted in a huge smile of delight, "Iris, that's okay! You can startle me anytime! Anytime you like!" Martin quickly dropped to the surface of the upper balcony and reached the narrow ladder that served as the only access to and from the catwalk. Sliding down the bars to land on the lower, railed porch he took two steps and reached the open entrance to the watch room. Entering the sheltered area he stopped his hasty canter abruptly and assisted the lovely visitor as she stepped down the last rung of the internal ladder. Martin brushed against the light fabric on the shoulder of her summer dress as she descended. Delightful appreciation filled him as he noticed how the dress became Iris' delicate form. His green eyes gleamed with a sense of wonderment and he exclaimed, "You look...lovely!" Martin's smile could not have been wider and he pulled his hat from his head, attempting to be a gentleman. He gave an abbreviated glance at the arch-shaped radio which rested atop the tool chest and then without turning from Iris he twisted the volume control to reduce the overpowering noise. He commented, "This is the second visit in one month. I'm honored!" Faltering for a second Martin continued in an uncertain tone, "Robby isn't here...."

"I know," Iris smiled and explained, "I saw him on the docks with Becky."

The pair stood smiling at each other for a moment until the silence was broken. A clanging on the metal steps drew both attentions and Ben appeared from around the tight curve of the spiraling stairway. The lad greeted the keeper, "Hey Martin!"

"Hey, Ben." Still smiling Martin greeted the boy, giving the lad's sister a quick but all-encompassing glance before returning his sight to the youth. He inquired of the chipper little fellow, "How's it going?"

"Great!" The lad completed the ascension and then turned to watch his friend finish the climb.

Vern reached the top of the stairs and accepted the extended hand of his pal. He hailed the keeper cheerfully, "Hi, Mistah Thurber!" The boy's overalls were rolled up at the ankles and it was plain that he was wearing hand-me-downs. "I' been thinkin' and I got a bunch a questions! How come there ain't no door ta that top porch? An' how come you keep those curtains closed during the day? An' what makes the light flash?"

Martin resigned himself to the fact that he would not be alone with the lovely Iris and silently sighed, but he remained happy for having the visitors. He laughed lightly and responded to the child, "Hey, Vern. You're a pretty smart fellow for thinking of all that. We'll have to sit down and discuss those things."

Assured of his companion's arrival into the cramped room Ben extended his hand to the keeper and announced brightly, "I brought my checkers this time."

Martin accepted the handshake and replied, "That's good. We'll have to play a couple of games." He looked up from the lad in time to notice Iris's amused grin.

~~~~

The following morning Darcy had not been out of the tent long when she received a guest. The familiar sheriff's car came to a stop and the occupant climbed out. He called, "You ready to open that lock?" Reacting to Darcy's enthusiastic nods Lester opened the trunk of the patrol car and removed a large pair of metal clippers.

Together the pair walked down the trail to the beach. As they reached the shoreline Lester got a good look at the tower for the first time in years. The outlines of dozens of painted markings still could be seen. In many places the turpentine had managed to remove the bold colors, but left an ugly, pink-grey hue. In disgust the officer said, "Jeeze…I see what you mean."

Darcy sighed, "And that is after most of a day of cleaning."

Lester shook his head. "To some people nothing is sacred." As the lawman approached the tower he slowed and then looked at the landscape around him. He gradually turned in all directions as he scanned the surroundings.

Watching the officer's guarded behavior Darcy asked, "What is it?"

"I'm not sure." Lester narrowed his eyes and remained focused on his examination of the area, "I've got this odd feeling...that we're being watched."

Darcy laughingly announced, "We are!"

Lester was not amused and turned to give his companion a glare. He firmly asked, "What do you mean?"

"It's Martin Thurber. He has been watching me since the first day I arrived." She cheerfully added, "At least I know his name now."

Shaking his head Lester flashed a skeptical, incredulous stare at Darcy before approaching the door to the tower. Feeling rather vexed he ridiculed her, "You don't really believe that malarkey...do you? There are no such things as ghosts. When you die, you're dead. You go to heaven or to hell. You don't hang around here." He raised the heavy clippers and captured the neck of the padlock between the blades of the tool while he continued to talk, "I've heard the story hundreds of times about Thurber jumping from the tower." He grunted a bit as he squeezed the handles together and the old metal of the lock bent, then broke under the force. Lester persisted, "And I believe he destroyed the light and killed himself. But that man is gone...left here a long time ago." He lowered the cutters and relaxed his grip on the metal-shearing device. Not getting a response from the young woman he looked at her.

Darcy stood there giggling and grinning widely. She shook her head at the fellow. With a chuckle she chided, "Oh, what you don't know. Martin Thurber is here all right, I guarantee it. I've seen him at the top of the tower...and you just broke the lock that has been there all along."

Lester would not admit belief in the spirit world, but with the lock broken he wasn't about to linger around the old lighthouse. Claiming there was work to be done elsewhere he left in the patrol car at an expedient speed. Darcy mused that the officer was probably telling the truth about needing to be elsewhere, but noted that the man had left faster than he had come.

Lifting the corroded old lock from the latch Darcy attempted to prepare herself for what she might find on the inside of the tower. She pulled at the door handle and the wooden barrier budged only slightly. A second and then a third try progressively moved the door a little further open. Finally a fourth tug opened fully the aged door and allowed a heavy odor of mildew combined with mold to escape its entrapment. Taking a few steps back and wrinkling her nose Darcy decided to give the tower a little while to breathe before venturing inside. Peering through the portal she caught a glimpse of broken glass and a number of empty beer bottles.

After taking an hour to trim some kudzu around her campsite, she returned to the tower with her camera, a couple of the plastic garbage bags, a flashlight and a shovel. She stopped short at seeing the door tightly closed again. Setting her items down on the sand Darcy again tugged at the door. It took another four efforts to get the entranceway truly open. Again the strong smell of musty air came from the tower.

Using the flash attachment on the camera she remained at the doorway of the tower, without actually entering the building, and took two photographs. The flash would insure that the images showed the interior conditions of the building for she personally could not see the details at that moment. Then she set the 35-mm equipment on one of the plastic bags with the camera lens covered again.

Darcy gathered another of the garbage bags and the flashlight. Breathing deeply she prepared herself to enter the tower for the first time. Stepping through the opening in the four-foot-thick wall she entered the round, musty chamber. She switched on her flashlight and directed its beam around the interior of the structure. Her heart sank at what she saw. A thick layer of sand had somehow been deposited on the floor. Mixed with the sand were shards of glass that reflected the light in shades of translucent brown and green. Along with the broken slivers were whole bottles and even a smattering of old trash—rotting rope, crumpled cans, unidentifiable metal, ceramic and plastic items. On the far side of the chamber was an indentation in the wall about a foot wide. Bricks had been torn from this spot and left strewn about, perhaps by treasure seekers. Even here on the inside of the building was a coating of painted graffiti. Darcy pointed the light upward along the wall. The foul remarks and slanders were sprayed on the surface as far up as she could see. She noted that there was one piece of good news in all this mess— the spiral staircase seemed intact despite some rusting.

A sudden chill came over Darcy. Just a moment earlier the interior of the tower had been nearly unbearable with a warm mugginess. She clasped her arms about her body, then shined the flashlight around, befuddled by the cold air.

"Get out."

Rubbing her hands across her arms to fight the chill she continued to look for possible origins of the cooling source.

"Get out!" Seeing that the woman was not going to leave he moved himself directly in front of her and waved his arm near her face.

The sudden cold draft caused Darcy to jump back. She had seen no reason for the sharp temperature decrease nor this movement of air. Now completely unsettled and bewildered she turned and hastily left the tower to check the outside temperature. On the beach the air was warm and comfortable. She looked to the sky, but saw no line of clouds. There was nothing that would indicate a weather change was imminent.

That was when Darcy heard the door slam behind her. She wheeled around and seeing the doorway sealed shut she stared in disbelief. In frustration she muttered, "Ghost!" She strode firmly back to the door and pulled hard on the aged, wooden panel. This time it opened on the second try with little resistance to her strength. Standing in the entrance she gazed inside and gave a scrutinizing search for the responsible door-closer, but knew that he would not be there.

Still with the plastic bag and flashlight in hand Darcy summoned her courage and once again entered the conical chamber. She opened the bag and spread the top wide while setting it on the sandy floor. Feeling that there was enough ambient light coming from the open entrance she turned off the flashlight and set it against the door frame. She spotted a piece of trash that had been abandoned against the wall and picked it up. Examining the item she found that it had been some kind of fish tin. The container could have been easily twenty years old. Darcy was about to place the piece of refuse into the plastic bag when she felt the air turn cool again. Without pause she released the fish tin, stood up straight and boldly exhorted, "Wait a minute...."

"I told you to get out!" Again he stood directly in front of her, stern and unhappy. "You don't belong here!"

Attempting to negotiate and reason with the presence that she could neither hear nor see Darcy pleaded her case, "...I just want to help."

"GET OUT!!!" He advanced on her and took hold of her shoulders. He shook her and yelled, "GET OUT OF HERE!"

Jarred by the specter's contact, Darcy's body flooded with adrenaline. It would have been natural to turn and run, but she stood motionless, combating the urge to flee. Every muscle in her was tense and ready for action. Her heart pounded hard. Her voice cracked as she tried to appease the belligerent ghost, "I want to help clean this place up."

"Help?!" He released her shoulders and spoke in bitter dismay, "No one ever wants to help! Not in all these years has anyone helped!"

Darcy breathed deeply in relief and chided, "You know...for a ghost who destroyed his own light, you sure are protective!"

"No!" Again he firmly grabbed the uninvited intruder and held her shoulders in a vise-like squeeze. He shook his head. "I didn't do that!"

Sensing the renewed contact between her and the dead man's spirit Darcy winced and exclaimed, "Jeeze!"

Easing his grip, he exclaimed again in frustration, "No...I didn't do that!!!"

Darcy's brow wrinkled and her eyes narrowed. A strange feeling had overtaken her and she knew now what she had to do. Calming her heartbeat, trying to empty her mind, she forced herself to relax. Her own internal chaos quieted and she entered a state near meditation.

"I didn't do that! Do you hear me?! I DID NOT DO IT!!!"

She could not hear the ghost, but somehow sensed his meaning and began to understand. With an unusual calmness she countered her own earlier observation and spoke aloud to the phantom, "But...you really didn't do it, did you?"

"That's right!" He was stunned at Darcy's comprehension. He released his grip on her shoulders and gently rubbed her arms, before ending his physical contact with her. Tearfully Martin answered again, "That's right! I didn't do it."

Chapter Six

Martin arrived at the Campbell household wearing his full-dress uniform and impeccably groomed. The dark blue, double-breasted jacket was pulled straight. The bow tie was stiffly flared. The metal U.S. Lighthouse Service emblem on his cap had been polished. He was on time to the minute when he rang the doorbell of the two-story house. The rambling, porch-lined building was a blend of formal Southern architecture with clean lines and columns mixed with a bit of frill that showed in lacy detail work attached on gabled eaves. On the exterior the house certainly did not seem like a manor, but was rather modest and functional. A warm, tungsten glow came from inside the home.

Caroline opened the door and found the lightkeeper tensely waiting. She greeted him pleasantly, "Mister Thurber, I'm so glad you could make it!" Pulling the door wide she motioned to her guest to enter and offered to take his coat and hat. The foyer was lit by a ceiling lamp which was encased in an ornately etched glass globe while the hardwood floor was covered by a fine, plush rug. The home was far more opulent and lush on the inside than Martin had expected despite the Campbell's part-ownership of the general store and the small fishing fleet. The pair were soon joined by a dignified seaman whom the matron introduced, "This is my husband, Ike Campbell. Ike…this is Martin Thurber."

As they shook hands Martin noticed that the seaman's palms and fingers were rugged and callused from years of pulling nets, working with ropes and hoisting cargo boxes. Martin figured his host to be approximately fifty years old. He was of average height, lean and firmly built. Ike's lengthy face sported a neatly trimmed beard that was more salt than pepper.

Approaching from the interior of the house was another man, broad across the shoulders, brawny and at least as tall as Martin. Ike introduced the new guest, "Mister Thurber, this is my business partner, Warren Hoffer." Looking to the boat owner he added, "Warren, this is Martin Thurber, keeper of the Saint

Rosabelle Lighthouse." Warren was more than likely a few years younger than Ike. He was dressed quite well and in a manner beyond the means of most fishermen. His hair was a mass of sun-bleached, dark blonde waves and he wore a full beard to match.

Hoffer extended his massive hand and chimed, "A pleasure." Martin met the handshake and quickly found that his strength was being tested. Hoffer's grip was near-crushing and the boatman engaged Martin's eyes in a test of will as he wore a closed grin. The lighthouse keeper took the challenge and aimed his gaze at the man while returning a sturdy hold on the confining hand.

As the men released their grasps Warren laughed in a deep voice and slowly nodded. He conceded, "Iris was right. You are a man of character." He turned and called sharply into the interior of the house, "Henry!!" Only when a strapping, young chap appeared did Hoffer turn back to face the keeper, "Martin…my son Henry."

As the slender, youthful man stepped up and received Martin's handshake Warren introduced the principle lighthouse keeper to his son. Henry's grip was also strong, but much to Martin's relief it was not challenging as his father's had been. There was something about the young man's eyes, however, that were edged and hard, causing Martin to be not entirely comfortable.

Beyond the men the keeper caught a glimpse of Ben peering around the corner and unwilling to join the crowd at the door. This shyness seemed unusual for the boy and Martin made a point to speak to him, "Good evening, Ben." Slipping entirely from view the child could be heard responding, "Good evening, sir."

As the gathering turned to venture further into the house they heard the sound of footfalls on the flight of banister-lined stairs which were adjacent to the foyer. Iris was gracefully descending down the dark, wooden steps. Her hair was drawn in fancy clasps and she was dressed in an exquisite azure dinner gown that accentuated her blue eyes. The snug, wide waistband fit her form perfectly and gave a clean tailored look to the silky, soft garment. Though unrevealing the dress subtly accentuated the gentle curves of the radiant lady's figure.

Martin was awestruck by her entrance and spoke unrestrained, "Iris…you're absolutely beautiful!" She smiled back at him in gratitude.

As the lightkeeper gazed in complete admiration, Henry briskly forged his way between the two smiling individuals and interrupted the eye contact shared between Martin and Iris. Firmly taking the woman's hand from the banister and holding it in a courtly fashion Henry lead her down the remainder of the stairs. His expression toward Iris was edged with possessiveness as he bluntly commented, "Yes, she is. All women should dress properly to please their man." Iris continued to smile, but a strained and uncomfortable look crept into the corners of her eyes. Martin's heart sank. Henry's possessive display all but completely confirmed Robby's warning about Iris being betrothed. Remembering his role as guest Martin opted not to rebut the young man, but remained silent, attempting to bolster his faded smile for the sake of those around him.

The dining places were set for the adults only and arranged so that Martin was in the direct company of the two business owners with Ike at the head of the table. Noting that Ben had not been included in the dinner Martin inquired regarding the lad's whereabouts.

Ike answered, "He will be eating in the kitchen with our cook and her son."

"Ben and Vern seem to be good friends," Martin commented and smiled.

The keeper heard a scoff come from across the table. With a sour look of disapproval Henry openly expressed his opinion to his host, "You shouldn't let your boy spend so much time with those blackies. It isn't right."

Caroline contested with a concerned reply, "I don't see that it is doing him any harm."

The youthful fisherman started a quick rebuttal, "It isn't helping to...."

"Henry!" Warren cut his son off in mid-sentence and gave him a firm look of warning. Succumbing to his father's command the younger Hoffer became quiet and a bit sullen. Satisfied that his son had been silenced, the imposing seaman's voice returned to cordial tones and he asked the lightkeeper, "So...Mister Bowsen is tending the light this evening?"

Martin nodded, "He's taking first watch." He took the folded cloth napkin from his place setting and spread it across his lap. Succulent aromas wafted from beyond the kitchen door and the guest found himself more hungry than he had previously realized.

Caroline inquired, "Aren't you afraid he may fall asleep?"

"Oh, no." Martin sounded confident, "Robby is diligent enough about his duties. And besides...I think he may have some company tonight to help keep him awake." He glanced in the direction of Iris and caught her hidden smile.

The main course arrived and conversation diminished. Orange-glazed roast duck with oyster dressing was served on fine bone china accompanied by a vintage wine served in crystal goblets. Side dishes of wild rice with slivered almonds, an herbed vegetable medley of baby carrots, yellow squash and string beans, plus warm rolls that were soft and fresh from the oven rounded off the main course. A berry parfait finished the wonderful meal and left absolutely no room for another bite.

Sherry was served in silver-stemmed snifters after dinner. Martin accepted Warren's offer of an imported cigar, but decided to reserve the tobacco for later use. The ladies soon took their leave. Iris was at first hesitant, but was ultimately guided by her mother's statement, "I'm sure the gentlemen have things they would like to discuss."

As the men settled in the parlor and relaxed, Ben slowly entered the room. Martin spotted the child and, not wanting to interfere, quietly observed his actions. The boy cautiously watched the powerfully-built Hoffer who was busy preparing and lighting his cigar. Carefully easing his way around the strong man Ben approached his father and tugged at his parent's sleeve to get his attention. In whispered tones the child asked the seated seaman for permission to go outside for awhile. Softly his father gave his consent, but warned the boy to tell his mother first. Nodding, Ben backed away and turned around...almost running directly into Warren. Stunned, the lad backed up a step and with a bleak expression on his face looked up at the man. In a frail voice the youngster apologized, "Excuse me, sir."

Stepping aside the brawny seaman responded, "Of course," and motioned with his cigar for the child to pass. Ben took the cleared path and left the room immediately while Henry openly laughed at the boy's timidness.

Martin commented to Warren, "Ben seems a bit afraid of you."

"I have little use for children, Mister Thurber." The man drew a long pull from the thick roll of tobacco and released the grey smoke slowly. He added, "At least not until they're old enough to haul nets."

"He should be getting close," Martin looked to the host and commented, "I have seen smaller boys onboard some of the boats."

Henry supported the observation, "Indeed."

Steady and firm with deliberate measure Ike stated, "I will be the judge of my son's capabilities." He packed the bowl of a smoking pipe and filled it with Sir Walter Raleigh tobacco.

"As is proper," Martin answered, confirming the man's authority over his own child.

Changing the direction of the conversation Warren inquired of the lighthouse keeper, "Have you ever considered being part of a ship's crew?" Applying gravity to his next question he continued, "Perhaps being a...captain?"

"No." Martin shook his head in surprise, "Can't say that I have."

Ike commented, "The wages can be good." Mr. Campbell's bright, blue eyes signaled confidence in his statement, and his voice was smoothly warm as he continued, "I'm sure it would be quite a bit better than the pittance the government has to offer you."

"That's quite possible," Martin countered, "but I know very little about commercial fishing."

Releasing a leisurely bellow of swirling, grey air Warren arched his thick eyebrows and claimed, "I'm sure that you would be a quick learner." His ample face displayed an overly-broad smile.

The younger Hoffer nodded and echoed his father's thoughts, "We are always in need," then adding extra emphasis, "of...loyal...captains and crew."

Martin was perplexed as he revealed, "I was told by Iris that your catch has declined...that you are not bringing in much these days."

There was a pause, then Henry looked at his father and laughed, "I never told her about the changes. That explains it." Redirecting his comments to the lighthouse keeper he clarified, "We have redistributed our boats and now most of our hauls are Menhaden."

Again there was a pause. Seeing Martin's quizzical expression Warren patiently explained, "Menhaden isn't a fish for eating. They use it to make fertilizer and oil products. We take it straight to the factories. It's good profit."

Ike drew a deep breath through the pipe causing the tobacco embers to glow red in the carved hollow of the bowl. Allowing the dense curls of aromatic smoke to escape from his lips the seasoned fisherman stated, "We could easily line you up with a boat in our fleet." Holding the pipe in his weathered hand, he explained, "You could spend a month or two learning the ropes and then we would let you take charge of her, of course with the understanding that Warren and I control the major decisions concerning the fleet."

"Well, I thank you for the consideration." Martin was struck by the men's proposal, but inwardly confused as to their reasons. "That's a very generous offer," he shook his head, "but the Lighthouse Service is in my blood. I have helped tend lights since I was a boy, from the time I could climb the stairs. This is what I know."

Henry moved, drawing breath to counter the man, but Warren gave his son a quick, hard glare. Looking back to the government employee, the elder Hoffer smiled and suggested, "You don't have to decide right now, Martin. A wise man thinks his decisions through. You think about it. You might find reason to join us. Our business is good." He sucked another long draw on the cigar and released a plume of rolling smoke.

"Becky, he's back." Giggling flowed down the tall, conical chamber and Martin grinned at hearing the young woman's playful sounds being echoed. Robby's voice again urged, "No. Listen." Martin deliberately stepped down hard on the metal stairs as he continued his upward climb. Nearing the top of the spiral flight he slowed and gave a resounding, guttural clearing of his throat. As he reached the watch room he feigned a slight surprise and cheerfully greeted the couple, "Good evening!" The twosome were now standing a full double arms' length apart which was somewhat difficult to achieve in the tight space of the upper tower chamber. With a formal politeness he commented, "What a pleasant surprise to see you this evening, Becky. Been helping Robby with the watch?"

Playing with her hair Becky smiled and quickly nodded, "Oh, yes."

Martin pursed his lips, shifted his view from the young woman to the assistant lightkeeper and stated, "You know...the General Instructions state plainly that no visitor should be in the watch room between sunset and sunrise." He paused just long enough for his words to register before continuing, "But perhaps we can make an exception this evening. Well then, what have we to report?"

Robby answered, "Nothing out of the ordinary. Six fishing boats caught the tide out." The assistant keeper handed a pair of binoculars over to his superior and asked, "So, did you have a good time?"

"It was pleasant enough." Martin's answer was delivered with an overly casual flatness and he moved toward the open doorway to the observation terrace as if looking for something.

Catching the dull tone in Martin's voice the youthful keeper pried, "Really?"

Not looking up Martin hesitantly nodded and said, "Vern's mother is an excellent cook."

Watching Martin stare out at the night horizon Becky carefully asked, "Did you like the Hoffers?"

He was slow in responding but finally said, "They're interesting people."

"They are awful, aren't they?" The young woman expressed her soured opinion, "Henry is a spoiled brat. He thinks he owns everything he sees."

Becky's tart tones caught Martin off-guard and he broke from his facade of surveillance. He looked back to the young woman and replied, "Well, now that you mention it…I did find parts of the evening a bit awkward." With an obvious sadness the tall keeper looked at Becky and asked, "Iris is betrothed to Henry, right?"

The lass screwed her face up in a look of disgust and spat out, "That's what he thinks! He says it's so, therefore it is supposed to be so." She scornfully smirked at the thought and shook her head.

Both of the lightkeepers were stunned by this latest revelation. Taking a deep, relaxing breath, Martin now realized that he had been jumping to conclusions. After an awkward pause, Robby queried, "Wait a minute. You're saying it isn't so?"

"That's right." With a smug smile she said, "Iris has never agreed to anything." Despite her defiant airs Becky's cavalier expression faded within half a moment and she sighed as she revealed, "Although it is just a matter of time. It's what their families seem to want. And 'what Father wants, Father gets.'" Sighing again she added, "Iris would never go against her father's wishes."

"But…she hasn't agreed." Martin stared at the auburn-haired lass and searched for hopeful signs. He pined for a confirmation, "Not yet…right?"

With a slight, sympathetic smile Becky answered, "Not yet."

Morning sunlight streamed down on the vegetable garden as Martin knelt and pulled some weeds from the row of tomato plants. He glanced up to see his workmate approaching, struggling with two large metal watering cans filled to the brim. Lowering his eyes, he resumed his inspection of the future crop.

Setting the pair of containers down Robby caught his breath and asked, "So…what really happened last night?" He watched as Martin shifted over a step in order to examine more of the plants.

Not looking up from his chore the principle lightkeeper asked, "What do you mean?"

Robby started, "You get invited to dinner at the home of one of the most influential people in the community. You go and meet one of the other most influential people in the community. And then…." The lad waited for the man to take the bait and finish the statement. When no response came he objected, "Ah, come on…what was it about?"

Pausing his weeding activities Martin answered, "They offered me a job."

"A job!?" The young man bubbled with curious excitement.

Still not displaying any notable enthusiasm the tomato gardener drolled, "They offered me a captain's position on one of their boats."

"You said yes, right?" Wide-eyed and eager Robby watched Martin as the keeper moved slightly to one side and once more began checking for weeds. When there was only silence the assistant inquired more soberly, "You did say yes…?"

"No." The answer was given with no harshness, but carried a flat resolution.

"What?" The young attendant disbelieved what he had heard and chided his coworker, "Martin, you're crazy!" Shaking his head he stared at the keeper. Finding it unfathomable that someone would turn down such an offer he appealed, "All that money…why on Earth not?"

Standing up Martin moved around the patch, took one of the watering cans and began to moisten the soil nestled around the tomato plants. "A couple of reasons." Catching the assistant keeper's attention he motioned to the other can and then to a waiting row of greens.

Insistently prodding for more information Robby quizzed, "Like what?" At a lethargic pace he lifted the container and set about sprinkling a portion of the garden.

Wrinkling his brow Martin responded, "It didn't feel right." Robby gave his superior a queer look and the lightkeeper explained, "To start with…I don't know anything about fishing boats, let alone trawling. They said they would train me, but why should they bother when there are plenty of men available…men who've had years at sea working nets." Looking over at his youthful partner he asked, "Don't you find that a little odd?"

Robby suggested, "Well…maybe they like you."

Doubtful Martin shook his head and asserted, "I just met them for the first time last night. Not to mention if Hoffer's son had anything to say about it they would be using me for line bait. He made it very plain that he considers Iris to be his."

"But all that money!" Robby made sounds of dismay and whiningly lamented, "You could be making so much more than you'll ever be paid by the government for working here…or at any lighthouse."

"I know," the lightkeeper said and scratched his cheek leaving a smudge of dirt that marked his sweat-dampened skin. Breathing deeply he sighed, "Sometimes money isn't what counts. I was born in the U.S. Lighthouse Service. I can't picture myself being anywhere else BUT at a lighthouse. This is what I was meant to do. I would be lost if I had to leave the Service."

~~~~

Darcy sat on a folded tarp and meditated in between the two brick structures. She had routinely practiced relaxation and mental awareness routines in the past, but with so much going on lately she had been lax. It felt good to get back to her habit of meditation. Though her eyes were closed and she was comfortably relaxed, she was aware of all action around her. She noticed subtle sounds and shifts in the breeze.

"*Darcy....*"

She noticed the morning doves cooing as they searched for seeds along the narrow path carved in the kudzu.

"*Darcy....*"

Her eyes fluttered open and she smiled. She spoke audibly though not loudly, "Martin?" She sat for a moment just looking forward and allowed herself to become adjusted to the morning light. Gradually she stood and stretched. Something not entirely seen drew her attention and she looked at the vine-covered brickwork of the larger structure. For the first time she noticed an opening in the masonry. It seemed to be a window. She advanced toward the building and examined the darkened indentation which the coarse tendrils of the voracious vine clogged and barricaded. Through the tiny gaps in the foliage she thought she caught a glimpse of movement. Not knowing what to expect she hesitantly inquired, "Martin…?"

Her progress in investigating the portal was interrupted by the sounds of car horns. She jogged out from between the structures and was stunned to see the approach of not one, but a number of vehicles. A pair of pickup trucks were followed by both Abigail's station wagon and a Honda that Darcy thought belonged to either Gretta or May. The trucks pulled to the side and allowed for more vehicles to move forward. As people disembarked Darcy noticed that they were wearing a variety of clothes, ranging from Bermuda shorts to faded jeans. Watching the cluster of arrivals she recognized most of the gathering and shouted, "Hi folks! What's going on?"

David Hoffer reached into the back of his truck and unloaded a chain saw. Eric had been riding next to his father and climbed from the elevated truck compartment while beaming at Darcy. "You won't believe what I found on the Internet!"

Having arrived with her mother and grandmother in the station wagon Kim moved quickly to join in the conversation and wasted no time. "WE found…" the young girl indignantly corrected her brother, "I was the one using the computer."

"But it was my idea," Eric protested and made a face at his sister.

David interjected, "Wait a minute, you two. Go help your mother." The fleet manager was joined by Lester McKay who was dressed in denim overalls. The children's father added, "We need to talk to Darcy for a moment."

"All right," Kim responded and stuck her tongue out at Eric as she left. Slightly disgruntled the boy followed and headed for the station wagon.

David offered, "We thought we would help you out here a bit, if you would like."

Happy, but befuddled Darcy replied, "I like!"

Lester eyed the tangled growth that was several feet thick in some areas where it covered the ground. He asked, "Where would you like us to start?"

"Well," Darcy pondered, "how about widening the path? If any work is going to be done on the lighthouse we will probably need to get vehicles a lot closer to it."

"Good idea." The men fetched protective eye goggles and work gloves from their vehicles. Soon the whine and buzz of motorized saws deafened the atmosphere as David and Lester commenced cleaving the aggressive weed. Sawdust flew as thick kudzu trunks were severed.

Abigail's voice sang forth a cheery greeting, "Good morning!" Gretta, Linda, May and Kim were followed by the storekeeper. Seemingly uniformed in gardening attire complete with wide-brimmed straw hats the women had armed themselves with shovels, pruning sheers and hand trowels. Enthusiastically announcing their intent to assist Darcy, they needed only the slightest instruction on what needed to be done. Directing them to the area between the buildings Darcy explained that she had been attempting to clear the remaining stubs of the kudzu so she could move the tent. The small but determined brigade of ladies marched forward and engaged the roots of the enemy. Eric, full of youthful energy, practically ran to the site and began to dig immediately, while Ben, older and more methodical, accompanied the ladies and patiently assisted as he was directed.

Darcy was astonished at the invasion of local residents. Finding it all a little odd and possibly a tad puzzling she watched in pleasured amazement as shovels were utilized and noticeable amounts of the plant fell victim to the roaring saws. Then a late arrival caught her attention. A vintage, green pickup slowly pulled to one side of the cluttered roadway. An aged man opened the door of the forest-colored truck and dismounted. He surveyed the terrain with his dark eyes studying the makeshift workforce in action. His weathered skin was the color of dark chocolate and a farmer's straw hat covered his wiry grey hair. His patched and faded overalls showed long-term use. Darcy guessed the man's identity and waved to him while she headed back down the path toward the parked vehicles. The new arrival waved back to the young woman.

Seeing Lester along the trail, Darcy attempted to gain his attention. The saws drowned out all her shouts. Approaching him, she touched the lawman's shoulder. He looked up and allowed the powered chain saw to wind to a stop. Following her pointing gesture Lester saw the older man slowly moving toward them. Speaking over the continued din produced by the second chain saw still being wielded by David, Lester announced, "My granddad!"

Together they walked to meet the fellow and after Lester motioned a retreat they returned back to the vehicles. Away from some of the noise, it was easier to talk. Lester proceeded with introductions, "Granddad, this Darcy Vornack...the lady I was telling you about." Then looking to the young woman he added, "Darcy...this is my grandfather, Vern McKay." The older man's eyes twinkled pleasantly and he smiled warmly.

With sincerity Darcy extended her hand to the weathered gentleman and feeling his roughened palm against hers she said, "The pleasure is mine." She watched Vern's smile broaden to display pearl-white teeth.

The senior announced, "I brought you a goat. Lester, here, says you can spare some of this vine ta feed him."

Darcy responded with a touch of glee, "Absolutely! He can eat just as much as he wants."

"What're they doin' here?" Vern surveyed the activities taking place in the kudzu-choked lot as pruning shears and shovels were being employed and David's power saw sent a plume of powdered wood airborne. Almost sounding dismayed he asked, "Cuttin' it all up?"

"They're just making a dent." She laughed, "Don't worry...there will be acres more left for that goat to eat!"

Relieved and encouraged the elder offered, "Well, then, let me lend a hand." He paused, then asked, "Is that Ben Campbell over there?"

His grandson responded, "Yes, sir. It certainly is."

"Well then, let me go say hello ta my friend." Vern began to mosey toward the location of the elderly fisherman who was attempting to assist Gretta with a stubborn root crown.

Darcy did well not to laugh at the efforts of the portly lady who was nearly knee-deep in a hole and tugging with all her might on the tuber, her flowered shorts discolored with dirt stains. Watching all the effort being done on her behalf Darcy figured that she had better go join in. As Lester once again revved the chain saw she made her way down the path to the space between the brickworks.

By noon much to the amazement of all concerned the path had been widened enough to allow even large vehicles to pass. The expanse between the two masonry forms had not only been cleared of vines, but also of the troublesome root crowns as well. Kudzu still remained in possession of the actual structures, but there was now more than ample room to relocate the tent. Satisfied with their efforts the group declared a lunch break.

The crew had come prepared with folding chairs, coolers of drinks and bottled water, plus sandwiches and bags of chips. There was more than enough for everyone. They found a spot not far from the assortment of vehicles and then commenced the midday meal with the same vigor previously given to vine elimination.

Now that most everyone was quietly stuffing their mouths with the simple delicacies Darcy remembered an earlier encounter. She asked Eric, "So what was it you found on the Internet?"

He swallowed his bite of sandwich and explained, "I had to do a report for school…and after the other night, well I decided to do it about lighthouses. So…" he looked over at his sister, "we…got on-line and started checking out sites."

"Mmm." Darcy smiled at the pair of youngsters, "What did you find out?"

The lad's eyes gleamed with true interest and enthusiasm as he spoke, "There are lighthouses all over the place…like Scotland and Japan and France."

"Well, I hadn't thought about it, but now that you mention it…it makes sense." Darcy reasoned, "Any place that has a shoreline would need some kind of navigational aide." There came the sounds of agreement from others who were listening, but most had their mouths too full to comment.

Kim added, "And some of the older ones have these huge, crystal lenses called Frensal."

"Frensal?" Darcy asked, "Maybe, Fresnel? The same design lens is used in many of the lights that are on movie sets."

The girl explained, "But these are really big and go all the way around the lamp."

Smiling Darcy said, "Sounds impressive."

Reclaiming the spotlight from his sister Eric continued, "We downloaded some pictures. They're real awesome. Anyway…the Coast Guard took over running the lighthouses in America in 1939 and have been automating them or shutting them down if they think they aren't needed any more or they aren't safe."

"In 1939." Darcy mused, "That's the same year Martin Thurber died. You didn't happen to find out on what day the Coast Guard took over, did you?"

Eric shook his head and quickly chewed a handful of chips.

"If you don't mind...please continue with your research." Darcy encouraged them, "It sounds like you have a good start and I would love to know more."

Both of the Brown siblings beamed at their newfound importance and responded in agreement.

Their father requested, "See what you can find about preservation, too."

At that moment a dark blue Toyota came up the road and pulled off to the side. A number of individuals in the gathering grunted at the sight. The driver quickly left the car and snatched a two-liter bottle of soda from the front seat before trotting toward the group. Breathing heavily as he arrived Peter Brown apologized, "Sorry I'm so late."

"That's okay, Peter," the unexpected absolution was delivered by Lester. He continued slyly, "I need to leave soon, so you can take over the chain saw." There were muffled chuckles as the smile worn by the late arrival faded a few degrees.

Though wearing a look of bemused perplexity Abigail offered, "Have a seat, Peter. Eat a sandwich before you get started. I brought a few extras."

Heeding Lester's motions Darcy followed him beyond the group of locals. At a slightly more private distance he informed her, "There's going to be a gathering at the church tomorrow night to discuss the prospect of incorporating the town. You might want to be there so you can let your California friends know what's happening."

Darcy nodded and agreed, "Sure, I'll come." After a moment she asked, "Lester...might I have one more favor?"

With a slight smile he responded, "What is it this time?"

"Could you look up the file on Martin Thurber's death?"

His brows furrowed as he asked, "Any reason...other than morbid curiosity?"

Darcy started, "Yeah...." She shook her head while she brooded, "But, maybe I shouldn't say anything yet."

"Come on." His deep voice verged on insistence, "Out with it."

Looking into the deputy's intense brown eyes Darcy responded flatly, "I have reason to think that he may not have destroyed the light."

"Uhhuh." Lester's expression took on a knowing look and he asked, "And just where did you come up with this insight?"

Almost bashfully Darcy answered, "I had…a real…poignant encounter…with Martin's ghost. And I know that…he claims he didn't do it."

"You talked with his ghost." Lester's voice was filled with obvious doubt as he folded his arms across his chest.

Recognizing the officer's disbelief Darcy began to feel slightly defensive and firmly replied, "Well…yeah."

Still maintaining his calm, official voice Lester continued, "And he told you that he didn't destroy the light." He watched Darcy carefully and studied her expression.

Her answer was blunt, "That's right."

"You heard him say it." His words were that of a statement, but were really a question.

"Well," again she hesitated and then carefully answered, "in a fashion."

Not satisfied by Darcy's vagueness Lester asked, "What does that mean?"

"Okay, look," now even more agitated by Lester's doubting Darcy expounded, "I went into the tower and I felt him touch me. When I accused him of ruining the light…he got angry. He grabbed my shoulders. I…I could feel his anger. It was like he was trying to make me understand. I don't know how I know…I just do. When I agreed and said that he hadn't done it, he let me go, and I felt this sense of thankfulness…like I had somehow connected with him…that he had made me understand something no one else had, but the feeling was also filled with this awful kind of longing. There's something wrong…maybe that's why he is still here. He wasn't ready to leave when he died." She drew a breath. "I know all this may sound a bit crazy, but I would like to find out what happened. Maybe help him, if I can."

The officer's tone was now a bit more uncertain, "You could feel him grab you?"

She blurted, "Oh yeah! It was like someone who had just had their hands in ice water. Cold, but I could definitely tell that they were a man's hands."

"Well," Lester slowly stated, "I believe that you believe that you had some kind of encounter. I don't normally look up files for ghosts, but for you I'll make an exception."

With some relief Darcy said, "Thank you."

"Of course." He gave her a mild, amused look.

Chapter Seven

By late afternoon the group effort had made a big difference in the appearance of the coastal tract. Not only had significant open spaces been carved in the solid, green mat of foliage, but Darcy's living quarters had been fully relocated with protective tarps now sheltering the diminutive tent. Nestled between the pair of brick structures the new campsite offered much more living space than the previous location. There was even a slight feeling of fortification about the setting.

An area had been cleared especially for the goat to roam in. The soft-eyed creature was tethered and given enough chain to wander around as he pleased. Despite the clearing that had been made, there was still plenty of kudzu for the animal to graze on. This was a temporary arrangement as the area would need to be eventually fenced in for both the goat's comfort and protection. Clyde, as the goat was named, was exceptionally friendly. A young dwarf ram, his coat was black with frosting save for his broad, white muzzle and one white tuft on his underside. To the delight of the children he proved eager for attention, nibbling all the carrots they held out for him. Clyde only stood about a foot and a half tall at the shoulder. Darcy was told that he would not get too much larger—maybe only an inch or two. Once he was established in his new location, he seemed to understand his duties as he immediately commenced munching on kudzu foliage. Vern McKay excused himself from the gathering, having seen that his ram was cared for, that fresh water was made available in a large pan. He waved goodbye, stating that his wife would be worried about him.

Borders had been created surrounding both of the old masonry forms, allowing people to survey the ruins from all sides. Most of the attached vines had been severed at their bases. It was agreed that much care was still needed to remove the tangled web of tendrils which held the buildings in their near-inflexible grasp. More damage than good might come from a careless pull. Already loosened bricks could be entirely dislodged from the weakened structures.

Looking around at the helpers Darcy noticed that Ben was not with the main gathering. Wandering behind the campsite she spotted him still laboring with a shovel. Quietly approaching him she recognized where he was working: Thurber's grave. She thought it quite strange as she overheard the normally laconic fisherman mumbling energetically to himself. After watching him for a moment she attempted to gain his attention, "Ben?"

The man jumped from being startled by Darcy's arrival. He looked at her for a moment with a weird expression on his creased features. Finally he recognized her. Then relaxing somewhat he went back to his efforts at digging. With resolve he heaved down on the shovel and audibly grumbled, "Not right."

Feeling puzzled she approached slightly closer and asked, "What's not right, Ben?"

"Roots." He lifted the loaded shovel blade of dirt from the depths of the hole. The soil was tossed onto an expanding pile to one side of the grave. Forcing the spaded tool into the bottom of the cavity again he grunted, "Gotta get 'em…out."

"You're right, Ben. It isn't right that anyone's grave should be left in ruins like this." She asked gently, "Did you know him?"

The aged man looked at Darcy without replying…in a few seconds he dropped the shovel, leaned over and applied his strength to pulling at the unburied tuber. As he strained, lean muscles showed in his arms and he gritted his teeth. At first there was no sign of movement…but ever so gradually there began to be indications of the root yielding—the slightest sound of creaking and a slow surrender from its hold. Suddenly with a deep, popping sound there was an airborne spray of dirt as the underground plant connections gave way. Darcy shielded her eyes as the shower of earth descended, pelting Ben and the surrounding area. Silently Ben carried the removed root crown from the grave and dropped it on a collection of other extracted roots. To Darcy's amazement he had already removed a half dozen or more of the tuber sets.

"Ben, I could use your help with something," she solicited him with some reserve, "that is, if you don't mind. If you were here when the lighthouse was still being used…maybe you could tell me about the grounds? Like…what are these buildings?"

He pursed his lips and paused, then looked back at the grave. Understanding his reluctance to leave the job unfinished Darcy assured him, "I'll work on it in the morning. It's getting a bit late in the day, now."

Again Ben looked at Darcy. He said, "Needs...grass seed."
"Yes," she smiled and agreed, "I'll buy it."
Ben brushed off the dirt from his shirt and shifted his view to the old, rectangular building. Walking around the deteriorated structure toward the rest of the crew he announced in his normal tone, "Keeper's house." His remark caught the interest of Eric who motioned to the others who were present. One by one the group became aware that something unusual was going on. Those who were still talking among themselves quickly became quiet. Eventually everyone directed their attention to the gathering's senior citizen and what knowledge he might have to share.

~~~~

Lighthouse Inspector Kern was dressed in his crisp uniform dramatically punctuated by snug fitting white gloves. He opened the kitchen pantry and scrutinized the contents. Looking over the cans of sweet peas, yams and beats the man twitched his carefully trimmed, greying mustache and commented sharply, "Needs better organization." Danforth, the assistant as keenly dressed as his superior scribbled notes on a tablet. Followed closely by the keepers the assistant trailed after the district level officer. They all proceeded to the next room.

~~~~

Moving across the newly established campsite to the second old, strangled brick structure Ben studied the odd, rounded shape. With a steady voice he declared, "Cistern."
Having grown up in primarily urban areas, Darcy did not understand what the old man meant. She shook her head slowly and asked, "Cistern?"
Gretta explained loudly, "You know...for holding water for drinking or for crops, maybe." The seaman nodded and agreed with the description.

~~~~

Climbing the ladder to the top of the cistern the inspector opened the cover and sniffed the air that rose from contact with the stored water. Not detecting any unpleasant odor nor noticing any contaminants the official silently returned down the rungs. Again the quiet parade trailed behind as the inspector moved toward the next location.

~~~~

No one had expected Ben to continue with his grounds tour, but given that he seemed to be volunteering no one objected. He moved half-way down the path that led out from the campsite, then paused and turned into the expanse that had been cleared for the goat. Striding across most of the open area he came to a stop short of the kudzu border. Pointing just beyond the edge of the plants he said, "Barn."

The crowd of dirt-covered workers that had followed Ben to the area now dotted with vine stumps looked at each other and then back at the patch of voracious greenery. All that was visible beyond the groomed space was a tangled mass of kudzu, perhaps as much as a yard deep. Neither bricks nor boards nor any other building material penetrated the growth. If there had once been a structure where Ben was pointing there was no sign of it now.

~~~~

Standing in the entrance to the humble barn the inspector watched as three Rhode Island Red hens scratched at the ground hunting for grains of feed. The birds' colorful plumage seemed mockingly cheerful. They seemed oblivious to the formal scrutiny. Abruptly Inspector Kern asked the two keepers, "No livestock?"

"No sir," Martin answered, "not yet."

"Very well." Kern moved on.

~~~~

Back on the path Ben now pointed to a place on the other side of the main trail across from the keeper's home and began, "Assistant...." He faltered momentarily, then concentrated and brought forward the words, "keeper's quarters." Again there was nothing where the man motioned to except a covering of vine and the remains of two or three strangled and smothered trees. His audience gave a few disbelieving mumbles.

"No, I think he's right." Abigail spoke in her uncle's defense, "I think I remember...a wood frame house. It was very small."

"What happened to it?" Darcy asked, "Do you know?"

Abigail frowned and shook her head, "It may have burned. I don't really remember. It's been some time ago now."

Peter quipped, "Kudzu ate it, that's what!" There were giggles and grunts of agreement.

~~~~

Running his white-gloved fingers over the edge of a table Kern lifted his hand and checked for signs of dust. The clean fabric of the glove was grey from soil. He glanced at assistant keeper Bowsen scornfully. Shaking his head he moved into the bedroom. Spotting a pair of work trousers draped over the straight chair he turned about. Pursing his lips he proceeded to leave the building. The inspector's assistant scribbled on the tablet as he hurriedly trailed the man. Silently Martin followed the two men out and was in turn followed by Robby who seemed baffled and hurt by the apparent disapproval. He just couldn't understand what the big deal was over a few minor details of housekeeping.

~~~~

Ben waded into the kudzu and pointed to just beyond where he stood. "Workshop."

~~~~

Viewing the wooden workbench Kern spotted a pair of pliers and a screwdriver that had been left on the surface. He said flatly, "Tools must be returned to their proper places after use." Again the district level assistant jotted notations.

~~~~

Ben moved toward the beach. The fascinated entourage followed. It seemed that he was heading for the tower, but he stopped short. Pointing to an elevated mass of greenery he said, "Oil house."

~~~~

Greasy rags left on top of a canister were enough to raise resounding condemnation from the inspector. "We MUST be ever on guard against fire." Lecturing the keepers Kern was fervent as he reprimanded, "NEVER leave combustibles unsealed. NEVER leave spilled oil untended to...and NEVER LEAVE FLAMMABLE ITEMS UNTIDY!" Making sure he got his point across he curtly tested, "Do you understand?"

Both men replied, "Yes sir!" Martin's visage was sour as he shot his partner a look. A blanched-faced Robby gave a slight wince.

~~~~

A few feet short of where the trees gave way to the shore the old fisherman wandered away from the path into the low brush. He stopped to indicate where he was standing and said, "Foghorn."

~~~~

The old oil engine, just over four feet tall and a yard long, had been installed in the signal building over thirty years earlier. The engine's exhaust served as compressed air, building up pressure to be released through the trumpet horn that could emit an incredible blare of noise easily heard miles away. Such blasts were said to have knocked unwary gulls from the sky and blown the eardrums of unfortunate workers leaving them forever deaf. The inspector was not interested in these aspects of the engine and horn. Instead he checked for excess oil and dust.

~~~~

Wandering out onto the sandy expanse Ben pointed out to the water and after a prolonged moment said, "Wharf."

David shook his head and commented, "The sea took it years ago." He walked over and placed his hand on the shoulder of the old man who was still staring out to sea.

"I have an idea," Peter merrily chimed, "why don't we have a cookout tonight? We could have it right here!"

Seemingly reluctant Linda asked, "On the beach?"

"Why not?" Peter remained exuberant and said, "I could go back and get hotdogs, maybe corn and potatoes…pick up some more drinks. We can build a fire…."

In her outspoken, burly manner Gretta surveyed the shoreline and blurted out, "What with? There isn't that much dry driftwood."

Not dismayed Peter answered, "Kudzu!"

"Peter, it's all green." Abigail sighed, "We just cut it."

Recalling her earlier efforts Darcy interjected, "Not all of it. There's some that has been drying for days now…down in the bottom of the piles."

"All right then!" David's confirmation sent his children cheering.

~~~~

Both of the Saint Rosabelle lightkeepers stood stiff and motionless on the wharf as they received the judgement of the inspector, "Not acceptable, gentlemen." Glaring at the pair as he paced the planks Kern snapped, "The tower needs painting. You shall begin on the project as soon as possible." He watched for any signs of dissension and then continued, "Your brass fittings need to be polished more thoroughly. There should be not one fingerprint, not one!" Lastly, with a grumble he begrudgingly added, "At least your books seem to be straight." Stopping short in front of the assistant keeper he turned and stared directly at the uncomfortable young man. In an overbearing voice the official boomed, "Mister Bowsen! You need to take better care of your uniform! Your buttons need to be shined and there should be not one wrinkle. Not one! And your living quarters need to be properly cleaned. Such conditions will not be tolerated and deserve disciplinary action. If I find such conditions again you may lose your position." Resuming his pacing he added, "Supplies, whether they are the government's or yours personally should be tidy and organized. All clothing should be folded neatly or hung…never left strewn on furniture. There had better be marked improvement by my next visit, gentlemen. There are many keepers that would like your assignment. Do I make myself understood?"

THURBER'S LIGHT

Grim-faced and in unison Martin and Robby both responded, "Yes sir."

"Good!" Kern turned sharply and strode down the aged, wooden wharf to the waiting launch. As he and his assistant boarded the small craft he called back to the men, "The chaplain has come with us. He waits at the tender and shall come minister to your spiritual needs." The small craft pulled away and headed for the waiting Lighthouse Tender. The ship was one of a fleet known as tenders because they tended to the needs of the lighthouses, transporting both supplies and personnel from the depot to the light stations. Without visits from the Lighthouse Tender many light stations would be completely cut off from the rest of the nation.

The keepers watched as the motorboat became more distant and they felt their blood pressure decrease. Breathing great sighs both men relaxed slightly and were glad for the inspector's departure. Looking over at his senior Robby smiled weakly and commented, "And I thought you were a hard butt!"

Martin glanced at the younger keeper, his flat expression saying all that needed to be said.

At the tender there was an exchange of personnel in the launch. A wood box was carefully lowered into the launch and the motorboat was again freed. The return trip only took a few minutes at most. With lines tied to the wharf and the tiny vessel held stable by the boat's operator the chaplain climbed the ladder. Without assistance he found his footing on the dock. The seafarer climbed up behind the clergyman and announced, "Gentlemen, this is Father..."

"Leo Richfield!?" Martin jubilantly beamed with obvious delight and asked again, "Leo!?"

"Martin Thurber?" The fair-haired, freckle-faced priest glowed in his own happiness. He closed the gap between them and the reunited pair clasped hands in a hardy and lingering greeting.

Robby stood watching the two conspicuous friends and then commented, "I take it you know each other."

"Oh...." With newfound energy Martin turned and introduced his partner, "This is Robert Bowsen, Assistant Keeper. Robby," he continued to explain, "Leo and I have been friends since we were boys. We went to school together and his father captained the local tender, so we were able to play together sometimes, too." Turning his attention back to the arrival he said, "It's been a long time...."

"It certainly has," the clergyman agreed. "We have a lot to catch up on."

Feeling suddenly like an outsider Robby watched the sole crewman as he worked the davits and hoisted the wooden box to the wharf. He commented idly, "Ah, good, a library box. New books."

Martin remained overwhelmed by the presence of his childhood chum and admitted to the fellow, "I wasn't sure if you had managed to finish the seminary." The two men laughed and began to walk down the weathered dock toward the light station.

"Well, I knew you would be in the Lighthouse Service," Leo teased the lightkeeper, "I just hadn't expected you to be so far south!"

"It's warmer here." Martin explained, "I nearly froze to death last winter." After strolling some distance along the wharf he realized that Robby wasn't with them. Looking back to see the young man dallying sullenly near the launch, Martin called out, "Robby! Come on! Join us!"

Robby's eyes brightened and he jogged up to the pair of old buddies.

~~~~

The fire crackled as the broken lengths of kudzu gave up the last of their moisture and glowing embers drifted skyward, lofted by the heat of the flames to be lost among the stars. An endless number of twinkling points speckled the evening's ebony dome. Damp, oceanside, night air brought the cluster of people close to the warmth provided by the little bonfire. Their laughter rose among the embers and served to warm the night just as much as the crackling fire. Jokes, fishing stories and tales of the sea…all were told with a neighborly flare and local flavor. Frankfurter packages were emptied as bellies were filled. Foil wrapped vegetables were cooked until tender in the edge of the flames. Lastly marshmallows were skewered on sticks.

As the puffy, white treats were browned Darcy stated, "I appreciate you all coming out and helping me like this, but I have to wonder what spawned this united effort." She added with a smile, "It must be a bit more than just coincidence that all of you decided to come on the same day."

The group became silent and then muffled giggles filled the quiet. Abigail spoke on the group's behalf, "We sort of have a vested interest in your winning the bet."

The camper wasn't surprised by the answer. She smiled broadly as she responded, "Ah, I see."

Peter looked toward the tower as it loomed in the darkness. His face was blushed by extended exposure to the day's sun. Contemplatively he asked, "So how do we save this lighthouse?"

Darcy sighed, "Good question."

In his usual cynical tones Eric inserted, "How do we stop the beach from going away...."

Giving his son a placid glance David said what seemed obvious to him, "It's going to take money."

Gretta scoffed, "Lots of it." She scraped a blob of crispy, brown marshmallow from her lengthy stick and then consumed the gummy delight in two bites.

May was bundled in a heavy sweater to fend off the cool, coastal breeze. As she thrust her hands in her pockets she asked, "What if we don't have enough?"

Linda answered the woman directly, "We DON'T have enough."

Becoming aggravated at the prevailing defeatism Abigail spoke up, "So, we're just going to have to raise more money."

"Who here knows anything about restoration," Darcy inquired, "or engineering?"

Loading his stick for another round of toasting sweets Eric squished a second marshmallow over the tip of the thin spear and shrugged, "Not me...."

Following Darcy's leading question, Abigail commented, "We'll have to hire some kind of contractor. Someone who knows about this kind of building." She fetched a bottle of water from the cooler which rested next to a thermos of coffee and a silent, portable radio.

David admitted, "That's going to be expensive."

"Look," Darcy thought aloud, "this place is a historical landmark, right? Even if just a local landmark?"

David confirmed, "Yeah...."

She continued her line of thinking, "Maybe there's some kind of government money that might be available."

Liking the idea Peter brightened. He nodded and exclaimed, "Yeah!"

Linda asked, "So what does that involve?"

Peter smirked and remarked, "Paperwork, no doubt."

"Yes...but we have to find the right paperwork." Gretta attempted to be practical, "What level of the government do we go to, what department, what office...?"

"What official do we bribe!"

"Peter...." Abigail began to scold her son, but seeing his immense smile and then the wide grins all around the circle saluting his tart humor she relented.

More soberly Linda queried, "So, what happens if the lighthouse falls before we have enough money to save it?"

May gasped, "Heaven forbid!"

Gretta continued to think of possible complications, "And how do we know that whoever is in charge of the money doesn't just keep it all for himself? Or herself?"

"You use a business account and keep financial books on your organization," a gruff voice answered from beyond the group, "that's how." The huddled group shifted their seated positions and those on the far side of the fire stood in order to see who had unexpectedly responded. Carl stood a few yards inland from the gathering. He was holding a bottle of brew and wearing his usual dirty undershirt. The firelight gave an odd illumination to his unshaven face, accenting the stubble with both highlights and shadows. A slight wavering in his stance revealed his mild intoxication. He huffed, "Well, I was wondering what you people were up to out here."

Peter responded in terse tones, "Well, now you know."

With a snide smile Carl mocked the younger brother, "Yes, I do."

Gretta huffed, "Carl, we don't need your trash causing trouble here."

Looking over at the stout woman he rebuked her, "Who says I'm going to cause trouble," then added, "you fat sow."

David took a few steps forward and warned the intruder, "I think you should leave, Carl."

"No doubt." As he turned slowly away he added, "Well, shit on you!" He strode heavily across the sand and headed back toward the path.

"Carl?" Darcy left the fire-warmed ring and pursued the loner, "Carl, wait a minute."

The man came to a stop and looked over his shoulder at the person following him. With a grunt he swivelled about and growled, "What?"

Darcy made deliberate eye contact with the belligerent interloper, but kept her voice calm and low as she admonished him, "That was very rude."

Carl furrowed his brow and sneered. He responded bluntly, "So?"

"Well," she contested, "you didn't have to be so ugly."

"It wasn't exactly like I was welcome." He began to turn away from her and aimed for the dirt road.

Shadowing his motions Darcy attempted once more to talk with the solitary man, "Maybe if you gave them a chance to be nice, they would be."

Again Carl halted and shuffled his feet to stabilize his footing in the loose sand. Gazing at Darcy he argued, "Look...all they want is something for themselves." Shaking his head he gave a grimace and flatly said, "They're not being nice to you for nothing."

Exasperated Darcy inquired, "What is it that you think they want?"

Carl looked at the woman as if amazed at her ignorance. He replied sharply, "They're helping you so their dumb old tower doesn't get knocked down. That's all."

"Well, then," she produced a strained, slight smile and said, "they and I have an interest in common. I don't want to see the lighthouse torn down either."

Taking a deep breath he scoffed, "What's so special about the damn thing?"

Darcy answered plainly, "It represents hope."

"Hope." He mouthed the word in silent repetition. Shaking his head he lowered his brow and raised his beer bottle to give a mock toast. Taking a long draw from the brown, glass vessel he veered again toward the path and shuffled off, continuing his retreat.

Darcy did not pursue him this time. She watched him wander away through the tree line and disappear down the newly widened trail. Sighing to herself she turned to rejoin the folks at the fireside. As she settled back into the lawn chair she simply said, "I don't think he will be back tonight."

David restarted the conversation and admitted, "Well, I've got to admit Carl has a point. Seems like we need to start a non-profit organization and get it registered."

"Non-profit?" Eric looked befuddled, "Don't we want to raise money?"

"It would be non-profit because all of the money we collect will be going to the lighthouse," Peter answered, "rather than into our own pockets."

Adding a few more sticks to the flames Abigail mused, "There must be someone who could help us with this."

Darcy pondered for a moment and then offered, "There are other lighthouses out there. Maybe there are people involved with them who have had experiences with this sort of thing. Perhaps they might be able to guide us a bit."

"I'll check on the Internet," Eric volunteered, "to see if there are, well, lighthouse groups and that kind of thing. And maybe we could have some kind of event...like they did at school when they needed to replace the air conditioner." He dug deeply into a bag of marshmallows and shoved the last two on his stick.

"That's a thought," Linda agreed without hesitation, "but what kind of event?"

"How about a raffle?!" May cheerfully exclaimed, "I can talk to the ladies at the quilting club and maybe we could make something!" Her eyes twinkled at having thought of a way to help.

"That sounds great." Darcy smiled and affirmed, "We should explore all the possibilities open to us."

Gretta declared, "What about a yard sale? Anyone can help with that."

"That would be good, too," Abigail agreed.

Looking sleepy Kim offered, "I'll make a canister and we can put it in the store for people's change." She leaned against her mother who put her arm around the girl as she yawned.

Poking at the fire with his kudzu stick David said, "I'll look at contractors that might be willing and able to work on this kind of project." After a moment he added, "It might be helpful in restoring the tower if we had the original plans for the lighthouse construction. I think those would have had to be filed with the county office."

There was a thoughtful pause. Then May inquired, "Mind if I take some of those kudzu roots?"

Suddenly concerned Linda questioned, "You're not thinking of planting them, are you?"

"Oh no," May laughed, "don't be silly."

In exaggerated relief Peter emitted a loud, "Phew!"

Responding to the teasing May declared, "I'm going to bake them."

"What!?" Gretta had no hesitation in showing her disbelief. With her hands on her hips she gave her friend a skewed look.

Sitting up straight May defended herself by stating, "My sister in Charleston says they taste just like sweet potatoes."

"You mean," Darcy hesitantly asked, "people eat this stuff?"

"Oh yes." May responded, "My sister is into all that organic stuff. She says people in China have been using kudzu as medicine for generations. They make tea out of the leaves and she's mailing me some recipes. You know...her son is a doctor and he knows all these good things. He's dating an aerobics therapist and she's...."

Abigail gently interrupted the woman's verbal wanderings and inquired, "May, when do you think you'll be getting those recipes?"

"Well, I don't know." May replied, "I just talked to my sister last night. I imagine they'll come in a few days."

Darcy smiled broadly and proposed, "Folks...this may be our big event. We are sitting on top of a whole crop of food."

Linda seemed adverse to the idea. "I have heard of kudzu festivals taking place inland, but I never gave them much thought." She admitted, "It always seemed like foolishness to me...bunch a people celebrating a dang weed."

Gretta revised the last statement and smoothly said, "A bunch of people spending their money to celebrate a dang weed."

Yawning again Kim drowsily asked, "Do you think the ghost would let all those people come see the lighthouse?"

"Not that ghost thing again." Eric chastised his sister, "There's no ghost here."

The children's uncle saw a good opportunity for mischief and began leering toward the girl while emitting his most ghoulish of laughters, "Whhaaahhahah...."

Protesting Peter's playful taunts Kim squealed at him, "Stop it!"

"Anybody mind if I turn on some music?" Eric briefly glanced around the circle and asserted, "It's too quiet out here."

Linda gave her son a tired look and said blandly, "Eric, don't."

"Aw come on, Linda." With a cunning expression Darcy countered the teen's mother, "Let him turn it on."

David warned, "You don't know what he listens to."

"That's okay...honest. Let him turn it on," she glanced at the youth, "and maybe set it over there." She pointed toward the lighthouse tower.

Eric took on a smug, suspicious look and asked, "What? Is the ghost going to get me?" He laughed and when he got no reply spat out, "Yeah, right!" Taking the radio from beside the cooler he clicked on the power and finding his choice of stations he increased the volume. With a cocky stride he went over to the tower and propped the radio against the wall's surface. Prancing back he quipped, "So? Where is he?"

May winced and covered her ears to protect them from the raspy music. She half yelled, "That's just awful! Do we have to listen to that?"

Abigail echoed her friend's sentiment, "Truly Eric, must we?"

The harsh, pulsating beat vanished in a frenzy of static. As the sounds skipped in a chaos of rising and fading noises the fireside group became silent. They looked in the direction of the radio and then not seeing anyone at the tower they looked back to each other. Then the static gave way as the musical strains of Gilbert and Sullivan floated from the radio speakers.

Chapter Eight

"You haven't heard 'im? Shewy! Who needs a fog horn…when you've got 'im bellowin' opera from the top o' the tower like that?" Both of the crew members laughed then one swallowed his mirth as he spotted the lightkeeper walking toward them. The taller fisherman attempted to silence his partner to no avail. Martin greeted the twosome as he proceeded past them and along the wharf lined with commercial fishing vessels. He had overheard part of the crew's conversation and realized the snickering resumed once his back was to the fishermen.

Martin continued on his way, leaving the dock behind him. He followed the road to the Campbell & Hoffer General Store. From the outside the business seemed quiet and he smiled at the thought of having a peaceful moment with Iris. He opened the door wide and stepped inside. Looking to the counter in anticipation of seeing the charming lass, he was taken aback at what he found.

Henry Hoffer leaned forward against the wall with Iris penned in between the unyielding wood and his firm body. He caressed her hair with one hand while keeping the young woman captive by blocking her way with the other. He cooed, "You know that you're mine." Iris' look was not one of affection, but one of great discomfort. She looked for a way out of the situation, but was practically unable to move due to the youthful fisherman's encroachment. Turning her head to avoid Henry's advances she spotted Martin who was watching the scene.

The lighthouse keeper jerked the door closed and caused the string of bells to clatter loudly. Startled, Hoffer straightened his stance and looked at the doorway only to find the keeper standing rigid. Martin greeted the seaman with a cutting tone, "Hello, Henry."

Pushing away from the wall, the firmly built young man gave the lightkeeper a spiteful look and returned the cold greeting, "Hello, Martin." Giving Iris a

110

final, sharp glare Henry strode past the new arrival and out the door, slamming it after him.

Glancing at the door Martin made sure that Henry had truly gone before he approached the disheveled Iris. He stopped short, careful not to crowd in where the other had just vacated. Martin was not sure if she would want him too close. Watching as she brushed her lustrous, golden hair back with her fingers he quietly asked, "Are you all right?"

She silently nodded and then sputtered, "He didn't mean any harm. He just...." She found herself unable to finish the statement.

"There are people who say that the two of you are betrothed. Becky says that you're not." He glanced at the wooden floor while adding, "I don't want to intrude where I shouldn't."

"You're not intruding. Please don't think that you are." She hung her head as she quietly continued. "No. We are not really betrothed. I don't love him, but our families want us together." She shook her head and drew in a great, stuttering breath. Looking up into Martin's eyes she expressed regret. "Henry isn't a bad man, but he is very possessive."

Mrs. Campbell came in the door and immediately saw the expression on her daughter's face. Alarmed she inquired, "What's going on here? What has happened?"

"Nothing, Mother." The young beauty's response only caused her mother to become all the more convinced of some wrongdoing.

Noting the older lady's agitation Martin offered, "An overly abrasive customer."

"Just a seaman passing through." Again adjusting her hair Iris said, "There was no damage done." Looking back to the lightkeeper she gave a slight smile and added, "I'm just thankful Martin arrived when he did."

The water along the dock reflected the images of the boats that were resting in the inlet, safely moored or at anchor for the evening. Lost in thought the lightkeeper strolled toward the small motorboat that had brought him to the town's wharf. His pondering was interrupted when he recognized his name being called from the back of one of the fishing boats. Turning to find the source he was surprised to see one of the crewmates he had overheard earlier when he arrived in town. The fellow motioned for the lightkeeper to come over to the boat and with some reluctance Martin complied. To his surprise the fisherman handed him a package that was neatly wrapped in butcher's paper.

The keeper was puzzled and inquired, "What's this?"

"Red snapper," the rough-looking man replied. "Thought you and Robby could use a good meal." With a lopsided smile he added, "We do appreciate the job you fellas are doin' over there."

Giving a quiet nod Martin looked at the tidy bundle and then responded, "Thank you." Backing away from the boat he went on his way.

~~~~

The townsfolk met on a fog-dampened night two weeks later. The community gathering totaled nearly three hundred people, albeit not all of them were of voting age. As they entered the old church each person was asked to sign an attendance journal and most willingly complied. Joining the line Darcy greeted the familiar person in front of her, "Good evening, Ben."

He smiled at seeing her and responded, "Good…evening." He stopped and took a deep breath. Looking down at the floor he closed his eyes and, concentrating, stammered, "Grave. Did…you…." He forced himself to continue his thought, "remove…."

"Yes, I did." Darcy assured him, "Hopefully I got the last of the roots today and I'll pick up some grass seed tomorrow." She watched as he signed the notebook. As Ben went to find a seat she took the pen and visually traced to the end of the list. One line above the blank space was the cleanly scripted signature, Benjamin Campbell. She signed her own name below his.

Casually glancing around the room Darcy's eyes caught on a man who was staring right at her. His look was not one of friendliness or welcome, but rather of intense scrutiny. His attire suggested that he had come from one of the commercial fishing boats. Immediately Darcy remembered her confrontation on the docks behind the general store. She was sure the man who was now watching her so closely had been one of the men unloading those boats.

Uncomfortable with the man staring at her, Darcy broke eye contact and scanned the crowded room. She noticed that Carl had somehow managed to make the meeting even though she had never seen a vehicle parked outside his old trailer. Wearing threadbare jeans and a worn-out denim jacket he stayed in the rear of the building. His personal odor seemed to insure that he maintained a liberal margin between him and the other attendees. Commercial fishermen still wearing their slickers and tall rubber boots mingled with retired yachtsmen and sports fishermen. Farm families and the few business people from the local area were all there to protect their interests. Things went as well as one could hope with such a diverse crowd. There were strong verbal clashes, but fortunately no physical confrontations occurred. The lack of actual blows may have been in part due to Lester and other resident members of the sheriff's department being in obvious attendance. Numerous legitimate concerns such as taxes and services were voiced. In the end, a committee was formed to investigate possible kinds of municipalities that might be right for the community. There was an agreement that it should come to a vote as to whether the community would become legally incorporated. The meeting lasted for over four hours.

As the crowd began to disperse Lester sought Darcy out, finding her just outside the building. Standing and watching the people depart the meeting, she welcomed his company. After a thoughtful moment he explained that he had attempted to locate the file concerning Martin Thurber's apparent suicide. There was no sign of the file as there were no files at all prior to the nineteen seventies remaining at the Sheriff's office. The files had all been purged by the previous sheriff due to lack of storage space. The only thing that Lester could offer was a suggestion—that Darcy try the county newspaper. If she could find the name of the investigating officer on that case then she might be able to track that person or a relative of that person to a local address.

Abigail had approached the pair without their noticing and had overheard part of the conversation. Giving Darcy an odd, curious look she waited for an explanation. When none was offered she simply proceeded with stating the reason why she had been looking for the twosome. She told them that in two days there would be the first formal meeting to discuss preserving the Saint Rosabelle Lighthouse. For lack of a better place Abigail had volunteered her home. It would be a casual event, scheduled for the evening. She had posted flyers at the store and also on the door of the church in the hope that no one would miss it.

Interrupting the conversation Darcy called after a lone, unstable figure mounting an abused bicycle, "Carl! Carl, wait a minute." Saying nothing the derelict awkwardly turned and looked over his shoulder at her. She asked him, "You're not going to ride that across the bridge, are you?"

He responded bluntly, "Yeah."

Darcy began, "You can't do that…."

"Why the heck not?" He added defiantly, "I rode it over here."

"Well, the fog wasn't as thick earlier." Before he could issue his rebuttal she added, "Let me give you a ride in my car." There was no response from the unshaven man other than a slight shake of his head. He resumed pushing the rusted bicycle toward the roadway. Darcy turned her appeals to the county law officer, "Lester, he'll get run over."

"Carl!" Lester's deep voice stopped the bicyclist's progression. "Technically you shouldn't be riding a bike at night without proper lights on it," the deputy stated, "so I guess you'll either have to take a ride with Ms. Vornack...or with me."

The odd pair had traveled all the way to the midpoint of the bridge without one word having been spoken. Finally Darcy decided to force the situation, "So, Carl...what do you do when you are not working for Brett?"
It took him a moment to look over at the driver and respond, "Whatever." He looked back out the window. "Mow lawns, sometimes...fix fences, mop floors. Whatever."
"Well...that's good." Not wanting to be judgmental nor let silence invade again she replied, "Not everyone needs a glamour job...just whatever it takes to get by. I understand."
He gave a muffled snort and retorted, "Yeah, sure. And you work in the movies."
"You think movie work is all glamourous?" Her voice was edged with amusement, "Well, I have spent my share of time on pooper scooper patrol."
"Dog shit?" His brow furrowed and his eyes narrowed as he looked back at the driver, "You mean...you've cleaned up dog shit, so you could work in the movies?"
Darcy answered unabashed, "Dog shit, horse shit...lately, just bull shit."
Carl gave an amused chuckle.
The driver grinned and commented, "You have a wonderful laugh." Darcy glanced over in time to see Carl attempting to hide his bashful blush.

The next day Darcy paid a visit to the newspaper. It was a twenty-mile trip to the county seat to find the business. Though located in a larger town there was still only one main business street and The Sawgrass Register was located prominently on one corner.
Armed with a notepad and a pen Darcy entered the brick building. She was greeted at the front counter by a dark-haired woman who introduced herself as the chief editor. Darcy explained that she would like to look at back issues dating from nineteen thirty-nine. The editor looked at the visitor with curiosity. Attempting to appear credible Darcy divulged that she was trying to do research on a particular person, Martin Thurber. Now seeming even more curious than doubtful the local woman explained that even though the paper had bound copies from that year the actual documents were not

open to the public. However there was microfiche available. She explained, "Martin Thurber was one of the more interesting, historical figures of our area. Is there anything in particular you are looking for?"

"Yes. The name of the law officer who was assigned to investigate Martin's death."

"That would have been my Uncle James." The editor watched as Darcy's expression changed from simple inquisitiveness to great surprise and then asked, "Why would you want to know that?"

With sincerity the researcher responded, "I would like to know more about the event if possible."

"Are you a writer?"

"No, no. I'm just curious. That's all." Darcy caught the dubious look on the editor's face and then reluctantly added, "I am looking forward to owning the old lighthouse property."

"Oh." The woman's voice took on a knowing timbre as she said, "You're the one."

"Yes," she introduced herself, "Darcy Vornack."

"Elinor Jones," the business woman responded. "Well, I still have my uncle's records. He died about ten years ago. He kept copies of all his case files." She motioned Darcy to follow her behind the counter and she lead the way into the archives of the newspaper. She continued to explain, "I didn't know what to do with them, so I've been storing them along with some other old files we keep here…research and photos we keep from past articles just in case we have to start writing about those subjects again. You know…they say Thurber still haunts the old lighthouse. There are occasional reports of him being seen in the top of the tower."

"Yeah, I know." The tone in Darcy's voice caused Elinor to glance in her direction.

Darcy was lead to a back room that smelled of old papers and stale air. Metal shelves held box after box of files, books, photos and other paperwork. The editor expressed some regret, "Unfortunately, I really don't have that much time at the moment to help you sort through this stuff. You're welcome to spend as long as you like, though. My uncle's material starts about here," she pointed to one box and then strolled down the length of one row of shelves, "and goes through about here. I'll be back in a while to see how you are doing."

Darcy began looking at the cardboard boxes that were alphabetically labeled with wide, hand-scrawled, black lettering. After a few seconds of searching she found the box marked "T." As she pulled it from the shelf she found that it was overly stuffed and quite heavy. Readjusting her hold on the musty container she hauled it to the one table in the room and began the chore of sorting through the files in hopes of finding the one that would answer her questions.

After pressing past several large, bulging files Darcy found what she was looking for. When she pulled it from the box she was disappointed to see that it was not nearly the size of many of the other files. In fact it was rather thin. Trying to keep her anticipation to a minimum she opened the manila folder marked "Thurber, Martin." The first thing on top of all the other contents was a scene photo. In black and white, in stricken detail, Martin's crumpled body lay partially embedded in the sandy ground at the base of the tower.

Darcy quickly closed the folder and deposited it on the table. She stood and turned away from the file, sickened and overcome from what she had just seen. Flushed and faint at the crushing reality of the keeper's death Darcy noticed her breathing had rapidly increased. Her pulse raced. Forcing herself to stay steady she regained her balance. Struck by her own reaction she chastised herself, "Oh for Pete's sake…what did you expect?" As she calmed down, her pulse began to beat normally again.

Regaining her resolve she returned to the table and slowly reopened the folder. She carefully began looking over the contents—reading the reports and notations. She made use of her own notepad by transcribing bits of information as she came across them. Two hours passed without her noticing. Looking up from a document Darcy was slightly surprised when Elinor returned.

"Did you find what you were looking for?"

"In part." The researcher showed frustration and said, "Your uncle made a notation that there was no suicide note left…or that none was ever found. I find that a bit odd."

"Well…it is commonly thought that he lost his mind," Elinor reminded her visitor. "Perhaps he wasn't disposed to write one or wasn't stable enough to do so."

Darcy slowly replied, "Perhaps…but also, there's no autopsy report. Why wouldn't there be an autopsy report?"

"Maybe they didn't do an autopsy."

Bewildered Darcy inquired, "Why would they not do an autopsy?"

"The guy took a dive off a seventy-foot tower." Elinor gave a bemused smile and suggested, "Maybe they thought the cause of death was obvious…you know, the sudden impact at the end of the fall?"

Darcy was not satisfied, "But what if it wasn't?"

"What if it wasn't...what?" The editor's eyes narrowed.

"What if the cause of death wasn't obvious?" Darcy argued, "He could have been dead already and someone threw him from the tower. He could have died in a way that wasn't obvious, like poison, maybe, or in some way that was covered up by the damage done by the fall."

"Why? I mean, even so, who would want to kill a lighthouse keeper? Every boat operator depended on the lighthouse. Why would you kill the guy who kept it functional? It doesn't make sense." Eyeing the visitor Elinor added carefully, "You make it sound like you think it was murder."

"Well, I think that is a possibility. As for who...was there an assistant keeper? Maybe they had a squabble that got out of hand. I have heard about a lover who jilted him. Maybe she had reason." Pausing for a moment she stated, "I haven't been able to read through this as carefully as I would like. Would it be possible for me to make photocopies?"

Seeing no real harm in the visitor's interests Elinor answered, "Sure."

"Thank you," Darcy added, "I would be happy to pay for all copies."

Chapter Nine

"All right, but I want prints!" Martin backed up to the tower wall and stood next to Iris. They joined the pose for the group photo with Becky, Robby and Vern already in position. As Ben adjusted the camera which was mounted on a sturdy tripod and set the timing mechanism, Iris reached over and took hold of Martin's hand. Delightfully startled the lighthouse keeper smiled and glanced at the beautiful lass. She beamed back at him.

~~~~

Returning from the newspaper building to Saint Rosabelle Darcy suddenly slowed the car. She noticed that the front door of the antique shop was ajar. Hoping that the business was open she pulled off the road and headed down the short, dirt driveway. There were no obvious signs of activity at the location, but she decided to check and got out of the car.

Walking in the doorway that had been propped open Darcy looked around. There was no one that she could see attending the store. She made her presence known by shouting, "Hello?"

From beyond a door in the back of the small showroom came a masculine voice, "I'll be with you in a minute!" A moment later a familiar man clad in a work apron appeared through the opening. His head hung down as he wiped his hands on his apron. He started to inquire, "How can I help…." Surprised, Peter Brown halted in the middle of his sentence and gained a sizable grin. He altered his greeting, "Darcy! Hi…I was just taking care of some items in the back."

"Hi, Peter. I didn't know this was your shop." She looked at the fellow, then smiled widely as she inquired, "Is that green paint…next to your nose?"

The dealer wiped a tarnish-colored smudge from his upper cheek with a workcloth. Slightly embarrassed at having been caught in the act of adding a little artificial age to his brass items, he asked, "Is there something in particular that I can help you with?"

"I was just curious what was in here." Darcy looked around the cozy, cluttered front room where even the walls were covered with items to sell. Old chipped mirrors, crackled paintings and faded art prints hung on every surface. She browsed among the tables and shelves that were covered in an array of peculiar items. On one shelf a collection of miniature pirate flags rested along with toy treasure chests piled amid packets of plastic doubloons. She jested with the shopkeeper, "I take it…these…are not authentic…."

"Authentic Chinese," he chuckled. "I started keeping them for the kids. I think I sell more of that stuff than anything else."

There was an array of brass knickknacks on one of the tables—bookends, doorknobs, other unusual items. Darcy examined the assortment, then asked, "What are some of these things? I don't recognize them."

"Some of them are from boat riggings." He walked over and joined her while she looked at the contents lying neatly arranged but crowded on the table. "That's a cleat…latches, pulleys, a boatswain's whistle…I have some nice bells over there." He pointed to a table in the rear.

"That is an odd piece on the back wall." She motioned to a unusual, curved length of brass that was perhaps two inches or more in thickness and nearly five feet long. The curve was composed of sawtooth-style indentations from which the shopkeeper had strung a number of other items like sun catchers, trinkets and various bangles.

"What? Which one?" Peter smiled, offering, "I'll be glad to get it down for you."

Darcy said, "No…I mean…the piece everything is hanging on. I wonder what that was used for."

The shopkeeper answered, "Honestly, I don't know. My father gave it to me a number of years ago. He said he found it in my grandparents' attic after my grandmother died. He told me I might be able to make a buck or two if I sold it, but I thought I could put it to use instead." While shaking his head he agreed, "It is a strange piece."

"Your grandparents' place," she asked contemplatively, "does it still exist?"

He laughed, "Oh yeah. You've been there. Mom moved back in the old homestead when she and Dad got divorced. Nice place."

Darcy agreed, "Yes, it is. I love the old wood interiors." After a beat she asked, "Will I see you there tomorrow night?"

Peter's expression was momentarily sour, but then he begrudgingly agreed, "Yeah, okay."

She smiled, "Good."

In the early morning Darcy's attention was drawn to the keeper's quarters completely covered with kudzu. The forlorn structure seemed to ask for her help and so she set about removing the net of greenery in which it was tangled. Working carefully but diligently Darcy found the slightly elevated entrance and struggled to clear the narrow portal. Once that was accomplished she continued to remove what kudzu she could without doing harm to the building. She spent the bulk of the day at the effort.

As she and the local volunteers had previously suspected, the entire structure was in gross disrepair and threatened to crumble in many places. The vine was doing a very thorough job of destroying the masonry. Making her way inside the structure she found that the weed had invaded even there. Spiraling through broken window panes, it crowded the apertures, seeking yet further growing room. Runners had begun to creep across the plank flooring of the front room while their brethren clung to the inside walls and began to break through the roof, thus allowing some sunlight to penetrate. There were a few, sheltered, dark corners within the snug building where the bricks had yet to succumb to the forces of nature and the prying actions of the foliage.

Darcy gave the inside of the quarters a cursory examination, but noticed that it was growing late in the day. She chose to continue at another time as she needed to prepare for that evening's meeting. Heading for the doorway she noticed the now familiar sensation of the ghost's presence. She could feel the change in temperature and the heaviness of his stare. She was no longer stricken by fear as she had been when she first encountered him. Rather she had learned that staying calm improved their communication. She mildly inquired, "Martin?" Darcy paused and turned around to face the interior of the historic living space. Standing before her, Martin's translucent form glowed faintly with a disturbing radiance. The very air touching him seemed imbued with an unearthly energy. All at once she was both terrified and exhilarated, never having seen him this close before. Though there was a misty quality to his presence the startled camper could see vivid details of Martin's face and person. His appearance was not horrid as one might expect from a crazed, lost soul, but was one of an ordinary man whose features reflected his strong mettle. His face indicated a life hardened by steadfast duty and perseverance in an austere environment, but was blended with a reasonable, mild demeanor. Darcy locked gazes with the tall man and saw that his eyes were beseeching and filled with an unnamed, unending yearning.

He was never quite sure why sometimes it seemed like people could see him and sometimes they could not. It didn't seem to matter whether it was day or night, if he was angry or sad. Sometimes he couldn't even be sure whether people were looking at him or through him. There had been rare occasions, rare sweet occasions in the past, when he could talk to someone and they would at least know that he was there. Darcy seemed more aware. This time he was certain. "Please, come with me."

Though Darcy could not hear a sound, she somehow knew that the keeper wanted something. She could sense his request. She appealed, "What is it?" Remaining unnerved by the ghostly presence and his deep stare she asked him, "Should I not be here? I don't mean any harm."

Without aggression he responded, "I know." He reached for the woman and took her hand, "You understood before. I can only hope that you'll understand this time too. Come with me."

Darcy was startled by the cold sensation of his touch, but refused to overreact or give in to her natural trepidation. There was something about the sadness in the spirit's eyes that kept her from running. Standing stiffly still she stammered, "Martin?? I don't understand. I don't know...what you want."

Martin was aware that she was afraid. He did not want to frighten her any more. When she had first arrived at the lighthouse he thought that she would be like the others who had come before...vandals, thieves or at best pompously indifferent curiosity-seekers. Now he no longer felt that way. She was unique, special. He now believed that she meant well, that he could trust her. He attempted to reassure Darcy, "It's alright. Just come with me." He gently began to pull her in the direction of the far room which at one time had been a bedroom.

Gradually becoming more adept at understanding what the specter was trying to relay Darcy vocalized the thoughts that came to her, "You're not angry...you want me to come with you...."

"That's right...." *The apparition faintly smiled and repeated,* "That's right...."

Slowly, cautiously, Darcy followed the ghost's lead. They passed through the interior doorway and entered the dim chamber. This room alone seemed undamaged on the inside by the kudzu's invasion. She was guided to the inside wall where the remains of a fireplace dominated the surface. There the urgent pulling ended and she felt the release of her hand. Darcy stood facing the brick masonry and was somewhat confused. Showing signs of mild frustration she implored, "Martin, I still don't understand." She continued to examine the fireplace when something odd caught her sight. There was an object protruding just slightly from the loose bricks. Looking closer she found that it was some kind of paper. Darcy reached for the yellowed document and gently pulled it from its hiding place. Studying the thick paper she determined that it was the remainder of a crumpled photograph. Carefully holding the found item Darcy noticed the warmth of the musty air and looked around to find that the ghost had gone.

~~~~

The oil engine was proving troublesome. The two lightkeepers examined the mechanisms and attempted to remedy what had failed during the previous evening. Both of the men had been awake the entire night due to the malfunction of the foghorn. They wearily worked within the confines of the small building housing the horn. Hopefully they would not have to spend another whole night pumping hand bellows, doing the work of the faulty engine.

Martin checked the valves as Robby examined the spiral gear, adjacent to the nearly three foot diameter flywheel. The assistant grumbled, "Wish they had sent the machinist instead of ol' man Kern last week."

"I know, but we have another two months before the annual overhaul." Carefully testing a pipe connection Martin added, "And besides, at least Inspector Kern was pleased this time."

Robby stiffened and furrowed his brow as he playfully mocked the district officer, "However, you should be sure to dust more often."

Their work was suddenly interrupted by the shouts of a boy, "Martin! Robby! Where are you?"

Calling over his shoulder the principle keeper responded in the direction of the door, "We're in here, Ben!"

A moment later the boy hurriedly entered the foghorn building and was followed closely by his younger companion, Vern. Smiling broadly Ben held out a brown paper folio and announced, "We got the photographs back!"

Showing the lad his oily hands Martin said, "Perhaps you had better hold on to those for the moment." Looking expectantly back at the doorway he puzzled, "We didn't hear the launch. Where's your sister?"

Answering candidly the lad said, "She didn't come with us."

"You drove the launch by yourself?" Robby gave the youngsters a suspicious glance.

Vern replied, "Nah…we got our own boat now." The boy's eyes twinkled as he stood tall, filled with pride.

Martin was truly surprised by this announcement and inquired, "Your own boat...really?" Watching both of the lads enthusiastically nod, a thought came to him, "Do your parents know about this boat?"

"Well...our mothers do." Ben's blue eyes sparkled as he explained, "We found it washed up, abandoned."

The assistant keeper gave a sideways glance to the two youths as he continued to survey the gear and crankshaft. With a notable sharpness he asked, "You're sure it was abandoned?"

Vern defended their claim, "We waited three whole days to see if anyone was using it. No one ever came."

Ben looked back to Martin and continued, "It was leaking a bit, but old Mr. Dinkle showed us how to fix it up with rosin. You should come out and see it!"

Sourly Robby responded, "We've got work to do."

"Well...." The elder boy started to say something, but then his boldness faded as he remembered past consequences of countering adults, particularly busy men. He decided against giving a rebuttal.

Seeing the boys' downcast eyes and sensing their disappointment Martin offered, "Would you like to help us?"

Vern and Ben exchanged surprised looks at each other and then the younger hesitantly asked, "Really?"

Reacting to the lightkeeper's nod Ben cheered, "Yeah!"

Drawing the lads closer to the malfunctioning foghorn air compressor Martin explained, "We've got to get this engine fixed before the next bout of bad weather or we won't have a foghorn." He sighed, but then smiled, "When we're finished we'll find someplace nice to put those photos. Then I would like to see that boat of yours."

~~~~

The home of Abigail Hoffer-Brown was aglow with evening lights as Darcy drove up. She parked her aged car among the numerous vehicles already sitting haphazardly around the house. There were nearly twenty cars, pickups and SUVs. It appeared that the hostess had gotten a good response to her flyers announcing the meeting.

May had convinced every person in her quilting group to attend. There were almost a dozen women in the membership. Much to Darcy's surprise the ladies were a varied lot and not at all what she had expected from such a group. A handful of crewmen from the commercial fishing boats was also present at the meeting. In general they were a rough-looking bunch, but they seemed genuinely interested. She noticed the entirety of the Brown clan was in attendance and that Ben had joined them as well.

There was also a new, but familiar, face busy mingling with the others. Approaching the newspaper editor Darcy gave a happy greeting, "Elinor? Good evening...covering the news?"

"Exactly! Around here this is a big happening."

"Well...good." Darcy commented, "We can use all the coverage we can get."

After a period of time that allowed stragglers to arrive Abigail called for the people to settle down and be seated as best possible. Every chair the hostess owned was set out in the large living room, but the space was filled to capacity. A few people remained standing by necessity. One or two even sat on the floor.

"My gracious!" Abigail cheerfully announced, "I am happy to see everyone tonight. We have had a better turnout than I thought we would. This is wonderful! Well, as you know we are gathered here to discuss saving the Saint Rosabelle Lighthouse. If something isn't done quickly we may lose it forever. It appears there are many things we need to do in order to save it, but they will only work if we all take part and do what we can."

One of the fishermen spoke up, "How do we know if we do all this work and fix up the place that then Ms. Vornack won't just shut us out?" All eyes shifted to watch the current speaker who was standing in the back of the room. He continued, "We're talkin' about her private property. How do we know she'll share?" A number of people in the gathering mumbled in agreement and again the focus of the group's vision shifted.

Suddenly the center of attention Darcy felt a swell of stage fright, but knew she had to respond to the fisherman's question. Drawing a deep breath she attempted to speak with clarity and confidence, "I'll be glad to arrange a limited, long-term lease to the organization." Looking back at the fisherman she recognized the rugged face. It was the same man who had stared at her during the community meeting, the same one she had encountered when the boats were being unloaded.

He stood with his arms folded and a dissatisfied expression marking his deeply tanned face, "Limited? And just what kind of limitations are you talkin' 'bout?"

"Well," she laughed, "I don't want to see the tower used as a hotdog stand or something like that. I don't think anyone here would want to do that kind of thing, but then ten, twenty years from now...who knows what someone might try to do."

The answer seemed to at least partially satisfy the seaman and the meeting progressed. Abigail called on her eldest son, David, who explained the need to create a non-profit organization for the purpose of raising funds, but before anything could be done they would need to elect officers. Nominations were opened and first thing Eric declared, "I nominate Darcy for president!"

Darcy was completely surprised by the lad's proposal. The room filled with mixed sounds of disapproving grumbles and rapid, hushed conversations. Recovering her composure she shook her head and responded, "Eric…I'm flattered by your confidence in me, but…I think that I should decline." She watched as the teen's expression faded then offered an explanation, "My work often requires that I travel…sometimes for extended periods. I think that it would be better if the group was represented by someone who is more likely to be in constant contact with the local community and better able to deal with whatever opportunities arise. With that in mind, I nominate Abigail Hoffer-Brown for president."

Pleased as punch, Abigail accepted the nomination. Not having any opposition she was elected quickly to the office. Nominations for vice president were then opened. Here was a matter of contention as two men were nominated for the post. The first was the local pastor, John Leroy Dinkle, and the second was Steven Rutton, the outspoken fisherman. After being allowed to speak on their own behalf it was decided the election should be done by secret ballot. Sheets from one of Kim's school notebooks were appropriated and torn into smaller pieces which were then distributed to the gathering. Silence fell as everyone scribbled their selection. A few minutes later a rubber boot was passed around into which the paper scraps were dropped. Being the only official officer Abigail counted the votes. Pastor John had won by a clear margin.

The nominations for secretary were opened and one of the quilters, Lynn Liebert, the young wife of a fisherman, was immediately suggested for the position. Plain, unassuming and of a short, boxy build, she did not offer a formidable appearance. Her distinctly oriental features served only to make her more undesirable to many of the mainly 'good old boy' fishermen. As the woman accepted the nomination Steven scoffed and brusquely asked, "Why should we vote for you? What makes you think that you're qualified?"

Lynn jutted her chin out and replied, "I have a bachelor's degree in business from the University of Louisiana." Steven just rolled his eyes and, sighing loudly, looked at the ceiling. Her credentials served to prevent further nominations. She was elected without opposition.

The last office to be filled was treasurer. Abigail nominated Lester McKay and the man balked, "Me?! Why would you want me to be treasurer?"

"If we can't trust the local law with the money," Gretta boisterously blurted, "then who can we trust!" A wave of laughter swept through the group.

Lester succumbed, "All right then." He folded his arms and gave a begrudging smile.

Steven managed to get himself nominated for treasurer as well by pressuring fellow crew mates. Again a formal vote was taken with torn shreds of notebook paper being scrawled on and then dropped into the yellow boot. Once again Abigail was the arbiter. She soon announced that Lester had been elected by an almost unanimous vote.

Now with a full set of officers it was further recognized that the group needed a number of committees to handle the group's varied efforts. Attempting to set an example Abigail offered to spearhead formalizing a charter document for the group. Following her lead David volunteered to head the committee for restoration and preservation planning. Much to everyone's surprise Peter volunteered to lead the committee for raising funds. Then Pastor John offered to organize efforts for grant research, applications and registry. Gretta took charge of the committee for immediate clean-up efforts. Darcy along with Elinor Jones became co-chairs of the committee for historical research. Again Kim's school notebook was borrowed and the tablet was passed around so people could sign up for participation in the various committees. Everyone wanted to take an active part, one way or another. David reported that he had found three contractors who were willing to look at the old tower to see if this restoration was something that they would be willing to bid on. They would begin their visits to the location within the next few days.

Peter followed his brother and stated that there had been the suggestion of holding some kind of benefit event. He added that Gretta had mentioned a yard sale. He said that it would be a good event, but he had bigger ideas. Though the details were yet to be worked out he proposed a "Lighthouse Festival." The yard sale and any number of things could be combined into the one big event.

With encouragement from the other ladies May announced that the Quilting Club would be delighted to donate their efforts to make a special quilt to be raffled off at the festival. They were already working on creating a unique design just for the Saint Rosabelle Lighthouse. Actual sewing would begin by the end of the week.

Abigail announced, "Thanks to the efforts of Eric and Kim we have been able to gather a fair amount of information quickly. Because they could find their way around the Internet we learned a lot." Looking to her eldest grandchild she asked, "Would you like to share some more of your findings with the group?"

Eric suddenly wavered, overwhelmed and a bit less confident. "Well," as his voice cracked a little he stopped and cleared his throat before continuing, "we found a magazine dedicated to lighthouses. Each month they include a list of all the lighthouses that they think are in danger of being destroyed soon…for whatever reasons. Kim and I counted over forty lighthouses in trouble in just the United States and a handful more in Canada that are all on the list. Our lighthouse has been on the list for about a year and a half. They have a lot of articles about lighthouses that weren't saved in time…at least two in just the past year. They also have articles about other restorations taking place and how to contact the people doing them. They feature when a lighthouse is relit…like the Tybee Island Lighthouse. We found a really good site connected to the National Maritime Initiative. Through that site we found information about a Historic Lighthouse Preservation Handbook which is published by the federal government."

David interrupted, "It costs thirty-five dollars and we have already sent for a copy, but it may take a while for it to get here. In the meantime we…that is, our computer-literate children…have been able to download some of the sections for us to read off the net."

Having regained some of his confidence Eric took the cue from his father to continue, "We also found a link to the National Register of Historic Places. It seems that if we can have the lighthouse entered into the registry then no one can knock it down without a lot of red tape. It also might make it easier to get grants to help restore the tower. We downloaded information on how to apply for the grants and also some forms I think we will need. It sounds like we will have to do a bunch of research about the history of the tower in order to qualify for the registry. From what I have read so far we will need someone to take photos of the area for documentation. I wondered about how we could get some of the history and I thought of the National Archives. I found their homepage on the Internet! They have a whole section in their holdings just about the Lighthouse Service. Unfortunately they haven't gotten much of the information available on-line, but they said that they could answer specific questions by snail mail…you know, postal mail. I found out that the closest actual location of the Archives is in Atlanta. I also found a site run by the United States Coast Guard, which took over the Lighthouse Service, on July 7, 1939." He paused, then glanced over at Darcy who was taking notes and added, "Other documents said July First, so I'm really not sure which it is.

"There are organizations that might be able to help us find information. One is the U.S. Lighthouse Society. Another is the Lighthouse Preservation Society and there is also the Great Lakes Lighthouse Keepers Association. These are all non-profit groups."

After some further details about sites that featured individual lighthouses and lighthouse photographs Madam President thanked Eric for his thorough report. His face was bright as he sat back down. With no further business to be presented by anyone on hand it was decided that the next meeting should take place two weeks after this initial meeting. Then Abigail called for adjournment.

As the meeting dispersed quickly Kim caught up to Darcy. The youngster urged Darcy to follow her down the hall, further into the depths of the house. Eric quickly fell in line behind them. They made their way to the den where Eric booted-up a home computer while Kim uncovered a folder from among a short stack of papers. As the girl handed the folder to Darcy she grinned and said, "These are photos of what the old...Fresnel lenses looked like."

Opening the folder Darcy found three prints each of which showed an amazing, crystal structure.

"They look better on screen." Eric loaded a display program on the computer and the images of the great crystal lens filled the screen. Even confined to the size of the monitor and captured as digitized pictures the beauty of the Fresnels was stunning. The leaded crystal prisms bound by their gleaming, brass frames glowed in a fiery delicate light as only true leaded crystal could.

After having stood for a while examining the images in awe Darcy straightened and inquired, "May I keep these prints?"

Kim answered, "Sure. They're for you."

"Thanks," Darcy responded then turned back to the computer screen in time to see another program loading. The screen filled with animated, bug-like creatures. She asked the lad at the keyboard, "What's this?"

"It's an extreme up-grade of a really, really old arcade game." He began punching the shift keys and moving a small image of a blaster turret at the bottom of the screen. Hitting the space bar Eric fired the illustrated weapon, shooting at the descending bugs.

THURBER'S LIGHT

"What was the game called?" She paused and then added, "It looks sort of familiar. I may have played it, when I was...er, much younger."

Furiously pressing the buttons, his eyes never leaving the screen, Eric replied, "Space Invaders."

Chapter Ten

Halloween Night 1938

"We've got to extinguish the light!" Robby's features showed pure anguish as he reached the tower's watch room.

"What?" Martin grabbed the assistant keeper's shoulder as the young fellow began to mount the ladder to the lamp room. "Wait a minute.... What are you talking about?"

"Earth has been invaded by Martians! Our light will just guide them here!" Again Robby attempted the climb.

Maintaining his hold on his assistant's arm Martin became amused, but remained concerned and mildly scolded, "Martians? Robby, where did you get an idea like that? Of all the nonsense...."

"It's true! I heard it on the radio!" With frustration Robby met his superior's dubious gaze. Relinquishing his ascent of the ladder the assistant charged to the radio and huffed, "Here! Listen!" He snapped the power on and the receiver came to life. Amid the sounds of sirens the rich, deep voice of an announcer flowed forth. His words were seeped in emotion as he relayed the great tolls that had been rendered by otherworldly invaders. After barely a moment of listening to the broadcast Robby resumed his advance to the iron rungs only to be intercepted by Martin's tall frame. Ardently protesting the youthful keeper blurted, "We have got to put out the light! We could be endangering the whole community!"

"We'll be endangering ships if we do that! You know that we can't put out the light for any reason whatsoever without a direct order from the Superintendent. Now...just calm down." Countering the assistant lightkeeper's attempt to pass him, Martin commanded, "Calm down!" He strained to listen to the information divulged by the increasingly chaotic noises of the radio. Pondering what he was hearing he mused, "That voice...it sounds familiar...."

Robby broke the hold of his distracted superior and heaved himself up

THURBER'S LIGHT

the metal framework into the lantern room. His actions did not catch Martin completely off guard however. The lightkeeper was close on Robby's heals. Before the vehement youth could reach the lamp Martin yanked him away. Because of the force of the pull Robby slipped and tumbled to the floor. Now fired with anger the young man raised himself up with his hands clenched in tight fists. He advanced on the principle keeper while shouting, "They'll kill us all!"

Martin readily dodged the youth's wild, sweeping attack then stepped behind him. With a swift motion the lightkeeper grabbed and locked his coworker in a hard, restraining hold. Robby bucked and kicked attempting to work free of his elder's firm grip. He strained while he squirmed and contorted to no avail. Finding no escape he shouted, "Let me go!!!"

"I don't want to hurt you," Martin spoke in the wriggling assistant's ear, "so don't swing at me again." He released his hold. The struggling lad flung himself from Martin's grasp, but his movement was without balance. The propelling energy sent the assistant keeper again to the floor of the lantern room. Robby hesitated as he tried to catch his breath. He sat on the textured metal, rubbing the smarting shoulder on which he had landed. Glaring at the lamp's defender he whined, "Cripes…Martin, they're coming! They'll kill us all! Isn't living more important than that…that stupid light?!"

Martin stared hard at his agitated partner and responded with deliberateness, "If that light keeps the crew and passengers of just one ship safe from harm then it's worth more than both our lives joined." He watched Robby as the less-experienced keeper looked dejectedly from him and then out of the lantern room windows into the misty night.

Suddenly the young man pointed toward the horizon behind Martin and in a voice trembling with fear he exclaimed, "There! There they are!!! It's a Martian rocket ship! They're here!!!"

Martin hesitantly turned to see what Robby was pointing to. There was something a distance down the shoreline, just offshore with lights that glowed white and green. He watched the eerie illumination for signs of motion.

The young man whimpered in unbridled terror, "They've found us!" Sounds coming from the radio drifted up from the opening in the floor.

"It's a ship all right," Martin studied the lights reflecting in the ocean water, "but it isn't Martian. We've got a freighter aground."

Slowly Robby began to comprehend the principle lightkeeper's words. Dazed, he asked, "What?"

Martin extended his hand to the assistant who still sat awkwardly on the lantern room floor. "There's a ship run aground. We need to take action."

The young man hesitated before accepting the offered assistance. His shoulder still ached from his hard landing. Slowly taking hold of Martin's hand he was pulled upward to his feet. Dumbfounded he sputtered, "A ship...." He looked again at the weaving pattern of reflected light that danced on the waves, then to the elongated form that sat nearly stable.

Determined to snap the assistant keeper back to his senses Martin ordered him, "Call the Coast Guard!" He preceded the young fellow down the ladder and rapidly descended the spiraling flight of stairs.

Martin approached the looming, metal hulk of the grounded freighter. Illuminated now only by dull emergency lights the ship dwarfed his tiny speedboat. He could see activity on the open deck as the stranded sailors peered over the edge. As he neared the stern of the great hull Martin was astonished to discover an arriving fishing boat. He had not noticed its approach while watching from the tower nor had he seen it when he lowered and freed the light station's motorboat from the davits of the wharf. The trawler's engines churned the dark water as it maneuvered as close as possible to the larger ship without risking its own entrapment in the sand.

Martin decreased the speed of his small craft and steered its glide in the direction of the surprise arrival. He recognized the vessel from the docks of Saint Rosabelle. It was a fishing boat dubbed "Lucky's Star." It was one of the boats owned by Ike Campbell and Ike himself hailed the keeper from the side of the trawler.

The men shouted back and forth over the drone of the boat engines, deciding upon a plan of action. Understanding that the fishing boat could carry far more of the stranded crew than the small powerboat could possibly transport, it seemed a logical choice that Martin shuttle crew members who descended a rope hanging from the grounded freighter to the waiting commercial vessel. In the darkness of the October night the air temperature seemed very cold with the sea mist rising from the modulated chop of the water, but both the rescuers and the seamen of the freighter understood that it could have been much worse. They were lucky the weather was tranquil, if chilly. A storm would surely have claimed lives among those involved.

Thankfully no lives were lost. There were a few injured. They were carefully lowered from the ship's deck to Martin's motorboat where they were secured and then delivered to Ike and his crew. Before the last of the crew left the stranded ship they raised a signal flag with a solid, black circle displayed boldly to show that the ship was not abandoned. It took the trawler a few trips to haul all of the ship's members to the nearest, safe landing which was the lighthouse wharf.

The team from the Coast Guard arrived much delayed by the pandemonium caused by the broadcast of H. G. Wells's 'The War of the Worlds,' performed with eerie reality by Orson Welles and the Mercury Theatre. It seemed that if Robby Bowsen had overreacted he was not alone. The switchboards of law enforcement agencies all along the east coast had been inundated by confused and panicked callers.

It took over an hour to document the beaching of the cargo vessel, to record the accounts of the bridge personnel and to tend to those few who had been injured during the shore impact. Those with more serious wounds—there were even two fractures—were transported to the nearest medical facility right away while the rest of the crew was debriefed. Eventually rooms were located for all of the shipwrecked men at inns or in homes of Saint Rosabelle residents. Far from their home port of Halifax, Nova Scotia the ship's crew were thankful for the hospitality.

Martin checked on Robby to make sure that he was still in condition to tend the light. Soberly the assistant apologized for his earlier actions. He was clearly ashamed of his overreaction to a fictional theater broadcast. The principle keeper easily accepted the apology while counseling his subordinate that the event might serve as a good lesson not to panic.

Martin left the Light Station under Robby's renewed dedication and transported the last of the freighter's crew to Saint Rosabelle. Guiding the trusty motorboat he ferried the ship's captain and pilot across the inlet. As they traveled the men talked about the night's strange events, eventually turning their conversations to unusual things they had previously seen during their journeys at sea. Reaching the town, the lightkeeper made sure that the men were safely housed for the night and their needs attended to by the shipwright Dinkle and his wife. The seamen were grateful, but tired from the ordeal. Once at the home they wasted little time before retiring to the waiting beds.

Taking his leave Martin ventured to the Campbell home. Seeing the lights still on he tapped at the front door. Dressed in her cream night robe Catherine carefully opened the door. The lightkeeper apologized, "I'm sorry for the late visit, Mrs. Campbell, but if Mister Campbell is still up...may I speak with him please?"

Martin was shown into the parlor where the seaman was just relaxing with a drink and his pipe of tobacco. Ike welcomed the lightkeeper and offered him a nightcap. Declining a brandy Martin explained that he would have to relieve his assistant when he returned to the light station. At the seaman's insistence he did settle into one of the plush chairs of the richly comfortable room.

Ike asked, "How can I help you…at this hour?"

Martin commented, "It was very fortunate that your boat happened to be passing at the time it was." He watched Ike's eyes.

"Yes…it was very fortunate." Campbell sensed the lightkeeper's scrutiny and cautiously took a sip of his drink.

Bluntly the keeper asked, "So…where is the rest of the fleet?"

"They will be back in a day or so." Ike clutched the bowl of his pipe and after an awkward moment explained, "We returned early. We were having some intermittent engine trouble."

"That may explain why I didn't hear your approach." Martin continued to study the fisherman and watched his reactions, "Though she sounded fine coming into port."

"As I said, 'intermittent.' We were lucky just then…." Taking a long pull from the pipe and dropping his head backward Campbell released the smoke in a swift swirling plume. He added, "Didn't have any problems getting back in."

"Mmm…lucky," agreed Martin, "luckier than the cargo ship." Still looking directly at Ike he said, "Her captain gave a strange story. He claims his navigational officer got confused."

Something about the crusty boat owner indicated discomfort as he responded, "Oh?"

"Yes. The pilot claims he saw two lighthouses." Martin watched as his host involuntarily blinked hard before he continued, "He didn't know which one to choose as marking the inlet, so he aimed the ship between them."

"Sounds like the captain needs to call his crew on sobriety." Ike attempted to laugh, but it was obviously forced.

"Possibly," Martin's voice was firm and unwavering, "but the officer seemed sober enough when I talked to him. Confused, but sober."

"Well, with all that confusion on the blasted radio," Ike took a swig of the brandy, swallowed quickly, then finished his statement, "who knows what he really saw."

"Mmm." Martin echoed, with a dull edge, "Who knows…."

~~~~

"Oh, my gosh! Who would do this!?" Darcy looked over the remains of her tent. The frame was still standing, the fabric had been ripped wide in a number of places. The beam of her flashlight revealed that the contents of the shelter had been removed and scattered around the ground. It was hard to say if anything was missing while she surveyed within the isolated patch of illumination given off by the beam of light. Clyde the goat had been freed from his chain and was at the far end of his grazing area. He remained alarmed and watched warily for danger. As Darcy began gathering stray items a pair of bright halogen headlights approached from down the dirt road. The light of a side beam searched the undergrowth as the vehicle progressed. The camper could hear the engine coming to a stop as the headlights pointed directly at the two brick structures.

Darcy shaded her eyes from the blinding brightness as she walked toward the headlights. She came to a stop when she heard the metal car door slam. A moment later a backlit figure cast shadows that shifted in the intense light and loomed toward Darcy. She strained to identify the approaching person. Her worries were relieved as a familiar voice called out, "Darcy...I got your message. Are you alright?"

"Lester! Yes," she sighed deeply and then reconfirmed, "Yes. I'm okay. I guess it's a good thing Troy gave me that cell phone after all."

Together they went back toward the buildings and now with the added light of the deputy's flashlight took a look at the disheveled campsite. Examining the tent Lester asked, "Is anything missing."

"I won't really know until morning." Darcy shrugged. With a lopsided smile she said, "Fortunately I keep my so-called valuables locked in the car. This must have happened during the meeting. Thank goodness I drove."

Spotting the wandering goat Lester called sweetly to the animal, reassuring him. After a moment Clyde cautiously approached and received a gentle petting from the large man who again secured the lead chain. Turning to the camp's resident with seriousness showing in his gaze the officer offered, "I have a hunch. Mind if we walk out to the tower?"

"No. No problem. You think...." Her eyes suddenly wide with concern Darcy was off at a trot headed for the unprotected and vulnerable landmark. The law officer did not trail far behind. Reaching the opening to the beach Darcy cleared the last visual obstruction and wailed in distress. The clean, outside walls of the tower had again been marred by graffiti. She swore an oath as she reached the lighthouse and saw the extent of the markings. Among random spray-painted markings were boldly printed the words, "WRECKERS

RULE." A large, red skull and crossbones occupied part of the wall. Swearing again she cried out, "Why would someone do this?" She turned to Lester and shaking her head in frustrated disbelief asked again, "Why?"

"Darcy…don't move, okay?" Lester gave a weak smile as he added, "There are footprints out here." He shined his flashlight on the sand and pointed out a set of tracks that were now partially obliterated by their arrival.

"Ah, crud." Embarrassed at her lack of forethought and upset over the negation of her efforts to clean the building Darcy lowered her head and gave a melancholy mumble, "Sorry."

"We're both at fault," Lester said. Attempting to answer Darcy's question, he continued, "Some people just don't understand the value of things or concepts like private property. They think that the world is theirs to ruin as they see fit. I don't know why, really." He continued to scan the ground shining the beam of the flashlight in a searching pattern. "It looks like there were a number of people out here." Following the abundant footprints he traced some to the water's edge and found a distinctive marking in the packed sand near the water's edge. Returning to the saddened camper he divulged, "Seems that at least some of them came by boat. That is where they put their anchor. Tide is coming in. They may not have expected you back this soon and were counting on the tide to cover some of this up…if they were thinking that hard."

Sounding a bit snide Darcy motioned to the painted markings on the building, "What is this 'wreckers' stuff? A bunch of rebel, auto mechanics?"

"We may be out in the country," Lester earnestly answered, "but that doesn't make us immune from gang activity. It gets worse every year. Given my guess, 'wreckers' refers to the old pirates."

"Pirates?!"

"Yeah," the officer gave a clarifying answer, "they were a kind of pirate. When a ship wrecked, wreckers would move in and tear it apart…sometimes before it was truly abandoned. They would take everything of value. Cargo first, but then anything else they thought would bring a profit…right down to the boards the boat was made of."

"But…I mean," Darcy insisted, "I don't get it. Piracy is a defunct business, right?" She gave her companion a befuddled look.

Lester agreed, "Mmm…pretty much…in American waters anyway. Coast Guard put a stop to most of it. Now would-be pirates have turned to things like drug running, bringing in illegal aliens…that kind of stuff."

Unhappy with the thought of any of the mentioned outlaws Darcy grunted, "Great."

Shining his light on the skull and crossbones the law official stated, "Much more likely…what we have here is a gang marking."

"That might explain why it looks like they tore things up rather than just stealing stuff." Thinking aloud Darcy added, "Although to be honest I wouldn't put it past Brett to hire someone to try and scare me off. He can be a sore loser when he doesn't get his way during film productions."

At a strolling pace the pair walked back to the campsite. Contemplating Darcy's comment Lester asked, "Have you seen Carl this evening?"

"No, actually." Darcy explained, "I always try and make sure he knows when I'm coming in. I honked this evening, but he never looked out. Hmm. He is working for Brett. You think he had something to do with this?"

"I doubt it," Lester shook his head and then added, "but he may have seen something. I'll pay him a visit on my way out. Also, I'll send a team out to take castings of those prints." Reaching the trail entrance to the campsite he paused and hesitated, before offering, "You don't need to spend the night out here. I, uh…could take you to my grandparents. I'm sure they would be glad to put you up for the night."

Giving a somber laugh Darcy replied, "Thanks…but no. I made a deal and I'm going to stick to it. If anything I may need for you to vouch for me that I stayed…and I don't want you to have to lie."

"Somehow I thought you would say something like that." He argued, "Your tent is ruined."

"I know." She sighed, "I've got a patch kit. I'll work on it in the morning. If worse comes to worse duct tape does wonders."

"Darcy…."

"Don't worry," she assured the officer, "I'll stay locked in the car tonight."

In the grey light of early morning the campsite was a wreck to behold. As Darcy attempted to reassemble her residence she dialed the Sheriff's Office and asked to speak with Lester McKay. She was informed that he had not come in yet, but that he had left a message for her. The female officer relayed the information that Lester had found emptied spray paint cans outside of Carl's trailer, but Carl had been too drunk to communicate coherently. Lester left the inebriated man at the trailer and would visit him later that day. Thanking the deputy Darcy returned to tidying her belongings. She tried hard not to jump to any conclusions about Carl.

Later in the morning she slowed her car as she neared the corner of the dirt road and the pavement. To her surprise she saw Ben and Kim pounding a sign made of yellow posterboard nailed onto a stake into the dirt. She rolled down her window and hollered, "'Good morning!"

Ben looked up from the project and returned Darcy's greeting, "'Morning!" Kim smiled and waved to the vehicle's driver.

Grinning widely Darcy asked, "What's happening?"

Kim's exuberance showed as she helped her great-uncle and she answered cheerily, "It's so people can find the lighthouse!" The posterboard was marked with a large arrow and a simple illustration of the tower.

"Good idea!" She gave them a thumbs-up. Glancing through the other window across to the tarnished trailer Darcy saw Carl dutifully peering out from between the faded drapes of the tiny window. She gave a deliberate wave in his direction. He seemed to wince slightly, but raised his hand to the windowpane in acknowledgment before letting the curtains fall back into place. Turning back to the twosome who were finishing planting the sign she said, "Got to go do some research! See you later!" As she pulled onto the paved road, the pair waved goodbye.

It had been decided that the easiest obtainable resource for historical information about the lighthouse was the county's very own newspaper. First having been published in 1914 the weekly paper would offer at least some information and potential leads for obtaining more valuable contacts. The ladies agreed on their strategy. Darcy would begin at the very first issue and work her way forward through time. Elinor would assist as her work would allow.

Hours passed as the women viewed roll after roll of microfilm and occasionally printed a hard copy of a relative story which was then added to a file folder. Evening came and they continued to work, bringing in cartons of carry-out food. The research stopped only as Darcy realized that she needed to return to her campsite in order to remain in compliance with the conditions of the bet.

The following morning Darcy reached the intersection of dirt and pavement in time to see Carl outside of his humble housing. Dressed in his usual stained undershirt he seemed to be examining the grounds surrounding the lusterless trailer. Over time great amounts of beer cans had been strewn about the place. The beverage containers had been piled in some locations and the piles were complemented by a few overflowing garbage bags. In truth the corner was becoming a sorry sight. Darcy waved a greeting to him and in her best cheerful voice called, "Good morning!" Looking back at her the disheveled man flashed an odd expression and began marching toward the car. A wave of foreboding coursed through Darcy as she watched his unexpected and rapid advance. Refusing to give way to her fears she swallowed the feeling and attempted to show only calmness. As Carl reached her driver's window she displayed a slight smile and simply said, "Hi."

He looked directly in at Darcy and said bluntly, "I didn't have any part in that."

"I'm sorry...." She gave a confused expression and looked back into the man's intense eyes. A sour odor came from his shirt and drifted through the car window.

Waving down the dirt road in the direction of the tower and Darcy's damaged tent Carl explained, "McKay said you thought I might be involved, because I take Brett's money." Without taking his gaze from the driver he said firmly, "I wasn't."

Releasing a caught breath Darcy answered, "I know that." Giving a slight nod Carl stood back from the car and allowed the driver to continue on her way. Steering the old vehicle onto the blacktop Darcy allowed the tension of the moment to leave. Though uncomfortable with the confrontation she was pleased that Carl had bothered to respond to the possible accusations. The driver's smile broadened and she continued on her drive to the local newspaper.

Research was again resumed and filled the day until eyestrain put a damper on their efforts. By then they had reached issues of the paper from 1937. They already knew that the lighthouse was decommissioned after the lamp was destroyed in 1939, so they were close to exhausting what the newspaper had to offer concerning the lighthouse's years of active duty.

They laid out a timeline on a legal pad with notations of events relative to the lighthouse. Names of keepers and assistant keepers along with the names of family members when possible were placed next to their date of arrival and departure at the light station. The reasons why they had left were noted if it was stated in the articles. Darcy and Elinor also made notes on other local events they thought might be of interest.

By early evening the timeline was fairly complete from the mid-1910s to the late-1930s. They examined their work and both women noted that there seemed to be more events centered around the lighthouse in the later years than there had been before. There were only two lighthouse keepers listed for the 1910s and 20s. The first keeper died in the line of duty at age seventy-three. The second keeper who had been promoted from assistant served for fourteen years as principle keeper before being retired after a total of twenty-one years of service at the Saint Rosabelle Lighthouse. That was in 1931 at which point activity seemed to dramatically increase.

Elinor gazed at the jumble of notes and asked, "What is all that?"

"Let's see...." Darcy began reading off the scrawled headline notations, "1931 - New Principle Keeper Phillip Sanders assigned to lighthouse. 1932 - Keeper leaves Light Service for seaman's life; Assistant Andrew S. Capps promoted. 1933 - Wreck of the Bratland. Also in 1933 - Former lighthouse keeper Phillip Sanders lost at sea - assumed drowned. 1934 - Wreck of the cargo ship Neptune's Delight, Lighthouse Keeper Capps honored for role in rescue of crew members. Also in 1934 - Lighthouse Keeper Andrew Capps killed in freak accident, struck by run-away horse and cart. Again 1934 - Arrival of new Principle Keeper Harold Reese. 1935 - Wreck of the Bright Union plundered. 1936 - Lighthouse Keeper Reese reasigned to northern post; Jorge P. Duncan assumes duties as Saint Rosabelle keeper. 1937 - Lighthouse Keeper Jorge Duncan found drowned; young assistant keeps light until new principle keeper's arrival. Also in 1937 - New Principle Keeper Martin Thurber on the job."

The women looked at each other pensively and Darcy asked, "Is it my imagination or does all of this seem...."

"Really fishy." Elinor completed the statement for her companion.

Chapter Eleven

"Hey!" Darcy exited from her car and called to Ben who was resting on the front porch of the general store. She asked, "Did you clean up the corner?" Her question surprised the old man and he gave her a very puzzled look. As she climbed the stairs she saw the fellow's expression and asked, "No?"

Ben answered slowly, "Nope."

Abigail came out the front door toting a broom and greeted Darcy, "Good morning!"

"Good morning." Darcy moved out of the way and found an unoccupied stool. As she sat down she cheerfully asked the broomwielder, "Were you the one who cleaned up the corner?"

Beginning to sweep the broad porch Abigail glanced over and asked, "What corner?"

"Oh." Darcy took Abigail's question as a negative response and answered, "Someone cleaned up the corner where Carl had tossed all his trash." She watched as the storekeeper gave an astonished look, then inquired, "Maybe Lori or David and the kids?" She looked from one person to the other, but again there was no confirmation and Ben just shook his head. "Peter, maybe?"

"I wouldn't think so," the storekeeper replied and the old gentleman grinned while setting up the checkers board for a new game.

"You think…Carl cleaned it up himself?" Shocked at the seemingly unlikely possibility Darcy carried on, "Well, it looks great! All the trash that had been around the trailer…it's all gone. Every last bit!"

The rain drizzled down wetting the ground just beyond the boundaries of the tarps. It had started during the night with a strong gust of wind that had awakened the coastal camper. Clyde soon became agitated and began circling his retaining spike, pulling hard on the chain. With effort Darcy removed the spike from its hammered location and led the young ram to the shelter of the campsite. Three seconds later Clyde was straining to one side pulling away from the ruins of the keeper's quarters. Darcy looked at the dwarf goat and asked, "What? What's wrong?" With wide eyes Clyde continued to pull in the direction of the cistern. Sighing Darcy agreed, "Okay, fine." She planted the spike close to the cylindrical, brick surface and attempted to console the animal, "It's okay to be afraid of ghosts, but I honestly don't think he would hurt you." The goat stayed under the shelter of the tarpaulin roof, but never ventured in the direction of the quarters.

Starting again on her way to the newspaper's archives Darcy reached the intersection of the dirt road and the rural highway. She glanced down the roadway, but then backed the car up and pulled it off to the side of the dirt road. She got out and stepped on to the ground which was still damp from the rain that had fallen the night before. She studied the corner where the posterboard sign had been the prior morning. There was no trace of the sign, not even the wooden stake.

Perplexed she wandered over to the dull and dented chrome trailer. Tapping on the door she waited at least a minute or two for the resident to answer. Eventually the drapes parted just enough for Carl to observe who had come calling. The door opened slightly and the roughshod fellow stood in the doorway with his undershirt partially tucked in and sleep still in his eyes. He mumbled, " 'Morning."

"Good morning, Carl." Darcy motioned to the corner and asked, "Do you know what happened to our sign?"

"Yeah." He scratched at his uncombed hair, "I threw it out."

"Threw it...." Darcy was annoyed by the man's seemingly callus, but honest, answer and inquired, "Why would you do that?"

Pushing the door a little wider a casual Carl answered, "The rain ruined it. The cardboard melted and the ink ran. It was unreadable. Stupid to make a sign like that."

"You shouldn't have just taken it down." Darcy complained, "We need to have a sign. You think you could do better?"

He responded flatly, "I already have. I just didn't have a chance to put it out before you came fussing around." Swinging the door wide open for Darcy to see inside he strolled into the depths of the trailer and a moment later returned. He thrust his constructed replacement at Darcy. It was a double-sided plywood sign supported by a sturdy two-inch by two-inch stake. The wooden board was painted in white enamel housepaint with the word "Lighthouse" boldly and neatly printed in blue.

Delightfully stunned Darcy was momentarily dumbstruck, but when she found her voice again she looked at the man and beamed, "Carl…it's wonderful!"

As he squinted and furrowed his brow, he looked away from the elated recipient and said, "Aw, stop it. I didn't…."

"Really, it's wonderful!" Still beaming at his donation Darcy exclaimed, "Thank you!"

Carl's voice became harsh as he boomed, "Shut up! I don't want to care about you…or about your stupid lighthouse." Now gazing beyond his neighbor into the distance he added, "God damn, I need a beer!"

Taken aback Darcy was at first silent, but then found a tone that sounded unintentionally tart as she spat in return, "Well, sorry for making you care about something."

Retreating into the trailer's interior the caustic resident yelled, "What the hell do you know?!"

Darcy sighed then drew in a deep breath. With a somber tone fringed with a touch of sadness, she spoke without bitterness, "I know that you…have something personal…that you just can't get beyond."

"Aww, fuck you!!!" Carl strode heavily back to the doorway. He slammed the door shut leaving Darcy outside, standing there holding the painted sign.

~~~~

There was a knocking at the door and Martin paused momentarily before yelling, "Just a minute!" He continued composing his entry into the journal and then lowered his pen. Rising from the roll-top desk he opened the door and was delighted to find his favorite visitors. He smiled as he greeted Iris and the two boys, "Good morning! Come in, come in!" Following the sounds of laughter he glanced outside and saw Robby swinging Becky around in his arms. The young lovers were clearly unaware of the late autumn frost in the air.

Ushering his guests into the room Martin closed the door against the nippy breeze. The quarters were comfortable with a lit heating stove that removed the stiff chill from the chamber. Iris handed him a warm and aromatic bundle that was wrapped in kitchen towels, "We brought you something."

He took a deep breath. "Applesauce cake!" He held the gift up, drawing in the luscious scent, savoring the delicious smell of the fresh, sweet cake. Placing the bundle on the only table in the room he warmly teased, "Oh, you do spoil me, Iris." With sincerity he added softly, "Thank you."

Iris' cheeks became rosy as she blushed.

Vern distracted the lightkeeper from the lovely lady, "Whatcha been doin'?"

"I've been writing in the logbook." Martin motioned to the leather-bound book on the wooden desk's surface.

Ben examined the official journal and then furrowed his brow. The child's eyes clearly showed his lack of understanding. He asked, "What's that for?"

"Well, it's part of being a lighthouse keeper." Martin explained, "We have to keep a log of everything."

Amazed and somewhat skeptical Ben inquired, "Everything?"

"Well," Martin nodded, "yes…pretty much. We need to record almost everything that happens here…like unusual things we've seen, the number and kind of ships that pass by, what kind of weather we're having, what supplies we've used, what we've done each day, when we have visitors and how many…or just special things that touch our lives."

Iris mused, "Sort of like a diary?"

Martin laughed, "A diary that the federal government gets to read."

Vern approached the tall man and asked, "Can we help today?" Eagerness shone in his deep brown, youthful eyes.

"Sure! We still need to clean the lens. You know…that's an important part of a lighthouse keeper's duties. It's a very serious responsibility. Would you like to learn how to polish the prisms?" The boys beamed with joy while literally bouncing at the thought. They announced their approval. The lads quickly headed out the door running toward the tower and leaving the keeper behind. He yelled after them, "Wait a minute…let me get my coat!" He looked over at his lovely visitor who was giggling at his exasperated expression. Martin took his coat from the hook next to the door and pulled on the dark blue wrap quite casually. Iris reached up and helped him straighten his collar. With the garment aligned she caressed Martin's dark hair for a second before allowing her hand to come to rest on his shoulder. Smiling at the unexpected assistance Martin took her hand from the shoulder of the jacket and tenderly held her delicate fingers and gazed longingly into her sapphire eyes.

His meditation was broken only when he heard Ben yell, "Come on, Mister Thurber, it isn't that cold! We want to clean the lens!"

~~~~

It was very early in the morning when the first of the clean-up committee arrived at the campsite. Darcy had barely finished showering and was not quite dressed when she noticed the vehicles parking on the dirt road. Hurriedly she pulled on her t-shirt and made sure that her denim shorts were zipped. Combing her wet hair with her fingers she went out to greet the first of the workforce.

Soon Gretta had her troop engaged in an attack against the kudzu approximately where Ben had proclaimed the assistant keeper's quarters had once stood. The crew set forth on their mission with shovels, rakes, trowels and saws. Darcy suggested that if anyone found something they thought might be a historical artifact, they bag it in one of the Ziploc bags she willingly provided.

The small group of workers had been active for about an hour when there was an unexpected arrival. Dressed in ragged but clean blue jeans with his undershirt neatly tucked in, a cleanly shaven man approached on foot from down the road. Darcy watched as the fellow walked toward the gathering. She was not sure if she could believe her eyes. She called to him, "Carl? Is that you?"

Stopping short of the group with his hands in his pockets he simply said, "I'd like to help."

Having been alerted by Darcy's words Gretta also watched Carl's arrival. She was not about to give him an inch of leeway. She was resolved and stated tartly, "We don't need your kind of help. Go away." The other members of the team heard the angry tone in the woman's voice and were attracted to the situation. Many stopped what they were doing to watch.

"Who asked you?" Carl's expression took a sudden bitter turn.

Propped sturdily on her shovel Gretta rebuffed, "We don't need white trash here."

There was a momentary look of hurt on the fellow's face and he started his rebuttal. "I'm not...." Swallowing the rest of the sentence his jaw became tight and he withdrew his hands from his pockets, folding his arms defensively across his chest. He aimed an insult at his opponent, "You over-stuffed busybody."

Gretta's eyes grew wide and she shot back, "Drunken panhandler."

His teeth gnashing Carl responded, "Sour kraut."

"Low-down scoundrel." Gretta's puffed-up stance dared the man.

Carl was ready for the challenge and retorted, "Loudmouth lump of...."

"Wait a minute!!!" Darcy was becoming tired of the disruptive squabble and attempted to intervene between the two sharp-tongued combatants.

Gretta started to deliver another verbal blow, "You...."

Darcy boomed in a now more powerful, unusually commanding voice, "I said wait a minute!!!" Her forcefulness took all present by surprise. Placing herself physically between the quarrelsome pair she first looked directly at Gretta and scolded, "He said he's here to help." Turning to Carl she sternly inquired, "You said you were here to help, right?"

Gretta tried once more to defend her territory, "Well...we don't need his help."

"And I can tell when I'm not wanted." Carl looked off into the undergrowth while avoiding eye contact with either of the women.

"Will you just wait a minute?! Both of you!" Darcy's frustration was complete, but she worked to control her emotions and moderated her voice. She flatly stated, "We can use your help, Carl." Looking back at the aghast committee leader she continued, "We can use all the help we can get." Again addressing the new volunteer, "I for one would be glad to have your assistance." Thinking for a second, she looked back and forth between the staunch pair. Deciding, she then continued, "We need to build a fence for the goat...the outside of the tower could use some more attention...and there is still plenty of that awful vine to be cut back. Certainly we can find things for both of you to do that would keep you two far enough apart that you don't get into a fistfight."

As the morning hours passed it was obvious that Gretta was still unhappy about the addition of Carl to the work group. There were exchanges of nasty looks and haughty glares. Finally as the afternoon neared Gretta, along with a supportive Eric, approached Darcy in protest. In a rare attempt to keep her voice low the portly woman demanded, "Why are you favoring him?"

Looking up from a half-exposed kudzu root Darcy glanced at the woman and responded, "Pardon?"

Again attempting to restrain her volume Gretta fired, "Why do you insist on letting him be a part of this?"

"He's working just as hard as everyone else." Darcy looked in the direction of Carl who was gathering cut sections of kudzu. She added, "As a matter of fact, I thought he was in better condition than this. He must not have been doing much physical activity lately...he's sweating like a waterfall."

Eric sniped, "He'll want to be paid or something...because he's actually doing some work."

"Well," Darcy responded flatly, "that isn't what he said."

"He's just a bum...no good...a good for nothing." The teen persisted, "Why do you give him the benefit of the doubt...when it's so obvious?"

"Look," Darcy sighed, "I don't advocate anything he has done in the past. I won't condone the abuse of alcohol...but I do know that none of us are far from where he is."

Gretta bristled, "What do you mean by that?"

Knowing that their inactivity was becoming obvious to the others working

Darcy prodded her shovel into the dirt next to the tuber before inquiring, "What do you know about him?"

Eric chimed in, "He's a bum."

Hefting the loaded blade of dirt out of the hole Darcy grunted, "What else?"

Gretta answered when the boy just shrugged, "He showed up about five…maybe six years ago and started leeching off of everybody."

"Anything else?" Placing the soil onto a small pile Darcy looked back at the twosome who just stood there. Thrusting the tool back down into the root's domain she said, "Figured that would be about it. So really…we have no idea why he is what he is." She raised the shovel again. Tossing the shovelful of dirt to the side she continued, "God doesn't mark a child at birth and say, 'This one is a bum.' Something happens along the way. No one is immune to bad times. All it takes is a slight twist of fate to ruin a good person. Money…looks…status isn't even enough to save someone from personal tragedy." Again the shovel hit the freshly exposed earth. "Some people have the strength to overcome great problems…others don't. I'm not saying that all of the people you meet on the street are fallen angels waiting to get their wings back, but it isn't good to generalize about folks. I've seen some mighty good people fall into some really low places." Pulling out a sizable load of dirt and placing it aside she concluded, "If Carl is willing to try and give back to the community even just a little bit…I don't want to stand in his way."

Screwing up her nose Gretta shook her head in exasperation, turned and walked away. Eric was torn by his loyalty to his neighbor and the weight of Darcy's argument. He hesitated, but then ducked his eyes and quietly returned to his work.

As the group took a lunch break all involved sought shade from the heat of the day. The coolers were raided for their chilled beverages. Bags of potato chips were opened and spread on the cardtable which May had donated to Darcy's campsite. Brown bag lunches opened as the volunteers fed their appetites. Clustered together the team gossiped and joked in between bites. The only person to be seated alone was Carl. He sat on the ground at some distance from the group without food or drink. Eric noticed the loner, contemplated speaking to him, but then felt awkwardly uncertain. Instead he turned to the camp inhabitant, "Darcy…."

She followed the boy's line of sight. Seeing the sweat-soaked, solitary volunteer she called to him, "Hey Carl…come on and join us!" Having seen the exchange, Gretta shot the boy an unhappy look, but withheld her complaints.

"Thanks...not hungry." Carl wearily waved to Darcy and the teen.

"Well...you should at least have something to drink. You've been working hard and we're all a bit dehydrated." Darcy went over to the fellow, offering him an assisting hand. She suggested, "Come on...we've got some Gatorade...or bottled water if you'd like."

Giving a weak smile he complied and accepted the assistance plus a bottle of grape Gatorade. With Carl now seated among the gathering, lunch went on much as it had. Neither Gretta nor Carl exchanged one word which was doubtlessly all for the better.

The effort resumed for another few hours, but as mid-afternoon approached the group grew tired of working in the hot sunshine and unanimously agreed that they were ready to call it quits for the day. Eric suggested they migrate to the general store where they could rest on the porch with a cold drink. Darcy offered to take Carl along for the ride. Though reluctant he agreed after the others encouraged him to join in. Looking at the shaved man Darcy thought out loud, "Carl, would you like a haircut?" He looked up at Darcy and gave her an inquisitive eyeing. She smiled at him and said, "I would be willing to pay for it...if you would like one."

"Sure." He nodded in agreement.

Abigail stood on the front porch of the general store as the lighthouse workforce wandered through the store. Ben offered to run the register as she prepared for the event. She placed her beautician's tools on the small table that normally held the checkers board. Though she had never pursued the trade for a living, she had once attended beauty school. Since that time the skill had come in handy with family and friends. Sensing the rarity of the situation she had readily agreed to give the normally unsocial derelict a haircut.

Looking a little apprehensive Carl sat on one of the stools and was draped in a floor-length plastic smock. A casual crowd of onlookers had gathered. Those that were not fortunate enough to have claimed one of the few stools leaned against the railings, icebox and wall. Attempting to melt into the spectators Darcy propped on the porch railing. Among the observers was Kim who originally had come to see her grandmother. The young girl was joined by her brother and Gretta who had sworn that this event was something she had to see. As the last of the shoppers left the store Ben seated himself on the porch as was his norm for this time of day. He was joined by a couple of the fishermen who were hotly debating the merits and disadvantages of the community becoming a formal town.

Abigail began by combing through Carl's perspiration-laden hair and carefully working through a few minor tats. She took the sleek scissors and began to trim the back of his hair. Her work was impeded as her patron wavered and began to tremble. Finding it difficult to continue she became mildly frustrated, but tried to be understanding. Attempting to reassure the fellow she mildly said, "Don't worry. I haven't clipped anyone's ear in a long time. Just hold still."

Carl shot a look over his shoulder at his barber and contested, "I am holding still."

"No, man," Eric grinned as he chided, "You're shaking all over the place. It's just a haircut. You don't have to be afraid of a haircut!"

Carl gave the teen a wrathful glare and fairly growled, "I'm not afraid of nothing, kid!" This response drew hoots from the observation gallery. One of the fishermen openly laughed at the tough-talking vagrant.

Darcy watched the smocked man as he continued to wobble and tremble. Carefully she asked, "Carl, what's wrong. Are you okay?"

Defensively, he snapped, "I'm fine!" After a moment he tried to calm his voice and shakily mumbled, "I need a drink."

Eric responded to the man's last comment and retreated into the store. A few seconds later he returned carrying a can of beer. He extended the cold beverage toward Carl and said, "Here you go."

Looking like a horse confronted with fire Carl pulled away from the stool, torn by mixed urges. His gut clenched in the need for the alcohol, but his mind attempted to overcome the awful desire. Wide-eyed and shaking he unleashed an agitated bellow directly at Eric, "No!!!" His body seizing, he shrieked, "I don't want…that!!!"

Stunned and not understanding the boy backed away from Carl. Abigail became fearful and quickly slipped from behind the explosive man. She grabbed Kim's hand and pulled the child into the store. Voices of objection came from the others on the porch. Turning away from the group to face the open space beyond the end of the porch Carl grasped the railing and yelled, "Just leave me alone!"

Darcy wasted no time in averting further confrontation between Eric and the upset alcoholic. Guiding the youth toward the store's entrance she advised him, "Get him a bottle of water instead. He's going through withdrawal."

"I don't understand." Hurt and exasperated Eric shook his head and asked,

"Why did he yell at me? I thought he wanted a beer. That's what he drinks, right?"

"Don't worry about it." Darcy tried to console the teen while still attempting to guide him away from the possibility of furthering a bad situation. "He isn't angry with you...*per se*. Just...get rid of the beer. Water will do fine." She gave the lad a weak smile.

"Hey, man," one of the fishermen moved toward Carl, "why are you giving the boy a hard time? He didn't do anything to you."

"Please...do as he asked and leave him alone, okay?" Darcy again tried to intervene by placing herself between the fisherman and his target. She pleadingly requested, "Please...?"

Unsatisfied the fisherman remained set on settling the matter until Gretta laughed and called to him, "Come on, Joe. He isn't worth the trouble. Let's go to the Spoon and I'll buy you a cup of coffee. Nothing you can do to him will match what the boy's mother will do if she hears about this." Begrudgingly the fisherman nodded and turned away to go down the steps. Heading for the steps Gretta gave Darcy a snide expression and then turned further to address the other seafarer, "You coming, Fred?" With a grunt the second fisherman rose himself from his propped position and followed the woman down the stairs and across the road to the tiny restaurant and tavern.

Sighing with minor relief Darcy noticed that Ben was still present...calmly, but warily, looking on. The porch was otherwise cleared of the audience. With a strangled smile she asked, "Ben...is there a doctor around here?"

"I don't need a doctor!" Carl did not turn his stance and continued gripping the crossboard of the wooden railing, but glanced momentarily over his shoulder at the pair.

Watching while Carl looked back out at the corner Darcy turned to the quiet Ben, softly beseeching, "Please...." Raising her hand to her ear with fingers folded, pinky and thumb spread, she motioned a phone call and nodded hopefully to the elder. Understanding the request Ben nodded in reply and casually wandered into the store. Waiting a moment Darcy considered the suffering man's disposition. Cautiously she moved beside him. She delayed speaking until he turned his sight slightly in her direction. Almost whispering she said, "Carl...I'm proud that you're trying to do this...but you don't have to go through it alone. We can try and help you."

"You mean you...you would be willing to try and help me." He asked with amazement, "Why?"

Not wishing to argue the point that others might help him she answered,

"You're not such a bad guy, Carl. Why didn't you tell me you were going to go dry?"

"I'm worse than you think." He drew a quivering breath and then answered, "I didn't really want you to know. I didn't want it to be a big deal. I just wanted to be able…to be in control of my life for a change…not all messed up all the time." He looked directly at Darcy and commented almost under his breath, "I had forgotten what it was like to have someone be nice to me."

The interior of the trailer was just as small as the outside made it look. Standing barely inside the doorway, still able to breathe fresh air, Darcy could not help but overhear some of the activities and conversation between the doctor and patient. Despite Carl's initial protests the one doctor who was willing to travel to the tiny community had been sent for. Much to everyone's relief when Dr. Susie Marsh arrived Carl had calmed down and agreed to allow her to treat him.

He was taken back to the trailer as it was thought to be the best thing for his comfort. In reality the trailer was cramped, incredibly untidy and pungent with a terrible, sour odor. Almost all open surfaces held masses of emptied beer containers. Dirty laundry was piled on the one sofa. A crumpled throng of sports, true crime and adult magazines was scattered in various places on counters and along the floor. Except for an emptied tuna can in the sink Darcy found no sign of food.

Opening the one small window she could not only find but also get to, she heard Dr. Marsh state, "I'm going to give you a Thiamine shot."

"Like hell!" Carl's exclamation was followed by what sounded like his recoiling and slamming against the trailer wall. "You keep that hypodermic away from me!" Fearing the outcome Darcy made her way through the clutter to the other end of the trailer where the action was taking place next to a twin bed.

She found the lady doctor with the prepared syringe and the quivering man, armed with an empty bottle, backed against the wall. His reddened eyes blazed wide as he flattened against the dull paneling. Trying to keep her voice light and calm Darcy asked, "Hey…what's going on here?"

"Tell her to keep away with that!" Carl defensively held out the bottle while clutching the container's neck tightly. His body continued to shake despite his attempts to maintain control. Sweat beaded on his forehead, ultimately running down his neck and body.

"Take it easy, Carl. It'll be all right." She turned to the unhappy doctor and asked, "You said Thiamine. That's vitamin…uhm…."

"B," the doctor answered.

Darcy inquired, "What's that for?"

Slipping into her professional voice, Dr. Marsh answered evenly, "To help prevent Wernicke-Korsakoff Syndrome. Heavy drinkers are often at risk." Seeing the question still in Darcy's eyes the doctor continued to explain, "It's an impairment of brain functions...a progressive deterioration that can have a number of symptoms...speech impairment, swallowing difficulties, weakness, lack of coordination, numbness, paralysis of eye muscles or even the whole face, muscle atrophy, contractions, even memory loss. In advanced cases it can lead to coma and death."

Darcy pursed her lips then looked over at the wary man, "Okay...well, you heard the lady. You need the shot."

"Uh uh." Continuing to balk Carl shook his head and stared at the doctor with suspicion.

Even Darcy was becoming weary of the standoff and her tone reflected the fact, "Carl...if you can face up to Gretta...you can face up to a little needle." Seeing no signs of his relinquishing the bottle she added, "Boy, she would have a good laugh at your expense right now...scared of a shot."

This final comment caught the man's ire and he shifted his gaze to Darcy. He spat out, "You wouldn't...."

She reached up and grabbed the amber body of the beer bottle. The move caught Carl off guard. He started to yank the glass vessel away from her, but found that she had placed her other hand on his arm. It was the first time they had made real physical contact and the sensation was odd to him. She held the bottle firmly, but her touch on his skin was warm and gentle. She asked him, "Please...let me have the bottle." She slowly moved her hand down his trembling arm and then covered his hand with hers. He eased his hold on the potential weapon. Darcy removed it from his relaxing, shaky fingers. Placing the brown container aside she said, "Thank you, Carl." He took hold of her hand. Though still distrustful of the needle-wielding doctor, he allowed himself to be led by Darcy's guidance to the side of the bed and where he apprehensively sat down. Closing his eyes and wincing he accepted the shot.

Putting away the emptied hypodermic Dr. Marsh announced, "There, it's over now." Next she handed him a pill and explained, "This will help ease the symptoms of withdrawal. I will leave you a four-day supply. I want to see you at the clinic after the four days are over." Watching the patient swallow the pill the doctor directed her next statement to Darcy, "It would be best if someone stayed with him for a while to make sure the symptoms don't become any worse. I don't think that they will, but just in case. I need to go back to the clinic. I have other patients coming in. Are you his girlfriend?"

"Uhm, no." Darcy gave a light smile and explained, "just a friend. I live down the road."

With a meekness uncommon to the man Carl looked at his neighbor and requested, "Please...stay." He swallowed hard.

"He'll need to stay calm," the doctor continued, "and as if I should have to say this...absolutely no alcoholic beverages. That includes beer and mouthwash."

Seeing the discomforted need in Carl's eyes Darcy agreed. It was true that no one else had bothered to come assist. As she nodded she stipulated, "Now you're going to lie down and close your eyes." Not wanting to be alone Carl complied without hesitation.

Accompanying the doctor to the door of the trailer, Darcy gave assurances that she would do her best to see to it that Carl would get to the clinic. After having thanked Dr. Marsh for having taken the trouble to come help Darcy gave a final wave as the physician climbed into her car and drove away. Knowing the hours ahead would be difficult, and stifling, Darcy took a deep breath of the fresh air before returning inside.

She heard Carl call for her and she responded, "I'm here." Entering the tiny bedroom she found the patient propped on one arm and nervously surveying the room. She lightly scolded, "Hey, aren't you supposed to be lying down with your eyes shut?"

He pleaded, "Please...don't leave."

"I'm here, aren't I?" She paused in the entrance to the cramped bedroom. Knowing the man's condition Darcy reluctantly probed, "Carl...I've got to ask...what about Brett? Do you need to call him?"

Carl's head seemed loose on his shoulders and rolled downward causing his words to be muffled into his chest as he responded, "Only if I think you're not going to be on the property."

"Ah. Okay...well, lie down." Darcy crossed to the bed and pressed gently on Carl's shoulder.

He dropped back to the mattress with his head coming to rest on the flattened pillow. She settled on the edge of the bed and looked into the man's glassy eyes. He groped the surface of the bed until Darcy took his hand in hers. He clasped his perspiration-moistened fingers around the offered source of personal contact. His tired eyes blinked and in a languid voice Carl muttered, "Thank you."

Offering a sympathetic smile Darcy massaged his hand and softly replied, "Of course."

There was an awkward moment as neither knew what to say next. Then Carl requested, "Tell me about lighthouses."

Darcy agreed, "Okay…but close your eyes. You should be resting." She gathered her thoughts and then began in a soft, lulling voice, "From what I have read so far…they think that the earliest lighthouses predated the Romans. The lights were bonfires lit on cliffs overlooking the sea and they showed sailors that they were close to the shore…that they were close to home. The first actual recorded lighthouse was the great tower of Alexandria…." As she spoke she watched Carl's blurred eyes gradually flicker closed and his breathing relax. She would talk to him until she was sure that he was fast asleep.

Chapter Twelve

Christmas Eve 1938
"Yes, I'm sure," Martin said, then added, "would you do me a favor though?" The young man answered without pause, "Sure!"

Martin handed the assistant keeper a small package, no larger than his hand, which was carefully wrapped in brown paper and tied with a string. There was a folded note neatly tucked under the knot. Taking a breath Martin requested, "Please give this to Iris Campbell if the chance allows." He watched as Robby slowly nodded with a huge grin. After swallowing he smiled back at his coworker and added, "Thanks…now go on and enjoy yourself." The principle keeper watched as his companion turned and headed toward the wharf to make use of the station's motorboat. It would be a quiet evening at the light station. Martin returned to his chores as he heard the motor gurgle into life. Then the skiff churned away from the dock.

Later that night the keeper stood outside the watch room on the narrow catwalk and looked toward the village. The colored lights played on the constantly irregular motion of the water. The waves and low swells broke the multi-hued reflections into a thousand shining points. For a moment he thought he heard the sound of Christmas music being carried over the waters of the inlet, but the faint melody gave way to the persistent music of the waves meeting the shore. Filled with a loneliness more powerful than he had ever known before he pictured in his mind the gala taking place at the Campbell home, but nothing about the event was clear save for the woman he loved, his beautiful Iris. He stood there alone, lost in the depth of the night despite the comfort of his brilliant beacon.

Having delivered Martin's gift, Robby left Iris alone in the kitchen. The sounds of the holiday celebration carried through the doorway. Iris carefully slipped the folded note from between the binding of the packet and then gently pulled open the slipknot in the string. Filled with curiosity, she unfolded the brown paper. A red-enameled metal pin in the shape of a star was the only contents of the gift. She opened the note and read:

Dearest Iris,

I was awarded this in Maine for my hard work and efficiency in tending a lighthouse there. I want you to have it now. Tonight you will enjoy the company of others and I will be here, tending the light. Though I am not with you, please know that you are the only star in my sky.

Adoringly yours,
Martin

~~~~

Waking very early in the morning Darcy found Carl still asleep. She took the opportunity to slip away and go to her camp to check the site. She made sure the goat had clean water and shade available for later during the heat of the day. After inspecting the area Darcy wandered out to the beach. She could not say exactly why she did this except perhaps just to make sure the tower was still there. It was...but so was a scattered mess of beer and soda bottles, emptied potato chips bags, a dozen or so cigarette butts and new spray paint stains on the walls of the old lighthouse. Shaking her head she went back to her shelter and fetched a garbage bag. She cleaned up the litter on the ground as best she could, though cleaning the tower again would have to wait.

Not wanting to be absent too long from the recovering alcoholic she made haste to secure the tent and again began the drive down the dirt road. She had just gotten underway when a buzzing noise came from under her seat. Startled by the sound she slammed on the brakes. Again the noise came from beneath her. Holding her breath she sat wide-eyed and apprehensive until she remembered the link to her "other" life, her cell phone. Relieved, she released a nervous laugh. Putting the car into park she dug under the seat and pulled the device from its hiding place. Pressing the green button she answered, "Hello?"

"Hey, lady...are you alive out there? You're a hard woman to get hold of these days. I was getting worried." Troy McGovern's rich voice flowed from the cell phone earpiece, "I haven't heard from you once your whole time there."

"I'm sorry." Darcy took a deep breath and relaxed slightly. She offered an explanation, "It's turned out to be a bit more of an eventful stay than I thought it would be."

With a touch of smugness the movie star retorted, "You told Brett when you two last talked that it was a bore."

"Uhm," Darcy winced remembering the event and replied, "oh, that was…a B-O-A-R…as in wild pig." She eased the car back into gear and allowed it to roll down the road at its own pace.

"Wild pig??" There was a tone of enthusiasm in Troy's voice as he exclaimed, "I didn't know you were a hunter!"

"Well, I'm not." She emitted a slightly strangled laugh and continued, "No, not exactly."

"Oh." There was a significant pause and then, "Are you okay?"

"Oh, yeah. I'm fine." Redirecting the conversation Darcy said, "It must be early as sin where you are. What's up?"

"The transaction went through, so the land is ours now. I wanted to warn you…they're going to begin clearing part of the area in the next couple of days…there will be a bunch of heavy equipment showing up…and a contractor with his crew and workers…and a lot of noise."

"Hmm…so much for the peaceful mornings. It has been nice."

"Sorry about that." Troy took on a serious tone, "So, you're getting on okay then?"

"Well, yes," Darcy allowed her voice to reveal her guilt, "but there are some things I should tell you." She explained how the local residents came to know about the development plans including Troy and Brett's involvement. Troy seemed unconcerned with this and answered by stating that the community would have found out sooner or later anyway. Now with the permits finalized there was nothing that the locals could do to stop the building. Darcy then explained how desperately the people wanted to help save the lighthouse. There was a pause and she assured him that it should not interfere with what would be going on nearby. With that point clarified Troy responded in good humor, wishing the project good luck.

He asked, "What about that bum Brett hired to keep an eye on you? He isn't harassing you, is he?"

"No." She hesitated while trying to think of how best to respond, "Actually…he…isn't so bad once you get used to him."

"Darcy?" The inflection in Troy's voice was unmistakably that of someone who knew the woman well, "What's going on?"

"Oh…nothing much, really." She attempted to make the situation seem casual, almost normal, "We just…are helping each other out with a few things."

"Darcy Vornack...you're not getting in over your head with this one, are you? Lady, you're the only person I know who would try to convert the enemy. I can't believe Brett would hire someone like that guy to begin with. He seemed like a pretty wretched hooligan...who knows what he's capable of."

Knowing that her friend was telling the truth, but unwilling to accept his fatalistic view Darcy started her slow reply, "Troy...."

The actor understood from experience that he could not alter her actions and so cut her off, "I know. You'll handle it. Well, you be careful. All right? You just be careful."

Having finished the conversation and bid farewell to her employer and friend Darcy tucked the cell phone back under the seat. Pulling the car up next to the trailer, she got out while still feeling emotionally far away. She lingered on thoughts of her friends among the film crews. Another world! They all seemed so distant at this moment. As she closed the car door a small convoy of pickup trucks pulled onto the dirt road from the highway. The lead vehicle slowed and David Brown yelled from the driver's window, "We're going to survey the tower!" Then, having been snapped back to the present, Darcy just smiled and waved to the man as he accelerated his truck.

Tapping lightly at the drab door of Carl's trailer but getting no answer she opened it slowly and peeked inside. She could see activity in the tiny wash area of the bathroom and called to the resident, "Good morning, Carl! How are you doing?"

Peering around the corner with his wet hair yet uncombed and his face splotched with shaving cream Carl responded, "Good morning. My head hurts like hell, but I think I'll live."

Lowering the volume of her voice to accommodate his hangover Darcy rather bashfully admitted, "Carl...I promised to meet someone in town today. We're doing research and I really should be there."

The man's eyes widened and a look of interest came to his rough features. He inquired, "About the lighthouse?"

Amused at Carl's change of attitude about the antiquated tower Darcy nodded and answered, "In part, at least."

"I...would like to go with you. Can't stay here alone all day." He looked down at his worn undershirt and tattered jeans, "That is, if it's...not too much trouble."

Concerned Darcy looked at Carl and asked, "Do you feel up to it? I mean...."

He nodded, "I'll make it."

"Okay." A smile grew across her face as she added, "Sure...you're more than welcome." Pleased with her answer the foam-faced fellow stepped back into the bathroom and Darcy could hear the tap running. Looking around in the cluttered trailer she asked, "Have you had anything to eat this morning?"

There was a pause as Carl thought about this question and then replied, "No. I guess not."

"Well...do you have anything here?"

"I think there are some saltines in the cabinet." Rubbing a towel across his washed and now clean shaven, if slightly nicked, face he asked, "Would you like some?"

"No...thank you." She hoped she hid her momentary humor at his sincere offer, quickly voicing her true concern: "Carl...you need to eat."

His rebuttal was honest and simple, "I haven't felt hungry."

"If you haven't been eating right you may well be nutritionally deficient. We can stop by the store on the way back and pick up some stuff so you can eat real meals...not just crackers." Seeing Carl's dubious expression she chided him, "You don't want any more of those shots do you?" She needed to say nothing more to convince him.

Darcy took a moment before their departure to call ahead and forewarn Elinor that she would be late and would be bringing a friend with her. The editor sounded chipper and responded that the delay was fine as long as they got there before lunch. Darcy laughed and answered that she hoped they would not be that late.

As the pair drove in the direction of the county seat they passed the general store. There was unusual activity there that drew Darcy's attention. She slowed the car in order to get a better look. Ben and Peter were out scraping off the old paint from the porch with a handful of onlookers scrutinizing the project. What's more, much to her surprise, the front sign had been fixed—no longer reading, "GENE AL," but the whole, complete "GENERAL." Sorry to see some of the local character being changed, Darcy still smiled, knowing that the repairs were in preparation for the events to come and ultimately for the best.

Driving on she commented, "I saw a thrift shop in town. We can stop if you like. Maybe we could find you a better pair of pants."

"I'm sorry." Carl's voice carried a beleaguered quality. "I probably shouldn't have made you bring me."

"What?" Darcy firmly asserted, "You didn't make me do anything. What's the problem?" She glanced over and noticed the passenger's deliberate, distant gaze out the window.

Carl swallowed and his eyes lowered before he answered, "I don't have any money. Just a couple of bucks."

Puzzled Darcy responded, "I thought Brett was paying you."

"He is." Carl paused and then said sourly, "I boozed it all." Darcy's startled expression served to inadvertently embarrass him and he felt the need to clarify matters, "Over the past couple of weeks." His shame was obvious. He breathed deeply and attempted to reassure himself as he spoke, "But that's over with. I'm through."

After a few seconds of silence Darcy lightly suggested, "Hey, well…why don't I just loan you a little bit of cash. You can get a few things and then you can pay me back when you get the chance."

Outfitted in a nearly new pair of jeans and a plaid, button-down shirt Carl seemed like a different person. Even his smile was a bit brighter. Satisfied with their purchases the duo left the thrift shop and went across town to the weekly newspaper's brick building.

Elinor studied Darcy's companion and extended her hand in greeting, "I'm sorry…I don't quite recall…."

Hesitantly Carl met the handshake and answered, "Carl…Floyd."

"Well, it's a pleasure." Adjusting her attention to her fellow researcher Elinor warned, "Darcy, we need to watch the time. We have a luncheon meeting."

"Oh?"

The editor announced, "Lester is going to meet us. I called him about our findings…and I've made some copies to take with us."

Carl inquired with an amount of apprehension, "Lester…McKay?"

Darcy nodded and smiled with her answer, "That would be the one." Noting an edge of wariness in her companion's look she explained, "We've found some interesting things. It seems that for various reasons the tour of duty for principle keepers at the Saint Rosabelle Lighthouse was much shorter than it should have been during its last ten active years. This seems a bit odd to us…and I have had my own reasons to believe that the last keeper may have been murdered."

"Whoa…." Something in Carl's eye caught fire and he seemed to gain yet more enthusiasm for the research. A long folding table had been dedicated to the organization of the information and items were added as they were discovered. Attempts were made to keep things in chronological order so that years unaccounted for could be readily seen and then researched. Looking over the collection Carl spotted a folder near the far end of the table. Placing a finger on the file folder he pointed to the contained records and asked, "What's this?"

Both women noticed a bit of a smirk playing across the man's lips. Darcy responded, "Well, now…you zeroed right in on the hot stuff, didn't you? That would be the police file on Martin Thurber's death and the destruction of the light." Watching as Carl glanced at the file and then back at the ladies she offered, "Would you like to look at it?"

"Yes," he replied quickly, "I sure would."

"Help yourself," she nodded to him, then remembering her own experience she warned, "Carl…some of the photos are…not pretty."

Soberly Carl nodded back to her and sat down at the table. He spent nearly a half hour reading through the information, studying the images and taking notice of the investigating officer's handwritten comments. When he had finished looking at the file he placed it back in its chronological position on the table. Now the women were sorting through boxes of photographs and negatives. Wanting to join in the effort he asked how he could help. Elinor cheerfully suggested that he could continue the search through the micro media archives.

As Carl got under way Elinor leaned over the table and whispered to Darcy, "What happened to the back of his head?"

"Huh?" Darcy showed her confusion.

"His hair…its all uneven in the back."

Remembering the aborted haircut Darcy grinned and replied, "It's a long story. Guess I had better get him to a barber this afternoon."

Carl proved to be readily versed in the operation of the media machine and had no trouble loading and advancing the microfilm. Quietly sitting at a small desk he slowly advanced the roll and checked the headlines as they went by. About twenty minutes into the activity he came to an abrupt stop. Suddenly standing he quickly asked, "Restroom?"

"Down the hall to the right." Elinor looked up from her stack of photographs and noticed Carl's pasty color and wavering stance, "Are you…." Before she had a chance to finish the question the man exited the room in a run. Watching after the fellow she said, "Darcy…I think your friend may be ill."

"Ah darn. I should have known better. That microfilm can give a healthy person motion sickness." Answering Elinor's inquisitive stare she explained, "He's been ill for some time and he's just now getting back on his feet."

"Oh." It was clear that the newspaper editor was settling for less information than she would have liked, but she did not press the matter. She returned to examining the photographs and whatever inscriptions that may have been marked on the back of them.

After a few minutes Darcy went to check on Carl. Knocking on the restroom door she entered the wash area with some caution. She found Carl washing his face and quietly asked, "Hey, fella…how are you doing?"

Wiping a slick substance from his chin he mumbled, "Sorry."

"Don't be." Showing a warm manner she tried to console him. "If you don't feel up to continuing with this…look…I'll understand."

"No. I want to help." Carl's eyes showed that he was being sincere and that for some personal reason he felt that the research was important.

Struck by the man's desire to participate Darcy simply said, "Okay…."

The Around-the-Clock Diner was a typical small town eatery. It was housed in one of the store fronts and open from eleven in the morning to eight at night. Specializing in home cooking the establishment offered locally favored foods from okra to meatloaf. There was something for almost every appetite.

Lester McKay met the threesome precisely on time. They, of course, were early. As a reporter Elinor had learned to be prompt or risk losing her news story, and working as a movie production assistant Darcy was required to be one of the first to arrive on location. Lester extended his hand to the women's companion and spoke with some amazement, "Carl?" The officer gave the fellow a scrutinizing study, "I…am…impressed." As they all entered the dining area Lester spoke softly to Carl, "By the way…no fingerprints on the cans."

"And what cans would that be?" Elinor asked the question as if the comment had been made directly to her. Finding a table near a window the group settled into wooden chairs lined with worn plaid cushions that clashed with Carl's new shirt—and nearly anything else, for that matter. The news reporter intently watched the lawman while giving him an expectant grin.

"That would be the spray paint cans…from a recent round of vandalism at the lighthouse."

"Ah, yes. Darcy told me what happened. Well, this is interesting information. I'll include it in the text for Monday's edition." Looking directly at Carl she asked, "So…how are you involved?"

Carl's eyes became narrow and hard. Perturbed, he chewed his cheek in annoyance. Deliberately moderating his voice he responded, "I'm not. It's just that the cans were found in my yard."

Lester attempted a rare sweetness in his voice, "Uhm...I would prefer if you didn't print all that, Elinor. Not at this time." Attempting a smile in response to the woman's inquisitive gaze he explained, "It would appear as if whoever did the actual vandalism tried to use Carl as a scapegoat...setting it up to look like he did it."

With a slight laugh and arched brows Elinor could not restrain her investigative habits, asking, "And of course you didn't do it, right?"

"That's right." Without anger or apology Carl said, "I was stone cold drunk at the time. I couldn't have stood up to piss if I had wanted to." He knew his overly honest answer would quell some of the journalist's nosiness and was not surprised when her smiling expression faded to mild astonishment. "Sorry if I've shocked you, but that's the truth."

Moving on to the main reason for the luncheon meeting Lester addressed the pair of women, "Okay, well...show me what you've got." Elinor handed him a manila folder which held copies of all the articles about the lighthouse keepers and their fates. The news editor explained the contents as Lester thumbed through the copies of old newsprint and photographs. He took time to study each one.

The proceedings were interrupted as a pretty, young waitress wearing an apron over her denim shorts approached the table with an order pad and pen. As she took their requests Carl was about to decline, but caught Darcy's expression. She suggested a cup of soup and the waitress eagerly announced that a fresh kettle of vegetable soup had just been made. Carl agreed, less from wanting the soup—more from not wanting to cause too much hassle.

With the orders taken Darcy told Lester, "Thanks to Carl's help this morning we have included a copy of the article concerning Martin Thurber's death."

Carl gave his opinion, "Those circumstances seem a bit suspect to me. It could have been suicide, but that doesn't make sense. He was decorated three times for his life-saving efforts. Once in Maine and twice down here. He openly shared the credit with a local fisherman on one occasion...made a point of it. He doesn't seem like the kind that would do what they claimed he did...even if he was jilted and heartbroken. There is a mention that the coroner declared it suicide...death from sudden impact, but there are no firm details. There is simply a file photo of the tower connected with the article, but I have been checking the photos that were included in the folder from Elinor's police files."

"Actually...my late uncle's," the business woman corrected.

Motioning to the second file in Lester's possession Carl continued, "I have a hunch that the site was tampered with prior to the law getting there." Taking the file from the local officer he opened the record and found the image he was after, "If you look at the sand...there are a number of footprints. It is hard to tell just how many sets. I would say at least two...one possibly a woman's...see how much smaller they look?" He indicated the area in question.

Darcy gave Carl a curious look and said, "You sound like you've done this before."

He silently nodded and was prepared to say nothing more. Lester nudged the man, but still there was nothing else from Carl. The local officer then leaned into the table and divulged, "He was a city policeman in Texarkana." Instantly Carl wheeled in his chair and gave the deputy a frosted, angry glare.

"How interesting," Elinor gushed. "Why did you...."

Elinor's inquiry was cut off cleanly by the former police officer's snap, "I don't want to talk about it!" Realizing he had raised his voice and had drawn a few glances from the occupants of other tables Carl sat back in his chair. He tried to calm himself while steadying his quickened breath.

Darcy was quick to respond and attempted to head off any further provocation, "That's fine...we don't have to." She moved to redirect the attention of the group by stating, "I have a hard time believing that Martin was jilted." Darcy opened the pocketed folder that had been given to her by the Brown children. Using her napkin to prevent any further damage from handling she removed the photo she had found in the keeper's quarters. She placed it out for the group to see.

"Darcy...where on Earth? This isn't one of the photos from the archives...is it?" Elinor was shocked and delighted as she angled herself to get a better view of the captured image. She exclaimed, "This is wonderful!" The group photo featured the two lighthouse keepers who were identifiable by their uniforms, two young women and two children. The younger of the keepers had his arm draped around the shoulders of one young lady and she clasped his side in a rather daring show of partnering. Pointing to the assistant keeper Elinor stated, "That must be Robert Bowsen. He's mentioned in some of the articles." Continuing to study the photograph her eyes followed the line of adults. "And that would be Martin Thurber...with his sweetheart. Aw, look at their expressions...." Clasping hand in hand the principle keeper and the young woman at his side shared looks of complete adoration. They were not looking at the camera, but into each other's eyes.

Swallowing her hesitation Darcy commented, "Martin wanted me to find this. He led me right to it."

Carl furrowed his brow and asked hesitantly, "We're talking about the dead man, right?"

"She thinks he's a ghost and that he haunts the lighthouse," Lester controlled the urge to snicker.

"He is and he does." Darcy's response was edged with defensiveness, "I wouldn't have found this without his direction."

"Okay," Lester still played light of the camper's beliefs, "well, where did he give you this?"

Answering flatly Darcy replied, "In the keeper's quarters. I think it may have been the bedroom."

Realizing it might be best not to poke too much fun at the woman Lester became more serious and asked, "Do we know who the others are? The women and the kids?" Watching first Darcy and then Elinor shake their heads he frowned. "Guess that's part of the mystery we're just going to have to work on."

"There isn't that much in the police record. It seems that the investigation was cut short...by order of the U.S. Coast Guard." Carl turned to a sheet in the file folder and read, "The United States Coast Guard officially took charge of the Light Station on the first of July and thus has declared this incident a military matter. As such, the Saint Rosabelle Police have been relieved of the investigation."

Drawing a breath Lester confirmed, "You all have found some interesting stuff. It does seem odd that there were so many coincidences between the changes in lighthouse keepers and accidents of one kind or another. I think that this is at least worth looking into. I will ask to have the case reopened. Mind you...it's up to the sheriff, but I think there is good reason to review matters." Indicating the aged photograph from Darcy's file he asked, "Care if I take this? I could have it back to you by tomorrow."

She hesitated and said, "Sure...just be careful with it."

Lester nodded, "My office can make a copy and I'll return the original to you."

Elinor declared, "I would like to have a copy too!"

Lester looked to the photograph's owner for approval. Darcy smiled and agreed, "Of course."

Eyeing the folder still in Darcy's hands Carl asked, "So...what else have you got hidden in that thing?"

"Well...just a couple of photo images that Eric and Kim found on the Internet." She removed the prints from the folder and spread them out on the table. "These are some lighthouse lenses from different locations. The children thought they could give me some idea of what ours might have looked like."

"Huh...." Lester looked at the digital prints and then moved one of the crime scene photos to the top of the stack for comparison. "Look at that...those pieces of glass," he pointed to a scattering of broken shards of reflective material dispersed in the sand around Martin's lifeless form. "Odd shapes...pieces of the lens, you think?"

"Could be," Darcy responded while examining the two images. She noted, "They have that triangular shape that would have fit into the brass framework...." Staring hard at the downloaded image her eyes grew wide and she gasped. With a wave of excitement she looked back at her table companions and declared, "And Peter Brown has part of the brass frame!" Uncertain sounds came from around the table as the occupants gave Darcy peculiar looks. "No, I'm sure of it! It's hanging in his shop...on the back wall. I remember asking him about it and he had no idea what it was. Now I know why! That isn't exactly your 'everyday' piece of brass!"

Chapter Thirteen

"This meeting will now come to order!"

The second meeting of the Saint Rosabelle Lighthouse supporters was held at the church, which could better accommodate a large crowd. The room was filled with heated conversation about the upcoming County Hall meeting concerning the incorporation of the Saint Rosabelle community. It had gotten so that everyone was embroiled in the topic—even the children. Lester kept his quiet as Carl and one of the local boat owners voiced differing positions. Ben surprised them by putting in frequent one-word comments. The ladies of the quilting club compared snippets of gossip concerning the members of the County Commission and where they might stand on various matters.

Finally Abigail clanked an old boat's bell and the gathering began to quiet. "To start with I am delighted to announce that we have our first donation for the historical museum...which should accompany the lighthouse. Peter Brown has contributed a piece of brass framework that once held part of a Fresnel lens...most likely the lens from our own lighthouse." She paused while the gathering murmured about the gift then continued, "We have a lot of business to take care of and we should now hear the minutes from the first meeting." Lynn stood and with an air of confidence read her notes. They were accurate, detailed and uncontested.

With the minutes officially accepted the meeting progressed to the treasurer's report. With a wide smile, Lester announced, "So far we have gained one thousand and seventy dollars from direct personal donations given to the overall project by some generous members of our community...plus twenty-six dollars and seventy-four cents from the store canister...seventeen dollars from raffle ticket sales for the quilt. That makes for a total of one thousand, one hundred and thirteen dollars and seventy-four cents!" There were excited sounds that came from the gathering, then they burst into a round of applause approving the total. When the group calmed down a bit he added, "We've made arrangements to open a savings account at the First

Coastal Union Bank and all we need is the official group name in order to deposit our funds."

Abigail acknowledged that Lester was finished with his report and cheerily announced, "Sounds like we're off to a good start! Next I think we should hear from David Brown...."

Despite the joy of the group at having learned of their good fortune David's face was oddly somber. Taking a long breath he said, "I have accompanied four contractors while they examined the tower. There is some structural rehabilitation that will need to be done. Beyond securing the foundation, there are some minor cracks that must be treated so the building doesn't ultimately crumble. Basically we have two options for saving the lighthouse. The first is to actually move it to safety…like they did with the Cape Hatteras Lighthouse…and the second is to try and secure it where it stands." He paused and again drew a heavy breath. Unhappy about what he had to say, but knowing it had to be said, he continued, "There is quite a bit of difference in the prices of the options. If we pursue the first option, we are looking at a minimum of two million dollars. If we choose the second option we are looking at close to a half million at the least. The lowest bid I received to fix it was four hundred, twenty-eight thousand dollars."

Groans and profanities filled the room. One attendee commented, "That one thousand we got isn't goin' ta do squat." One of the quilters complained, "We can't possibly raise that much!" A murmur of equally despondent voices echoed after her and a fisherman added, "It might as well be a billion."

"Wait a minute!" Abigail was plainly irritated as she clanged the boat bell and hollered, "Wait just one cotton pickin' moment, folks! What is all this negative talk? It's just like what my mother always told me…you can do anything! Anything you want! You just have to figure out how! So alright…we're talking more money than we thought it would be. All that means is that we just have to work a bit harder, but we CAN do it."

Protests still came from some of the attending members until Gretta stood up and scowled at the complaining individuals, "She's absolutely right. What a bunch of whiny wienies! What would you have us do? Give up without a fight? It's our lighthouse…it's up to us to do this!!!" She scanned the room of abashed faces, of shut mouths. Not receiving any further argument she sat back down and muttered, "Good."

David glanced at the outspoken woman and then out at the rest of the group. With a weak grin he said, "I would also like to add that I have found space in one of the warehouses to store the items collected for the yard sale.

To make it easy, you can drop your items at the general store and either Ben or I will take them out to the warehouse...or you can drop them directly at the ol' Slawyer warehouse, but only on Mondays or Tuesdays." He returned to his chair.

Abigail quickly summoned the next speaker, "Eric, would you like to tell us what you have been doing?"

He stood up from his seat and, still trying to overcome his nervousness at the prospect of speaking in public, relayed what he had to announce. "I've set up a web page for our group to tell the world about the lighthouse and how it needs help. I think it looks pretty good so far if I do say so myself, but it could use some more photos. I've got the site listed on three search engines and should have it on a couple more by the weekend. We've had a couple of hundred hits so far." He started for his seat, but heard some of the older members of the audience mumbling to the others about the possible meaning of his last statement. He stopped and explained, "Hits are good...it's when people look at the site." Detecting a vague, possible comprehension by the elders Eric sat back down.

"Now if anyone has some snapshots of the lighthouse...would you please share them with Eric and the rest of the group?" Abigail called for the next report, "Peter?"

Unlike his nephew, Peter Brown was more than comfortable taking the spotlight. With almost a flamboyance he proclaimed, "Our committee has decided that our first event should be held during the second week of July. That way it will correspond with National Lighthouse Day. We'll hold the yard sale that Friday and Saturday at the corner and have the kudzu festival at the same time...just stretching the event down the road. We can invite people to walk down and see the lighthouse. They can have their picture taken there with the tower. Thanks to Watkins' Used Cars and Boats we'll have flag streamers to hang from the booths to make things look more festive. Also, we have a lot to thank Ocean View High School for...they're willing to loan us nearly two dozen folding tables...and the use of their kitchen. Magnolia May Dubin, the school's chief cook and Lester's aunt, has made the kind offer to help us whip up as much of those kudzu recipes as we would like. All we have to do is supply the ingredients!"

"Second week in July...that's pretty close." The group's president calculated the dates and then asked, "It gives us just about a month, right?"

"That's right! But we can do it!" Peter beamed, "We're already on the way...so get into those closets, attics and basements and dig out those buried treasures! We're going to need them all!"

"Well, okay then." Struck by her son's enthusiasm Abigail grinned broadly while addressing the next chairperson, "Gretta?"

"Well…as you all might know by now we had some vandalism at the tower. Someone came and spray painted graffiti on the tower, again. So, we have once more removed all the filth. If they come back…we will do it again. And if we catch whoever it is…they're going to be sorry!" Trying to soften her disposition Gretta paused before moving on, "We've made good progress in removing the vines from around the keeper's house and we've marked the location where the other buildings would have been. If anyone would like to volunteer their help…even for just one day…even for a few hours…we would love to have you!" She sat down while still glancing around the room.

Abigail agreed, "Yes, please do volunteer your time! Every effort helps…and is needed." She then turned the floor over to the historical research committee, "Okay…Darcy? Elinor?"

As the women looked at each other Darcy took the cue to make the progress report, "We've found the lighthouse to have a rather interesting history. We have begun composing a list of keepers and assistant keepers…and are hoping to hear back from the National Archives regarding some of our inquiries. We've been thinking that it might be good to document the stories that local community members have about the lighthouse…whether they are from direct memory or remembrances that were passed down by older family members. Even if what you have is a legend or a tall tale it might help us to find details of the real history. If people are willing we would like to begin tonight and record what some of you have to recall." Still feeling awkward at public speaking, Darcy retreated quickly.

With committee reports finished the meeting moved on to other necessary business. After a bit of discussion the group voted on a name. At Elinor's suggestion they unanimously chose "The Saint Rosabelle Lightkeepers' Association." A rather brief constitution had been compiled by the officers. It was read by Abigail and approved in a matter of minutes. With no further business presented the meeting was called adjourned.

A majority of the members departed, but a good dozen stayed behind to either share a story or listen to the accounts being told. As the members gathered around, Elinor set up a tape recorder and placed it on the table. She hooked up a microphone and set it in an adjustable holder. Placing a chair in front of the device Elinor requested, "It would be good if you will begin by saying your name."

One after another brief anecdotes poured forth from the older members.

One remembered hearing the keeper singing from the tower and waving back to passing boats. Another recalled visiting the lighthouse during the warm summer months and playing checkers with the two keepers under some trees near the beach. Yet another remembered her mother giving the keepers a pie.

Much to the surprise of those still present Steve Rutton, the prominent and outspoken boatman, approached and took the seat in front of the microphone. Clearing his throat he began, "My name is Steve Rutton…and here is a story as told to me by my late father, Captain Fabian Rutton. The lighthouse keeper…Martin Thurber…was a strange one all right, but not for lack of bravery. It was on a day in late winter…."

~~~~

January 1939

The day began with lustrous blue skies, but by afternoon the weather had begun to change. At first the water and air seemed still with an alluring calm that would enchant anyone unfamiliar with the sea. Soon enough white billows marked the horizon and streams of low flying clouds began to race by, skimming the water and shore, dulling the visible boundaries of ocean and air. Temperatures dropped at least twenty degrees as the wind freshened and filled with a wet mist. Soon gusts whipped the loose sand from the beach sending the grains into uncontrolled flight. They blasted against windowpanes, stung exposed skin, hurt unprotected eyes. Darkened, textured skies matched the inky, slate grey waves. As the wind grew more angry, tossing surf foamed caps thick with froth. The ocean rolled hard, then roared as it collided with the shore to race, hissing up to the beach. By late afternoon the rain began, heralded by great flashes of lightning. The last of daylight was consumed by the tempest.

The moan of the fog horn was blaring from the building below as the two keepers talked in the watch room. Robby was uncomfortable as yet another flash of lightning illuminated the storm-darkened world. He began, "When was the last time we…."

The fog horn released its bellowing call: MWHOAAAAAAH!!

"…checked the grounding lines?"

Martin who was still in unbuttoned foul-weather gear answered, "I looked at them…." He habitually ceased talking a moment before the MWHOAAAAAAH!!

"…last week."

"That's good." Robby glanced down at the metal flooring. The entire tower was connected by metal work. The stairs, the floors, the railings, even the roof was metal and without proper grounding the lighthouse could be an electrical deathtrap.

MWHOAAAAAAH!!

The young man toyed with a piece of stationery and Martin noticed the envelope that was set next to Robby's raincoat on the tool chest. Climbing the narrow ladder to the lantern room Martin asked, "Letter from your parents?" He began to check the fuel reservoir for the lamp.

"Yes." Robby's voice came from below, "Martin...I just filled the lamp!"

"I'm just making sure." Seeing that the supply would last at least two hours Martin again closed the container.

MWHOAAAAAAH!!

The voice from below called up, "My brother moved to Brunswick. He got a good job in the shipyard there, but that leaves just Mother and Dad to work the farm. Dad's asthma has been pretty bad lately."

MWHOAAAAAAH!!

Robby continued, "Why don't you go get some sleep. You'll be wishing you had later." He quipped, "I'm not taking both watches, you know."

Martin gave a light laugh and answered, "Yeah, I know." MWHOAAAAAAH!! "And you're right...I'd rather not be tired later." Reaching for the ladder he paused and watched the rain strike at the windows of the glass room. His eyes refocused beyond the pane of glass and looked out into the gloom. About to turn for the ladder he caught himself. He was not sure of what he saw out in the darkness. MWHOAAAAAAH!!

Sliding down the ladder Martin hurriedly began fastening his raincoat and made for the door which opened onto the rain-washed balcony to get a better look. Robby watched his superior with concern and simply asked, "What?"

"There's something out there."

Not questioning further Robby took his coat from atop the tool cabinet and slid the wrap on. A gust of wind blasted in as the door was opened. Martin stepped out, forcing his way onto the narrow...drenched...slippery catwalk. Pressing forward he began moving around the tower's curvature with both hands grasping the railing. The strength of the wind was brutally strong on the outside of the building and was unhampered by obstacles that would slow its rate at ground level. The assistant keeper ventured after Martin. MWHOAAAAAAH!!

Nearly a third of the way around the metal balcony Martin stopped and he felt his heart race. Pointing he yelled to his coworker, "There! Look!"

THURBER'S LIGHT

A sudden brilliant bolt of lightning followed by a timpani of thunder caused the assistant keeper to cringe and duck, momentarily blinded. Recovering his senses he looked up and beyond the railing in the direction of Martin's urging. There from what seemed to be just beyond the village, if they could have seen the village, was a light. The unidentified beacon was not as high as the tower and definitely not as bright, but it was strong and elevated.

Robby hollered over the wind, "What the heck is that?"

"I don't know!" Martin studied the second light. As the fog horn began to emit another of its mournful cries yet another spectacle occurred. Some distance off from the shore a sparkling streak rose into the sky. MWHOAAAAAAH!!

Momentarily confused, Robby braced for another round of thunder. Then he watched as the bright light silently peaked and diminished to fall toward the blackened, boiling surf. Now realizing what was happening he yelled out, "Flare!" Still clinging to the railing he turned about and headed back for the doorway.

Taking a final look backward toward the unidentified light near the far shoreline Martin was just as befuddled when he saw that beacon suddenly fade, vanishing. Cursing and shaking his head he made his way back to the safety of the watch room.

Robby shoved the door closed behind Martin. Catching their breaths the keepers looked at each other. Knowing what had to be done Robby offered, "I'll radio the Coast Guard."

"All right...good." Martin replied, "Tell them I'm out there."
MWHOAAAAAAH!!

"Martin...." Robby quietly shook his head and gave his superior a worried look. He could have tried to argue, but he knew that it would be to no avail. Martin just nodded in acknowledgment of his coworker's expressed fears and then began down the staircase.

The yacht had struck a shoal and its belly was lodged in sand hidden by the shallow, moving water. Now heaved and battered helplessly by the angry swells the trapped vessel faced the possibility of having its wooden hull broken by the merciless forces of the ocean. The distress was further confirmed by three rain-soaked people on the boat's deck. Spotting Martin's tiny motorboat approaching they hailed the keeper with cries for help.

It took much of Martin's concentration just to keep his craft from being swamped by the waves. Unable to approach closer for fear of the small boat being tossed against the stranded vessel the keeper attempted to survey the situation. His heart quickened as he noticed a dinghy, overturned and barely floating, a few yards from the motor yacht. As he searched the scene, he spotted a figure clinging to the lifeboat, struggling to hold his head above the frigid surf.

Martin quickly grabbed the life saving ring tethered by a long rope and took aim at the battered man. The ocean would quickly drain the warmth of life from the overboard sailor and he might easily succumb to hypothermia, dying of exposure. The very moment Martin let go of the tossed ring his own boat was hit by a swell and his aim was spoiled. The buoy was sent too far to the side. He pulled the tether in and drawing the whitewashed cork hoop from the water aimed again for the hapless man. As Martin let the ring fly it hurled toward the drifting, capsized boat and landed just beyond the desperate seaman. Gently drawing in the extra length of rope Martin watched as the man reached for the buoy, grabbed it and pulled it to himself. The sailor let go of the almost totally submerged lifeboat and hugging the ring allowed himself to be dragged through the waves to the side of the motorboat. Martin was careful of his timing so as not to tip his own boat into a swamping swell as he pulled the nearly drowned and frozen victim into the craft. Still alive but severely weakened the man could do little to help.

Martin returned his concentration to the trio of individuals who remained on board the pummeled motor yacht. Again bringing the motorboat as close as he dared Martin took the life buoy in hand. He gave broad arm signals attempting to show those aboard the rocking vessel what he intended to do. He flung the ring hard through the wind-torn air and nearly missed his mark. Seeing the line coming toward the yacht one of the men on board reached out and snatched the rope loop strapped to the ring before it had a chance to fall to the ocean surface below.

There was a brief discussion between the two men and one woman. The rain beat heavy against the men's yellow oilskin slickers as the woman's sodden dress clung close to her pale skin. Soon they seemed to come to some kind of an agreement. One of the men took the ring and holding it tightly jumped from the unstable deck. Hitting the water he surfaced moments later with the buoy still in his possession. Wasting no time Martin began to haul in the rope, drawing the man close. Wary of the angry oceanic motions the lighthouse keeper again timed his actions as he pulled the fellow into the boat. Looking into the eyes of the new passenger under his securely tied rain hat Martin was surprised to see the fellow was only in his teens.

Meanwhile, a new difficulty had begun. The bottom of the motorboat was filling up with water. Rain and surf were working together to slowly sink the little boat despite Martin's best efforts to keep from being broadsided by the waves. Pulling the hat from the lad's head Martin placed it in the teen's hands and yelled, "Bail!" Weary, numbed and confused the boy held the hat and stared at the lighthouse keeper. Again Martin shouted at the lad to bail water. This time he grabbed the fellow's hands and pushed them, hat and all, down to the floor of the boat. Allowing the sou'wester to fill with water he forcefully yanked the boy's hands up and to the side causing the brine to fly from the rain hat. The rescued passenger was stunned by these actions and continued to stare at the keeper. Suddenly he understood. The teen began to feverishly work at his assigned task, scooping the salt water from the motorboat and dumping it overboard.

Once more Martin returned his attention to the yacht and the stranded couple still clinging to the rain-slicked deck. Picking up the buoy Martin realized that he could no longer feel the weight of the cork in his hands nor could he feel his grip on the rope. His fingers had become numb from the cold. Nonetheless he took aim at the deck, pivoted and drew his arm back for the throw.

Before Martin could deliver the toss the ocean rose in front of him. The yacht groaned as the mighty swell caught it from the side, pushing the entrenched vessel hard. The wooden hull creaked and cracked as it listed, leaning into the brink. The sudden angling of the deck found the stranded pair unprepared. They floundered while sliding on the wooden surface, each grappling for any handhold. The woman was knocked completely off her footing as the ocean continued to shake the vessel. Unable to find anything to grasp she tumbled overboard into the churning surf.

Martin was thrown off-balance by the passing rush of sea and caught himself on the bow of the motorboat as he tried to avoid falling into the surf himself. Regaining his footing he cursed as he heard the small boat's engine gurgle and cough. A cry from the yacht pulled his vision back to the dying vessel and he saw the man straining and clutching the deck's thin railing. In a heartsick wail he called to the woman who was missing from view. Realizing the man's intentions Martin shouted, "NO! WAIT!"

Disregarding the warnings, the man dropped to the waves though he lacked both safety line and flotation buoy. Surfacing he could only think to call to the woman again before diving again below the turbulence. Martin swore out loud. Shedding his own coat and hat he worked to secure the tether line around his waist with the life buoy capping the rope at a few yards length from the keeper's middle. Glancing behind him Martin saw that the teen was aware of what was happening. Then the lightkeeper dove into the dangerously cold water.

Cutting his nerves like a frozen dagger the temperature of the water reached inside Martin making it difficult for him to force his body to obey and move. His clothing was quickly saturated and heavy, slowing his progress further as he began a lumbering swim toward where the man had gone under. The buoy which remained secured to the line trailed behind the keeper as he battled the fluctuating surges of brine. Suddenly the yachtsman broke the surface of the water and gasped for air. He was coughing and sputtering, but would not give up the search for his companion. Before Martin could reach him he vanished again beneath the foam-tipped crests. Reaching approximately where he had last seen the man Martin pulled the life buoy to himself and scanned the waves for signs of the other man. A moment later the yachtsman surfaced nearby, choking and thrashing as he struggled for breath. Martin swam to the stricken boater, captured him from behind and held his head above the churning water.

Now barely able to move himself, Martin clung to both the ring and the regurgitating man. He sensed the line go taut and the pull of the ring, but felt nothing else. The world was growing dim. The yachtsman was pulled from Martin's arms and then he himself was hefted upward. Unable to remain conscious Martin was unaware of the approaching boat horn, the search light, the calling voices.

"Sir...I think he's waking."

The aching, deep burning pain of his body thawing caused Martin to wince and vocalize a soft moan. Stirring he remembered the water, the waves, the need to keep moving or drown. His eyes fluttered as he fought to wake, panicking from the thought of the inevitable death sleep induced by hypothermia would bring. He discovered constraints against his movement and began to gasp for air while struggling to free himself.

"Steady...steady now!" Restraining arms held against his torso as his eyes fully opened. "You're safe, now. You'll be all right."

Trying to focus, Martin thought he heard a woman's voice, but remained confused and disoriented for another full minute while he took in his alien surroundings. His breathing slowed as he came to recognize the noises, sights and smells of medical treatment. He fell back to the bed trying to remember more of what had happened. The nurse gave him a comforting smile and raised the thick blanket back over his chest. A pan filled with hot water had been placed on the nearby night stand. Soaking a cloth in the water and then gingerly ringing it out she placed it on his hand and worked his fingers with the saving warmth.

A uniformed man entered the stark room and neared the bed. He waited until Martin had refocused his vision on him before speaking, "I'm Captain Phillip Roberts of the Coast Guard."

Martin swallowed and struggled to speak, "The boat...there were...."

"You did a very commendable job." The captain spoke reassuringly, "Those men would certainly have perished if you had not been there for them."

"A woman...there was a woman...." An unexpected cough erupted from the keeper's lungs cutting off his words.

With a look of regret the visiting official shook his head, "We haven't found her yet. We are still searching."

~~~~

"They found that woman washed up on the shore a couple days after that," Rutton continued to spin his tale, "all pasty blue and bloated." He watched for the disgusted expressions of his listeners. "It seems everybody around knew Thurber had been a bit strange up to that point, but that's when my father said Thurber really started acting touched." He raised his finger to the side of his head for dramatic emphasis. "He began claiming there was a second lighthouse or some such rot. Well...you know everybody laughed at him...and then it came to him to jump off the tower. Imagine that!"

Chapter Fourteen

The last people to leave the second meeting of the Saint Rosabelle Lighthouse Keepers' Association exited the building. Standing behind the chapel, Carl and Darcy bid Elinor goodnight while Lester scuffed at gravel in the unpaved parking lot. Picking up a couple of rocks the muscular man reminded Darcy, "You said you had something for me?" He pitched the stones one by one across the parking lot, now almost empty, sending them into the depths of the neighboring woods.

"Yeah," Darcy dug around in the pocket of her car door and found the roll of film. Handing it over to Lester she explained, "I took these snapshots of the tower before I removed the graffiti the first time. I've been thinking that it might be helpful to make a few prints of them to compare with the latest rounds of vandalism. I think I remember there being something about the Wreckers then, too." Lester took on a smug, questioning expression while holding the small canister slightly elevated. With a light smile Darcy justified the lack of prints, "Alright…yeah, well, I haven't had a chance to have them developed yet. I just remembered they were in the camera this afternoon." The deputy pocketed the roll of film with a laugh.

Carl's mood was more pensive. He glanced at his companions and asked, "So…what did you think of Steve's story?"

"Well," Lester answered, "we know for a fact that Thurber was honored for his rescue efforts early that spring. The newspaper gave us that much."

Darcy shook her head and mused, "I don't recall any mention of a second lighthouse though…or the woman. That adds a new twist."

Cocking his head Carl warned, "Steve has been known to, uhm…embellish a bit."

~~~~

Martin opened the door to the tavern and scanned the room. He noted each of the seven occupants and found Ike Campbell seated alone at a table. The boat owner was aware of the lighthouse keeper's arrival and as Martin crossed the plank flooring Ike casually greeted the sullen-faced arrival, " 'Evening, Martin." The seaman leaned back in his chair.

"You had something to do with it...didn't you, Ike?" Martin gave the lean seaman a cutting gaze and repeated, "Didn't you?" Across the room the bartender quietly picked up his rag and retreated to the far end of the bar. Once there he gave the pretense of busying himself gathering emptied glasses. Uncomfortably the aproned man continued watching the confrontation with dodging glances. A few of the customers, all local fishermen, began shuffling about. In an exodus they placed their tips on their tables and withdrew out the front door. Only a couple of scruffy fellows who were members of Campbell's crew stayed behind.

Placing the nearly empty beer mug down on the table Campbell calmly replied, "Pardon?"

"That second light was a deliberate attempt to mislead ships! Are you engaged in piracy?"

Ike's eyes flicked downward before he met Martin's glare, "I don't know what you're talking...."

"Bull shit! A woman is dead because of that light!"

"I wasn't the one who lit it."

"But you know who did." Martin's green eyes were intense as he studied the seaman for revealing clues. Determined he demanded, "Who was it, Ike? Was it Warren?"

"There are some things you shouldn't involve yourself in. It isn't healthy. You should leave well enough alone." Ike raised the mug and drained the last of the contents before setting it back firmly on the tabletop.

The keeper's voice bristled defensively as he queried, "Is that a threat?" His eyes darted from one hulking crew member to the next as he watched for their possible attack.

"No...no. Just a warning." Ike stood and placed some coins next to the glass mug. He continued, "And I don't want you coming around to see my daughter any more. You'll just hurt her...break her heart...when you're gone."

Firmly, defensively, Martin replied, "I am not planning to leave."

A bittersweet smile edged into the boat owner's trim beard. He looked at the lighthouse keeper and his eyes held an odd expression—perhaps pleading, perhaps sad. Lowering his sight he shook his head and moved past Martin. He was joined by the other crew members as he opened the tavern door and stepped out.

~~~~

"It's nice of you to come over and help me sort through this stuff." Abigail Hoffer-Brown surveyed the cramped space. The attic was stacked high with the collection of stored belongings. Some of the contents were generations old. Small boxes were piled on larger boxes, concealing old chests and a smattering of aged furniture. Cobwebs hung drowsily, adorning hat stands as well as cupboards. Paintings and other framed items were wrapped in plastic or sheets and coated in years of dust.

"It's my pleasure." Darcy's eyes confirmed her delight at having the chance to explore the noble house's hidden spaces. Glancing about she added, "You sure do have some wonderful things up here. I was wondering…."

"Yes?" Abigail shifted her eyes and gave Darcy that curious expression the older woman was so good at displaying.

"Peter said that piece of brass from the lens…it came from up here when his father was cleaning things out." Eager for a new tidbit of insight Darcy looked hopeful as she asked, "Any idea how something from the lighthouse ended up in this attic?"

"No, not really. I never ventured up here much when Mother was alive. Then after she passed my marriage was falling apart and I just didn't take the time to sort through everything. It must be years since I've even looked at these things. I don't think I've been up here much since the divorce and then it was basically to get my ex-husband's stuff out. I don't have any idea what all we'll find, but I'm sure we'll find some things I can donate to that yard sale!"

"You bet." Darcy smiled and assured Abigail, "I've got a good feeling that we'll need everything people can donate."

"You know…after Peter set the date Eric spent almost the entire night on the computer getting the word out." Every bit the proud grandparent Abigail bragged on the youngster, "That boy has quite a knack for all that modern, technical stuff."

"He sure seems to." Darcy used the opportunity to give her companion an update on someone else making an effort, "By the way…Elinor is not only announcing the events in *The Sawgrass Register*, but she's working on contacting other newspaper and magazine editors that she has met in the past. She's asking them to give the festival some space in their publications as well."

Abigail grinned as she replied, "That's our gal. I've heard she spent a few years in Atlanta at one of the newspapers after she finished college. Guess she decided that the city life wasn't really what she wanted after all. She came back home…and we're glad to have her here."

Before the women could reach the tiny window at the end of the room, boxes had to be shuffled. With some effort they managed to jar loose the crusty, wooden window frame and slide the aperture open. The tiny orifice allowed for a minute, but welcome, amount of air circulation in the dusty attic. Starting near the staircase they began opening cardboard cartons and discovering the surprises inside, stirring up memories for the home's resident. The contents included a wide range of items. Clothing that had gone out of style, an old croquet set, glass Christmas ornaments with their paint fading, all were discovered early in the effort. As each container was carefully searched and sorted Abigail wrestled with the choices of what she would keep and what would go for the benefit of the lighthouse. Those items that she opted to keep were either resealed or moved to the living room for sharing with friends and the family. Those boxes to be donated were carried down the narrow stairway and ultimately organized in the carport.

Returning to the attic they discovered more clothing, old luggage, rolled rugs and dusty flotation devices which were removed to reveal a bottom row of boxes and an antique sea chest. The chest had an unfastened padlock hanging from the lid's latch. The twosome looked at each other for a brief moment, but each knew what they wanted to investigate next. Together they wiped a layer of dust from the old trunk.

The finish on the wood of the chest had darkened with age and the brass bindings were dulled by tarnish. Gently sliding the lean neck of the open lock from the closure Abigail removed the slightly corroded device and laid it aside. Kneeling in front of the wooden box she contemplated the hefty container, "This must have been my mother's. We never did finish going through her things after she died." The lid was stubborn with the old hinges stiff from lack of lubrication. The women worked together to pry the wooden top open. As the lid was raised the contents were revealed: a bevy of old photo albums, loose photographs, antique postcards and a small jewelry box.

After lugging the chest down the stairs and setting it near the living room coffee table the two women needed a bit of a break. With iced tea in hand and resting back in the leather couch Abigail began looking more closely through the chest's contents. She set the painted jewelry box aside for lingering over later. Some of the photographs were so old that she had to check the back of them in hopes of finding out who the people were. Removing a framed image from the back of the trunk Abigail smiled and announced, "Here they are. These are my parents."

Darcy leaned forward from her seat next to her hostess and slightly angled her head to look at the pair in the photograph. The woman was stunningly beautiful and the man was dressed in some kind of military uniform. Pondering aloud she asked, "What's the uniform?"

"Navy. This was taken at the start of the second World War. I've been told that my father was quite a hero. He joined the Navy early on and he rose to command a P.T. boat in the Pacific. He and his crew sank six Japanese submarines," Abigail somberly continued, "before a sub's torpedo sank them. It was a direct hit. None of the crew had a chance. I don't remember my father, really. My mother often told me that my father always wanted the best for us. He left her the entire Hoffer portion of the fishing fleet and the store...which he had inherited when my grandfather died in an accident."

Darcy could not help but ask, "An accident?"

"I was told that it was all sort of queer. There was some kind of hidden debris that snagged his trawling line. He tried to cut the line free, but the boat listed and he fell overboard. He drowned before the crew could stop the engines and pull him in. All my family said he was an experienced fisherman and it made no sense. But when you live with the sea...it occasionally calls in its dues. You can't take it for granted." Studying the framed images Abigail dreamily smiled and commented, "Mother was a beautiful woman...don't you think?" She passed the photograph to her guest.

Taking the picture Darcy looked at the woman in the yellowed photo and replied, "Yes." Held static in time the lean and wispy woman's image was exquisite. Her eyes held a special depth, a special quality. In that moment Darcy realized that she had seen the face before. With shock in her voice she asked, "This is your mother?"

Abigail's voice was edged with concern as she answered, "Yes, Iris Hoffer...Campbell before she was married." Her expression revealed that she had seen her guest's revelation, but also that she was bewildered by the insight.

"I think there is something I had better show you." Raising a finger, motioning that Abigail should give her a moment, Darcy trotted out to her car and fetched the folder from the front seat. Returning inside she opened the folder and withdrew the photograph that she had found in the keeper's quarters. The aged print was now protected by a clear plastic cover. She handed the image over to her perplexed hostess.

Smiling Abigail began to study the photo and queried, "This was taken at the lighthouse?" There was a pause and her smile wavered as she continued her examination. She looked up at Darcy while questioning what her own eyes had seen. Setting the somewhat faded group picture next to the portrait of her parents it was plain to see that it was the same woman in both photographs. Abigail attempted to comprehend the discovery and began sputtering half questions, "Where did you…who…oh, my gosh."

"I found it in the old keeper's quarters…." Darcy corrected herself, "Or rather…it was given to me. The man your mother is standing next to is Martin Thurber."

Glancing at Darcy's picture and then back at her visitor Abigail questioned, "Are you sure?"

With a slight laugh Darcy answered without any hesitation, "Oh yes, I'm sure."

Abigail again looked at the group image and the expression shared between the gallant Martin Thurber and her mother. The older woman reflected, "You mean…it was my mother…who jilted him?" Shaking her head at the thought she asked, "Who gave you this photo?"

"Martin Thurber." Darcy's hostess gave her a shocked and harshly skeptical gaze. Settling back down onto the couch Darcy began relaying her accounts of the ghostly encounters she had thus far experienced with the keeper, his lingering sorrow and his overwhelming sense of need. She explained how she had been led by Martin to find the photo hidden in the wall, how he had confronted her in the tower and how the goat never wanted to go near the house. She even told how she had set up the checkers board so she could practice for her matches with Ben, but had sometimes found herself playing an invisible opponent instead. At first dubious Abigail soon became intrigued. She brimmed with questions and Darcy did her best to answer. The conversation continued even as they returned to the attic.

Chapter Fifteen

February, 1939

Father Leo habitually rubbed the rim of the coffee cup while seated at the small wooden kitchen table. His thick fingers seemed unusually active against the surface of the white, United States Lighthouse Service-issued china. The kitchen was cozy and had been built to government specifications which eliminated the luxury of extra space. At close proximity both of the Saint Rosabelle lightkeepers listened intently to the words of the clergyman as he lamented, "It's gotten bad. The rumors are everywhere and no one seems to really know what is going on. It's been known for some time that F.D.R. has wanted to reorganize the federal agencies. He tried last year, but it didn't get past Congress."

"I remember." Martin cuddled his own cup of warm coffee with both hands, hoping it would chase the chill of the gloomy day. Despite the presence of the fueled and lit coal stove he wore his wool uniform jacket which provided extra comfort against the cold. He remarked, "People said the President wanted too much power."

"It's just a matter of time before he tries again and if it passes there's no saying to what extent things will be rearranged. I'm afraid it will be inevitable that the Lighthouse Service will be involved in the shuffle." Leo stroked the red embossed trim of the cup before raising it to his lips for a slow sip and swallow.

Robby was befuddled and looked to his elders. He inquired, "Why? The Lighthouse Service is one of the most cost-effective agencies the government has. They have to have lighthouses, right?"

Leo responded with a noticeable melancholy, "Yes…that's all true, but chances are pretty good that the Service will go under the control of the Coast Guard."

"But why?" Robby was becoming almost belligerent in his confusion.

Raising his eyes from his coffee Martin answered, "Among other things Roosevelt thinks that it will save the government money."

"What does that mean?" the assistant keeper hesitated while looking to his superior. Then, nearly wincing, he continued in a bleak tone, "We'll lose our jobs?"

Martin sighed and shrugged, unable to answer. Seeing his friend's troubled features Leo interjected and relieved the keeper of the required response, "Everyone is worried, Robby…but no one knows for sure. It isn't fair to hold the keepers in the dark, but even the superintendents don't know. There will be a lot of people that will be affected…one way or another." He paused long enough to take another sip, then added, "You know, you fellows are rare…most light stations have families living at them. The Paskowski family has three daughters. If they have to leave their post it will totally disrupt their way of life. They will have to move and find not only a new income but a new home. The children will have to adjust to new surroundings, new schooling, new friends…all at the same time. And what of the men who are close to retirement? Will the Coast Guard honor their pensions? This may be very, very stressful for a lot of folks. As I said before, you are not alone in being worried."

Robby glanced downward as he came to realize his selfishness. Taking minor solace in the clergyman's words he slowly nodded. Without speaking he shifted his stance and when he raised his eyes he seemed to show an amount of shame.

Looking from one keeper to the other Leo attempted a smile and added, "All we can do is pray for the best and have faith." Both keepers silently nodded in agreement.

Chapter Sixteen

May 1939

Martin held the opened letter and studied the typed words as he slowly entered the workshop.

Robby examined parts of a small boat motor as he cleaned them with a darkened, oily rag. His fingers matched the murky shade of the cloth. Noticing Martin's arrival and the opened envelope he asked, "What's that?"

With paced words Martin answered, "It's a circular from the District Superintendent."

The slow, weighty tones in the keeper's voice alerted Robby to the possibility of bad news. Setting his project aside he solemnly inquired, "Is it serious?"

"It, uhm…yes. Roosevelt is truly going to…." Unable to put it into his own words Martin paused and said, "Well, I'll just read it.

"To all employees:

"You have no doubt learned from the press reports that Executive Order No. 2 under the Reorganization Act, read to Congress on May 9th, provides for the transfer of the Bureau of Lighthouses to the Coast Guard in the Department of the Treasury.

"Under the terms of the Reorganization Act, the Executive Order becomes effective 60 days after it is read to the Congress, unless by concurrent resolution of the two Houses of Congress the plan is disapproved.

"This office will keep you advised of further developments in the matter, and bespeaks in the meantime a continuance unabated of the same loyal public service which has characterized this Service in the past."

"What does all that mean?" Robby wiped his fingers on the greasy cloth.

Soberly Martin replied, "It means we may lose our jobs in sixty days, but the Superintendent wants us to continue doing exactly what we have been doing."

"Oh."

~~~~

Darcy woke in what seemed to be the middle of the night to the noise of heavy rumbles and deep hisses. The sounds seemed too big for any natural animal. Her first thought was that a storm was nearing. Soon the call of rough, masculine voices made her realize that the contractor had arrived to clear the land. Making sure that she was decent, she groggily exited the tent. Finding her sandals, Darcy slipped on the shoes before looking around.

"Hey! Hey!!! You can't stay here!" The foreman shouted gruffly and began to approach the still sleepy-eyed camper. He bellowed, "You hear me? I said, you can't stay here!!"

"I heard you just fine." Darcy calmly zipped up her tent and walked to meet the man toting a clipboard. She levelly stated, "This is my home. I live here."

Giving an amused, uncaring laugh the burly man proclaimed, "Not anymore. You're going to have to move." Then he punctuated, "So get your stuff and get out!"

Working to keep control of herself Darcy explained, "I have permission from the development owners to be here."

"Well sorry, but there's no place for you here. All of this is getting cleared off." The foreman motioned to the two brick structures and everything around them.

"Now…you just wait one minute…." Darcy was becoming more and more agitated.

"No. You've got ten minutes to get off the property or then my boys will help you off!" He began to stride back to the idling diesel trucks, but the flash of red and blue lights stopped his march. Turning to face the arriving patrol car he cursed, "Now, what the…."

Leaving the klaxon lights shining the car's occupants sprang from the two front doors. The young officer who climbed from the driver's seat commanded, "We need to speak to the person in charge."

Gruffly the foreman replied, "That would be me."

"Good." Carl appeared from the passenger's side of the official county vehicle. Stunned, Darcy kept her silence while watching the new arrivals. Carl continued to address the husky man who wore a hard hat, "We have a county court injunction stating that none of the structures on this property may be damaged until the question of proper ownership is settled. Furthermore, we have a court order signed by Judge Howard S. Beisacker that states that any and all land developers doing work within a five-mile range of the Saint Rosabelle Lighthouse must take every precaution to avoid damaging the light station and may in no way hamper the effort to preserve the Saint Rosabelle Lighthouse tower." He paused only long enough to breathe before adding, "A light station, by the way, is defined as not only the tower but all the structures that would serve to assist the lightkeepers in the performance of their duties." Darcy felt her heart race as she heard Carl's saving words. It was all she could do to squelch the urge to shout with triumphant joy.

"What!?" The foreman's irritation became now utter anger and he blasted, "That's crazy! Let me see!" As he grabbed the documents and moved into the headlight beams of the patrol car to read them his anger merged with a defeated frustration. Swearing profusely, he stomped off barking new orders to the crews who were unloading heavy equipment from the trucks.

~~~~

Martin attempted to quell his anticipation and recited in his mind all those things he wanted to say. His pace was swift as he approached the general store. Unsure of what he might encounter he was tense but felt resolute. He would simply have to face whatever confrontations would arise.

The keeper's eyes brightened as he saw Iris sweeping the front porch and he mounted the stairs with renewed strength. She had noticed his coming and excitedly dropped the broom, crying out in anxious delight, "Martin! I've been so worried for you!" Without thinking she reached for him and ran her hands up his arms, grasping his muscular shoulders, bringing him close to her. "There has been so much talk...Robby said that you were ill, but a lot of the fishermen said that you...had lost your senses. Martin?"

"I'm all right. I did have a touch of flu, but that has passed." He brought her hand down and held it gently between his own two hands. Looking into her eyes he tried to explain, "Your father and I are...at odds. He doesn't want me to see you."

She shook her head. "But why?"

"Someone is deliberately trying to wreck boats." Swallowing he confided, "I think your father may be involved. Have you ever wondered where some of that salvage stuff comes from?" Watching Iris' shocked expression he quickly continued, "I think it would be best if you didn't say anything. I don't want you involved, Iris. It could be dangerous and I...I don't want you hurt." Her eyes filled with even greater concern. She began to speak, but Martin raised his hand to her lips and softly hushed her unspoken words. Caressing her cheek he could not help but reveal his innermost desires, "I don't know what the future holds. There's going to be a reorganization in the government and I may have a job...or I may not. I'm going to try and stay on, it's the only thing I can do. If it doesn't work and I'm released I'll have to try and learn another trade. But I do know that if you are willing to be with me...I will find some way to provide for us." He paused, swallowing. Taking a slow, full breath, he continued, "Whatever happens I know that my world won't be complete unless you are there with me." He looked deep into her eyes. "I love you, Iris. You fill my life. I want you...not just during clear, summer days, but always." His heart beat hard as he lamented, "I used to never be lonely at a light station...now I'm lonely every day, every night you are not there with me. I've been willing to wait for you, but now you're going to have to make up your mind. If Henry is the one you want...please let me know. I can't spend the rest of my life like this. Not knowing...not knowing from one day to the next if I'll hear you've married him...if I'll ever see you again...it's torment." He shook his head as he continued, "I can't give you a big home and lots of fancy things. I can't give you servants to cook your meals and wash the clothes. But I'll give you everything I possibly can...every day, for as long as I live. You're the one I love...the only one." Searching her eyes he implored, "You have to choose, Iris. You are the only one who can decide. I'll live with your decision, whichever way it falls."

Martin let go of Iris' hand and his fingers again softly stroked her face. Lowering his eyes he began to turn from the lass when the heavy sound of shoes on the wooden stairs startled both of them. Looking up too slowly Martin could not avoid the direct punch delivered to his head. The lightkeeper reeled backward slamming against the door of the store. Iris gave a piercing cry that filled the air and drew the attention of people passing by.

Henry Hoffer assailed the momentarily-stunned keeper, grabbing him by the shirt, then pushing him against a porch post. Releasing him with one hand the seaman prepared to deal another blow and coarsely roared, "You keep your hands off her! Wickie filth!"

If the physical attack was not enough to anger the keeper, the command and insult to his profession were. Martin pushed the red-faced attacker, causing the latest punch to go into the air. While Hoffer attempted to recover his balance the angered keeper responded aggressively and grabbed the seaman. With his adrenaline rushing Martin pressed the fiery young man into the wall of the store. The force of the impact caused both men to audibly grunt.

In total distress Iris wailed at the pair, "Why are you doing this!? Why!?"

Caroline Campbell threw open the front door and stared out at the brawling men. Aghast, she attempted to scold them into retreat, "What on Earth!? Henry Hoffer! Mister Thurber! What is this!?"

As Henry broke from Martin's hold he attempted to kick his foe, but the attack fell short as men from the street pulled the keeper back and restrained him. Henry began to take advantage of Martin's confinement. Anticipating the attempt, the gathering of townsfolk moved to obstruct the charge. Most of them held Henry at bay while three more removed Martin from the porch, forcing him to descend the stairs. Henry spat out loudly, "This isn't over, Thurber! I swear…this isn't over. Iris is mine!"

Touching the bruise over his eye Martin called back to the heated young Hoffer, "If you really love her…if you really care about her…you'll let her make up her own mind! Her happiness depends on it!" He took one last look at the occupants of the porch—the fierce-eyed seaman, Caroline who showed concern mixed with reflection and especially the one woman whom he had ever truly loved with her eyes now moist with frustrated tears. As he walked toward the docks the sun was lost behind flaxen, billowing clouds and the breeze stirred restlessly. Boat riggings clanged against their masts.

~~~~

The workforce was a strange sight to behold. Gretta in her flowered shorts, shirt and straw hat led the brigade which consisted of nearly two dozen cub scouts, a smattering of scruffy seamen, a quartet of keenly-dressed members of the yachting set, and one or two displaced artists. Lester McKay was on watch to make sure things did not get out of hand. It was not an entirely comfortable situation. The construction crew was barely tolerant of the citizens who were constantly moving in harm's way and slowing the progress of preparing the ground for building. Tempers were tested, but were kept in check by the presence of the uniformed deputy.

Following the bulldozer the locals quickly gathered as much of the uprooted kudzu as possible while throwing the roots into plastic bags. They then ran full bags to waiting pickup trucks. The size of the harvest was amazing as bag after bag filled the truck beds to capacity. The rare, heavy rocks that were exposed by the backhoes and bulldozers were hefted into a wheelbarrow and then carted out to the shore where they were placed on the ocean side of the lighthouse. The team began to build a breakwater in hopes of slowing the shore's erosion as the loss of land threatened to topple the historic tower. Much more effort would be needed to create an effective barrier, but at least they had a start.

Not far into the morning a familiar old truck arrived and parked in the midst of the gathered vehicles. Vern McKay stiffly climbed down from the cab of the pickup and examined the activities. With an alarmed and dubious look he approached his grandson and demanded, "What in the world is going on here?"

"They're clearing the land for construction."

"I don't understand...."

Lester paused, slightly amused by his grandfather's confounded expression, "Well," he explained, "when people move into million dollar homes they usually don't want kudzu growing in the backyard."

"And these folks?" The elder man waved his hand at the strange array of people scurrying about gathering plant roots and rocks.

"May Baker got some recipes for cooking kudzu...so they're collecting the roots. We're also finding some big ol' rocks and they are moving those to help protect the lighthouse."

"Hmpf...." Vern spat with almost an edge of anger. "Well, I had better help with this."

Lester was now the one confused as he watched the older man walk away with an air of agitation to join the group rummaging in the dirt. He called after him over the din created by the equipment, "Granddad?" Not getting a reaction he just shook his head and continued to watch the endeavors.

~~~~

The raindrops struck at the tower's windows, so big they spread and then ran down the surface of the panes. This spring storm had started not long after Martin had returned from town and his confrontation with Henry Hoffer. The weather seemed as bleak as he felt. Robby would be resting now in preparation for the evening's first watch. There was no one to talk to. Idly polishing brass Martin gave only part of his attention to the cleaning and allowed his mind to wander.

Looking out beyond the land he watched the grey surf peak and dip as it was roughed up by the blowing wind. In the inlet a private boat bounced in the increasing chop. As Martin continued to watch he wondered why anyone would be deliberately leaving the port in a small craft during the deluge. Watching more carefully the keeper sensed that the boat was familiar. Laying his rag aside, he fetched a pair of binoculars. Peering through the lenses, he focused on the vessel as it traveled. It was the Campbell's launch! The craft was hit by a large wave and slowed in speed, drifting to a stop. Martin was certain that its engine had stalled. He could see the launch being jostled by the growing surf. Without a second thought the keeper left the tower. The saturated sand clung to his boots as he ran across the wet ground. Martin strode the length of the slippery wharf with the boards slicked by the salt spray and precipitation. Uncovering the station's tiny boat, he released the davit cables and dropped himself into the craft as it floated free. A light puff of exhaust rose as the trusty motor fired, gurgling into life. The rain was coming down with increasing strength and Martin had to work hard to move the boat in the right direction.

    As the motorboat approached the stranded and battered launch the keeper could see Iris armed with a paddle and still attempting to move the launch forward through the rough surf. Spotting Martin she called to him. Hearing her voice his hand clinched harder around the steering handle of the small motor. When the two boats touched Martin quickly tied the mooring line to a stern cleat on his small craft and then handed the line across to Iris. Rain-drenched, her hair hung down in a wet mass. She attempted to move her golden mane aside as she ably knotted the rope to the bow of her craft. It was all the little motor could do to pull the stately launch, but shortly they were safely moored at the lighthouse wharf.

    With the boats secured Martin assisted Iris from the her family's vessel. As she found her footing on the wet boards the lightkeeper placed his arm around her waist and together they began to run for the shelter of the keeper's house.

    Martin opened the door and ushered Iris inside. Water puddled at their feet as he closed the door behind them. Iris was soaked and her dress, like her hair, hung down limply. The keeper was not in much better condition with his shirt clinging to his chilled skin. They looked at each other and despite their sodden appearances they could not look away.

    Spontaneously they were drawn together until there was no space between them. Without regret they embraced each other. Joining in a forceful kiss, they unleashed a passion that had been denied for too long. Their hearts quickened as they realized that at last there were no more barriers. Their bodies craved each other in uncontrollable, ardent desire. There was no questioning, no faltering. The wet clothing fell aside and their skin, sensitive with anticipation, urged for the intimate contact. Their damp bodies warmed as they found the pleasure of each other's touch. Beyond the protective shelter of the keepers' quarters the storm lashed at the windows and lightening streaked the darkening sky. As thunder crashed and rumbled fiercely, the impassioned lovers inside no longer noticed the foul weather. Their rapture was total; their joy in each other unbounded. Sharing themselves completely, physical craving surrendered to release. Even in exhaustion they rested still entwined, their love at last unrestrained and consummated.

Chapter Seventeen

On this spring afternoon the cozy living room of Martin's quarters was comfortably warm. The keeper and his two young guests engaged in one of their favorite activities. The lightkeeper studied the checkered game board, then reached for one of the black discs. Moving it forward he asked the one spectator, "How's your sister?"

"She and my Dad had some kind of big fight." Ben sounded uncomfortable as he explained, "I think it was about that evening when she got stuck in the inlet and you towed the launch over here. Anyway...Dad sold the launch 'cause he said it was dangerous."

Vern cautiously moved one of the red markers toward his tall opponent then looked up at Martin expectantly. The lightkeeper's expression caught the lad by surprise and he asked, "Mista' Thurber...are you all right?"

"Yes." Martin attempted to fain a smile, but inside he felt ill. The launch represented almost the only chance for Iris and him to meet. Now it was gone. The keeper glanced at the game and choked on his words, "That...was a nice boat."

Ben agreed with a sigh, "Yeah."

Martin moved another of the black markers forward before asking, "Ben, does your Dad know you're here now?"

With minor hesitation the lad answered, "He's out on one of the fishing boats." Looking into Ben's eyes the keeper could tell that the youngster was telling the truth, but had probably failed to inform his father when he had the chance.

Giving the adult an odd, inquisitive stare Vern reached for his red game piece and proceeded to jump one of Martin's discs, landing his token in the last row closest to the keeper. With a slight scold in his voice the brown-eyed boy commented, "Mista' Thurber, you not payin' much attention ta' the game."

Taking a red marker that had been previously jumped from the edge of the table the keeper placed it on top of the safe piece, kinging Vern's man. With a faint smile Martin replied, "Guess you're right, Vern. I'm sorry."

~~~~

"Old man Carson's cow is not exactly headline news, but it's better than nothing." Elinor propped herself against the front desk at the sheriff's office. In the back of the room two men joked about the poor heifer and its plight while another officer dutifully sat and pecked at the letters of a computer keyboard, writing up the official report.

"Aw come on, Elly. It took four of our finest to get the ol' girl unstuck." Lester smirked at the newspaper editor, reporter and photographer all rolled into one. "Just think of those soiled uniforms!" Seeing the woman's begrudgingly sour expression he grinned and defended himself, "Well, I do my best to keep you informed. It isn't like we're in a big city with a murder every day...thank God."

"Amen to that," she said wholeheartedly.

A young woman entered the front door wearing a pair of cut-off denim shorts, a loose cotton shirt and carrying a substantial navy blue satchel of mail. Chewing on a large wad of gum she brightened at seeing the conversing pair. "Mail's here, Lester...hey, Elinor! What's up?"

With a casual cunning Elinor replied, "You'll just have to read about it in the *Register*."

"You betcha'. Got your photos back." Handing Lester a padded envelope she also extracted a handful of other materials from her satchel and passed them to the officer. He accepted the small stack and sighed as he sorted through the bills, letters and junk mail. Not wasting time, the postal worker scooped up the out-going mail and tucked it into her bag. Glancing up from the correspondence Lester said, "Take it easy, Peggy."

Watching Peggy pop a bubble as she left the office Elinor questioned the deputy, "Photos by mail?"

Placidly Lester answered, "We've got to keep within the budget somehow."

"Well?" She anxiously eyed the envelope and when no explanation was offered she bluntly asked, "What are they?"

The deputy, with deliberate coolness, taunted the woman, "Curious...aren't you?"

"Oh, you tease! You know that's my job." She furrowed her brow and crinkled her nose at the man, then gently pushed at his broad shoulder.

"Okay, okay." Succumbing to her insistence Lester divulged, "Darcy gave me this roll of film. She said that she had taken photos of the tower before she cleaned it up the first time…and that maybe there might be something to compare with the recent vandalism." He looked at Elinor who was glancing back and forth from the envelope to the officer. "I suppose now you want me to open them."

"Of course!" With an exasperated expression she beamed and joked, "You have to ask?"

"All right, then." He held the padded package and ripped open one end. As he tilted the envelope the folder of photos slid into his large hand. Removing the prints he sat the stack on the desk and took the top few to look at. Elinor reached for the stack and helped herself to about half.

The pair were momentarily quiet as they examined the images, setting some aside while studying others. Elinor suddenly sucked in her breath and emitted a muffled squeak. At the same time Lester grumbled aloud, "What the heck…." They looked at each other. They were both stunned but eager to know what the other had found. They exchanged their photographs and studied the other images.

Within moments it was obvious that they each were confused as to the other's reactions. Lester was the first to speak as he shook his head, "So…it's some guy in a uniform. It got double exposed, I guess. I don't get it…."

"That's not just some guy!" With her eyes wide, Elinor exclaimed, "That's Martin Thurber…inside the tower." Lester gave a blank stare at her and she again tried to convey the importance of the photo, "See? He's standing on the stairs!"

"Are you trying to tell me that this is a photograph of a ghost?"

"Yes!" Elinor effervesced with excitement as she continued, "Exactly!"

"Oh, Elly. Not you, too." He gave a smug smile and shook his head. "Come on. She's got friends in Hollywood, remember? That's some kind of trick photo." He leaned over and pointed to the print still in Elinor's grasp. Reaching for another photo she held, he stated, "This on the other hand…."

"What? Rutton's warehouse?"

"This is an honest photo…showing what could be a dishonest activity!"

As the last of the evening's glow began to fade the three women sat outside just beyond the french doors of Abigail's home. They finished their meal while laughing and talking about all the things they had found while sorting items for the sale. Abigail's eyes twinkled as she exclaimed, "Wait till you see what I've uncovered!" She opened the glass doors and eagerly led her friends into the living room.

A clutter of items which had been brought down from the attic now filled the room. There were rolled charts and cardboard boxes with knickknacks. Old Mason jars filled with seashells shared room on the table with stacks of books. It was the old sea chest however which she chose to share. As she opened the latched lid their attention turned to the contents of the wooden trunk as a collection of photograph albums, portraits and other journals were revealed. Firstly, Abigail selected the photo of her mother and father. Showing it to her companions she explained, "Darcy was here helping me bring things down from the attic when we discovered this picture of my parents. I thought she was going to jump out of her skin when she saw my mother...then she showed me this." She brought out a printed image and showed it to her two friends. "We scanned her original into my computer and made this print."

Staring at the picture May smiled widely and exclaimed, "Gosh! Is that your mother?"

Abigail glanced at both May and Gretta before answering, "Sure looks like it...and that's Martin Thurber beside her." She let her friends study the image a few minutes before setting it aside.

Removing the top album Abigail randomly opened it to show the age and quality of the prints. She turned the page and commented, "There has been so much going on lately I haven't taken the time yet to go all the way through these things. I do want to sort through the photos and choose some to have reproduced. I'll give some to the children and grandchildren. I thought they might like to have pictures of their family tree."

May peered at the images and cheerfully responded, "But of course!"

"This picture of your mother and the lighthouse keeper is weird." Gretta studied the open page of the book while glancing at Abigail from the corner of her eye. She asked, "Do you think that the photograph is legitimate? Or is it some Hollywood special effects trick?"

"Well...there is no reason to think that it isn't real." Abigail's brow furrowed and she displayed an air of seriousness. Looking at the thick-set woman she asked, "How would Darcy know what my mother would look like? And why would she bother creating such a thing? That doesn't make any sense."

May began reaching over to the volume then stopped short and pointed to the edge of a document in the back of the book. She asked, "What's that?"

"What?" Abigail looked at the album. Following her friend's poking finger for the first time she saw the inserted, yellowed sheet of paper. "I don't know." She gently tilted the book closed and then reopened it to the location of the ill-fitting document. The fine parchment had been carefully folded in half resulting in the seam being pressed for years, neatly undisturbed. Carefully extracting the discovery Abigail set the volume down and used both hands to gently unfold the sheet. With intense scrutiny she studied the filigreed borders, the penned signatures, the inscription.

"Oh my! What a find!" May peered over her friend's shoulder. "Your parents' marriage certificate! Now, that is a treasure!"

Holding it out for both of her guests to view Abigail was spellbound. She just stood shaking her head. She finally stammered, "Of all things...."

Gretta's eyes narrowed while looking at the official document. "Abigail...what's your birth date? It's in March, right?"

"Yes...the nineteenth."

"What year?" Gretta gave a slight, awkward smile.

A strange look crept into the corners of Abigail's eyes as she responded, "Nineteen forty." Gretta failed to respond and instead directed her eyes elsewhere. The hostess was growing perplexed and with some impatience inquired, "Why?"

Looking back at her friend Gretta flatly stated, "Your parents were married on the twelfth of November, nineteen thirty-nine." Dramatically she counted the fingers on her left hand. "That's only five months. Abbi...you were conceived out of wedlock."

Chapter Eighteen

June 25, 1939

Entering the store Robby looked around and examined the situation. Iris was standing silently behind the counter. Her somber, glazed expression showed that her thoughts were somewhere other than the general store. The assistant keeper also spotted Caroline who was sweeping the hardwood floor in the rear of the business. Easing the door shut he was careful not to jostle the hanging bells.

Without a word he approached the melancholy Iris. Somewhat startled by Robby's unannounced presence, her eyes opened wide and she drew breath to speak. But before she could utter a sound Robby put his finger to his lips motioning for her to be quiet. Swallowing her gasp she looked at him questioningly.

Robby reached in his pocket, then handed her an envelope simply marked with the printed name, 'Iris.' She took the delivery, slowly opened the flap and removed the white note paper. Delicately unfolding the stationery her eyes began to water as she read the handwritten message. Seeing her mother staring in their direction Iris tried to remain calm and fought back the tears. Stashing the note under the register she said, with a slight crack in her voice, "We will do our best to fill this order."

Without thinking Robby glanced in the direction of the matron then back to the counter attendant. Not knowing what else to do he responded, "Thank you." Hesitantly he headed for the business's door.

"Mister Bowsen! One moment!" Caroline's words caught the assistant keeper as if he had been struck by a harpoon. He reeled for a second and then turned around to see the older woman striding intently in his direction. He thought to flee, but it was much too late.

She confronted the youthful lighthouse keeper who clearly showed his nervousness, "Just what is this special order?" Her tone was not exactly hostile, but it was firm and demanding.

Robby swallowed and glanced at Iris, then stammered, "Cloth. We need cloth."

"Cloth?" Caroline studied the young lightkeeper and added, "That shouldn't be too much of a problem. What kind of cloth do you need?"

Mustering a twitchy, little smile Robby answered, "White."

"White is the color." She examined the nervous young fellow from under her brow, her broom still in hand, then continued, "but what kind do you need?"

Again the young man was dumbfounded. Not waiting further for Robby's response Caroline turned to her daughter and requested, "Let me see that order."

With hopes of alleviating her mother's curiosity Iris interjected, "Sailcloth. They need sailcloth...two bolts worth."

Caroline knew her daughter well and though the lass's words were spoken with confidence there was something in their tone that alerted the older woman. Moving around the counter she spotted the stationery tucked under the register. Reaching for the paper she said mildly, "Here now...let me see the order, just the same."

"Mother, please...." Iris moved to intercept her mother's overreaching grab and their hands both took hold of the note at the same moment. Caroline saw the pleading expression in her child's eyes, but maintained her grip on the sheet of paper. Her steady, insistent gaze became more edged and finally Iris relinquished the note. Robby shuffled uncomfortably not knowing what to do.

Taking the message in both of her hands Caroline read the scribed words. Her expression softened. She looked up at her lovely, watery-eyed daughtger, then back at the note. Finally, placing her hand on Iris's trembling shoulder Caroline gave an agreeable smile and gently corrected her child, "This isn't for sailcloth.... This is for satin and lace."

~~~

June 30, 1939

The Lighthouse Service Tender was anchored offshore with its presence noticeable to all the boats that sailed or motored by. Having delivered its load there was only one more matter left to be dealt with prior to its departure. A special request had insured that Father Leo Richfield had been among the passengers. Now dressed in his finest clerical apparel he watched his friend nervously pace the limited floorspace of the tower entrance while waiting for his beloved. Leo's voice betrayed his amusement, but remained amiable and attentive as he advised his old friend. "Martin, calm down. It's going to be fine. You look good. Just relax."

Martin did look good wearing his full-dress uniform. The brass buttons on his jacket gleamed and the dark blue fabric accentuated his tall, firm build. He had taken great care to make sure every aspect of his official suit was perfect, from the crispness of his tie down to the shine on his shoes. He turned and looked at his friend and began to explain, "Sorry, I just...." Realizing that Leo had probably assisted any number of couples with this same effort Martin swallowed and inquired, "Do all grooms go through this?" He laughed tensely as he received an unsurprising nod from the freckle-faced priest. Martin's hands locked behind him as he tried not to resume his pacing. In an attempt to distract himself he managed to ask Leo, "So have you decided to continue your service with the Coast Guard?"

"I'm afraid not. The church has seen fit to send me abroad to Britain. It seems that my efforts are needed more there right now." The clergyman shrugged, smiled and asked, "And you? Are you going to join?"

Shaking his head in contemplation Martin answered, "I'm going to try and stay on as a civilian keeper. I'm not sure how I would get on...as part of the Guard, but I do know how I feel about the Light Stations. It is a shame Inspector Kern is going to retire, but I'm sure they haven't made it easy on the older men." The keeper peered around the corner of the lighthouse entrance and looked in the direction of the assistant keeper's quarters. Robby had propped himself on the railing of the tiny porch. Also attired in his complete uniform, the young man looked amazingly dapper.

Following his companion's gaze beyond the stonework of the tower Leo commented, "It was nice of you to agree to let Robby leave this evening."

"I'm not sure he was ever really meant for the Service. I always had the feeling that he would rather have been working with the land. When he got that last letter from his parents and he read that his father was needing help...I felt he wouldn't be staying long. With the Coast Guard taking over in the morning...what's one more night?"

"Do you think his girl will be going with him?"

"Becky?" Martin laughed, "She's been looking forward to it."

The priest quietly asked, "Are you going to be alright tonight...carrying both shifts?"

"As if I haven't done it before." The keeper grinned broadly and added, "And anyway...I won't be entirely alone."

"That is exactly what I mean!" Leo's quip caused the men to exchange a light laugh.

Movement at the wooden-frame house caught their attention and both men watched intently as the bride's maid came out on the porch. Becky was dressed in her best church clothes—a yellow chiffon gown with puffed shoulders and a trim lace collar. She was a lovely sight. The bride next appeared from the assistant keeper's quarters. Martin stared in awe at this beautiful vision in white, then his smile grew wide. Inspector Kern followed out of the quarters and Iris gracefully placed her hand on her escort's arm. As the procession began toward the tower Leo patted Martin on the shoulder and with all the enthusiasm of a schoolboy he announced, "Here they come!"

~~~~

Darcy was nestled under the lightweight sheet, dressed in a loose, sleeveless t-shirt and comfortably baggy khaki shorts. The humid heat of summer made the night air heavy and the camper was soundly sleeping. She sprawled on top of the sleeping bag in the cozy little tent that was now held together with patches and adhesive. Waking abruptly, she blinked. In an instinctual reaction she gathered the sheet close to her as a chill brushed her shoulder. Aware of the odd but now familiar feeling of not being alone she rolled from one side to her other and looked up to see Martin's pale, luminous form crouching beside her.

"Get up!"

Momentarily startled by the ghost's mood her eyes grew wide. "Look…I know you're not happy about the construction…."

"Please…get up! I need your help. They're here." He seemed to look beyond the dome of the tent and then slowly faded from Darcy's view.

"They? Who are they? Oh, no, Martin. Please…I like you, but one ghost is enough." Darcy paused as she felt the air warming around her. Suddenly regretful of her rebuttal to the phantom she tried to reconcile, "Martin? I didn't mean…. I just…." She fell silent knowing that he had gone.

Darcy scratched her head as she sat up. An odd feeling crept over her and she felt compelled to leave the comfort of the tent. Stepping out of the small dome she slipped on her sandals and stretched. Quietly looking around she took in the night sounds which she loved. Frogs croaked to attract mates and insects created a constant buzzing, chirping din. Neither hearing nor seeing anything unusual she was about to go back into the tent when she heard whispering. The chorus of frogs abruptly quieted, leaving only the shrill sound of flying insects and whatever presence had disrupted the night. Concentrating Darcy could make out voices talking low. The muted sounds soon ceased and memories of her second day at the site came flooding back to her. She remembered the whispering voices—that is, if there had truly been more than one.

Her uneasiness was partially dispelled as she caught a glimpse of a light. Some distance from the tent, possibly on the far side of Martin's grave, a yellow beam of illumination flickered, disappeared and then flickered again. Soon she heard the sounds of a shovel being carefully prodded into the ground. Whoever these people were they were of the living, not of the dead. Her view of the scene was partially blocked by the side of the keeper's quarters. Not knowing who or even how many people might be beyond her view she tried to think of a plan of action. She thought about phoning for help, but then remembered that the cell phone remained charging in the car.

Her mind raced. These intruders were working under the cover of darkness and so probably had something to hide. And people with something to hide often became violent in order to keep their secrets. The sounds of dirt being moved was unmistakable. She surmised that they were either digging to hide something or uncover it. They might be treasure hunters seeking to steal a piece of history from the site, but who could tell? There was no way to see from her current location.

Moving as silently as possible Darcy picked up the flashlight from where she kept it inside the tent, near the door. She hefted the light's heavy, metallic barrel in her hand and was pleased. It might have to serve as a weapon should the need arise.

Without turning on the flashlight she slipped out the side of the tarp-covered compound. Facing the main trail and not the newly cleared land, she thus avoided exposure to the intruders. Constantly scanning the darkened terrain Darcy edged her way along the front of the old keeper's quarters. She had progressed halfway along the building when a new, quietly crunching sound caught her attention. Looking down toward the dirt road she saw an unlit, shadowy form slowly approaching in the darkness. It was some kind of vehicle with its headlights off, possibly a pickup truck. There was no way of knowing whose vehicle it could be—whether the owner was friend or felon.

Exposed in the open and sure to be seen by the driver of the truck Darcy could think of nothing to do except quickly slip into the doorway of the deteriorating building. Still moving without the assistance of light she tangled her foot in the remains of a kudzu vine and fell ungracefully to the deteriorating plank floor. Her landing was hard and caused a resounding thud. Darcy managed to swallow the instinctive, guttural response to the bruising, but the silence had been broken nonetheless. Quickly feeling around her prone position she retrieved the dropped flashlight.

From a distance a muffled male voice asked, "What was that?"

Darcy thought the question came from behind the building. She quickly moved to regain her footing while fearing that at any moment she might be discovered. Feeling her way along to a front window she peeked out. The truck had come to a stop. It looked like both of the cab doors were opening and two men were getting out.

"I didn't hear nothin'," a man's voice that crackled with a touch of age answered from behind the building. Though the voice sounded familiar to Darcy, she was unable to identify the speaker. She continued to watch the men from the truck. The shadowy forms split with one heading toward the cistern and her encampment while the other moved toward the keeper's quarters. Much to Darcy's discomfort she saw that the one approaching her was armed with a pistol.

She quickly backed away from the opening and went as far into the dark room as possible, all the while feeling for more of the greenery snags. She had thought that the building had been cleared of such things, but her ungraceful entrance had proven her wrong. Reaching the back wall she crossed over and ducked into the bedroom just as the man reached the brick structure. Darcy held her breath and stayed statue-stiff, hugging the wall, until she thought that she had given the armed figure enough time to pass the area.

Easing to the edge of the interior doorway she slowly moved to look back at the building entrance. Suddenly she was grabbed and forcefully yanked forward. As she drew breath to yell a large hand firmly clamped over her mouth. Darcy's first thought was to fight, but as she began to shove hard against her assailant her intuition kicked in. It took a few seconds for her to be completely certain who had taken hold of her. The inside of the building offered little in the way of light and Lester McKay's dark skin served to make his identity all the harder to confirm.

Now understanding that she was in no immediate danger Darcy nodded to Lester's signal to stay quiet. He released her and motioned for her to stay put. Leaving her behind in the building Lester drew his weapon and cautiously crept out of the quarters.

Darcy could agree to being quiet, but it was not part of her nature to be left out of the action. Waiting only a beat after Lester's departure she ventured out on her own again. She first moved to the door and peered out. Seeing Lester slip around the far corner of the building she sneaked outside. Darcy inched her way along the front of the quarters and reached the corner. As she was building up the nerve to look around the edge of the brick she heard Lester's voice shout, "Oh, for crying out loud! What in the devil...."

These were not the words that Darcy had expected to hear from the law officer. In puzzlement she peeked around the corner and saw a cluster of flashlight beams. Openly walking toward the scene she began to distinguish the people present. Exposed by the yellowish tungsten torchlight a dumbfounded Vern McKay and equally flustered Ben Campbell stood next to a hole they were digging near the lightkeeper's grave. The other person having arrived with Lester was now discernible. Carl stood to the side, but was still visible in the ambient light. Darcy joined the gathering as she turned on her own flashlight. Lester gave her an annoyed look, but voiced no objections to her arrival.

Putting away the pistol Lester looked at his grandfather with a mixture of irritation and confusion. He inquired, "Granddad, what are you doing?"

Earnestly the old man answered, "Diggin' a hole."

"Well...that much is obvious." Unamused the deputy asked, "What's the hole for?"

There was no immediate response and the two older men looked at each other. Finally Vern said, "Guess you'd better arrest us."

Lester tried to maintain his patience, but was growing frustrated as he requested, "Why don't you just tell us about it first?"

The elder McKay glanced to the hole and admitted, "I...concealed evidence."

"I don't understand." Lester shook his head and asked, "Evidence of what?"

"We were here when Lighthouse Keeper Thurber died. I hid some things...in a pickle jar. I later buried it near ol' Martin so he could have 'em close." Looking up from the pile of earth Vern mused, "How'd you know we were here, anyways?"

The deputy confessed, "I didn't. I was actually coming to talk to Darcy about her photos when I found Carl, here, jogging up the road."

Carl looked at the pair of excavators and commented, "I saw your truck go by without its lights on...didn't know it was you, though." He shifted his stance and continued, "I figured that there was some kind of trouble."

Darcy smiled at the idea of Carl coming to her aid, but her curiosity could not be contained. She asked the officer, "So...what were you going to tell me about the photos? They didn't get lost, did they?"

"No. As a matter of fact some of them are now being held as evidence. You had taken a few shots on the docks and had managed to catch Rutton's warehouse with illegal cargo. Most of his crew are being held on charges of poaching. They were collecting sea turtle eggs and then smuggling them south. The eggs can be sold at a high price in the Caribbean because they're thought to be an aphrodisiac. Seems Steve was using this stretch of beach as a collecting area. The walks you took along the beach at odd hours made him nervous that you might see his crew in the act. That's why he had them trash your camp—hoping to scare you off. He sure didn't want you to win that bet. With the lighthouse potentially becoming operational, lighting up the area and folks again frequenting the shore, Rutton and friends would have been out of the poaching business in a hurry. We've been unable to find Steve and a couple of his crew…and I thought you should be warned."

Carl suddenly waved to the group in exaggerated movements and motioned for them to be still. Each person watched the man for further explanation. After a moment Vern began to grow impatient and blurted, "Well…are we goin' inta town or not."

"Granddad, quiet." Seeing that the elder would not stay silent unless given a reason Lester urged in a hushed voice, "Listen…there is someone on the beach." As the group listened the muffled sounds of profanities uttered by rough, masculine voices drifted in from the direction of the tower and the surf. Immediately the deputy switched off his flashlight and motioned for all present to do the same. Now in the complete darkness, save for the soft light of the moon, the law officer quietly began to move toward the voices. It took him only a moment to realize that the entire group was attempting to follow him. Shaking his head at them he pantomimed that they should remain where they were. Almost in unison the rest of the impromptu gathering pointed fingers, shook heads and motioned that they too were going to go see what was happening. Lester wiped his face with his hands. He was unhappy but whispered gruffly, "Okay, but stay back."

Vern who was clutching the shovel like a long-handled club looked to Ben and asked, "What'd he say?"

Lester was about to turn around once more when the voices coming from the beach altered in intensity. No longer muffled the words were shouted and plainly heard, "Steve! Get out of there! Mother of God!" No longer waiting Lester pulled his pistol and ran for the beach. As the group followed at their various paces the sounds coming from the shore filled the air. Dull banging reverberated through the darkness and an awful scream that was somehow smothered came from the tower. The stench of gasoline wafted in the stagnant atmosphere.

As Lester reached the scene two robust seamen were struggling with the door of the lighthouse. Half a dozen emptied gasoline containers lay strewn at their feet. The door was sealed, resisting their tugs from without and a pounding bombardment from within. A panicking voice from the other side of the portal pleaded for escape. Spotting the lawman both of the sturdy crewmen ceased their efforts on the door.

One of the men ran for a dinghy which had been pulled ashore while the other stood his ground aware of the deputy's readied gun. As Lester took aim at the fleeing suspect the second crewman saw his chance. Slinging sand into the officer's face he made a grab for the firearm. His footing slipped in the sand and he crashed into Lester, sending the gun flying through the air. The pistol landed on the beach, just out of reach. With his eyes stinging from the grains of sand Lester grappled with his foe, attempting to prevent the seaman from reaching the weapon.

Arriving in time to see the flight of the dislodged firearm Carl made a dive to recover the pistol. The first seaman had managed to push the boat clear of the sand and now pulled the motor's cord trying to fire it into life. Taking aim Carl squeezed the trigger and the sound of the shot exploded over the roll of the waves. Startled seabirds left their roost, squawking and calling in alarm. Spotting the bullethole in the boat's hull perilously close to where he sat the seaman immediately raised his hands and froze in place.

As Darcy surveyed the action she saw the deputy wrestling with the determined crewman. Not knowing what else to do she joined the pair and wrapped her arms around the suspect in hopes of impeding him. The threesome lurched and stumbled around struggling. A sharp metallic sound resonated in their midst and the seaman abruptly dropped to the sand, limp. Vern McKay stood a mere shovel-length away, firmly gripping his makeshift weapon. Finding themselves without an opponent, Lester and Darcy looked at the victorious elder in astonishment. With a toothy smile Vern asked, "You kids alright?"

Darcy nodded to Vern and then joined Lester in scanning the scene for more trouble. Ben had teamed with Carl and was in the process of securing the prisoner from the boat. There was a momentary silence. It seemed that the event was over when a sudden, hollow thump from the tower entrance caused the startled threesome to flinch and jump. As they watched the building's entrance the door drifted open. Carl also had noticed the sound of the door coming ajar and quietly joined those outside the entrance. Lester motioned to Carl. The former policeman understood the unspoken request and handed over the pistol to its rightful user. Approaching the portal the deputy fanned his hand in front of his face as he got a whiff of the concentrated gasoline fumes. Lester took a deep breath of fresh air before he carefully crept down the thick wall of the entryway. At the last minute he clicked on his flashlight and shined the beam into the chamber, hoping to blind whoever might be hiding. Steve Rutton lay cowering on the floor whimpering with his arms wrapped around his head. Entering the conical room Lester moved toward the puling figure. From out of the corner of his eye Lester caught a glimpse of movement on the lighthouse stairs. "HOLY…!!!"

Outside of the old tower the sound of the Lester's voice was as clear and loud as if he had not been inside the structure at all. Carl began to charge for the door, but the deputy came rushing out of the lighthouse towing the boat captain as if he were a child's blanket. Lester shrieked to the group, "Don't go in there!"

Alarmed by the large man's exclamation Darcy tried to determine what the officer had found. "Lester? What's in there? What is it?"

With a horrified expression on his face the deputy bellowed, "Your freaking ghost is real!"

Chapter Nineteen

"Ben!" Through the glass panels Abigail spotted her uncle seated in the austere side room of the sheriff's office. The man's forlorn expression matched the stark furnishings—a heavy table and eight straight-back chairs. Making a direct line for the door to the meeting room she was intercepted by a slender, young officer who told her that she was not allowed to enter. Already agitated Abigail shook off his raised hand and gave him a lethally sharp glare. She began to give the man a verbal debasing, but was interrupted when the door to the partition opened. Lester McKay gave the youthful deputy a nod and thereby saved his fellow officer from the complete onslaught. He motioned for Abigail to enter the meeting room, holding open the door for her. She quickly entered.

Ben stood as Abigail approached. She clasped the old fisherman, embracing him. Nearing tears she pleaded, "Where have you been? I was so worried! I've been trying to find you since this afternoon! And then I get a call saying you've been picked up for questioning!" She looked around the room at the odd gathering of people. Darcy, Carl and Vern all sat quietly either unable or unwilling to say a word. With labored smiles and uncomfortable glances they silently acknowledged the woman. Lester and a junior officer leaned against the backs of chairs as they watched the reunion. With a touch of desperation Abigail implored, "What is this all about?"

Lester motioned to the old pickle jar which rested centrally on top of the meeting table. The rusted lid had deteriorated through the years and become brittle, thin, and melded to the jar's rim. The contents of the deep glass container were profoundly significant. Broken portions of large, curved prisms filled the glass bottle. Brown stains could be easily seen where blood, long since dried, had smeared on the shards of the once magnificent Fresnel lens.

In a low voice the young officer addressed his superior and suggested, "Maybe these folks should wait outside." He motioned to the three people who were not directly involved with concealing evidence.

"I don't mind if they hear," Vern sounded his opinion. His voice sounded tired and weary.

With sad resolve Ben forced out the words, "I want...them to...hear."

"It's okay," Lester assured his coworker and then turned to Abigail, "but you'll have to sit at a distance. These men need room to think...and remember." Gently guiding her to a seat, he gave the still-befuddled woman a reassuring pat on the shoulder.

The side room with its glass partition gave the group at least partial privacy and a moment of quiet. Staring at the aged jar, Vern sat forward in one of the chairs. He motioned to the container and said, "That ain't all of it. I've never been a thief in my life, not before, not since...except fo' that night. But I had to then.

"I had gone inta the store to get my mama some ointment fo' her hands. I was twelve then. I liked ta look at the comic books, 'specially Superman. I couldn't read a lick...still can't...but I would look at the pictures. I was in the back...lookin' at the books when I overhears these fellas talkin'. At first I didn't pay them no mind, but then I got ta listenin'. One says, 'You heard the Commander. We go first thing in the mornin' and take charge. If Thurber ain't ready...that's just too bad. Once we get there, we're under orders to get rid of everything with the Lighthouse Service emblem on it.' I couldn't believe what I was hearin'. I put up the book and tried ta peek at these fellas. They all be dressed in clean, white uniforms. Then the other one says, 'Well, what are we gonna' do with the stuff?' The first one says, 'I don't know...dump it in the inlet, most likely. They'll probably order this one shut down soon anyway...replace it with a radio buoy.' The other one was lookin' at the stuff on the back shelf...the stuff ol' Ike salvaged and sold. He says, 'Can you believe they sell this stuff?' I guess I must'a been standing there with my mouth wide open 'cuz one of them sees me and shoves the other fella. They both got quiet, lookin' at me...then one of 'em says to me, 'Guess you neva' seen a uniform before.' I says, 'None like yours.' Then I hear Mrs. Campbell yellin' at me, 'Vern! You get that ointment ta your mother!' I says, 'Yes ma'am,' an' I leaves the store, but I hears one of them...one of the men...say he's staying at his sista's fo' the night and he invites the other along.

"Well, I had ta find Ben an' tell him what I heard. So, I went ta the Campbell house. My mama was fixin' their dinner. I gives her the jar of ointment, then went ta find Ben. I was about ta talk ta him when he gives me the sign ta hush. He was ease-droppin' on his daddy talkin'. I knew the other voices that was with him...it was Warren Hoffa' an' his son, Henry. Henry, he was a bully...always taken' stuff from us...an' his ol' man was no nicer. I was gettin' scared an' I wanted ta tell Ben what I'd heard. I tried ta pull Ben away, but he wanted ta listen ta what was going on in the parlor. So I stayed with him...an' oh, what we heard.

"Mista' Campbell was so angry he was spittin'. He says, 'What you mean, you saw Iris goin' with Dinkle to the lighthouse? I told her ta neva' go there again!' Next I hears Henry sayin,' 'She's in love with him, Mista' Campbell. I hate it, but maybe we should leaves thems alone.' I remember...that shocked me. That was about the kindest thing I'd eva' heard Henry Hoffa' say. Ol' Ike, he scream back, 'No lighthouse wickie is goin' ta steal my daughta'. Over my grave!' Warren, he says, 'Enough. I don't care about your daughta' or what you do 'bout her. We got otha' problems. Tonight is our best chance. If we wait till the Coast Guard takes over, we'll neva' put that light out. We gotta have it dark ta have any chance o' catching that shipment.'

"Now I was real scared an' I pulled Ben out'a there. We gets outside an' we agree...we gotta go ta the lighthouse. The sun was low in the sky when we sets out. Ben an' me, we had a little boat...a rowboat we used for fishin' an' all. We'd been over ta the lighthouse many times in that boat...but always goin' over in the mornin'. Well...here it come gettin' dark an' there was a strong tide. Ben, he was strong an' all. Fourteen, I think. An' I worked them oars too, but it was hard work ta get the boat across. It must'a taken us hours. It was real dark, but we could see the ol' lighthouse lamp glowin' an' it would flash 'round, lightin' up the place.

"By the time we done got the boat ta the far side of the inlet...an' ready ta pull it down the beach, we saw some high fallutin' speedboat comin' up the channel. We hurry an' pull that rowboat up on the beach and tries ta hide it in the sea oats. We watch that mota' launch race on by an' I swears I saw 'ol Ike standin' at the wheel. I don't think he ever saw us hidin' in the shadows an' all. We knew we had ta get to Martin an' Iris an' warn them. But by the time we reach the light station...Ike's boat already be there an' we knew there be trouble already. We hid as best we could while tryin' ta see what was goin' on."

~~~~

"Martin?" She pulled him down toward her again and gripped his back under his nightshirt. He surrendered to Iris' wants. He leaned over her prone body as she lay on their wedding bed. Her lips were moist and desirous, her caress imploring him to stay as he kissed her. After rubbing his forehead gently against hers he raised up and softly stroked her hair, her face. She protested the inevitable, "No, please, don't go...."

Martin gently removed her hand from his side and kissed every finger before tenderly placing it on her chest. "I won't be long...."

"Please...."

"You know I have to tend the light." He stood and stepped into his work trousers. He finished buttoning his pants and with one more fond glance at Iris he left the room and his young bride. "I'll be back. I love you, Iris Thurber."

Stepping into the night beyond the warm glow of the quarters Martin pulled on his suspenders. He set about taking care of the required chores as expediently as possible. As he fetched a full, five-gallon canister of fuel from the oil house he hummed a hearty tune. His heart, mind and desire were back with his lovely lass. With an unusual spring in his step he mounted the spiraling tower stairs. Reaching the watch room the keeper hefted the canister up the ladder to the lamp room and then filled the lamp reservoir with the fuel. Sliding back down the ladder Martin set the emptied canister down on the metal floor and then took the binoculars from the top of the tool cabinet. With the barreled glasses in hand he went out onto the narrow observation balcony.

Breathing in the moist night air he began his routine survey of the waters for signs of mariners in distress. His eyes searched the horizon and then lowered to the line of the shore. His scanning drew to an abrupt halt when he saw a small, dark form revealed in the rotating light of the beacon. It was a tiny boat, Ben's boat, pulled ashore at some distance from the light station. Martin mused to himself, "Now what are those boys up to?" He continued to look along the shoreline while scanning for the possible, uninvited, juvenile guests. His eyes grew wide as he saw the sleek, unexpected motorboat moored at the wharf.

~~~~

"We hears screamin' comin' from Miss Iris an'...Ben, he move ta run ta her, but I holds on ta him. Then we sees ol' man Campbell an' Henry Hoffa' draggin' Iris toward the launch. Henry, he was carryin' a shotgun and they was yellin' at Iris ta shut up and get in the boat."

~~~~

They must have known the keepers' schedules, aware of their reliance on timing. Martin's mind raced, focusing on the possibilities. His bride's cries pierced the still night air, confirming Martin's worst fears and filling him with complete anguish.

~~~~

"Martin, he come bustin' out o' the tower door. He starts ta charge at Ike an' Henry, but Henry, he pulls up that ol' shotgun and he points it right at poor Martin an' he say, 'Don't come no closer!' Martin, he stops short, not knowing what ta do. He says, 'She's my wife. We're married now. There ain't nothin' you can do about it.' Ol' Ike, he shout, 'The hell you say,' and drags Miss Iris ta the boat. She was all cryin' an' fightin' an' callin' ta Martin, then beggin' her ol' man ta let her go. Martin, he try and go ta her, but Henry held that gun up and says, 'Martin, please don't make me.' Ol' Ike says, 'Shoot him, Henry. Jus' go ahead and shoot him!' Henry, he don't respond, but just stay still...aimin' that gun."

~~~~

Martin's heart pulsed hard and his mind reeled. If he charged Henry he was sure to take a full round of burning lead, but he could not just stand still while they took away the one woman he had ever loved so dearly. In a desperate attempt at reason he cried out, "Don't you understand what I'm saying?! We've been wed!" He began to step forward.

There came a terrible crashing noise from above. Martin instinctively ducked as a shower of broken glass dropped from the height of the tower and landed all around him. As the barrage subsided he turned to see what had happened.

~~~~

" 'Twere a horrible sound, that crystal an' glass breakin,' an' then it come again from up the tower. I could jus' see that man up there. Martin, he had ta decide what ta do, but as he look up at the tower Henry run fo' the boat and they were off. That boat ripped the water leavin' so fast. There was no way ta stop that launch...so Martin, he run fo' the tower. He must'a flown up those stairs...."

~~~~

Breathing heavily Martin spiraled up the interior of the tower. The sounds of more breaking crystal reverberated through the chamber like cannonballs smashing musical notes from a score, each explosive shatter falling into a cacophony of discordant tinkles. Traversing the dizzying and ever-narrowing stairs, his emotions spiraled like his flight. They had taken his beloved, his bride. All of his hopes for the future were held captive. Would he ever see her again? How could he have stopped them? He must find a way to free her, but how? In time he'd resolve matters, but now he had to fight for that which he also held dear, his sentinel, his life's labor given to the Light Service, his honor and his history. Tiring from exertion, but determined to try and protect the beacon for which he was responsible, Martin continued up the stairs.

Reaching the lamp room ladder he took to the rungs. As he reached for the top bar he received an abrupt, harsh kick to the head. The blow was solid. Martin clung to the metal rungs and hung there though his senses were reeling. As the vandal peered down at the keeper Martin recognized the hulking form of Warren Hoffer.

Jumping down the ladder Hoffer plucked the dazed keeper from the rungs. Martin had not been thrown to the floor as the attacker had expected. Instead, the keeper wrapped his arms around the burly, wild-haired seaman in an attempt to restrain him. As Martin grappled his opponent's shoulders the powerful man twisted about, slinging the keeper to and fro. Catching an instant's opportunity Martin found his footing and used the immense man's own motion to send them both to the floor. Together they tumbled out of the watch room door onto the catwalk.

The embattled pair rolled around amid glass shards on the textured metal, kicking and straining nearly seventy feet above the ground. The sharp slivers tore into the embroiled men's clothing, cutting and embedding in their skin. Warren's strength was greater than that of the tower's defender and he pressed Martin between his back and the metal flooring. Raising up, the seaman slammed back down repeatedly using not only his strength but also his weight to knock the air from Martin's lungs and the strength from his grasp. Succumbing to the pounding, the keeper's hold weakened and the seaman broke the restraining grip. Warren stood up with a malicious delight in his eyes. Gasping for breath Martin was unable to avoid the seaman's grab. Martin was yanked from the floor and hoisted into the air. Grinning wickedly, the blood-crazed mariner propelled the hapless keeper outward above the railing.

Martin caught the metal crossbar and dangled with his feet finding nothing but emptiness below him. His knuckles grew white with strain as he struggled to maintain his grasp on the railing. Warren sneered and looked around for a useful battering tool. A broken section of curved prism with its jagged end glistening caught his eye. The seaman laughed as he snatched the makeshift weapon. Battling gravity, Martin involuntarily groaned as the burning pain of his fatigued muscles increased. Finally using the last of his strength, he labored trying to pull himself up to the level of the railing.

~~~~

"I could see the flash o' that prism comin' down on Martin's hands…not once, but twice. It musta' smashed his hands on the railing, 'cuz then he fell. He didn't cry out or nothin'…but that heavy thump…what a sickenin' awful sound, him hittin' the sand. Ben screamed an' he got up an' ran fo' the keeper. I tried ta stop him, but he was bigger 'n me and wouldn't be stopped. I jus' dug in an' prayed the man in the tower didn't see me. Ben run ta poor ol' Martin where he lay."

The sound of sobbing halted Vern's dissertation. Ben's emotional, but stable, voice caught everyone in the meeting room by surprise, "He wasn't dead...." Abigail wanted to go to her uncle, but Lester placed his hand on her shoulder. She reluctantly remained seated. Ben wiped his eyes and continued, "He...looked up...and saw me. I tried...calling...to him...trying...to tell him...not to die. I didn't...know any better. I didn't...want...to...believe it. He...tried...to talk. I...leaned over...to hear him...his voice...was so...soft. He said..., "You'll...have to...keep...the light, now, Ben."

~~~~

"And...tell........Iris...I............love...her...."

~~~~

"That's...about all...I remember...of...that night." Ben paused, but then chokingly whispered, "I never did...tell her." Lowering his head the old fisherman's tears fell freely, now unrestrained after years of denial.

Vern put his weathered hand gently on his friend's back in an intimate display of genuine comradeship. He continued where Ben had left off, "Martin, I don't know how, but he clung ta life. The fall musta' broke his back, 'cuz he wasn't movin' his limbs none...but I could see him laborin' hard ta breathe. I saw Warren Hoffa' come out o' the tower an' I wanted ta yell ta warn Ben, but I must'a been too scared...nothin' came out. Warren was on Ben in a flash an' held him up like a rag-doll. He laughed like somethin' wicked...like a devil. Ben, he screamed an' kicked, but ol' Hoffa' was a monsta' of a man, huge. He just drug Ben into the water an' pushed him unda'. Hoffa' pulls him up an' he says ta Ben, 'If you eva' say a thing, I'll kill you...an' your nigga' friend, both!' He pushed him back unda' the water an' holds him there. Then he pulls him up an' demands Ben say where I was. Ben, he coughed an' gasped, but he didn't say nothin'. Again an' again Hoffa' pushed Ben back unda' an' pulls him up...each time yellin' fo' Ben never ta say a word, or else. He kept doin' this...till Ben, he jus' run out o' energy ta fight. He jus' went limp in that ol' monsta's grip an' all the while Hoffa' kep' yellin' at him. It might'a been jus' a few minutes, but it seem like fo'eva' when finally this boat come by an' wave ta Hoffa'. He jus' drug Ben up on shore an' dump him there.

"Hoffa' was 'bout ta go, when he musta' seen Martin still breathin'. Hoffa' cuss'd a streak an' rips off his own shirt. He wads it up and stuffs it on Martin's face, leaning heavy on it with his whole self. Martin, he couldn't help himself none…not even able ta raise so much as a hand in defense. Seem like Martin's chest heaved up, shakin' for a full awful minute…all the while Hoffa' cussin' at him ta die. Finally Martin just collapse an' lays still. Hoffa' gets up, takes his shirt, an' then goes down ta the end of the dock. He got inta that boat…an' they left an' didn't look back.

"When I come out of hidin,' I go over ta Ben. I thought he was dead. He lay there, all pale an' grey-like. I lean over him and beg him ta be alive an' lo' if he didn't start ta coughin' out water, breathin.'

"Lawd, what a mess. By the time I reached Martin he was jus' layin' still, starin' up at the tower. His eyes was all fixed, waxy an' distant…an' he was growin' cold. Lawd, I was scared. I couldn't tell nobody. I was a nigga' boy an' nobody want ta hear what a nigga' boy have ta say back then. I'd be lucky if they didn't put the blame on me an' hang me up fo' it. 'Sides, I knew fo' sure that if either of us told we would be killed by ol' Hoffa'. Ben wouldn't move. It was all he could do ta' jus' be alive. I knew we had ta get out'a there. It wouldn't take long fo' people ta notice the light bein' out.

"Then I remamba' what those fellas in the uniforms said 'bout sinkin' all the Lighthouse Service stuff in the inlet. I was near panic, but I knew somehow some o' these things had ta be saved. I tried ta think what Martin had taught us was important. We had this ol' pickled egg jar in the boat we used ta hold fishin' minnas.' I dumped it out and started collectin' as much of the lens as I could, fittin' it down in the jar till no more could go in. I put that in the boat then run back ta Martin's house. I found the journal in that ol' rolltop o' his and took it. I saw Martin's uniform hat and jacket, but I was thinkin' that they would be buryin' him in 'em. I grabbed a jar o' preserves and a loaf o' bread from the pantry…an' a roll of waxpaper, then went back. By the time I got ta the boat Ben was stirrin' and crying. I got him ta move an' help him ta the boat. I shoved us off an' rowed fo' the inlet as hard as I could. We got caught up by the current an' was swep' fast along the bank. I could see the lights o' boats headin' fo' the lighthouse…ta find out what happen'. I tried ta get Ben ta help with pullin' against that tide, but Hoffa' had done scared him so bad he didn't know day from night.

"We got washed way up inta the delta before I could get us stopped on the bank. I jus' tied the boat ta an ol' falled-down tree an' we stayed there till mornin'. Come dawn I used the waxpaper ta wrap up the book…then I went ashore an' hid the bottle an' book unda' an ol' log. Ben was lookin' at nothin' and not movin' much, but the tide had turned an' we went downstream...til we was found by some dayfishers.

"As we was bein' towed back ta port I look out an' see those Coast Guard fellas dumpin' stuff overboard from their mota'boat. They dumped the clock from the mantel...they dumped the rest o' the lens...they dumped papers...they dumped the dishes...an' they dumped the uniforms. They dumps them all in th' saltwater...even the uniform Mista' Thurber should'a been buried in. Made me sick.

"Folks made a big deal 'bout us havin' been missin'. Poor Mrs. Campbell jus' about went insane with her daughta' upstairs cryin' an' grievin' an' not comin' down at all...an' her son half drown dead, dumb an' barely in this world. It took a long time fo' my friend ta come back ta us...an' then he couldn't talk none. Soon afta,' Mista' Campbell took an axe ta that ol' boat of ours. Broke it inta a hundred pieces, sure 'nough. He forbids me from comin' back ta his home, even. Mama still work fo' 'em, but it neva' was the same.

"Ol' Mista' Dinkle...he was a boatwright...he told us, he went over an' he saw what went on over at the lighthouse. He say, the day afta' the light went out, the sheriff an' his men come ta investigate what happen. They'd not much more than started when those Coast Guard fellas came an' takes over. They says, 'This is a military situation an' no need fo' locals ta be involved.' Once the sheriff left they cleaned the place out. They bury Martin in a begga's box dressed in nothin' but the clothin' he die in, work trousers and his blood'd nightshirt. They give the stone carver some money fo' the stone, but the carver...he say that there weren't enough fo' the job. They give him no mo' money so all he carve was jus' the initials.... Few months afta' that...Miss Iris married Henry Hoffa'."

The junior deputy could not believe Vern's last statement and blurted out, "What? After all that?"

Having calmed his emotions Ben answered, "Henry knew what his father had done, and... maybe...had some guilt. He changed. He no longer took his father's orders. He was never a nice man...but he stopped...being abusive. He...no longer took Iris for granted. He was good to her...and he tried to be a good father to Abigail. I don't...know...if Iris ever truly loved him. It lasted...only a few years...because Henry...signed...to the Navy. It was...the war. He went down...in the Pacific."

Vern added, "Then I hears ol' Warren Hoffa' done drown.'"

Ben nodded, "The night...after...we heard about Henry's ship...Warren showed up...at the house. He...was babbling...about Abigail...how he knew the truth…and that…he was going to drown her. Dad threatened to call…for the law…so Warren left. That night…Hoffer was…out…on one of his boats…I think, alone. They said…he must have been…drinking. They…found him…overboard…tangled in his own net. Everyone knew he'd been yelling…at my Dad…but…Dad…was at home that night. They called it an accident. There…was…no way of telling…what really happened."

Chapter Twenty

The Saint Rosabelle Lighthouse Festival was underway and the event had attracted lighthouse enthusiasts from across the region. What had earlier been a quiet, country corner was now transformed into a bustling center of activity. A team of locals served vat after vat of cooked kudzu to hungry visitors who eagerly tried the unusual foods. Local politicians made their appearances to show their support and make popularity points with the public. There were even game booths set up to provide the children with their own amusements.

Gretta had her hands full just trying to keep the crowd under control at the yard sale. Masses of bargain hunters rummaged through the tables of items searching for those hidden, unique treasures that they could take home as souvenirs. The cash box filled quickly as they paid for their findings.

If all the planned activities had not been enough to make the event special then the arrival of Troy McGovern and Brett Jarrett added plenty of excitement. They had given only a few days forewarning and had asked that their attendance not be advertised, knowing that ultimately the news would be spread locally just the same. The sheriff's office provided as many deputies as possible to insure the safety of the famous pair from Hollywood. Both stars were warmly welcomed and in turn happily endured long sessions of signing autographs.

During the day a steady flow of people had walked the distance from the festival grounds to the site of the lighthouse. The tower was now cordoned off by temporary fencing and partially shrouded in scaffolding. Yellow streamer tape marked the border of the path to the lighthouse in an attempt to keep the visitors from disturbing the work in progress. As dusk approached the stream of tourists had slowed to a trickle, but soon members of the local community began to gather behind the keeper's house. Some of the tourists lingered to see what the day's final event would be. Conversations increased in level as renowned locals, and soon members of the Brown family arrived.

Finally assembling together, the Brown family stood at the foot of Martin Thurber's grave—now within the confines of a metal bar fence. The freshly placed sod told of a recent disturbance to the burial place. At the head of the plot a hip-high marker remained hidden beneath a satin cloth. David walked to the head of the grave and stood facing the crowd. The background conversations ceased when he raised his hand. "Thank you all for being here this evening. On behalf of my family I would like to thank everyone for their kindness, help and support during the past months. We would especially like to thank those who have offered their legal depositions to help clear Martin Thurber's name. In his honor, we dedicate this monument." He carefully removed the cloth, exposing a lustrous engraved marble stone.

As David stepped aside, Judge Howard S. Beisacker came forward. After clearing his throat and straightening his shoulders, he announced, "By the power vested in me by Barker County, I hereby clear Martin Thurber of all charges of criminal wrongdoing as might be held within this jurisdiction. In the eyes of this county magistrate, Lighthouse Keeper Thurber was not only a law-abiding citizen, but a true hero." Following an enthusiastic round of applause, Father Dinkle lead a prayer.

As the crowd began to disperse, Peter spotted the two movie stars and their escort, Lester McKay. Leaving the rest of his family to greet well-wishers, Peter made his way to the celebrities. "Gentlemen! Mister Jarrett? Mister McGovern?" Keenly groomed and dressed in his best sports clothes the antiques dealer looked every inch the serious entrepreneur. He asked, "I was wondering if you've had a chance to think about my proposal…about supporting the lighthouse and using it as your community's logo?"

The taller actor laughed, responding to the organizer of the day's events, "Just call me Troy, all right?" He smiled over at his partner and prodded, "Well, Brett, what do you think?"

"I don't know," Brett answered lightly, "supporting a landmark that we aren't even going to own sounds like a shaky proposition to me."

Peter frowned at the reply and rebutted, "We wouldn't do anything to endanger it. I assure you it will be well cared for."

"That's right!" Darcy chimed in as she stepped forward. She commented happily, "Peter, I noticed that you were right on time!"

Looking over at Darcy, Brett smiled coyly and pointed at her while noting, "You! All right, I underestimated just how stubborn you could be." He chuckled as Darcy cocked an eyebrow. Then he added, "I still don't understand some things, though."

Grinning, she responded, "Such as...."

"You went to all this trouble...and now you give it all away! I just don't understand you."

"I'm not giving it away," Darcy corrected the taunting star, "I'm leasing it. The contract is arranged with the understanding that I, along with a caretaker, will be able to maintain a portable residence on the grounds while both of the keepers' quarters are being restored. Then I will be able to keep a permanent home in the assistant keeper's quarters and there will be a museum in the principle keeper's home. The caretaker will eventually have a room in either the reconstruction of the foghorn building or the workshop."

A slightly acrid tone seeped into Brett's voice as he questioned, "And ol' Carl gets to be the caretaker?"

Darcy nodded in agreement, "He certainly does."

"You're not worried that he will hit the bottle again?" Troy voiced his concern, "It seems that he had been living with alcohol for some time before you met him."

"That is a possibility," Darcy admitted and then continued, "but I'm willing to give him a chance. He seems to have taken the lighthouse to his heart. I think he has found something that he believes in and it is helping him come to terms with his mistakes from the past. Besides, I don't think he'll be alone in the community any more. He'll have people to talk with on nearly a daily basis." She looked across the gathering and spotted Carl. Motioning to him she added, "Well, just look at him...." Dressed in a replica Lighthouse Service uniform that fit him perfectly, Carl was enjoying visiting with the remaining tourists. When he saw the group looking his way, he pardoned himself from the stragglers and gingerly moved to join his friends.

With a slight touch of verbal tartness Brett looked at Darcy and asked, "Just how did you con these people into helping you?"

"Brett!" Darcy glowered at the actor.

"I'm just kidding with you," Brett defended, "but all the same...."

Lester interjected, "We chose to help!" He smiled, then brightly added, "Whether Darcy liked it or not."

She nodded and shrugged, "They're the ones who organized the effort and they're the ones who continue to volunteer their time. They took the initiative to try and untangle all the governmental red tape...."

"And trust me," Peter jeered, "there's a lot of red tape...more than I ever thought there would be."

"They've poured their love into saving the tower." Darcy looked thoughtfully to her local friends.

"But why?" Brett shook his head in amazed confusion. "I still don't understand what the big deal is about lighthouses."

Carl spoke up, "It's because they represent hope. The hope of knowing that you are near a long journey's end…that home is near…that there is someone out there watching over you. We all need hope. It's hope that keeps us going, that keeps us alive." Expressing his feelings so adamantly caused a deep flush to come to his cheeks.

Lester added, "They also embody a sense of selflessness, that those who served here were willing to lay down their very lives to save the lives of others. The keepers sacrificed for the good of strangers…sacrificed comforts, everyday conveniences, often even human companionship. They faced boredom, low pay, constant repetition. They served while ill or injured, with medical treatment often unavailable. They served in the face of all kinds of hazards, natural and otherwise…all for the sake of others. We need to remember these values…we want to remember them…."

After a moment of silence Peter renewed making his pitch and pointed out, "The developers of Sea Pines on Hilton Head Island went to the trouble of building a brand new lighthouse so they could use it as a symbol for their community. Heck, this one's already built. This one comes complete with a history!"

Brett quipped, "They probably spent less building the new one than it will take to fix this one up." Something in the man's tone alerted Darcy and she looked at him through narrowed eyes.

"You've already made up your minds…haven't you?" Darcy looked back and forth between the celebrities and watched them intently. She goaded them, "Come on. I can tell you're hiding something!"

Troy caught a glimpse of his partner shaking his head in mock despair. Ignoring Brett he replied, "We did talk about it on the way here."

"And!?" Darcy could not help feeling anticipation as the two business partners looked at each other. She could tell that Peter was holding his breath in anticipation.

"And," Brett slowly answered, "we've decided to fund the effort…." He was cut short by the elated advocates and found himself being embraced by an ecstatic Darcy. Attempting to remain a grounding factor he raised his hands in a motion for the others to calm down. "Wait! Wait a minute. It's just so we can get the buildings stabilized. It's to get the tower out of danger…that's all."

Troy looked to Darcy and emphasized, "The Light Keeper's Association will have to cover the costs of the cosmetic refinishing and then maintaining the structures once they're secure." Watching the production assistant's expression he pressed, "Right?"

Darcy raised her eyes to meet Troy's and lightly, but jubilantly, replied, "That's right."

"Well, that isn't a problem!" Peter showed all the energy of true enthusiasm. "The kind of turn-out we're having for this event shows that people love lighthouses and are willing to help! You have no need to worry. This is a worthy investment."

"Investment is right," Brett grumbled.

Troy wrapped his arm around his assistant and told her, "You have a couple of days to finish up here, but then I'm going to be doing an ad campaign in Japan and I could really use your help."

Darcy quietly nodded and agreed, "Good. I always want to be part of your crew." She gave him a pleased smile.

Carl had been patiently listening to the conversation while enjoying the presence of the famous guests. His cheerfulness was suddenly dampened as he realized what had just been discussed. He confronted the production assistant, "Wait…you're not leaving, are you?"

"Yeah…for a bit. It's part of the job." Darcy sensed the man's heart sink, a sadness filling his eyes. Knowing that Carl had been using her presence as a reason to stay strong against the urges for alcohol she reached over and hugged him. She attempted to give him reassurance, "But I'll be back. I have friends and a home here now, right?" Watching him nod she added, "And I know that you'll look after the place until I get back, too."

"Hey! Can we have a photo with the lighthouse keeper?" A tourist family waved from beyond the flapping yellow tape and motioned for Carl to come near. A smile spread between the neighbors and with a wink Darcy released the uniformed man. Backing away Carl took a quick glance at the new grave marker before striding toward the lingering family of sightseers. With a clear, confident voice he welcomed them to the Saint Rosabelle Lighthouse.

Lester and Peter had been engaging the two celebrities in conversation about fund-raising when a golf cart pulled up. Having transported a number of less physically capable sightseers during the day the pretty teenager who sat at the wheel of the impromptu shuttle checked for more stragglers. Seeing the renowned actors she eagerly invited them to ride back with her to the festival booths. All four of the men boarded for the trip to the far end of the road. With Troy taking the front and Peter quickly filling the rear cushion next to Brett, Lester resigned himself to cramming his large frame into the small space normally reserved for golf bags. As their assigned guard, he had to stay with the celebrities, no matter the discomforts.

As Darcy watched the men embarking, she noticed that Troy's eyes twinkled as he seated himself next to the bubbly girl at the wheel. The assistant laughed to herself.

She joined the small gathering of friends and family that remained examining the newly placed marker at the head of the grave. The carved, polished marble block bore the emblem of the long-abolished U.S. Lighthouse Service and was formally engraved with the name, "Martin L. Thurber." Below the name were the words, "Principle Lightkeeper, United States Lighthouse Service, January 12, 1902 - July 1, 1939, Died in Loyal Service."

Darcy smiled, then turned towards Ben and commented, "It's a nice stone, Ben. I think he'd be pleased."

The elder spoke circumspectly, "It has been a long time…coming, but he finally…has a suitable vault…and marker. Martin deserved that much…and more."

"Especially now that the tower will soon be ready to serve as a navigational marker again." David observed, "When the grounds are open for the public to visit, it will be good to have the grave kept up and properly marked. That way the people will be able to see that Martin gave his all…that he sacrificed everything for the light."

"And that he didn't die insane," Abigail added softly, "but while fighting for what he believed in…trying to protect the lives of others." She smiled bittersweetly as she glanced down at the red star pinned to her blouse.

Kim interjected excitedly, "We're going to relight the light, right?" Her young face held a joy unequaled in the past months.

Her father answered the girl's question, "That's right! Come on, now." With a look of comfort David proposed, "Let's get some of that kudzu chowder! I can't wait to try it." Taking her hand he led Kim toward the yellow plastic straps and was joined by Linda along the way. He called back to his son, "Are you coming, Eric?"

With his grandmother at his side, the lad was still concentrating on the grave as he answered, "I'll be there in a little bit, Dad." Eric looked to the new property owner and asked, "Would it be okay if we went out to the tower?"

Darcy glanced at Carl as he accompanied the last of the tourists who began their trek down the dirt road. He was clearly delighted to share his knowledge with the group and was keeping them well occupied as they walked. Looking back at Eric, she replied, "Okay with me. We'll have to watch our step and stay clear of the work areas. But sure."

As Abigail and Darcy followed the boy's lead down the short path, Iris' daughter reflected, "I was in high school when my mother began coming over here on and off. My boyfriend at the time got all huffy, asking her 'wasn't she afraid of the ghost?' She would say the shelling was better over on this side of the inlet. Finally one day I asked her if she had ever seen the ghost. Mother got the most wonderful expression on her face...as if I'd just given her a present. She answered, 'Oh yes.' When I asked her why she wasn't afraid, she just smiled."

The calm, rose hue of dusk filled the sky and the gently moving water lapped the shore while the threesome surveyed the aged and trusted building. As they stood on the beach Eric looked to Abigail and pondered, "Do you think Thurber, I mean...Great-Grandfather...minded being dug up?"

Abigail shook her head, "I don't think so. I think he understood. Besides, it didn't take that long for them to do the autopsy and take genetic samples."

The boy winced slightly and asked, "They didn't take that much of him, did they?"

"Not that much, hon. Just a little scrape." His grandmother put her arm across his shoulders and reminded him, "And they were able to compare his fingerprints and Vern McKay's with the ones on the prisms. We now have proof that he wasn't alone that night...and that someone else ruined the light. I don't think he would be angry about us verifying that."

"No, I guess not." Eric paused to think and then said, "It was good of the judge to say all that...but the Coast Guard still doesn't believe that he didn't do it."

"They will," Darcy assured him. "They will in time. They've had to open their own investigation. There's an awful lot of new evidence now that they didn't have the first time...thanks to Ben and Vern. Not only the prisms, but the journal...which is a treasury of information. Seems Martin detailed a lot of things in that book." She paused before continuing, "You know, a number of people who served with the Coast Guard are helping with the preservation of various lighthouses around the nation. Maybe that's a bit ironic, given the harshness of the takeover, but I think that the members of the Guard who took the jobs of the Lighthouse Service keepers came to respect the lighthouses and the people who took care of them. I think some of the Coast Guard are trying to put things right."

Still pondering, Eric asked, "Will Great-Grandfather's ghost leave now?"

"I...don't know." Abigail shook her head, then looked to Darcy.

"I don't know for sure, either, but I don't think he'll leave immediately." Taking a breath Darcy continued, "As a matter of fact he may want to stick around for a while. With the tower being restored I'm sure he will have an interest in the restoration. Then he'll probably want to make sure people take care of the place properly. From what I've read it seems many lighthouse keepers were that way."

Eric lamented, "This is so weird...having to relearn the family history. Who would have thought that we could have both pirates and lightkeepers as our ancestors."

Abigail hugged the boy and mildly contested, "You're telling me!?" She gently began to guide the lad back in the direction of the path.

Looking to his grandmother Eric inquired, "Do you think Great-Grandfather would mind...if I helped take care of the light?"

Abigail smiled and replied, "Somehow I get the feeling he wouldn't mind at all."

"I would be proud, Eric."

The boy and his grandmother hesitated, for the first time aware of the unnatural sensation of the specter's presence. Almost certain they had heard someone speak, they glanced around for the source of the voice. Darcy swivelled in time to see the fading form of the darkly uniformed man standing at the railing of the lighthouse balcony.